COZY NIGHTS IN VERMONT

Volume 1 - Dyslexia-Friendly Edition

Fall Inn Love
Falling in Vermont

Elise Kennedy

Copyright © 2026 by Elise Kennedy.

All rights reserved.

No part of this book may be reproduced in any form or by any electronic or mechanical means, including information storage and retrieval systems, without written permission from the author, except for the use of brief quotations in a book review.

For content warnings about this book, please go to https://elisekbooks.com/

Also by Elise Kennedy

Cozy Nights in Vermont **Novellas**

Fall Inn Love

Falling in Vermont

* * *

Only One Cozy Bed **Novellas**

Pumpkin Spice & Pour-overs

Apple Cider & Subterfuge

Hot Cocoa & Mistletoe

Snowed In & Snuggle Weather

* * *

Love in Fairwick Falls **Novels**

Accidentally in Bloom

Wallflower in Bloom

Conveniently in Bloom

Unexpectedly Bookish

Falling at the Barre

Forever in Bloom

Table of Contents

Fall Inn Love .... Page 1

Falling in Vermont .... Page 207

FALL INN LOVE

CHAPTER ONE

IRIS

Iris Bertone snuggled into her train car seat, picturing the next two blissful weeks to calm the nervous butterflies somersaulting in her stomach.

Don't think about what's on the line. Picture making leaf angels—her preferred type of angel-making, much warmer than snow angels—*in a fluffy pile of orange leaves.*

She'd nabbed the most coveted freelance reporting assignment ever: a two-week, all-expenses-paid trip to review Vermont's 'hidden gem' romantic inns. She'd be on assignment for the 'Romance Travel' issue of *Discover & Dwell*, the foremost leisure magazine for women ages 25 to 45 with bold, elegant pages and international reach. She'd stay at seven inns and write an article on the three top, most romantic places to stay from the list *Discover & Dwell*'s research staff made.

She'd worked her ass off for years, paying her dues at small newspapers and magazines. Five years at the

Elise Kennedy

Buffalo Weekly News, two years at the *Finger Lake Scallywag Magazine for Boating Outdoorsmen* (barf), and a year at an online magazine for equine enthusiasts called *Hay Girl Hay*.

Finally, she was ready for her glamorous life as a writer and journalist to start.

Only took me 29 years, she grumbled to herself as she smoothed her corduroy slacks into place.

She cuddled her apple cider latte closer and inhaled the spicy, syrupy sweetness. Mentally, she was already on a sheep farm, covered in flannel, frolicking through the crunchy leaves. She'd write down every detail to convey how perfect the inns could be for the readers of *Discover & Dwell*.

She flipped open her planner. Iris preferred a paper planner she could triple-check whenever her BFF, anxiety, came knocking (she was a clingy bitch). The next two weeks were planned into fifteen-minute chunks. Some might call it overkill, but she called it being prepared.

The pumpkin spice-infused success practically leapt off her schedule.

She looked at her watch. Jo, her professional better half, was the photographer for the assignment and was late. They'd partnered on a ton of freelance assignments together, and time management had never been Jo's strength.

They'd be traveling on a dreamy train from Boston to Brattleboro, Vermont, designed to celebrate the start of leaf-peeping season. It was her absolute favorite time of year, and she couldn't imagine a better way to spend the early weeks of fall than getting paid to explore the coziest, most romantic places in Vermont.

Iris tapped her foot to control her nerves. What if Jo missed the train? What if she got stuck in traffic, or Oswald was sick with an ear infection again?

What if she'd accidentally tripped on the sidewalk, breaking all of her camera equipment as she landed on the hard pavement outside the train station, and was currently limping towards the train, unable to text? *What if the train takes off and all I have is an old iPhone with a broken screen to capture beautiful vistas at the best time of year that can't be replicated?*

Iris had failed her photojournalism class and knew her strength was writing. She desperately needed Jo's photos to make *Discover & Dwell* happy.

"Last call, all aboard!" a booming male voice called outside her train car, and people scurried on the platform.

Jo's face lit up Iris's phone and she swiped up immediately. "Where are you? Do you need help with your equipment?" Iris tried to keep her voice calm. "The train is about to leave."

"I'm not coming. Oswald fell and broke his arm this morning." Jo sounded miserable.

"Oh no," Iris gasped. "Poor little Oswald." He was three, and the most accident-prone toddler ever.

Elise Kennedy

"I'm so sorry. I know this was a banger of an assignment, but I couldn't leave him." The faint cry of a toddler wailing in the background made Iris's lip pout.

Poor little guy. "No, no. Of course. I understand."

Shit shit shit. Could she expense a camera for the assignment? Would *Discover & Dwell* accept blurry selfies for a national magazine?

"I didn't want to call until I had my replacement lined up, but good news, I found someone. You'll be in...uh...great hands."

Iris heard a nervous tone in Jo's voice.

"Jooo," Iris said slowly, warning in her voice. "Do I have to hang out with a rando for two weeks instead of my freelance work wife?"

"Not exactly a rando..." Jo said, audibly wincing. "Which train seat are you in?"

Iris whipped around to see the decorative plaque above the car's sliding door. "47A?"

"Okay, let me text him."

Iris's heart thumped hard in her chest. How was she *more* anxious now?

"*Him?*" Iris yelled. "You're gonna send me off with a random dude for two weeks? What if I get murdered? Worse, what if he's bad at the job?"

"Pshhh," Jo responded. "There will be no murder.

Probably," she added quickly. "Plus, the editorial staff already approved the switch, so you're good to go."

"Jo. What. Is. His. Name?" Iris said, spitting urgency with every word.

"Well, if it isn't Bun-Buns," a voice called from behind her.

Iris turned with a slow-sinking dread.

"Iris," Jo called from the phone. "Don't be mad, don't be mad, don't be mad!"

And there he was, her new photographer: the man who had towered over every accomplishment her entire college and high school life. Her long-standing rival: Sam Larsson.

"Joanne. Elizabeth. Lee. How could you," Iris's voice zipped like acid into the phone.

"Don'tbemadI'msosorry. I panicked and didn't know who else to call," Jo said.

"I can hear you, you know," Sam said, sauntering into the car as the train lurched into motion.

"You're gonna have a great time. Love you!" Jo sing-songed as she hung up the phone.

"Jo. Jo," Iris called as the line went dead. She closed her eyes and took a deep breath through her nose, trying to remember her gratitude exercise from therapy. *I love Jo, I love Oswald. I love reporting. I love Vermont in the fall. This will all be fine. Maybe I fell asleep and I'm having a nightmare.*

She opened one eye.

The *bump bump bump* of the train flopped the brown hair she knew so well on the man sitting across from her. His smug smile showed his absolute delight in her misery.

Damn.

Sam had been a pain in her ass since first-period lit class freshman year of high school when she'd first met him. They'd had a knock-down-drag-out argument about their assigned summer reading, *To Kill a Mockingbird*, and competed for fucking everything since.

Class president? Check.

Editor-in-chief of both their high school and college newspapers? Check.

Debate team captain? Super, triple, very checked.

"You look lovely, as always," Sam said with a sarcastic smile.

"You look…" She paused, taking in the useless small scarf around his neck that reminded her of journalists in the field, the designer green army-style jacket, fashionable jeans, and boots that had seen the sands of many far off places. "…like you're on the wrong train."

"No can do, old friend." He stood up to heft his camera equipment into the luggage spot above her seat, towering over her with his broad shoulders and thick arms as he stepped into her space. He wrestled with the bag, and the edge of his shirt lifted up, revealing the solid muscles of his abs underneath. "Jo called and said she needed a favor."

Cozy Nights in Vermont

Ugh. She hated that he was hot. Someone this annoying should at least look like the dweeb he'd been when she'd first met him in freshman English class. "I didn't realize you two still talked," she said, her jaw grinding hard enough to mill flour.

"Here and there." He flopped back into his seat across from her, taking up the full space of the empty bench. "Sometimes we call each other with assignments when one of us is slammed."

Sam and Iris had independently decided to attend the school with the best journalism program near their hometown. They'd tried to convince the other to go to a different school, but Iris had dug her heels in on principle.

They'd met Jo in college and pulled many late nights in the journalism building working on *The Daily Jaguar*, a student-run daily newspaper. Jo and Sam had both excelled in photography, whereas Iris had focused on human interest features. She wanted to push the world to be a better place by showing the heart and possibility of humanity.

Sam had barely changed since the last time she'd seen him a few years ago at a mutual friend's wedding. He'd looked devastating then, and not much had changed. He still had a gorgeous smile, strong eyebrows, and his once-clean shaven face now had an artfully curated five o'clock shadow.

"You look good, Buns," he said with a smile that made his stupid brown eyes sparkle.

She never knew if he was teasing or not.

"Oh my god, stop calling me that," she said, frustration simmering under her skin. "I'm not sixteen." She'd worn her thick, wavy hair in space buns for one week junior year, trying out a new look, and still hadn't lived it down.

He looked good too, but unlike her, Sam was well aware of it.

He'd always been tall, wide, and brawny; one of those annoying combinations of a jock and nerd that made him insanely popular in high school and created a constant stream of girls in and out of his dorm room in college.

Not that she'd ever tell him that she noticed.

Given how far out of her league he'd always been, she'd put him in a non-sexual competitor box. His only purpose was to be defeated. About half the time, she'd managed to win.

"So the dynamic duo is back together," he said with a shit-eating grin.

"That was one time, and you know it was punishment for me." That's what she got for "wasting" fifteen minutes of their ethics class "grandstanding against Sam's arguments."

Her professor's words, not hers.

"I'm looking forward to a nice two-week vacay," he said, stretching his hands behind his head. "Just taking it easy and shooting photos of leaves."

Ugh, this man. "This is not a vacation. I have a full itinerary," she said, showing him her planner. "We will not 'hope it all works out,'" she said, using air quotes. "*Your famous last words for the junior prom budget."*

He smirked at her with his stupid smirky lips. "Can't help that *you* overspent at the homecoming dance, Class President Bun-Buns."

"You were the class treasurer," she said, growling. "What about when we were covering the student protests in college? You got the date wrong. There was nothing but litter left."

"I got an award for those photos," he said, snorting and looking—again—smug.

She rolled her eyes as she watched suburbia shuttle past them outside. "Of course you did."

Sam Larsson was god's gift to photojournalism. He'd been handed practically everything while Iris had scraped by, vying for every story, trying to get her foot in the door at every shitty hometown newspaper after college.

Sam nodded. "I didn't think this sort of 'media for the masses' would be your kind of thing. Wasn't this the kind of story you made fun of in college?"

Yes, it was. Because she was an egotistical kid who didn't know better. The world didn't want impartial journalism; it wanted someone to tell them how to organize their closet for less. She'd rolled with it because experience was still experience. "Shouldn't you be off in a desert somewhere capturing a story for *Newsweek* about the declining camel population?" she spat back.

Every teacher and every editor had always avoided pairing them together. Their insane competition would turn any article into mush.

"You are still mad I got that internship," he said, realization dawning on him.

"Of course I'm still mad. They said I had it."

He shrugged. "Maybe my interview was better."

"Maybe it's because you got all the better assignments."

"Maybe it's because I had better grades," he said, getting heated.

"Maybe it's because you took all the easy classes."

"French Film Studies wasn't easy and you know it," he shouted as the door to the train car opened up from the hallway.

A greasy man in a shirt buttoned to his ribs walked in and sat down next to Iris.

"I didn't even get to be captain of the debate team because of you," Iris spat. Their teacher had gotten so tired of their arguing that she'd made them co-captains. "If you will be quiet for the rest of the ride, I can enjoy my cozy drink and the views."

Sam threw his hands in the air in surrender and opened his phone.

The man sitting next to Iris on the bench leaned in close to her. "Where you headed?" His breath reeked of alcohol.

Cozy Nights in Vermont

"Um, Vermont." She wouldn't give a strange man her exact location, but she didn't want to be rude. At least he hadn't insulted her in the last five minutes, unlike the bad penny across from her.

"I'm going to meet some buddies there," he said.

Iris went back to her phone, hoping he'd get the hint.

The odorous man pointed at the logo on her water bottle. "The Old Button Factory Downtown Lofts. That where you live?"

Creep sounded in the back of her mind as her spine tingled. "I need to work on my planner," she said and turned away from him.

"You live alone?" he asked and scooted closer, not taking the hint.

"Darling," Sam called as he stood up. "Do you have a pen?" He stood so he was knee to knee with her.

Uh, darling? Her stomach jolted as she realized he was talking to her. What was he thinking?

She handed him the third-best pen from her planner. He grabbed it but didn't move.

"Sorry. My girlfriend's territorial about her pens." Gesturing to the seat the creepy man was in, he added, "Mind switching?"

Oh lord.

The creepy man shrugged, got up, and left the car.

Sam sat down with a wide grin. "Thank you, darling," he said too loudly as the man was leaving, enjoying the ruse. "Jo said you were going to pretend to be a couple so the places didn't know you were reporters. Thought it was kind of dumb, but if pretending to be a couple irritates you then there's a bright side."

"The inns would behave totally differently if they knew they might be on the cover of a huge magazine." She grabbed the pen back. It would be lost in ten seconds otherwise. Sam was as organized as a toddler who'd eaten seventeen popsicles, though he took his camera equipment seriously.

"But we don't have to be a *couple* couple, right?" His eyes narrowed, which meant he was watching her for a reaction.

"God, no," Iris laughed unconvincingly.

She'd nursed a tiny, irritating, against-her-will crush on him since he'd started to grow into his lanky frame senior year of high school. He was objectively good looking, and she found competence sexy. He pushed her to be her best, and she was humble enough to admit she'd learned a thing or two from him over the years.

Not that she'd ever tell him. Over his dead body.

"What's that face?" he said, gesturing to her nose.

"Well, you know." She gestured between the two of them. "We're not a couple. We wouldn't be believable."

"Because you find me so disgustingly unattractive?" he said, knowing exactly what he looked like. He had a classically handsome face and looked like he belonged on a rugby field with his ruddy cheeks in a Ralph Lauren Polo ad. His jaw was angular and covered in light brown stubble. It, unfortunately, only highlighted his impish smile so that you hoped he pressed you against a wall and made out with you.

"We're going to be professional about it." She pressed her shirt down, feeling prim about the whole thing. "This assignment is a big deal."

"I know it's a big deal. Your editor, Ben, is a buddy of mine. He said there might be a spot opening on D&D's staff, so I figured I'd test it out. See if it's someplace I wanna work."

"Oh, right," she snorted. "To see if they're good enough for you."

Nerves twisted in her stomach. She was competing against him for the spot she'd talked to Ben about? The one that might open up? She'd wanted a full-time role at a name-recognizable company her whole life. It was the first step to getting her life started.

Well, restarted.

He settled down in his seat, crossing his arms and closing his eyes. His wide shoulders took up a lot of space, but she didn't hate the feeling of them pressing against her.

There was a familiarity in being next to someone you'd known for so long. He was comforting even if he was annoying, like an old shoe she hadn't thrown away yet.

"It would be a change of pace." He stretched out his long legs. "But I like the idea of paid vacations where I take some photos, even if I'm paired with anal-retentive writers."

"I am not—" She slammed her mouth shut, refusing to yell the word 'anal' in public.

"I'm surprised you're not interested in it"—he opened one eye—"or maybe Ben didn't talk to you about it."

"Maybe he did," she said with a triumphant head nod. She'd had to ask about a full-time role, but he'd said there'd be one available soon.

"Sure, Bun-Buns. Whatever you gotta tell yourself," Sam said with a sigh.

Her mind whirled as fast as the train wheels thundering under them.

She'd have to handle this 6'3" thorn in her side while also nailing the most important assignment of her life.

CHAPTER TWO

SAM

Sam Larsson jogged through their first stop in Vermont to catch up with the curvy brunette six paces in front of him. Iris still walked with the conviction of a Baptist minister on the way to burn some naughty books.

Must be a benefit of the stick up her ass.

One thing that hadn't changed since high school was how gorgeous she was. She'd only gotten prettier as she'd grown more confident after college. He'd seen her at weddings of mutual friends since then, but Jo had always been stingy with details when he would bring Iris up. She hadn't, for instance, told him why Iris's left hand was missing the engagement ring that had been there so long.

Interesting.

He'd meandered through the town, photographing the sights after they'd hopped off the train. Town ambiance was a big part of the appeal for an inn, and Sam loved photographing everyday life. He'd already taken countless photos of cute corner stores and fall decorations.

Brattleboro, their first stop, was quintessentially Vermont with its quaint Main Street and mom-and-pop shops that had been there for decades. Stores decorated for the fall season with hay bales and pumpkins outside, and a few leaves had started to turn, making for gorgeous photos in the sunny afternoon light.

He stopped to capture the swing and bounce of Iris's ponytail with his camera as she marched into their first inn.

Orchard House was one of the oldest inns in the country. The stately structure of brick and wood had seen wars and presidents come and go and stood through hundreds of autumns like this one. The gardens outside of the inn were serene, interspersed with yellow leaves beginning to fall.

He took photos in the grand foyer for a full minute. It boasted an enormous crackling fireplace, despite the warmth of the afternoon. Spindly, historic-looking wooden chairs sat in front of it. The afternoon light was turning golden and he wanted to capture the charm and gravitas of the historic inn. It had operated since Revere had made his ride, and it would be a serious contender for the final list of most romantic inns for the Valentine's Day issue of *Discover & Dwell*.

The lobby had a hushed tone to it. The rugs and decor were understated, historic elegance. The dark wood of the floor shone, and Sam idly wondered how many different styles of shoes had passed over it. Certainly, there'd been hoop skirts going up the staircase behind the reservation desk? Or stockings with lines on them during World War II? What would it be like to be this inn? To have witnessed so many couples coming in and out year after year?

Iris's heel-tapping brought him back to the present as she waited behind an older couple at the registration desk.

A smile crept onto his face as he recognized her nervous tic immediately. Iris was always nervous. He'd spent his time from age fourteen to twenty-two hearing the *tip tip tip tip tip tip tap* of her foot.

He'd honestly missed the sound.

Sam came up beside her, but she didn't acknowledge his presence. Only the *tip tip tip tip* of her foot greeted him.

Soon, a couple waited behind them. "I can't believe we booked the most *romantic* spot for our first night of our honeymoon," the woman said.

Tip tip tip tip.

"Baaaabe," said the young man behind him. "This is going to be fire."

Tip tip tip tip TIP TIP TAP TAP.

"Bertone, this inn has survived ten major wars, but it might not survive your foot." Sam gently put his foot over hers to quiet it.

She rolled her eyes at him, yanking her foot away. "We are late because of you."

He checked his watch. It was two minutes past check-in. "Oh no, they may not have a room for us. How terrible. Then we'll have to go home and I won't get the pleasure of your *calming* company."

"You are going to ruin this for me on purpose, aren't you?" she said, fire kindling in her eyes. "Maybe it's not a big deal to you, Mr. Reporting Live From the Scene of the War Crime, but it's important to me and I take my work seriously, so," she stood straighter and folded her arms, "you can't fuck it up."

He had to admit, he fucking loved getting her riled up. Her usually smooth and put-together exterior hid what he knew was a fiery heart. There were more than a few arguments he'd extended for the sake of seeing that liveliness in her, that spark.

The smacking of mouths behind them made them turn. The newly wedded couple made out like those fish that sucked on a tank to clean it.

Iris grimaced. "God, they look like pleco fish."

"*That's* what they're called," he said, shooting a pointer finger at her. "I always loved watching them at that greasy Italian place on Locust."

"Please do not call that deep-fried swill 'Italian.'" She shuddered. "My nonna would roll over in her grave."

"How are your parents, by the way?" Iris's mom had made the best lasagna he'd ever had. He'd wheeled and dealed an invite to her house between debate matches or after-school events whenever he could.

Cozy Nights in Vermont

She sighed. "Good. My mom retired and is begging for grandbabies. My dad's doing half time in his painting business." She pulled out her planner. "Ugh, you wouldn't think check in would take this long. We're going to miss the"—she checked her list—"historical tour of the inn."

"Oh no, then we'll have to get a cocktail and enjoy ourselves. How terrible," he said with a feigned pained face.

More sucking mouth sounds behind them made his skin crawl.

"I "—she snapped her planner closed—"did not allow for us to be late. I wanted to be here ten minutes before check-in, so by the time we got checked in"—she took a deep breath—"we would have our key, we could make the tour, we could then report on all the things we needed to report on, and I could—" She stopped herself and hit his arm repeatedly as the older couple walked away from the registration desk. "Oh oh, it's happening."

"You know, I just can't remember what I found so annoying about working with you," Sam said dryly. It was like working with a firecracker that was perpetually about to burst.

"Don't forget, we're a couple," she whispered.

Sam made a zipping motion against his mouth and then pretended to drag the keychain around his neck and hang himself with it. "Super excited about this, as you can tell."

"Two to check in," she said as a command rather than a question.

"How's your day going..." Sam said, finding the attendant's name tag, "Jonathan?"

"It's going better now, thank you so much," Jonathan said with a sigh of relief.

"Don't mind this one. We're excited," Sam said, pointing at Iris.

"Baaaaabe," the suckerfish man behind Sam said. "I, like, love you so much, I might die. Babe, you're, like, my *wife*," the suckerfish man said as though it was the most insane revelation he'd ever had.

"Baaaaaabe," the wife-suckerfish said back in return. "That's, like, the most romantic thing I've ever heard." And then, having gathered enough breath, their mouths met like magnets fighting for dominance.

Ugh. Sam turned back around. He was not emotionally or physically prepared to be surrounded by this much romance for the next three weeks, especially with a spiky former rival next to him.

Then he remembered her comment about Ben discussing the full-time role. The one he wanted.

Oh god, and current rival? He wiped a weary hand down his face. *Christ.*

"Have we definitely missed the historical hotel tour?" Iris asked with a plea in her voice.

If there is a god in heaven, please say yes.

"I'm sorry," Jonathan said with a frown. "It starts

promptly at three, but we have them once a day. I can book you for tomorrow's."

"Oh, great! Yes, let's do tomorrow. I'll bring my notebook," she said with excitement in her eyes. Like she'd won an actual prize.

Jesus, why was that so fucking cute? She'd always been the biggest nerd, and he was still a complete sucker for it. She'd always had matching binders, pens, and organizational tabs in high school. Around junior year, he realized it didn't irritate him because she was over-prepared; it irritated him because it made her adorable and he couldn't do anything about it. She'd already been with her long-time boyfriend then.

Jonathan presented them with two key cards. "We have you down for our queen suite. It features one queen bed with a lovely seating area and complimentary coffee and tea."

"Only one?" Iris asked with surprise.

"Only one bed, yes," Jonathan said, smiling, nodding as he set the receipt down for them.

I'm certainly not mad about it. As Sam met her eyes though, he saw panic in them. Maybe she wasn't comfortable sleeping next to him.

Time to save the day, Larsson.

"You know"—Sam leaned in—"she has just the worst gas at night, god love her." He squeezed Iris's shoulders. "You sure you can't find two beds for us?"

A thwack to his gut made him nearly break his serene smile.

"Oh no, I'm so sorry," Jonathan said, looking pained at Iris. "I am, however, happy to send complimentary Gas-ex to your room—"

"That"—Iris interrupted him, sending Sam a death glare—"will not be necessary. He was joking. What a great, handsome, and not at all punchable boyfriend. I saw online that you have an apple-picking tour. Do you have room for two more?"

Sam shook his head no at Iris. He didn't want to be on a tour bus with screaming kids.

"In fact, we had two cancellations for tomorrow," Jonathan said setting down a brochure. "It includes two bicycle and helmet rentals, a guided bike tour of our apple orchard, a picnic, and an all-you-can-pick basket."

"Sounds fun. Let's do it," Iris said.

"You're the worst," he mouthed silently while Jonathan looked at the computer.

"Should I get a bellhop to get your bags?" Jonathan asked. "Our elevator is out of service, unfortunately."

"Oh, no, that won't be necessary," Sam said quickly. "This one. Such a ballbuster. Insists on no help from any man," he said, throwing an arm around her as she shrugged it off with a growl. "And you said we're what, on the second floor?"

"The third," Jonathan said.

"Perfect. Let's go, darling," Sam sang as Iris scowled at him. "This is going to be a fun two weeks."

CHAPTER THREE

IRIS

As Iris hefted her heavy bag up the staircase of Orchard House, she threw mental daggers at the unfortunately biteable backside of Sam. He walked ahead of her, toting his photography equipment and bag with ease.

She paused on the landing to gather her breath and hefted her bag onto her shoulder again.

"You know, you didn't have to wave off the bellhop when he offered a *third* time." She blew hair out of her face as she panted. *I gotta do more cardio.*

Great. She'd be sweaty and stuck in a small room, in one bed with Sam. *Just perfect.*

"You hated it when I opened doors for you in college," Sam said, already at the top of the next floor.

"Because you'd rush ahead and hold it open while I was a half a block away, so I'd have to walk faster."

Baritone laughter rolled out of him. "And you'd fall for it every time."

Two weeks. Two weeks of this. He'd irritate her to the point where she wouldn't smother him with a pillow, but she'd think about it all fucking night.

"You are the worst." She finally got to the top of the stairs but took the corner too quickly and swung backward, being off-centered with her enormous bag. With horror, she realized she might careen backward down the steep staircase.

With a steady hand, Sam snaked his arm around her waist and yanked her back up to standing. He turned away from her once she was settled back in place and unlocked the room.

Whoa. "Th—" She cleared her throat. "Thank you," she whispered.

He shrugged without looking at her and opened their room door to reveal a gorgeous suite. It was complete with a working fireplace, a wicker basket of logs tucked in next to it, a cozy seating area with a basket of muffins and scones, and a white chenille blanket all set in a sage green room.

In the middle loomed a queen-sized bed covered in a snowy white duvet and four tall dark oak spindles on each corner.

She brushed past him to set down her things, and he grabbed her arm.

"Hold on. Before you explode all of your Iris-ness, I need to take photos."

"There is no Iris-ness to explode," she countered. "I wasn't the one who made a stack of ramen cups high enough to build a fort in the *Daily* editorial bullpen."

He moved around the room, crouching and ignoring her, which was fine. She didn't need one of his retorts, pointing out a character flaw she'd rather not think about.

Goddamn, she'd forgotten how hot he was when he was in photographer mode. Tight t-shirt around his arms, confident, no-nonsense. He focused with a sincerity and seriousness that she never saw from him outside of work.

His jaw clenched as he swept his hair out of his eyes. "Go stand in the window," he said, pulling back the curtains.

"I am not going to be in these photos."

"Unless you have a very small model hidden somewhere in your enormous bag, go stand over there."

"I can't do that," she said, fussing with her chambray shirt and corduroy pants. She'd dressed for girl's trip comfort, not to be featured in a magazine.

"Oh, no one's going to look at you."

"That's not any better." She cocked her head, annoyed at him.

"You know what I mean. You're part of the decor. You'll hide behind this gauzy curtain. It looks dead in the shot if it's only furniture." He shooed her to the window and she scowled but obliged. "Now, pretend your long-lost love is returning with Little Nicky's Donuts."

She couldn't help herself and cracked a smile. *One thing is for certain in this world: I do love a carb, especially from the bakery in our hometown.* Their room overlooked a main square full of hay bales, a corner store, and families traipsing back from an elementary school harvest festival.

"Done with the wide shot of the room. I'm going to make a fire for close-ups of the fireplace," he said, moving to the center of the room. The large brick fireplace went up into the ceiling in one large column. It looked original, and the opening was large enough for a toddler to stand in with room to spare.

"Good. I'm freezing." She shuddered as she searched for a sweater to put on. She'd cooled from the hike up the steep stairs, and the dried sweat was now making her chilly. She couldn't wait to luxuriate in the smell of burning wood while she warmed her toes.

The crackle and pop of the firewood sounded in the quiet room. She liked poking at Sam more than the quiet between them. It was filled with this other chemistry-filled tension, like they were two tigers circling each other.

It had been a long two years of being alone since Bart had broken the engagement, and she'd forgotten what it felt like to have this kind of chemistry with someone.

"Sit," he said, pointing to the seat in front of the fireplace.

She raised an eyebrow.

"Jesus. Fine, please...Princess of the Type As, High Priestess of the Holier Than Thous, willst thou sit upon this old chair?"

Iris slowly settled into one of the chairs in front of the fireplace. Its wide oak seat was bound with a burgundy leather covering, and it felt worn and comfortable.

Sam turned off the lamps and shut the drapes to give more of a moody lighting effect.

"Here, hold a glass. I want a more natural shot of the fireplace."

She eyed him skeptically. "I don't even have any makeup on."

"You look great," he said offhandedly.

She decided to ignore the thrill that gave her. Just concentrate on not looking dumb in the photos.

The fire now roared, licking up into the chimney of the fireplace. She felt the warmth seep into her bones and wished she had a bourbon in the glass she was holding.

She tried to not be self-conscious at the sounds of Sam and camera clicks moving behind her. "Turn your head to the left," he said.

She marveled at how his professional voice was so different from the one he used with her. It was calm, in command, polite.

Kinda hot.

Cozy Nights in Vermont

"What, no 'Buns' at the end of it?" she said, turning her head.

"I"—click—"am a consummate"—shutter, click, beep—"professional," he said, standing up. "Okay, we're good. I'm gonna get ice and water to throw on the fire."

"Don't you dare," she said, turning around quickly to stop him. As she stood up, her nose smacked into his bare chest.

"Why aren't you wearing a shirt?" she yelled, staring at the sheen of sweat on his —apparently—defined chest and shoulders. The scent of the cologne he'd always worn wrapped around her and tugged somewhere deep inside.

"Because it's a hundred fucking degrees in here," he said, setting his camera down and walking past her.

He flung open the windows. A cool breeze curled through the windows instantly, blowing the gauzy lace curtains.

Holy moly. She had not been expecting that to be hiding under his designer t-shirt. His chest was so...was so... something. *Jiminy Christmas.*

"While you finish clutching your pearls, I'm going outside to cool down. Maybe get some exterior shots once the sun sets."

"Pfft," she called back. "As if I'd clutch any precious stone at the sight of *that*," she lied, waving her hand at the vague vicinity of his abs and chest.

A smug smile curled onto his face. "You can stop staring at it anytime you want." He threw his t-shirt back on, pulling it over his head and flexing his abs while he yanked it down.

"You're the worst," she yelled, sitting back into the chair and facing the fire as he left.

She hated that he still smelled so good. And that he looked like a grown-ass man with hard, firm muscles. He'd started to bulk up in college, but...

Lickable! She snapped her fingers. *That's* what his chest was. *Get your head out of the gutter and into this inn.*

She pulled out her notebook to capture her thoughts, keeping things as factual and fair as possible.

Twenty minutes later, her phone buzzed. She was surprised at the pang of disappointment that it was Sophia instead of Sam. She loved her sister, truly, but she'd forgotten the invigorating feeling of volleying insults back and forth. It burned her muscles and woke her up, like a good swim.

> **Phia the Famous**
> How's your trip? Get any hot mountain man tail yet?

Her message was followed by a series of emojis including the peach, ax, maple leaf, shirt and bearded man emoji. Iris snorted.

Sophia was three years older and about a million years ahead in her career. Her successful cooking blog had turned into a successful cookbook and recipe media empire with two million followers. She was more of a successful writer than Iris would ever be.

>   Iris
>
>   Not exactly...

> **Phia the Famous**
> ooh, tell me more

>   Iris
>
>   How much do you remember about Sam
>   Larsson?

Sophia's face filled her screen as a phone call came through and Iris swiped up, bracing herself.

"You're *fucking* kidding me," Sophia yelled through the phone.

"What did I do to the universe to deserve this, Phia?" Iris paced in her room. "I donate to the needy. I pay my taxes. I even compost! With *worms*. Karma's got the wrong number." Her sister had sat through every outraged venting session about Sam for eight long years.

"No, this is your perfect opportunity. Bart's out of the way."

"Oh, come on," Iris said with disbelief.

"Seeing the two of you in your debate team matches, the way you talked about him at home. There was *obviously* some chemistry there. You said he was a nice guy, right?"

"I mean, define nice. Is he gonna murder me in my sleep?

No. But would he ever respond, 'Well, *actually*' after me in a meeting? Definitely."

"Iris," Sophia said in a chastising tone. "You liked him."

"What? No. That's gross. I was dating Bart. Sam was literally the bane of my existence."

"The bane of your flirtatious existence. And near the end of college, he wasn't so bad-looking, right?"

"Well he's not bad-looking *now*," Iris said without thinking, imagining his chest in front of her again.

"Haha!" Sophia shouted with vindication. "So? You're finally gonna have some fun after living a cloistered nun-like existence for two years?"

"Absolutely not. We're colleagues."

Sophia hummed and Iris pictured the waggle of her head that usually accompanied it. "But not like actual colleagues, like freelance colleagues. Free agents."

"Sophia, this is work. I take it seriously. Not all of us can be perfect and famous at twenty-two like you."

"That was a *long* ten years ago," Sophia said, grumbling. Iris could practically see her swishing the red wine in her glass now. "All I'm saying is don't count yourself out."

* * *

That night, Iris and Sam stood on either side of the bed like giant, middle school chickens.

Cozy Nights in Vermont

"It's no big deal," Iris said defensively to no one in particular as she stared at the smallest queen bed in existence. "I mean, we're adults. I know you."

"Right," he said, shrugging, scratching the back of his head and staring at the bed. "This isn't weird. I mean, you could argue we're... f-friends." He stumbled over the word, swallowing it like a boulder he couldn't get his throat around.

"Friendly rivals feels more appropriate." She pulled back the covers on the left side.

"You can never just agree, can you? Mind if I take the left side?" Sam asked.

She sat down and squeezed the pillow so her cheek landed on it with glee. "I literally just claimed it."

His eyebrows furrowed at her, a face she recognized immediately. "Are you marking your territory like a cat?"

Maybe. "I usually sleep on this side."

"Me too." He tossed his phone and wallet onto the other nightstand with the frown he reserved purely for her.

She lay down, feeling victorious. "Then it's going to be a hard two weeks for you."

"Tell me about it," he yelled as he disappeared into the bathroom.

She mentally prepped herself for the next ten minutes. *Just fall asleep, Iris. Don't think about who you're sleeping next to. It's like sitting next to a stranger on a plane. You're not going to think about who's next to you,* and you're not going to think about that one sexy dream you've had a few times about him.

You are not—absolutely not—going to imagine his hand drifting over to you in the night, sliding between your thighs. Pulling you close, kissing your neck. Just fall asleep by naming the presidents in alphabetical order like you always do.

"Light on?" Sam said as he stood around the corner with the dim light of the bathroom behind him.

He'd taken off his shirt again and had on low-slung gray sweatpants. The deep V of his abs was absolutely ludicrous. She slammed her eyes closed because she was physically unable to rip them away from how his sweatpants sat on his hips.

Jesus Christ, was she gonna get a break this trip?

He sat on the bed and she got a whiff of his aftershave. Why oh why oh why did he have to smell so good? "Are you sure you can't put a shirt on to sleep?" she said, facing him.

"I'll feel like I'm being strangled. Plus, it's 100 degrees in here." He turned over with an irritated huff to turn off the bedside light. "It feels all wrong on this side," he said, tossing and turning.

Something *did* feel off. What was it?

Oh. She had pants on. She whipped around under the covers trying to get comfortable. "I hate sleeping in pajama pants. I feel like a mermaid wrapped in seaweed."

Cozy Nights in Vermont

A long-suffering sigh came from the other side of the bed as she tossed and turned for a solid thirty seconds.

He huffed, waiting for her to stop flip-flopping like a dying fish. "Just take them off," he finally yelled as if it was the most obvious thing in the world.

She stopped mid-flop. "But then I wouldn't have any pants on, and we're..."

"What?" He lifted his head. His eyes met hers in the dark.

"...I don't know, next to each other. Isn't that weird?" *And a little sexy?*

He shrugged. "I don't have a shirt on."

"But you're a boy."

"Fuck gender norms. Plus, you're welcome to take your shirt off any time," he said with a sly grin.

She grabbed her pillow and hit him with it as he burst out laughing.

He leaned on the pillow, shifting to get comfortable. "I'll be asleep. Do whatever you want."

He looked bemused at her frustration, per usual, and her heart pounded faster as he stared at her in expectation.

She hated that she trusted him implicitly. "Fine. But, you know, keep everything over there."

"Aye aye, Buns," he said, saluting her.

She snaked out of her pajama pants and felt the welcome relief of free movement.

As they both found a comfortable spot in the lumpy mattress—*I'll be noting this in my review*—a loud thumping started on the other side of their headboard.

A rhythmic thumping that could only be one thing at ten o'clock at night.

"Oh my god," Iris said in mortification, putting one of the extra pillows over her face.

The rhythmic thumping stopped. She caught Sam's eye in the dark with a lifted eyebrow as they waited. Then a loud groan of "Babe" and the loud thumping started again.

Iris and Sam burst out laughing.

Thump—thump—"Baaabe." Thump—thump—"Baaaabe," sounded on the other side of the wall. Tears sprang to Iris's eyes as Sam buried his face in his pillow, wheezing with laughter.

Thump—thump—"Baaaabe."

Her face heated, and she felt a tiny tug of desire.

Nope. No. You cannot get turned on by comical lovemaking. "This is so stupid," she muttered. She re-situated herself and threw back the covers down to her waist.

"Is this doing it for you?" Sam snorted as he leaned up on his elbow, obviously not getting any sleep. Their bedside tables shook from the thrusting against the wall.

"Don't be ridiculous," Iris said primly. She took off her long sleeve shirt she'd thrown over her t-shirt.

"You are. You're getting hot and bothered," Sam said with a sly smile.

The cries grew louder, more urgent. The "babes" grew faster.

Yes. "No," she said as if he was being juvenile rather than exactly correct. "It's *warm* in here. You said so yourself." She settled onto her side, facing him.

The snort-inducing babes had stopped, and the babe in question started making low, guttural, sensual moans.

It was slow, needy, obscene.

It was, in a word, erotic-as-fuck.

Iris's stupid eyes found Sam's in the dark. He'd already been staring at her. He didn't look away, and Iris felt a challenge from him. That fucking chemistry she loved to hate and hated to love.

She could never tell if that pull of more was just on her side though. She'd seen Sam's girlfriends. She wasn't his type.

But he stared at her as moans circled in the air between them, creating a perfume of lust.

He licked his lips, and desire curled through her body at the swipe of his tongue. How it would feel against her breasts, her clit. On her neck, tasting it against her tongue.

Their breaths became heavy, needy, as the moans and thumps and dirty words surrounded them.

Sam's eyes moved across her face. Her pussy had started throbbing—*we will have words later, girl*—and she squirmed to keep her lust at bay. She never let her eyes drift from his though. She could swear she saw his breath quicken as his eyes dipped down to her lips.

A strangled, long "Baaaabe" called out, and the thumping stopped.

Sam cleared his throat as he punched to reform his pillow and turned around, the moment having been broken. "Finally."

Iris rolled her eyes at herself—*so embarrassing*—and pulled her eye mask down.

He let out a long sigh beside her. "Night, Bun-Buns."

It was going to be a long two weeks.

CHAPTER FOUR

SAM

Sam pushed the thoughts from last night out of his head as Iris spoke with the bike rental attendant at Orchard House. Her smile was warm, and those dark blue eyes looked navy in the afternoon sun as they laughed. Her sweater hugged her body and he ripped his eyes away, thinking of how hard she'd breathed last night as they listened to moans. How the outline of her breasts moving in the dark room were still etched in his memory.

He shook his head to clear it and walked his bike out to the dirt trail. As they buckled their bike helmets in front of Orchard House, Iris's face went pale.

"You okay there, Bertone? Think you can handle the wild and rugged terrain of a mile of dirt path down to the apple orchard?"

"Sure," she said, shrugging it off.

"We can skip it, you know. Do something that doesn't involve dead fruit on the ground and a truckload of bees."

"No, this is part of the experience. I need to write about it." She stared straight ahead with a serious face, psyching herself up for it.

He swallowed a chuckle. She wouldn't appreciate him pointing out how adorable she was. "When's the last time you rode a bike?"

She shrugged and tightened her helmet more. "I mean, college, but you know. There's that whole saying about how you don't die when you try it after ten years."

Sam kicked up his kickstand and pushed off. He looked over his shoulder, waiting for Iris, and saw her feet still planted on the ground.

She stood, concentrating, staring in front of her, trying to get the courage to move forward.

"Put your feet on the pedals. C'mon, we're losing daylight."

"I'm coming," she grumbled. She put one foot on the pedal and caught her balance.

She lifted the second onto the other pedal and looked triumphant, but as he watched in horror, she forgot to push forward. She slowly fell like timber into the bushes next to her.

"Push!" he called far too late as a strangled yell came from within the decorative bushes surrounding the backyard of the inn.

Don't laugh. Don't laugh, he thought as he biked back to her.

Cozy Nights in Vermont

"Maybe try to pedal next time," he said, hopping off of his bike. Her bike wheel slowly spun in the air, and he found her arm in the bushes, pulling her slowly to standing.

"Apparently, that metaphor is shit," she said, a twig stuck between her helmet chin strap and her hair. She was completely frazzled but, goddamnit, pretty fucking cute.

It had always been easy to put her in the not-datable box because she'd always been with Bart, the opportunistic fucker. He'd seen a good thing sophomore year of high school and stayed with Iris through college. Sam didn't creep on other people's girlfriends, but now...maybe she was fair game.

"You okay?" he asked, still trying to bite back the laugh. He pulled the twig from her hair.

"Yes," she said primly, responding as if she knew she looked ridiculous.

"That's the slowest I've ever seen someone fall." She chuckled with him, despite herself. "Why didn't you take your foot off the pedals?"

Iris wiped the dust off of her pants. "I forgot it's not like spin class. I'm usually clipped in."

"Well, the last time I fell off my bike, my dad told me I had to get back on immediately because otherwise I'd be terrified of it. So, on you go." He shooed her toward the bike still on the ground.

"But your dad's an asshole." She grimaced at her banana-seated enemy.

"Yeah, tell me about it," Sam scoffed. Iris knew of what she spoke, but it turned out his asshole dad was right about this one thing. "Unfortunately it's Larsson's family rules."

She grumbled as she picked up the bike and hopped on. Sam grabbed the back of her bike seat for stability.

"You're gonna put both of your feet on the pedals while I hold you steady, and *then* you're going to push. And if you need to stop again, what are we going to do?"

"Take our feet off the pedals."

"Louder for those in the back," he yelled.

"Take our feet off the *fucking* pedals," she yelled back.

"Language, darling," he said as an older couple walked by.

"Ugh!" was her delicate reply.

"Annnnd...aim away from the bushes!" he said, pushing her bike off as she pedaled away.

"I'm doing it!" she called with excitement, wobbling from side to side. He pedaled harder to catch up with her.

A half hour later, they wandered through the orchard as Sam snapped photos. Iris walked back from grilling an orchard worker about the apples.

"This is not an exposé, Iris," Sam said as he focused his lens on the bikes against a tree as the sun set behind them.

"I want to add color and specificity to the article. I can't say, 'The apples were juicy.' I have to say, 'The Macintosh, in-season, Grade A apples were tart and had juicy hints of the berries grown next to them."

"Okay, Virginia Woolf." He changed the focus on his lens. "Either scoot into the shot or out of the shot. Your shadow is in my view."

She scurried behind him as she snacked on an apple.

He'd already found himself taking a few candids of her as she'd spoken with the orchard worker. His lens tended to drift to her face as strands of her wavy brunette hair danced across her forehead in the breeze.

Iris had this ruddy, healthy complexion that belonged outdoors. She wasn't made for an office. She was made to experience the world, for adventure.

"How are the photos coming?" she asked, not looking at him.

"Gorgeous," he said, his lens again finding her face as she was backlit against the sunset. She turned around to see him and stuck her tongue out. "Or at least some of them."

"Hungry?" She lifted their picnic supplies.

"Starving. The breakfast buffet only had grits by the time I walked down this morning."

He unfurled the picnic blanket with a *whuff* and laid it on a table under the arch of two apple trees. Lazy bumble bees buzzed through fallen apples and wildflowers around them.

All in all, this was a pretty great way to earn a living.

Iris spread out their food, already picking out her pickle and putting it on his plate and grabbing his hard-boiled egg and putting it on hers.

"Hey," he said in surprise.

Her eyebrow quirked with a knowing look. "Did you grow a love of hard-boiled eggs since the last time I saw you?"

"Surprised you remembered. That's all," he said, impressed. "Thanks baaaaabe."

She smirked as he crunched into one of the pickles.

The day turned idyllic as the sun began to turn everything golden in the late afternoon.

And to think he'd woken up yesterday morning, miserable with a hangover, thinking his life was amounting to nothing. Now here he was less than 48 hours later, sitting on a bench in a beautiful orchard with a beautiful woman, getting paid to do what he loved.

The silence settled between them as they ate their early dinner. He bit into an apple that had been picked off the tree five minutes earlier. It was warm from the sun—tart, juicy, sweet.

A lot like the woman across from him.

He wanted to know where she stood. Was she still engaged? Was she getting the ring resized? Shit, maybe she was married. Didn't some people have to get the engagement and wedding rings melted together when they got married?

Cozy Nights in Vermont

"So no ring?" he said, choking on his sandwich as the question stumbled out of his mouth.

"That happens when you break off an engagement," she said nonchalantly with a brief, sardonic smile.

Jackpot.

He swallowed, trying to play it cool. "I'm sorry. That sounds hard. How did he take it?"

She picked at her food. "He broke things off, actually."

This time he really choked on his sandwich. It slid down into his throat like a rock.

"*He* broke it off?"

She had been together with Bart since their sophomore year of high school. Bart was the human equivalent of a walking beige flag. Bart was fine, but nothing like the go-getter spitfire full of sparkle across from him.

"He never wanted to set the date," she said, picking apart her sandwich, taking the crusts off. He loved that she still did that. "He said I was 'pressuring him' after five years of being engaged, and then decided to finally end it. That was two years ago."

He'd felt some strange relief. "I can't say I'm sorry, but it sucks he wasted your time."

Her back straightened, a thought visibly passing over her face.

Oh shit. Did I say the wrong thing? Maybe she's still in love with him.

"Thank you," she said with genuine appreciation. "He did waste my time." She looked at him with a narrowed gaze, trying to suss something out in her head—he knew that look. "Why did you agree to this gig?"

"I heard I got to hang out with a woman who hates me and thought, 'Sounds like a neat way to spend two weeks.'"

"I don't hate you," she said softly with a shake of her head. "You irritate the shit out of me because you're so competitive."

"Just because I won our 'how many apples can you pick into your basket as fast as possible' competition, doesn't make me competitive."

"You cheated. You're taller than me."

"Grabbing a branch and shaking it is not cheating."

She rolled her eyes at him as he laughed at himself, hearing the competitiveness in his tone.

She shivered as a breeze blew past them. It was cooler here than in Boston, and Iris had always been cold-natured.

"Come on." He grabbed their trash and walked over to a nearby wastebasket. "I got all the photos I need for now. Let's go back inside."

She picked up her bike with a sidelong glance at him. "You still didn't answer the question. How does a Peabody-nominated photojournalist who's covered international conflicts find himself on a train to Vermont with little ol' me?"

If only she knew. He sighed as he walked to his bike.

He hadn't shot that many international assignments, actually. He'd ridden the coattails of a couple of splashy gigs. But he'd gotten tired of trying to mentally compete with his father, famed Pulitzer-prize winning author. He wanted to settle into a life that was *his own* rather than chase awards anymore. Maybe a role at *Discover & Dwell* could be it.

"Because Bertone, sometimes you want to be with the person who makes you irritated beyond reason."

She threw a middle finger at him again as she got on her bike. Gritting her teeth and pushing off with a vengeance, she wobbled so hard that he sucked in a breath, waiting for her to crash. But he knew Iris, and she was not to be underestimated, whether it was on a last minute deadline or on an endearingly wobbly bike.

Maybe it wouldn't be so easy to grab that full-time role after all.

* * *

A moan crawled through the air and through Sam's skin as he lay on the cool grass under an impossibly purple sky. His cock stirred as heavy breasts pressed against his face and Sam moaned back, sliding a tongue between them. Plush and heavy, they felt luxurious. He craved more. Fuck, he'd never tasted something so perfect. Salty, like a living sea. Crashing waves and sea wind whipping around them, they intertwined together as she rode his cock up and down.

Iris's face was twisted in delicious agony as she rode him hard, every curve bouncing so hard that he'd come if he looked any longer. Yes. She fucked like she lived—passionately. He rolled on top of her and into a feather bed in one fell swoop.

Somehow a fire crackled behind them now in a cobblestone cottage. Her tits were lifted into the air, firelight licking over them. He salivated at her dusky nipples. Licked his lips and thought only of them. Of burying his cock between them.

But she shoved his head down, and he ate, and ate, licking so she arched under him. He pinned her down, not wanting her to miss a lick. Her nails raked into his hair, keeping him in place. He was made to eat her pussy. Her tart, needy taste made his hips thrust involuntarily.

"More, Sam, more," she chanted again and again. He sucked her clit, wanted to push her higher, make her remember him. Claim her so she'd never go back to before, wherever before was in this moment.

She was his, his, *his*, as he sucked harder and her cries went higher. Thick thighs clamped his ears as she broke under his tongue, until he couldn't take it anymore.

He stood up to where she was on the editorial desk now, the setting having moved as though by magic. Her pussy was out and her skirt piled around her waist. They'd get caught so he'd have to be fast.

He grasped her ankles together in the air, playing with her pussy, sliding a finger in and out, getting her ready. She arched her back, papers sliding everywhere, but for once, she didn't care. Just needed him like he needed her.

"Fuck me, Sam," she pleaded. He wanted her to beg. To want it as much as he did. He circled the head of his cock at her entrance, still holding her legs in the air pressed together where anyone might walk by and see her thick, round ass hanging off of his editorial desk.

"Say it," he growled. He pushed his cock in an inch and she squeezed.

"I..." He pinched her clit. "I always wanted it to be you," she sobbed. And he slid into her, tight and wet.

She clenched around him, permanently. He'd live here forever now, he realized, and he grasped her thighs, pressing her calves against his face with a rapturous smile. He pulsed once, twice. "Fuuuuu—"

Sam shot up panting out of bed. A sheen of sweat covered his body.

Where the fuck am I?

He got his bearings. Dark room. *Hotel?*

No, inn.

Not having sex. His cock throbbed, hard as a rock. He hated his weird, intense dreams that made no sense.

Iris slept safe and sound on the other side of the bed with a solid foot between them.

He wiped a hand down his face, leaning over to catch his breath. *Jesus. H. Christ.* He hadn't had a sex dream in years. And never about someone he knew, only a vague sense of feelings and lust.

He lay back down. *Maybe it's a one-off. Just a few days since I handled things and all my hormones are fucked up because I'm living with an annoying goddess.*

Closing his eyes, he tried to drift off back to sleep. But images of dream Iris riding him flashed in his brain. He'd have to learn how to handle this so it didn't get out of hand. He generally didn't fantasize about real people when he jerked off. Too weird when he saw them later. He needed a clear division, and his brain needed to get onboard.

He tossed and turned for an hour until he finally gave in at 4 a.m. and went to the bathroom to think of anyone but the woman beside him.

CHAPTER FIVE

SAM

"You're lost."

Sam gripped the steering wheel and gritted his teeth twice as hard.

How did I have a hard-on for this woman fourteen hours ago? "I'm not lost."

Gone were the visions of Iris from last night looking scorchingly sexy. Now, he wanted to throttle her.

He'd stopped himself—twice—from thinking about her as he'd handled his cock last night. She was curvy and luscious, and she was more confident and more gorgeous than ever before. His dream made him think of everything he pushed to the back of his head when it came to Iris Bertone.

"You're definitely lost." Her smug slurp made him grind his teeth harder.

He'd taken the back roads to their next inn, and they'd lost cell phone coverage.

He wanted the real Vermont experience away from the highway. They'd passed small general stores winding through different towns, and he'd already hopped out twice to get photos.

"We wouldn't have found that apple cider stand had we been on the highway," he said, pointing to her drink as he stopped at a stop sign in the middle of nowhere.

Were they facing east? Left was *probably* the way to go.

Iris's emo indie music crooned through the SUV with renewed vigor, mocking him.

"We're going to need coffee if this stuff keeps playing," he said with a sigh.

"It creates a *mood*," she said, as if it was the most obvious thing in the world. The emotional, angsty sounds of an acoustic guitar echoed around them. "You can't drive through misty Vermont fields in the fall and listen to EDM."

"Great, then just inject caffeine straight into my eyeballs instead." The gray skies darkened as the afternoon fell around them. Green and saffron-yellow trees were bursting through the countryside in the gray autumn day as he drove down the curvy road.

As he turned the curve down a rolling hill, a three-story block of glass and wood emerged in the mist-covered field in a thicket of trees.

Cozy Nights in Vermont

"Aha!" He was triumphant. They'd somehow found the next inn. "We're here. Totally knew it all along."

Though, *inn* was maybe the wrong word for what was in front of them. It looked like a glass paperweight had plonked down into a fall wonderland entirely in contrast with the organic leafy trees surrounding it.

"And it's cozy, too," Iris said with a sarcastically raised eyebrow.

"Should make for some good photos, though the research staff is playing fast and loose with what constitutes an 'inn.'" He pulled over to get a long-distance shot of the exterior.

Ten minutes later, they stood in front of the building with their bags, trying to figure out how to get in. Every single panel of the building was a giant window with no entrance.

"Maybe we should call?" he said, scratching his head as he hoped an underground entrance would appear by sheer force of will.

Suddenly, the bottom glass panel of the structure moved upward. It lifted vertically to reveal a stylish young woman in an oversized wool poncho and one of those hats white women loved to wear in the fall.

"You are back in nature, as you belong," the stylish woman said in a low, meaningful voice with her arms still wide open. Her poncho swayed in the breeze as she waited for them expectantly.

Iris silently turned to him, fighting back a smile. She'd

never had a poker face; that was why it was so fun to tease her all the time.

"Hello," Sam said, waving a friendly hand.

"Welcome to the Oasis at Canterbury." She emphasized the Oh with a guttural oomph and stared at them expectantly.

Oh lord. Could he make it through two nights here?

"Should we come in?" Sam asked.

"Whatever your destiny may be," the blonde host replied with a solemn voice and a veneered smile.

"This is gonna be fun," Iris whispered with glee as she picked up her bag.

They walked across a large patio and into a sparse, chic open-air lobby. It reminded him of expensive desert houses in Palm Springs. Harsh concrete and steel contrasted with a lone wood sculpture and animal hides on the floor. It was an interesting change from the homey coziness of a normal Vermont B&B.

"Come gather and we can settle into the energy of the space," she said, sweeping her ponchoed arm into the middle of the sunken seating area. They set their bags down and gingerly climbed down into the living room where oversized white fluffy armchairs lined the space.

"You must be Jessica. I've read so many great things about Oasis," Iris said.

"I prefer Jess," Jess said with a placating tone.

Cozy Nights in Vermont

"Is this where we check in?" Sam said, still trying to piece together what was happening.

"Technically yes." Jess wrapped her poncho further around her as she braided her limbs into a knot and sat on the oversized chair. "We don't like the words *checked in*," she whispered the last two words. "They feel so corporate, and not what we're about. The inn experience here is about welcoming you back to nature."

"Wow. Do all your guests get a personalized welcome service?" Sam asked.

"Oh my gosh, you're *so* funny," Jess said, putting her hair behind her ears.

Yikes. Openly flirting with him even though he was here with someone else?

No thanks. Instant ick.

He'd had a hard and fast rule about cheaters, given how public his parents' divorce had been, how obvious his father's cheating had been. He'd won a fucking Pulitzer Prize for it. The memoir of him being torn between two women. Sam would never, ever be like him.

"I only book a maximum of two guests per day so I can give them my undivided attention. And so, you know, I can, like, chill," she said, sending him a flirty little shrug.

Sam ventured a glance at Iris, and she was unamused. Maybe even sliding toward disgruntled. When her single eyebrow arched toward her hairline that meant she was in revenge-plotting mode.

He'd seen it *plenty* of times.

"Well, my girlfriend and I are excited to settle in." Sam reached out a hand toward Iris, and she sighed but took his hand. His thumb brushed over her fingers with affection.

"Oh, your *girlfriend*," she said slowly, staring at Iris. "Oh my gosh, that's sooo cuuute." Her *so* and *cute* were pinched and unconvincing. "Well, you guys definitely need a romance package. I'm so sorry. I wasn't getting that vibe from you at all. Let's see what we can do to reignite that spark, okay?" She tapped Iris's leg as if they were girlfriends set on a mission to make Sam get his act together.

"Okay, well." Jess clapped her hands together, suddenly down to business. "You're in our nature experience."

"Uh, experience?" Sam asked.

Why didn't this woman use normal words for things?

"Some might call it a, quote, 'room,' but you'll see it's an experience. Can I get you any chicory root or bark-infused teas before I unveil the experience?"

He heard a snort on his right.

"They're great appetite suppressants," Jess said with a happy shrug at Iris.

"What the fuck?" Sam blurted out as Iris looked murderous.

Jess patted his arm. "Oh, us girls always want little tips

and tricks to snatch those waists, right?" Jess elbowed Iris.

"My girlfriend is perfect as she is," Sam said protectively.

Jesus. Some people. Iris was, in fact, perfectly shaped and sized. She had full, powerful thighs. A stomach that he'd describe like a luscious Renaissance painting. Full and sexy. Great tits and an ass that wouldn't quit.

Not that he had any particular feelings for *her* though. These were just facts. She was hot and he was man enough to separate the annoying I'm-always-right personality from her looks.

"Why don't you follow me?" Jess hopped out of the sunken living room as he and Iris climbed out less gracefully.

"Thanks," Iris said with a curious look up at him.

He held out a hand to help her out of the awkward sunken living room. "Just doing my job."

Jess guided them to a tall staircase. "Each experience has its own entrance. Yours has a staircase or a rope ladder if that would be more fun," she said with an impish smile as if she and Sam shared a joke.

Not happening, blondie.

The steep, thin spiral staircase wrapped around a single black pole leading up two stories above. Jess flitted up the stairs, her poncho-covered arms wide as if gliding.

Iris threw her head back in exhaustion. "Why are there always *stairrrrs.*"

"Go ahead. I'll take your bag," Sam said, grabbing the bag from her.

"It's fine, I can do it," Iris said, wrestling it back from him with a resigned grimace.

"You said you wanted help last time." He grabbed for it. *This woman.* It was like she was put on this earth for the sole reason of arguing with him.

She dodged him. "No, because then you'll remind me how I needed your help for *five more inns*," she whispered.

"*Fine.*" He threw a hand up. "Then at least go first so when you fall, we can *both* die."

And so I get a nice view of your ass in front of my face.

As he walked into the glass covered room—er, experience—his mouth gaped open.

Okay, I kinda get why she calls it an experience now.

The room had floor-to-ceiling glass windows overlooking the rolling multicolored hills below. Green and orange leaves intertwined for acres and acres as a moody mist crawled through them.

He peeked his head around the corner, and Iris stared open-mouthed at the bathroom that had completely transparent glass walls. "This is my actual worst nightmare," Iris muttered in horror.

A toilet and shower sat overlooking the gorgeous view. Anyone in the room could see straight into the bathroom.

Cozy Nights in Vermont

Iris peeked her head in the door of the bathroom. "And there's no curtain?"

"It's so our guests can submit their vulnerability to nature," Jess said with a mansplainy tone, as if this was a normal feature of a guest room. "Make sure to try our handmade soaps. I make them myself. And your cleansing crystals are in your experience sommelier basket." She picked a red one and held it out to Iris. "These will cleanse those root chakras so you can connect on a physical level." Iris looked about two steps away from chucking the crystals at Jess's poncho.

After Jess left, Sam grabbed shots of the room and bathroom. He pointedly ignored the cozy, chenille-covered bed. He'd been thinking of his dream about her too often today as he looked at Iris. She'd worn a figure-hugging dress with a loose jacket thrown over it, and any time his gaze lingered on her, he'd flash back to the dream.

What she'd look like if she lost control for once, wasn't three steps ahead of everybody else, didn't have an ordered 15-minute-chunk agenda to go by. Didn't feel so on and responsible for every fucking thing and every fucking one.

Sam walked back to their bags at the entrance with his tripod. "All done," he called.

Iris stretched her neck. "After three hours of bumpy back roads, I need to stretch my legs. There's an art installation on the property. Though given what else she created here, I'm expect it will be concrete blocks tossed into a hollow tree."

"I could go on a hike." Sam grabbed his camera bag and slung it over his shoulder, honestly excited for her commentary on what was sure to be a ridiculous installation.

* * *

After Iris took five minutes to climb down the staircase, butt-scooting the entire time, they were finally out on crunchy fall leaves. The crisp air was thick with the scent of firewood and Sam breathed it in by the lungful.

He'd get one more hour of light before it turned too dark for photographs. Iris pulled out the paper map she'd brought from the room and turned it around and around in a circle, trying to find her bearings.

"I think we go through those trees." She pointed to an archway of leafy yellow and orange trees. They'd gone farther north, and fall was kicking off in earnest here.

He snapped pictures of her walking along the path, flailing her arms while stepping on stones to try to avoid the muddy patches.

"Oh, shit. I'm in your shot, aren't I?" she said, turning around suddenly, laughing. He captured that burst of her smile.

He waved her to the left and she managed to avoid the big puddles as she danced around piles of yellow and brown leaves on the ground.

"I think if we cross the wooden bridge, we can see her

experiences," she said, lowering her voice with a husky tone like Jess had.

They crunched their way into the path through the thicket of fall foliage and he couldn't resist baiting her. "I dunno... you sound a *little* jealous."

"She hand-makes her soaps. She lives in a gorgeous glass house. Of course I'm jealous. Did you see how hot she was? And she flirted with you."

Jess had toned thighs, a blinding white smile, and long blonde hair she'd probably paid good money for.

Sure, Jess was conventionally hot.

But Iris?

She was exquisite. A stunning knockout who was a spunky nerd, hell bent on besting him at every turn. With surprise, he realized he'd much rather share a bed with that than conventionally hot.

He couldn't resist teasing her. "Yep, you definitely sound jealous, Bertone—"

"I mean, she openly flirted with my 'boyfriend.' Plus, I can't imagine how that room is ADA compliant."

"Did you check for smoke detectors, too?" he joked as he lined up another shot of the tree archways.

"Yes, I did. Thank you *so* much," she said with smug satisfaction, hopping over a puddle. "I'm adding it to my list." She pulled out her planner and jotted down more thoughts.

She cared a lot about this assignment. She took it more seriously than he'd ever taken anything.

"What were you doing before you got this gig?" he said, trying to sound nonchalant as they walked over an old wooden bridge with a creek running underneath it.

He'd known she'd stayed in the journalism field, but he never checked professional social media, and Jo was cagey about giving him details.

"Aha! I found it," she said, pointing ahead on the path. A large black cube with rounded corners sat in contrast with a half circle of trees. She whirled on him with triumph in her eyes. "I told you. I'm sure she was going for *The Contrast of the Human Experience: A Man-Made Something-Something Against Nature's Bounty*. Also, this isn't a hike apparently, it's a 'pilgrimage,'" she added seriously, pointing to the map.

He couldn't resist baiting her again. "After she flirted with me, I don't know if you can be an impartial journalist. C'mon, let me see your notes." He held out his hand.

She shielded her notebook away from him. "Absolutely not. I don't need you to weasel your way into the byline with me by becoming my co-author."

"Look, there's the next cube," he said, distracting her. As she turned, he snatched her notebook.

She was a solid five inches shorter than him, and she pummeled him with her fists as he kept the notebook out of reach.

He jogged ahead backwards, trying to read her chicken-scratch handwriting. A pang of recognition hit him, as he remembered it on chalkboards, papers, and whiteboards in his past. Even on a sign in an insulting "Larsson is a Lughead" smear campaign for junior class president.

"Use Walden quote to open article," he read aloud. "A little on the nose, don't you think?" he said as he flipped through the rest of her notes which were facts about the inn. "How do you *feel* about where we've been?" He riffled through it, looking for any sort of adjective.

"I feel like...they're inns?" She shrugged.

He continued flipping through the pages as she grabbed at the notebook. "You're one of the most passionate people I know. Let it shine through in your writing." He handed it back to her with a smile. "As long as it's not motivated by your obvious jealousy."

Snatching it back, she silently marched down the path toward the next black cube. *Uh-oh. Must have struck a nerve.*

The only thing worse than a mouthy Iris was a silent one.

Sam got shots of the black cube, but as they rounded the trail back to the inn, something still pulled at him. "You never answered my question. What's kept you busy the last few years?"

"Just little nothing jobs." She shrugged.

"Oh, come on. Tell me. Every story is worth telling," he said, trying to catch her eye. That had been the motto of their Feature Story professor in college.

She nodded with a faint smile. "I did a couple years at an online site, trying to build up my portfolio of modern pieces. I was in Buffalo for so long—" She started to say something but stopped herself. "But I'm not trapped anymore. That's in the past."

"Trapped?" He stopped with a crunch in the gravel on his hiking boots. His stomach bottomed out and in that moment he realized he'd break Bart's legs if he'd hurt her.

"Metaphorically. Bart and I had been together since forever, and I thought when we got engaged...I don't know. Our life would finally start. But we just stayed in Buffalo even though I'm cold—"

"All the time," they said at the same time.

"Right?" She laughed, pointing to him. "I'd put in two years at the *Finger Lake Scallywag*."

He barked out a laugh. "That is not a real thing."

"It is, look it up," she said with smiling insistence. "I dreamed about having all these adventures, solving the world's problems and writing all the best words, but in the end, I was writing about boat maintenance in Upstate New York winters."

"That sounds..." He paused, thinking about how to soften the blow, but thought fuck it. He knew her. "God, that sounds awful."

"It was," she said with her face in her hands, laughing. "It was awful. Thank you. I feel seen."

Cozy Nights in Vermont

The gigantic garage door opened as Jess welcomed them back in a different poncho.

"Good evening, you two. How was your pilgrimage? Did you connect on a spiritual level?"

Sam met Iris's laughing eyes and, without missing a beat and without lying, he happily responded, "Yes."

CHAPTER SIX

IRIS

Iris sipped her pumpkin spice-flavored coffee as Sam took another turn up into a dense forest. She somehow only wanted silly, sweet lattes as it turned chilly. It felt like a kickoff to something special, like an extra twinkly Christmas or an extra crisp fall.

They'd had an uneventful rest of their stay at the Oasis at Canterbury. She'd honestly found the experience kind of boring. How many leaves could one peep, really?

She and Sam had been eager to leave that morning and find a bathroom that did not require the other person to climb down two flights of stairs.

They were on the way to their third of seven inns, Happy Glamping. "I've read up on the founder of the next place," Iris said excitedly.

"Shocker," Sam retorted as he peered at the GPS. They drove around a huge, mirror-still lake with mist creeping in at the edges.

Cozy Nights in Vermont

"He's a former tech mogul who sold off his company and doubled down on his investment in green tourism. He's written five books, including a guide on how to turn the world around by making everything more *intense*."

Sam raised an eyebrow at her.

She loved that challenge in his eyes. It meant he cared as much as she did. Bart had been easygoing and rarely paid much attention when she got going on a tirade. He'd been interested in a cookie-cutter life, and she'd fooled herself into thinking that he was the only one who'd ever make her happy.

But as it turned out? She could make *herself* happy.

And she wanted more than a cookie-cutter life. She wanted it all, and she wanted a challenge. *Maybe if I nail the article, Ben will see how adventurous I can be and give me the Discover and Dwell role.*

"It looks like you have some opinions you'd like to share," she said.

"Mmm, I know this founder guy's type." Sam rubbed his chin. It was his version of rolling his eyes.

"He might be at the inn. I'm hoping I'll get an exclusive interview with him. He's considered one of the top one hundred geniuses of our time. It says so on the back of his book," she said, pulling out a copy from her bag.

Sam snorted as he drove. "If they have cups filled with Kool-Aid, please don't drink any."

She thwacked him with the book as the car turned onto a gravel road. "You're jealous because he's so young and he's done so much."

"I know the Venn diagram between sociopaths and CEOs has a pretty big overlap. And I think his might be a circle."

They drove past a sign that said "Happy Glamping: an intense-forward, low ecological impact community."

"I thought we were only going to inns?" Sam said as he slowed onto the gravel road.

"They have a main building that's an inn, but also tiny homes and 'ecological super stays,'" she said, checking her notes. She shrugged. "Maybe the editorial staff wanted to mix it up."

It felt like camp to Iris as they drove onto the property. "Did you ever go to camp?" she said idly. They drove down the meandering gravel path, past unique tiny houses, makeshift tents, and tiny cabins all strung together with Edison lights.

"I did. So my father didn't have to deal with me for three months of the year."

Robert Larsson had been—and still was—a celebrated author. Iris was envious at Sam's leg up in the publishing world. He had an instantly recognizable last name, whereas she had two loving parents who gave terrible job advice ("Don't put money in a 401k. That's the company taking your money." "Make sure to stay in one job for seven years before moving on. You don't want to be flaky."). They'd never had money for sleepaway camp, so she and Sophia had slept in a tent in the backyard until they got too covered in bug bites.

Maybe Happy Glamping could fill the camp void in her life.

They passed a group of smiling people chatting away. One chopped wood as they laughed with the people sitting across from them. They all wore puffy vests and flannel, and sipped from handmade ceramic mugs.

Her nose pressed to the glass as they drove by. "I hope they have a place to make pottery." *This is going to be the best place yet. Fresh air, more happy people than I've seen at the other two inns.* She'd start drafting her article and put *feeling* into it.

But not because Sam said to. *Because I want to,* she decided.

Couples of all genders and ethnicities walked hand in hand through the campsite, chatting and smiling. Some carrying baskets of hand-picked greenery or bushels of apples. Some leisurely strolled between the cabins as an acoustic guitar played somewhere.

As they walked into the main inn, the smell of pastries and baking bread enveloped her like an old friend.

"Smells good," Sam said with a noncommittal shrug as they walked in with their bags.

They looked for a reservation desk and instead saw even *more* smiling people walking past them. "Maybe we're in the wrong building?"

Elise Kennedy

There were several small, old buildings reclaimed from past lives as maybe a schoolhouse or a farm on the property. The one they'd walked into had wide, dark oak planks that felt sturdy under Iris's feet. She peeked around the corner to see a kitchen with enormously tall ceilings, tall windows, and honest-to-god pies cooling on the windowsill, covered in latticework and sugar.

"Can someone help us find the reservation desk? Do you work here?" Sam asked.

A serene woman with long hair appeared. "I'm Ember. I don't work here, but it is my pleasure to furtherance our mission. Come with me."

"Yeah, that's a totally normal thing to say," Sam said, leaning in to whisper into Iris's ear.

Iris elbowed him in his side. "No worse than two ponchos and a pilgrimage," she whispered back.

Candles were lit throughout the dim space flanked by antique books and dried flowers in old vases. Workers wore flowing dresses, organic material like flannel, and worn canvas pants, reminding her of a high-end photography shoot.

"You see no one's on their phones?" she said with excitement over her shoulder, as they followed Ember. "This is a simple way of life," she said as they curved around the winding building.

"Let me get Tags," Ember offered.

"We're meeting Tags Cunningham, the founder? Oh my

gosh." A flutter of nerves and excitement rolled in her stomach.

This was it; this was the chance she'd been waiting for. A chance to interview a notable executive. Maybe this could even be a sub-feature within the article. Oh! Or maybe she could form a connection with him and come back for another outlet. Grow her empire—

"There's something creepy about the vibe here," Sam said, searching for hidden cameras.

"Welcome, welcome. I'm so glad you all are here." A spindly white man with long hair and a beanie pulled over it, wearing an expensive watch, walked toward them. "I'm so thrilled you were able to make time for us in your schedule."

Sam stared at Iris with confusion.

"Oh, we're here celebrating our two-year anniversary," Iris said to Tags, but mostly for Sam's benefit.

Tags clasped her hands. "Yes, and you're spending it with us. We take that seriously." Tags looked Iris dead in the eyes with an intense sincerity that was overwhelming.

"I'm a big fan. I've been reading your books," Iris said, her hands still clasped in Tags. *Was he gonna let go soon?*

"Thank you. I appreciate you. That means a lot to me, Iris and Sam. It's good to meet you, brother," he said, sticking a hand out and clapping Sam on the shoulder like they were old friends.

Oh god, maybe Sam was right? Was Tags a teensy bit weird?

"Let me show you where you're going to stay with us. Since you're celebrating, we've put you in one of our extra *intense* stays," he said, jogging ahead of them as Sam leaned over Iris's shoulder and picked up her bag without her asking.

"If there are any handcuffs involved, we're running."

"I'm surprised you have time for this," Iris said, catching up with Tags and ignoring Sam. "I know you're involved in a lot of businesses."

They were practically jogging to keep up with him through the rows of tiny houses, cabins, and tents.

"I like to take a hands-on approach to Happy Glamping. It's an important part of the way the future will work: us all being in an intense community together. Here's where we have you, our Wanderlust Wagon."

A delighted squeak leapt out of Iris's mouth before she could contain it. "Oh my gosh, I've always wanted to stay in one of these," her voice filled with genuine awe.

A sunburst-pink 1960s VW bus had been converted into a tiny home. It was connected with glowing string lights to the buildings around it and had a cute welcome sign, a little welcome mat, and a table and chairs outside.

She wiggled side to side with excitement. Sam looked less than impressed.

Cozy Nights in Vermont

Tags leaned against a tree. "We hope you'll be so comfortable here. We want to be intentional about our ecological footprint, so the facilities are shared and completely organic," he said, pointing to a row of outhouses.

Sam groaned behind her. He was going to ruin her one chance to connect with a *mogul*.

She brightened in response to make up for his bad attitude. "I'd love to know more about how you're offsetting your carbon footprint," she asked. They still used some electricity with the string lights and fans she'd seen in the houses.

"Our volunteers take turns powering our lights and any needed generators with bike power. By the way this location also comes with a tent if you'd rather sleep under the stars," he said, pointing as Ember came to escort him to the next appointment. "I have to counsel a couple I'm going to marry this weekend, but I hope to see you at the bonfire later."

Tags and Ember floated away, heads together, emphatically planning something with wide smiles.

She bounced on her toes, trying to contain herself. "I've always loved VW buses, especially the old ones," Iris said with an excited clap as she climbed into it.

Sam set his things down on the ground outside of the van as they climbed in. "I'll sleep in the tent," Sam said with resignation. Sam was built like a Viking and took up a comically large amount of space in the antique bus.

It had a small sink, drawers for toiletries, a driver's seat, a record player, and a nearly queen-sized bed with additional string lights lit up over it. A fluffy linen duvet covered the mattress, and handmade quilts sat at the foot of the bed. She couldn't wait to make a cup of tea and curl into bed that evening all by herself. Plus, she could finally work out the lust that had been building with a little *self-care*, since she wouldn't be next to Sam.

"You sure you're okay sleeping outside?" she said, second-guessing herself.

"I'd need to see a chiropractor if I was in here for too long," he said, looking around. "Before you set your things down—"

"I know, I know. Photos, photos, photos," she said, flapping her hands as they hopped out.

After a few hours of downtime, they wandered through the campground to find the bonfire. They grabbed vegan sandwiches from a tray and found a log to sit on at the bonfire.

Sam sat next to her, closer than normal, and he looked around warily.

Tags was strumming on a guitar as several others banged tambourines, singing along to an old seventies hippie acoustic classic. The firelight sparkled, highlighting the smiles of people around the campfire.

Ember walked by with a tray of large, homemade, hand-cut marshmallows. "I made cinnamon marshmallows today. Would you like some?"

Cozy Nights in Vermont

Iris smirked at Sam but said with genuine excitement, "One thousand percent we would."

Sam smiled politely as he took one. "I didn't know cults could make such great desserts."

"Oh, we're not a cult. We're an intense-living community," Ember said without malice. "I hope you enjoy."

They both stuck their huge marshmallows onto whittled branches.

"It *looks* good," Sam said, inspecting the marshmallow the size of his hand. "But will we end up on a documentary if we eat it and they find our bodies ten days from now?"

"C'mon, *embrace* the experience, Sam. What I wouldn't give for an enormous chocolate bar and Graham cracker, but I will be happy with my low ecological impact marshmallow all the same."

Sam leaned. "So, you're really not getting a culty vibe?"

It felt intoxicating to be here. Like nothing could go wrong. They were safe and happy, enjoying nature. "It looks like a lot of people who have the same values enjoying their time together, including guests who are here for a short weekend stay."

They rotated their marshmallows over the fire in silence.

"And the vibes from Tags, the man who goes by not one inanimate object, but a whole bunch of them? Super weird."

She bumped his shoulder. "He can't help his name."

"He can help what he goes by as an adult," Sam said, inspecting his marshmallow to see if it had been properly roasted. "Watch it." He pointed at Iris's marshmallow that was currently ablaze.

The small ball of fire at the end of her stick was perfect. "I'm *roasting* it, Sam. This is how you do it."

"Roasting is not a synonym for ruining, Bertone," Sam said with alarm and grabbed for her stick. She dodged with practiced ease.

"*This* is how you roast a marshmallow."

His eyes were large with dismay. "*That* is how you lose a marshmallow to the fire. It's gonna melt off your stick."

The amount of alarm in his voice for a block of sugar made her laugh out loud. "You worry about the dumbest things." She blew on it until the flame fizzled out.

A charred blackened husk remained around the marshmallow block. "See? Perfectly done," she said happily, pulling it off of the branch and feeling the gooey meltiness of it hit her tongue. The crackle of the burned and smoky marshmallow contrasted with the cinnamon and sugar, swirling into a mixture of smoke and caramelized edges.

She closed her eyes and moaned around it. "Oh my god. I don't know what we paid to stay here, but it was worth the price of this."

"You literally put a coal in your mouth," Sam said as he showed her his perfectly browned marshmallow. "See? All you needed was a little patience for perfection."

Cozy Nights in Vermont

"Some of us don't have time for patience. Some of us like to grab life by the marshmallows and burn them."

"Let's see if this is worth the price of the Kool-Aid," he said, taking a bite of his perfectly roasted marshmallow. His eyes closed in much the same way that Iris's had.

"Oh fuck," he muttered as he moaned, savoring each bite. "I mean, how bad can one cult really be?"

Iris clutched her heart. "Did you agree with me on something?"

"Baked goods have never been a problem between us. Whether a hot dog is a sandwich or a taco, however…"

"Or whether a taco is a sandwich," Iris countered.

"See? We can't even agree on that."

Their infamous debate had finally broken the high school advisor. She'd made them debate team co-captains because they'd filibustered for four hours about it and she couldn't take it any longer.

"It's not so bad here. People are happy, there's not a selfie in sight, no one's zoned out with a partner next to them. Everyone's connecting over a shared love of burnt sugar." She licked the goo off of her fingers and Sam's eyes traced the movement.

It kind of made her want to lick her fingers again.

"You should be put in front of a war crime tribunal for what you did to that marshmallow." The warmth in his smile belied his words though.

As she sucked in a breath to respond to his outrageous accusation, a giant drop of water hit her eye. The pitter-patter of a sudden rainstorm started as people around the fire looked up. Thunder cracked and suddenly, sheets of rain poured down as everyone ran for cover.

The ground was a mushy mess of leaves and mud as they ran, trying to find their van.

As Iris ran, each step got harder and harder, pulling on her shoes until she stepped forward and found one socked foot in mud. Her shoe had been completely stuck in ankle-deep mud.

Sam was steps ahead of her but looked back when she dropped his hand. She hadn't even realized they'd been running hand in hand through the rain. They were completely drenched.

"My shoe!" she cried. She struggled on one foot, trying not to fall over. She grabbed for her shoe covered in mud.

"Come on," he yelled, bending down and pointing to his back. "Hop on."

"I can't do that," she yelled back. Iris was a sturdy girl. She rarely thought about her size, but it came crashing back in times like this. She wasn't a simple person to pick up like the featherweight girls she'd seen Sam with in the past.

"C'mon."

"Absolutely not!" she shouted to be heard over the thunder and rain as she struggled to put on her shoe,

Cozy Nights in Vermont

falling off to the side and her socked foot squishing in mud.

"Woman," he yelled. "Get. On." He blinked at her through furrowed brows, rain rolling off of them.

God, he does look like a Viking. "Alright. But if we both go down, you have to concede."

"Never," he yelled with a growing smile as thunder cracked. He knew exactly what she'd meant.

She slapped her hands emphatically. "By the laws of logic, a hot dog *is* a sandwich, Larsson!"

"Well then I won't fall, will I?"

Ugh, fine. She wrapped her arms around his neck and put one leg around his hip and jumped up with the other leg. To his credit, he didn't miss a step and instead ran the last 300 feet in the pouring rain to their VW bus.

They unlocked the door, and he turned around so she could hop onto the first step, rather than step in mud.

She turned around as he walked away.

"Come in," she yelled. They had stored his bag in the VW bus. "You can't sleep out there tonight."

The tent was pummeled as rain shot down in thick sheets.

He stepped into the van. "But you were rid of me for one night."

He wiped the water out of his eyes and puffed out a

breath, waiting for her response as it thundered outside the open door.

His hair was curled from the water dripping down the side of his cheek. It glistened against the stubble of his beard, and she wanted to brush it away with her lips. Feel the plastered shirt against his chest that was two inches from hers. She ached at the thought of putting her head against his chest and having his arms crushed around her. A low throb started. Raw, unfiltered desire overwhelmed her.

Oh no. A crashing realization hit her: she *wanted* him.

His attractiveness had moved out of the theoretical and into her pants.

They were out of breath from the run, and in the low light between them, a moment caught. He stared at the lips she bit as she tried to sort out the tilting world in front of her. Neither moved in the open door of the van.

"Stay," she said, her eyes never leaving his.

Water dripped off of his cheek, and she reached out a hand to wipe it away but then yanked it back.

"Okay," he whispered. "I'll stay."

CHAPTER SEVEN

IRIS

Iris crawled to her normal side in the shorter-than-normal bed of the VW bus an hour later. Sam still slept without a shirt, which she was starting to look forward to each night, seeing the dips and grooves of his muscles.

She couldn't stop marveling at the boy she'd known who had turned into the man in front of her. It felt like when the optometrist added the lenses until you could finally see the picture clearly. He'd come into focus with two images blurring in and out of each other: the distant past and the present of who he was now.

"Tell me something that's happened to you since college," she said.

"You want my resume?"

She knew his resume, but she'd never tell him that. She'd poked around his portfolio as she'd drowned her sorrows in tequila sodas and pecan cluster ice cream, feeling like an absolute failure as she edited yet another issue of the *Finger Lake Scallywag*.

She tapped her fingers, thinking. "Something a girlfriend would know. In case we get tested."

He threw back the covers and crawled in next to her. She now looked forward to the intimacy of sleeping next to him. It'd been a long two years since she'd been with anybody. She'd had a couple of one-night stands (no thank you) but no one she wanted to sleep over.

"Since senior year in college, I..." He thought for a minute. "Got a pierced ear," he said with a grimace.

"No," she gasped. Shocked, she sat up to look at his earlobes.

A small scar marked his lower left lobe. "Just this one, and I hated it. Did it on a dare from a journalist friend when we were on assignment in Paris."

"Oh, that sounds not even a *little* fabulous and glamorous," she said, mocking him with a pouting face.

"It is not glamorous when it gets infected and you don't know the word for antibiotic in French."

"So you became a bad boy for two weeks. What else?" She leaned on her elbow a few inches from his face. He'd had to curve his body around the mattress since it wasn't quite long enough for him.

"My favorite type of food is ramen, but only when it's cold outside. When it's hot, sushi, obviously."

Cozy Nights in Vermont

Her jaw dropped. "You famously made a whole thing about not ever eating raw fish."

"Well, I was wrong then. And young and stupid," he said, laughing at being called out.

She sat up straight in bed. "Stop the presses. I should roll down the window and yell, 'Sam Larsson admitted he was wrong and I was right about one fucking thing,'" she said as she poked his side.

"A broken clock is right twice a day," he said as he laughed. He grabbed her hand to stop her from poking him again and held it against his chest. Their eyes connected and they stilled.

There was that moment again.

That pause of maybe...more. This *something else* that had been growing in the air between them.

Flutters somersaulted around her midsection and danced lower at his heated look. Warmth flowed from her hand still against his chest. She wanted to flex her hand to feel it but clenched her core instead.

"What about you? What's changed with you?" he asked, finally dropping her hand.

"That's the worst part," she sighed, moving to lie down. "There's hardly anything to tell."

"Come on," he said, nudging her. "You can't possibly still be into *Twilight*."

"I stand by that movie," she said reflexively, pointing a warning finger at him.

"What would a boyfriend know?"

She sighed, hating to tell the story. To get into it and relive her failure.

"That I was relieved when Bart called off our engagement because I hadn't been brave enough to do it. That I feel like a gigantic failure because I—of all people—followed a boy instead of my own career. That I'm twenty-nine and waiting for my life to start. That maybe it started a few days ago." She gasped for air as it had all rushed out.

Realizing with a crashing wave of anxiety that, yep—she'd overshared. She'd said too much, and given him all the ammunition. She looked over with one eye open, waiting for a smart comeback.

Instead, he stared at her, a small smile on his face. "Then I'm glad I'll witness how your extraordinary life will finally start."

A lump caught in her throat and she looked away, blinking through unexpected, sudden emotion. Her sister was crazy successful. Her parents didn't understand her dreams. Friends were kind but constantly reassured her she was 'crazy and already killing it.' It had been a long time since she'd felt seen.

And for better or worse, Sam saw her.

The bed smelled like a campfire from where the smoke had blown on them, and dim string lights swayed in the now gentle rain outside. This was the most perfect way to fall asleep, she decided. A kind man next to her, listening to the sound of rain in a warm bed on a chilly night, covered in heavy quilts.

"Thanks," she whispered.

"Night," Sam said in the dark.

"Night."

* * *

SAM

Sam awoke the next morning to an empty spot beside him. Sunlight streamed in through the windows of the VW bus.

Around 2 a.m. the night before, he'd woken up with his arm around Iris with her tucked into his side. She'd looked so innocent as she slept. He was used to the Iris that was his verbal fencing partner, but last night he finally saw a glimpse of the soft underbelly she hid so well.

As she slept, her hair had fanned out beside his face, smelling like plums and vanilla. He'd allowed himself a moment to enjoy just holding her, soaking in that scent, before he moved his arm. She'd always had gorgeous, thick, wavy chestnut hair. It felt surprisingly soft against his face as she cuddled into him. He didn't mind it spread out over his pillow.

He didn't mind it at all, in fact.

He sat back and took in the bus. As far as romantic rooms went, he had to admit, this was near the top of what they'd experienced thus far. The first two inns were gorgeous but stately and grand, overwhelming. Here, all you had was each other, and it turned out, sometimes that was all you needed.

A strange chant outside shook him out of his daydreaming. He peered out the window; an orderly line of people waited to chop wood, happily chanting and clapping their hands.

Something didn't feel right. His gut was never wrong, and he'd trusted it to save his life more than once out in the field in dangerous conditions.

This was a sleepy, camp vibe of an inn, but something felt off. The people were too happy. They all wore the same expression and similar clothes, aside from a couple of guests like him and Iris.

They were scheduled to stay there for one more night to get a feel for everything that Happy Glamping had to offer. During the car ride the day before, Iris had babbled on about all the activities she wanted to try—pumpkin harvesting, a naturally occurring hot spring, and a guided tour through the hills on a nature walk. He hated to ruin her adventure, but safety first—always.

He tossed back the covers, still feeling the dread in his stomach that was never wrong. Tossing clothes in his bag, he packed his camera equipment and even took the liberty of packing Iris's things. Thankfully, she'd kept all her clothes in her bag, so all he had to grab was her toiletries and toss it in with his.

Cozy Nights in Vermont

Once he found Iris, he'd convince her that they needed to cut this short. He still wasn't exactly sure why, but the creepy founder, the weird words they'd been using, it didn't add up to 'inn' to him.

A few minutes later, his hiking boots met the floorboards of the first activities building as his eyes searched for Iris. She wasn't in the crafts building or out doing autumn yoga. She wasn't in the ominous wood chopping line (thank god), and so finally, he entered the main building.

The whitewashed walls of the kitchen were worn but fashionable, as though they'd been weathered on purpose. Sam searched until his eyes finally landed on the face he'd never expected to feel relieved to see.

Iris had an apron on, rolling dough using an old wooden rolling pin. A streak of flour was dashed across her nose. Her curly hair had been pulled into a high ponytail, and she laughed as Tags showed her how to use the rolling pin. He had his arms around each side of her, talking beside her ear.

She laughed, looking over her shoulder at him as they chatted. Everyone else in the kitchen was happily working and chatting away as if nothing was amiss.

Sam's blood boiled at the lecherous look in Tags's eyes as he rolled the pin for Iris with his arms around her. *It's fine. I'll be calm.*

"Good morning," he barked. *Okay, maybe not that calm.*

Iris snapped her head up to see him.

"Oh, hi! Good morning," she said, happier than he'd seen her the last few days. "I'm making Tags's famous cinnamon rolls." She looked positively delighted.

"I see," he said, his eyes never leaving Tags.

Why are his arms wrapped around my Iris?

Damnit. He wiped his hand down his face in frustration at himself. *Just Iris.*

"Hey, man. Good morning," Tags said, squeezing Iris's shoulders. "This one is a lost cause when it comes to properly rolling out cinnamon rolls."

Sam stared at him, gritting his teeth.

"Oh," Iris said, breaking away and wiping her hands on a towel, moving out of Tags's orbit. "I was going to bring you a latte, but I got distracted. I'm sorry. It's probably cold."

She held out an earthenware mug with foamed milk and cinnamon.

"It's really good," she said, a happy light in her eyes. "Tags is going to lead the nature walk through the leaves. I figured we could go if you're up for it. Would make great photos."

"Hey, man, it's going to be *amazing*. We take the gondola up through the trees, soaring over everything, and then we have a leisurely five-mile walk back down to camp. It's part philosophical salon, part commune with nature."

People walked through the kitchen with the same loopy

smile on their face. How did Iris not see all the weird signs around here?

"Would you excuse us?" he said to Tags.

"Sure. See you in fifteen minutes at the base of the gondola lift entrance," Tags called.

Sam grabbed Iris by the elbow and pulled her to the door. "We need to go."

She scowled up at him. "Absolutely not. I'm so close to getting time with him for an exclusive interview."

"Look around." He gestured outside. "Something doesn't feel right."

"All I see are heaping piles of vegan baked goods that smell like nutmeg and people connecting with each other. You're probably just anxious. Maybe take a nap"—she untied her apron—"and I'll go on the gondola ride."

As she started to walk away, he grabbed her hand. He'd haul her over his shoulder if necessary. "Absolutely not."

"Excuse me? You are not my"—she lowered her voice to a hissed whisper—"real boyfriend. I am an adult woman and I can do what I want." Her foot stomped to emphasize her point.

"Iris, people were lined up for some sort of wood-chopping ceremony this morning, and don't you think it's weird how they all sort of adore Tags? I mean, the guy was given $10 million by his parents and sold a company for $8 million, and they think he's some sort of genius?"

Okay, so he'd gone down a research rabbit hole when he couldn't sleep last night. "He's not who you think he is. He's not some prophetic genius who knows how to make the world a better place. His real name is William. He chose Tags. Come on, let's go anywhere else. Please."

"I think you're just jealous." She threw the apron over her arm with smug satisfaction. "Because he was flirting with me."

A fire stoked in his belly. "Oh, like you were jealous of Jess?"

"Of course I was jealous of her. She practically shoved me off of her tiny staircase so she could have you herself."

Happiness bloomed in his chest at the idea of her being jealous. Ha.

"Fine, and maybe I was a little jealous," he admitted, "that his hands were all over you. You don't even know him. I'm gonna down this coffee and we're getting the fuck out of here."

He sipped the latte as he tugged Iris's hand to bring her through the kitchen toward their car. He stopped in his tracks and looked in his cup. "Wait, what is this? Is this oat milk?"

Ember called from across the room with a happy smile. "It's ferret milk made from our own free range ferrets on site. We're vegans otherwise."

Sam spit his coffee back into the cup. "Ferrets?" he yelled, wiping his mouth. Iris looked as shocked as he was.

Cozy Nights in Vermont

"They're so cute," another woman said beside Ember.

"We gotta go." Sam slammed the mug down on the table, not caring who heard it anymore.

"Oh, you can't leave early," Ember said as she stepped in front of him, serene expression still in place but eyes burning. "We'd love to extend your stay. You'd be a great fit in this intense-living community."

Tags came over behind Ember. "Yeah, we were talking about it last night. We love the vibe you have."

"Extend our stay?" Iris said with her head cocked to the side. "I don't know if that's in our budget," she added with a nervous laugh.

"Oh, no," Ember said. "You wouldn't pay as long as you signed a promise to the land and joined our collective. You'd stay for as long as we like."

...As long as they *like?*

Iris took a step toward the door with panicked eyes. "Oh no, we can't do that. We have a..."

Sam threw his arm around Iris as they backed away slowly. "...a baby. Yep, we have a baby at home."

"We love kids here. They have their own school. You can stay here while they're brought to you." Tags smiled at them with his stupid floppy hair hanging over his eyes.

A man with long, waist-length hair popped into the kitchen. "Last call for the eleven o'clock commune."

"Oh, that's us. We'll see you at the lift, okay guys?" Tag said, tapping each of them on the shoulder as they left.

"Oh my god." Iris turned to Sam slowly. Her shocked face went pale. "Sam, this is a cult."

He interlaced their fingers and tugged her outside to their car. "If you'd listen to me one time—"

Iris pulled away and jogged toward the VW van. "I have to get my stuff," she hissed.

Sam grabbed her around the waist and hauled her to him to speed up their walk to the car in the opposite direction. "Already in the car. Let's go."

They hustled through the gravel, walking quickly so they didn't draw attention.

A group of people waved to them heading in the opposite direction. "See you at the lift."

"Sure thing," Sam said with a laugh. "Gotta get our reusable water bottles."

"Way to be intense with your ecological impact," the stranger called with a thumbs-up as they walked away.

"Oh my god. Oh my god. This is a cult," Iris said as her breath came in short, shallow breaths.

"Just play it cool," he said, walking slowly and waving to another couple walking toward the lift.

Only two hundred feet until we get to safety.

"Don't leave yet, come meet the ferrets." A tall woman in an apron stood in front of an enclosure with a long animal in her arms. She waved its little paw around with a wide smile.

"Sam," Iris said, her voice wobbly. "She's waving a ferret at us."

"Don't look at the ferret. Look at the SUV," he said, fully realizing the ludicrousness of the words coming out of his mouth.

They unlocked the SUV, and Sam let out a sigh of relief when the car started. Tags hadn't pulled a nuns in *The Sound of Music* situation and cut the lines of the car.

Sam tore down the gravel driveway, trying to avoid pedestrians as they popped out. He slowed down to take a sharp curve back toward the main road as people stopped and waved to them with wide smiles.

"They have crazy eyes, Sam," Iris said, shrinking back in the seat.

Sam pressed on the gas as they peeled out of the gravel driveway.

Once they were back on paved road, safely out of the campgrounds of the inn, Sam realized his fingers were still intertwined with Iris's in a death grip.

He watched out of his rear view mirror to make sure this wasn't going to turn into some sort of *Texas Chainsaw Massacre* situation where they couldn't get out. Once they were on the highway going south, they breathed a sigh of relief.

He wasn't going to move his hand. *Hopefully, Iris won't either.*

As the reality of what they'd just escaped settled in, the image of a ferret being waved at them crossed Sam's mind, and he bit back a laugh.

"What are you laughing at?" Iris said.

A bubble of laughter burst out. "I just–"

"It's the ferret, isn't it?" she said, cracking a smile. "Did you see"—she started laughing as he wheezed—"her little paw?" She wheezed silently with him. "She was screaming, 'Take me with you!'" she said in a high-pitched voice.

Tears of laughter streamed down Sam's face.

"We were almost in a ferret cult," he said. "I don't think they're gonna make the cut of the top romantic hidden gems in Vermont."

"Oh, but the VW bus was so cute," Iris said, wiping her eyes from laughter and unfortunately letting go of his hand. "And the cinnamon rolls, oh my gosh. They were delicious."

"No cults, Bertone. Think of the American public."

"At least it wasn't a sex cult." Iris shuddered. "Can you imagine Tags's spindly body making sex moves on me? Bleh."

Sam said nothing, despite wanting to point out that that was *exactly* what Tags had been doing earlier in the day.

Cozy Nights in Vermont

He handed her his phone to punch an address into the GPS. "Let's go to the next one early. Maybe we'll stay there an extra night if they have a room available."

"Maybe they'll even have *two* beds," Iris said with hope.

"Maybe." He looked over at her with a smile. *Hopefully not.* He'd already gotten too used to being next to her. "Remind me of the town it's in?"

Her smile was hopeful as she finally relaxed in her seat. "Benning Falls."

CHAPTER EIGHT

SAM

Sam had never been so relieved to see a normal reservation desk in his life.

The entire lobby was a welcome respite from the insanity of this morning. The Maple Inn had a large fireplace crackling in the center and a wooden chandelier hanging over the cozy entrance. Cobblestones surrounded the fireplace, and masculine, hunting-themed portraits in reds and deep forest greens hung on the walls. Plush chairs sat in conversation throughout the cozy lobby and old oak beams lined the space.

The cheerful attendant at the front desk waved, and thankfully she had on a normal outfit and sported a name tag that said Amanda. "Hello! Welcome to the Maple Inn," she said with a wave.

"Hi," Iris said warily.

I know how she feels. "We're a day early. Our other travel plans fell through," Sam added.

Cozy Nights in Vermont

Amanda dove to her keyboard. "Let's see if we can find something for you."

"Just to be sure," Iris added, "your bathrooms, are they see-through?"

"Uh—" Amanda looked confused.

"Any cult-like vows we need to take?" Sam asked.

"Or ferrets?" Iris asked with panic in her voice.

Amanda counted on her fingers. "Uh...no, definitely no, and I've never seen a ferret," she mused, pausing, "so I'm pretty sure that's a no, too. We do have a continental breakfast. That's about as crazy as it gets."

Sam let out a sigh of relief. "Perfect."

"It looks like"—she peered closer at the screen—"the only available room we have for today is the Presidential Suite in the VIP Kissing Bridge Fall Festival package. You'd need to book it for three days."

"The what in the what now?" Sam said, not understanding how a room related to a kiss or a bridge.

"The Kissing Bridge Fall Festival. It starts today." Amanda pointed outside where traffic barriers were being placed and vendors set up their tables.

"I read up about everything on the festival," Iris said, her face bursting with excitement to tell him. "It started two hundred years ago when a farmer wouldn't let his daughter get married because he didn't think her fiancé was strong enough to provide for her. If he won the race against the men in the town, he was allowed to marry her."

Amanda clapped her hands with excitement. "And it's evolved into this huge family-friendly festival with activities, and the best food."

Sam was completely out of his element, playing catch-up. "But what's a kissing bridge?" *And where can I get one?* he thought absentmindedly, thinking back to the night before. He'd thought about kissing Iris about ten different times before finally falling asleep.

"They used to call covered bridges kissing bridges because people could drive through them in a carriage and sneak a kiss," Iris said with a dreamy look in her eyes.

"So romantic," Amanda said, swooning. "So, I'll book you in the presidential suite then. It has one king-sized bed..."

King? Maybe he wouldn't be tempted to put his arms around Iris while he slept while they were here.

"...with a lovely seating area, fireplace, wet bar, and includes our continental breakfast, which"—she handed the keys over to them—"does not include any religious vows or wildlife," she said with a wink. "Here are your two VIP Kissing Bridge Festival passes. It includes an entrance into the main race."

They spent the rest of their day exploring Benning Falls. They perused the general store, found Benning Falls gifts at Benning Books (Iris got the *One Hundred Year Of Kissing* book about the festival, Sam had opted for Vermont-shaped gummies). They grabbed lunch at Two

Cozy Nights in Vermont

Dog Coffee, and even watched the opening pumpkin smashing ceremony that kicked off the Kissing Bridge Fall Festival.

Their room in the Maple Inn was warm and comfortable, if dated in style. The maroon walls were lined with dark oak trim, and the enormous king-size bed had a sleigh-style bed frame. Their presidential suite had extra chairs, a remote gas fireplace, and all the amenities a modern hotel would have. A nice upgrade from the last two inns.

"You excited to have extra space for a couple nights?" Sam asked as they got ready for bed.

"It'll feels like you're in New Hampshire with how big the bed is," Iris said through a mouthful of toothbrush as they brushed their teeth.

They got ready for bed much the same way they'd done the last few nights. Iris was pretty tidy, and it turned out she was one of his more compatible roommates.

They sat down on the bed at the same time, and it felt like there was an acre of bed between them.

As he got under the covers though, Sam felt like he'd been pulled to the center of the mattress, as if it was dipping.

Iris flopped and flipped and flipped and flopped on her side of the bed. Not unusual for her; she was a bad sleeper, but one extra flop had her in the center of the bed.

"What are you doing?" Iris said as she landed against his chest with an *umph*.

"What are *you* doing?" he replied, her body pressing against him from his knees to his neck.

"I'm trying to fall asleep," she said, pushing against his chest.

"No, you were moving around, and I rolled into the center of the bed from all your flopping." He grabbed her hands to keep her from pushing against him uselessly.

"No, you rolled *me* into the center of the bed with your giant man body."

"I think there's a dip in the mattress or box springs or something."

They both got out, and sure enough, there was some crater in the center of the mattress that made them both roll toward the middle.

"We can call the front desk," Sam offered. It was 11:30, though.

Iris scratched her head, looking at it. "Then move all of our stuff to a different room? Or you think they'll wheel in the backup mattress they have for all their suites?" she asked dryly.

"Let's just go to sleep." He didn't sleep well last night since the mattress in the VW bus was practically child-sized, and he'd had visions of being recruited into a marshmallow cult.

"Then I guess we'll just have to roll against each other," she said as they tentatively edged into bed but then found themselves rolling toward the center again, nose to nose.

Cozy Nights in Vermont

He scooted back. "This is ridiculous. This mattress is the size of Montana." It was like the universe was literally pushing them together.

"Then you're welcome to find your own small cowboy ranch somewhere around the bottom corner."

"But then I'll be sleeping by your icicle feet, no thanks," he said with a snort.

They tried sleeping diagonally, that was worse. They tried lying horizontally on the bed—also somehow still worse. Sleeping the normal way, rolling toward each other, was the least of all evils.

"I don't think two people have ever had worse luck than us," Iris said. She lay on her back with her arm pressed into his.

Could have been worse, Sam thought. He could have missed this assignment entirely.

"This is not comfortable," Iris yelled in frustration, flipping again on her side, but losing her balance as she had been trying to stay on her side of the bed and flopped onto half of his chest.

"Sorry," she said, pressing up off him.

"Why don't we do this?" he said, raising his arm and putting it around her. "Half the time when I wake up in the middle of the night, we've somehow wound up in this position anyway," he said, settling his arm down over her back and onto her waist. "Is this okay?"

Her cheek was lying against his bare chest. "It's, um... fine," she said, settling in. "My hip feels a little weird like this. Okay if I move my leg?"

She moved her leg so it lay over his thigh. "My lower back is always so tight and this helps." As she moved her thigh up to resettle, she grazed his cock.

He sucked in a breath. This was going to be dangerous. He could feel she wasn't wearing a bra. Her leg in pajama shorts was nearly stroking him as she moved her leg up and down. He put a hand on it.

"You're going to need to stop that."

"Why?" she said, pulling back to look at him with earnest confusion.

"Just go to sleep," he said, closing his eyes and thinking of the least sexy subjects he could. Her hair smelled so good against his nose, though. All he had to do was just draw his head to the right and he could bury it into her waves.

She settled against him, and as he fell asleep, he actively debated with himself whether to ask the front desk for a new bed so he wouldn't have this torture for two more nights or to take advantage of something he never thought he'd look forward to—snuggling.

***

"Is it weird I want another caramel apple?" Iris said as they walked idly through a bustling fall festival. They'd gotten a large container of caramel popcorn to share.

Cozy Nights in Vermont

"Live your best life, but don't be surprised if your dentist materializes out of thin air to smack it out of your hand," he said, throwing a piece of caramel popcorn up in the air and catching it with his mouth.

They'd spent the previous day taking photos of the room, the inn, and taking in everything the Maple Inn had to offer. There was a spa service package included in their presidential suite, which they'd both enjoyed. Breakfast each morning was full of maple cinnamon scones, and Iris had dragged him to at least two different historical tours: one about the town and a bus tour covering the kissing bridges for the Fall Festival. He would have died from boredom, if not for Iris's adorable geeky questions during the tours.

They'd also snuggled as they had the night before, falling asleep in each other's arms. He'd stopped himself from stroking her arm as they talked before bed.

She'd put on her "autumn AF" outfit today (her words). She wore an oversized cardigan slouched around her, a crop top that showed a tantalizing hint of her stomach, a plaid skirt that hugged her curves, and tights with low little booties. He'd wanted to stare at every inch of her so badly the whole day they'd been together.

Kids ran around the festival with painted faces, and each booth had pumpkins decorating it on either side. Families took photos on decorative hay bales covered in fall leaves. A local cidery's tent was set up and couples stood drinking their adult beverages, enjoying the cool breeze of the afternoon.

"Do you want to grab a cider?" he said, pointing to the beer tent.

"No, it's time for the Syrup Race," Iris said with a waggle of her eyebrows.

"Oh, we're not doing that, are we?" Sam had a good guess who would be running the race since Iris was more than a little accident-prone.

"It's important. It's part of our VIP package. They're expecting us."

"But I can't take photos if I'm in it—" He almost called her Buns again but stopped himself.

Why? He wasn't quite sure. Maybe because *I want to move past who we used to be.*

The snarling competitors who put distance between themselves so they didn't have to address their feelings.

"Oh, come on. It's an important part of the article. This is the culmination of the entire fall festival before we leave tomorrow." She tugged his hand toward the race stage with a pleading smile.

"Fine, but if I win, you're buying me unlimited ciders."

Ten minutes later, a fully registered Sam and Iris stood with the other entrants as the emcee shouted the rules into the microphone. As part of the entry, Iris had to make a fall flower crown and place it on one of the posts at the finish line.

"Welcome to this year's Kissing Bridge Syrup Race, sponsored by Miller Family Syrup Farms." Applause came from the sidelines where hundreds of people watched. "Remember, you'll run a wheelbarrow full of pumpkins from here to the covered bridge. Then, you'll take a shot of bourbon and maple syrup, and pick up two full pails of maple syrup and run back without spilling any."

Sam looked at the table lined with shots and pails underneath. He looked at the other contestants. A couple of young guys about his age, a woman who was pretty fit, and an older guy who was currently chugging a cider. *Maybe I'll jog it. It's just a friendly race.*

"Now," the emcee continued. "When you get to the finish line, grab a fall crown and claim your prize."

"What's the prize?" he asked Iris, thinking about how hard he wanted to work at this.

"Your prize," said the emcee, "is a two-hundred-dollar book shopping spree at Benning Books. And, of course, the most important prize of all, a kiss from the person whose flower crown you pick up at the finish line."

Sam's head whipped up to the emcee on the podium and then to Iris.

A kiss?

The stakes for this race just got a lot higher.

"I probably won't win," he said, shrugging at Iris, even though a fire was lit inside of him. He couldn't take his eyes away as she bit back a smile.

Those lips that've smiled at everyone but you.

The smirk when she teases and you can't help but laugh back.

The tongue that licked her finger covered in marshmallow.

That was the best fucking prize he could think of.

"On your mark, get set..."

And at the sound of a cowbell, Sam ran as hard as he could to the cheers of the crowd.

He engaged his core, dodging a pothole in the road as he balanced the heavy, wobbly wheelbarrow. He was second place and he kicked it into high gear, thinking he might lose.

He tossed the wheelbarrow aside, slammed the shot of bourbon and maple syrup as fast as he could, not even swallowing as he picked up the pails of syrup, jogging back.

Jesus fucking Christ. He could kill a man with one of these if he needed to, they were so heavy. The woman was still ahead of him but slipped on the hay in front of her, and her syrup pails crashed to the ground, spilling slow-moving amber liquid everywhere.

"Disqualified!" the emcee shouted.

He thought of those lips he'd been staring at for the last fifteen years, and goddamnit, he was going to kiss them today, come hell or high water.

He pushed into overdrive. *I can breathe when I cross the finish line.* The pails pulled at his arms, and he was cautious not to spill a drop. His arms burned as he held the pails away from him.

His heart pounding and his lungs burning, he dropped the pails at the finish line and grabbed the fall leaf crown Iris had made when they registered. It had orange and yellow sparkly leaves intertwined with tiny sunflowers and chrysanthemums. He leaned over, catching his breath as the remaining competitors finished behind him.

He'd won. He'd sprinted the length of a covered bridge all so he didn't have to admit to his biggest rival that he so desperately wanted to kiss her.

God, I'm pathetic. He wiped a hand down his face as the sweat cooled.

"All right, young man, come up here and claim your prize!" the emcee shouted. "Here is your check for two hundred dollars for Benning Books." Sam panted as he shook the man's hand, grabbing the comically large cardboard check.

The partners of the competitors slowly walked off the stage after Sam had won.

"You have one more prize to claim," the older man said with a sparkling smile. Iris slowly walked to him on the stage.

She was perfection, he thought, panting at her as he placed the flower crown on her head. It sparkled against her chestnut hair in the fading sunlight.

Iris dropped her eyes. Sam cleared his throat. "You don't have to," Iris said, looking embarrassed.

Elise Kennedy

He could make a joke, laugh it off for the article.

But he was done with that.

He focused on her lips, willing her to look back up at him. "Don't you think we should?"

CHAPTER NINE

IRIS

Does he actually want to kiss me?

Her heart hammered in her chest as if she'd run the race instead. His eyes were trained on her lips as he stepped closer and—mind blanking—all she could do was nod.

Yes, we should.

His hand came to her jaw. Their eyes locked as he swiped his thumb there, so subtle. Almost like a caress.

They stood at the gate separating their past and the *more* that'd danced between them for so long.

"Finally," he sighed, bending down.

The sound of the crowd cheering fell away as their lips brushed, like a match igniting. Fire licked up inside of her as she opened, and he kissed her again with a moaning neediness that made her knees buckle.

His hand anchored on her hip, pulling her in, and she melted against him, as if they'd done this their entire life. His spicy cologne scent she'd always loved wrapped around her as she breathed him in, feeling the press of his lips against hers. She wanted to take and take, needing more.

He angled her head to deepen the kiss, and lust ignited like a brush fire at how he moved her possessively. Her hand grabbing the material of his shirt, she kissed him harder, her tongue caressing his bottom lip. His fingers dug into her hair, heady lust pulling at every nerve ending. Her nipples ached as they brushed against his chest, and he teased her with his tongue.

She wanted to crawl out of her skin at how much she wanted him, craved him. What was he doing to her?

Ruining her for everyone else.

Iris pulled away and gasped in a breath, coming up for air as if from the deepest depths of the ocean.

It could have been like this. It could have been like this my whole life.

The crowd still clapped. Only a few seconds had passed but the enormity of decades lost crashed down on her. She pulled away. "I...I need to go."

You have wasted your life.

"Wait," Sam said, grabbing her hand as he followed her off the stage. "We should—"

Cozy Nights in Vermont

She pulled away, walking backward. "No, I—I need a minute. Please."

He stopped and she ran away as tears welled in her eyes.

All that time, and my life could have been like this.

* * *

Two hours later, three shots of tequila down and a fourth on the way, the same phrase rang again and again and again in her head.

You.

Wasted.

Your.

Time.

You wasted a decade of your life. If a kiss from a man who irritates the shit out of you can make every nerve ending in your body stand at attention…how did you spend ten years with someone who never made you feel anything in particular?

And kneecap your career at the same time?

"Because I'm a multi-tasssker," she muttered, hearing the slur in her own voice.

Her fourth shot was placed in front of her, along with a glass of water.

"I don't need your opinion, thankyousomuch," she said to the bartender who smiled as he walked away.

Benning Falls had one restaurant-slash-bar, so she'd walked down the street and plopped herself on the farthest stool, hoping she'd be left alone.

She threw back the fourth shot.

"Ten years," she muttered. "Ten years I could have had great kisses, maybe great sex. I'll never have a twenty-two-year-old body ever again. And yet, what was I doing with it? I was in Buffalo, covered in a parka, researching boat culture in upstate New York. Barf-ola."

She hiccuped and sucked on the lime to make it all go away.

"I'm halfway to death, and I've wasted my life," she muttered as she laid her head down on her arm, drawing a sad face in the condensation on the old, wooden bar.

That was the whole point of the schedule and the notebook. If she was ultra-prepared at all times without missing anything, she wouldn't miss a chance at what her life was supposed to be.

I could have been in Paris. I could have had a hundred one-night stands in New York City. Maybe I'd be a one-night-stand girl if I knew kisses like that existed. "Ooh, I could have had a threesome," she said, slapping the bar.

An older couple at the end of the bar looked over at her with surprise.

Shit. Didn't mean to say that part out loud.

Maybe it's time for a teensy sip of water. And a good ol' fashioned vent.

Cozy Nights in Vermont

Iris

> i thught i did everting right and that I wa doing lifee perfectlyyyy

Phia the Famous

> Oh, yello drunk Iris. Hon, you've done everything perfectly. You're killing it.

Uggggh, why didn't she understand?

Iris

> no, with bartttttt. he wasted my seezxxxxxxxyness

Phia the Famous

> I love you, but he was the equivalent of a beige wet blanket, and I told you so.
>
> Now drink some water.

Fair. Her sister never lied to her, that was for sure.

Maybe Bart is the only person who will ever love me. She'd always been too much and too loud and too competitive.

Her lip trembled. She desperately wanted to cry, but she had too much dignity to do it in public.

She slammed three twenties down on the bar. That probably covered four shots of tequila in a tiny town in Vermont, right? Blearily marching forward, she walked to the ladies' room where she could respectfully cry her eyes out.

Elise Kennedy

She made it to the door before tears streamed down her face as she texted her sister.

> Iris
>
> thiss why I dn't drink tequuuila....
>
> t's the crying juice

> Phia the Famous
> Want me to fly to Buffalo and belatedly punch that balding dickhead for you?

Bart wasn't a dickhead; he just didn't set her on fire. Another wave of tears crashed down.

I didn't even know I could be on fire.

She yanked the roll of toilet paper in a stall so she could blow her nose. *All those years, wasted. All those years, wasted. All those years, wasted,* thundered through her head.

Another yank on the toilet paper roll. *Aren't your twenties supposed to be the best decade of your life? You're supposed to be free and sexy, then settle down in your thirties.*

Yank, yank, yank. *And all those teenage years where I could've learned how to date, failing at relationships when everyone else was failing and it didn't matter.*

Wasted with Bart the Wet Beige Flag.

She'd thought kisses weren't that special. They couldn't make you feel that much. Apparently, one kiss from Sam proved, yet again, she was really wrong.

Cozy Nights in Vermont

Now, here she was: thirty, making up for fifteen years of lost time.

With a basketball-sized wad of toilet paper.

Iris sat on the toilet and sobbed into her ball.

A few minutes later, the door of the bathroom opened. Two women walked in, chatting.

"When he said that about you and the baby, oh my gosh, I swooned," said a sprightly voice. "You go first. You're peeing for two."

"Thanks, though I hate peeing with this belly in these tiny stalls."

"Oh shit." Iris had, without thinking, set up camp in the larger accessible stall.

"Here," Iris said through a stuffed up nose as she opened the stall door. "You can go in here. I was, um... pondering." Seemed like the best way to describe the life crisis she was in.

"Oh, honey. Are you okay?" the nice pregnant woman asked. She had a kind face that was full of concern.

Her friend immediately came to Iris's other side. "Oh my gosh, are you okay?" She wore a bright cardigan and 40s-style wide-leg pants with a fabulously high waist.

The women looked...familiar.

"Oh, I'm fine." Iris waved them off with an embarrassed grin. "Just a lot of feelings and tequila."

"Tequila can have its upsides." The pregnant woman laughed as she walked into the stall. "It's entirely responsible for the beginning of my relationship."

"Are you sure you're okay? Do we need to call anybody? Oooo, or fight anybody?" The other woman stood with her hands on her hips, ready to throw down. She cocked her head. "Wait, weren't you at the race earlier?"

That's why they looked familiar. They'd been waiting with her while their partners competed. "Uh, yeah, I was."

"And you had that swoony kiss. I'm Becca," said the woman standing across from her. "And that's Josie in there."

"Hi!" a happy voice called from the stall.

"I'm Iris," she said in a watery voice.

Everything felt a little less overwhelming now for some reason. If heaven was real, it was probably a women's bathroom at a dingy bar.

Becca rubbed a comforting hand on Iris's back. "Are you okay? I mean, I don't know you...but I will fight him if you need me to."

"Ooh, me too! Well, as much as I can with a stowaway in my uterus." A flush sounded, and Josie walked out of the stall. "Do you need help?"

"Not like that. It's only..." Iris's lip wobbled. "I was with this other guy for, like, ten years. Then we were engaged, but he didn't want to get married. I thought maybe there was something wrong with me and I tried dating, but..."

She sucked in a shaky breath. "...but nothing was as good as that kiss."

"Ooh!" Josie clapped her soapy hands at the sink. "So go get him, girl!"

"But we can't really be together."

"Says who?" Becca said as she walked into a stall. "You?"

"Um," Iris realized. "I guess. We've been rivals and sort of friends for so long...wouldn't it be weird?"

"Look." Josie leaned against the sink, pressing a fist into her lower back. "I know a thing or two about mooning over somebody for a long-ass time. Too long, and I know what it feels like to have wasted all that time. The next best time is right now. Trust me," she said, patting her rounded stomach with a smile.

Becca looked at her smartwatch as she walked out of the stall and to the sink. "Max just asked if you fell in."

"He's very protective," Josie said with a smile as she pointed to her stomach again. "Don't overthink it, and go after what you want, okay? He's lucky to have you." She waved at Iris as she walked toward the door.

"Good luck!" Becca waved as they walked out of the bathroom.

You could always count on the women's bathroom to have your back.

Iris wiped mascara from underneath her eyes. She was still pretty drunk. Four tequila shots when normally she drank a grand total of a glass of wine a week had her reeling.

The next best thing is right now.

Like she'd unknowingly put her career on hold, she'd apparently done the same thing to her love life.

"Now I need to do something about it." Throwing her shoulders back, she swung the bathroom door open and ran into Sam's chest. "Wait. Oh, shit."

"There you are!" Sam said at the exact same time. "Are you okay?"

"Yeah, I just…" She almost played it off. She almost said, *"It's fine. Don't worry about it."*

She stood up and stared at his handsome face, swaying slightly on her feet. He looked frustrated and worried and hot.

Right now. She wiped her puffy eyes again, still worried she had makeup everywhere. "That was a good kiss."

Someone tried to get around them in the narrow hallway, and they scrunched to the side into one another. She moved against the wall, and Sam turned toward her. She shamelessly reveled in being close to him for that split second. *Bury my face in his chest and make everything go away.*

Sam started to respond, but old habits died hard, and she had to keep talking. He couldn't tease her if she kept talking.

Cozy Nights in Vermont

"And I know it was for the thing and there's some chemical reaction because we've spent so much time together. But it made me so sad," she said, her voice breaking as she wiped a tear away from her eye with irritation. "That kiss made me realize I wasted my time with Bart. So thank you, I guess."

Sam stood there with his mouth open, blinking for a solid two seconds.

Iris bit her lip. "It's a lot easier to talk about your feelings"—she grimaced through squinted eyes—"when the room spins a little bit."

A ghost of a smile flirted onto Sam's lips. "How many drinks have you had?"

"Enough," Iris said.

"Enough for what?" he said, moving closer to her as two more people came through the hallway with trays.

"For being brave," she said with a big sigh as her eyes fixed on his mouth. He leaned against the wall in the hallway facing her, almost nose to nose. *Just a few inches.*

He looked so fucking good that morning, and this afternoon, and right now. Large muscles wrapped in flannel—which was a very slutty thing for him to do, to look that good in all that flannel.

"I was thinking we should try that kiss again," she said, swaying toward him.

CHAPTER TEN

SAM

Every fiber of Sam's being wanted to respond "yes." He'd push her up against the wall, slide a thigh between her legs, and pin her the way he'd dreamed of.

He'd taste her mouth again because once wasn't enough.

Licking his lips, he searched for the taste of her. He'd almost skipped dinner so he wouldn't lose it. Instead of taking everything he wanted, he pushed off the wall and held out a hand.

She was far too many sheets to the wind for any of that.

She swayed toward him but he stopped her. "You're drunk, Bertone."

"I'm an adult, Samuel L. Fartface. And I want to kiss you again."

He furrowed his brows. Her pout was fucking adorable.

Cozy Nights in Vermont

She huffed, swinging her arms out wide. "I was going to do a thing. Jiminy Christ on a Cracker, you interrupt everything. 'Iris, don't do the news beat, be on features. Iris, don't join the debate team, stick with the tech crew.' 'Iris, don't kiss my face real hard, you're drunk.'"

She stumbled toward him, god love her, as he caught her and steadied her. He turned her toward the exit of the bar. "Let's get you copious amounts of water, and tuck you in early."

As they walked back into the bar, Iris waved excitedly at two women and gave them two thumbs up. They whooped in her direction.

Women are so weird. "Do you know them?"

"It's a girls' bathroom thing. You wouldn't understand." She swayed a little as they walked back to the inn, but she was largely silent for once in her life.

They walked up the stairs to their room, and he fished out his key card from his wallet.

She lay her head against the wall as he unlocked the door. "You have handsome nostrils." She rolled her head to the side and looked up at him. "It's my favorite thing when you're mad at me. I like the way they flare," she said as he snorted with laughter.

She pointed up at him. "See, there they go. Flaring. Shame we can't kiss again." She shrugged as if to say, "Your loss."

He opened the door for her. "Nothing beyond tucking you in with a giant glass of water is happening tonight."

Elise Kennedy

Tomorrow morning? That's a different story.

"Water is stupid. You know who drinks water? Bart." She flailed off his jacket that he'd thrown over her shoulders as they'd walked across the road. "Now tequila, there's a sexy drink. Goes perfectly with flared nostrils."

She fell onto the bed like a starfish, face first.

He poured two glasses of water—both for her. By the time he came back to the bed, she was dead to the world, snuffling and asleep.

He set the glasses down on her side and pulled the duvet over on top of her, making an Iris taco—not a sandwich, he thought, smiling.

His mind whirled as he tucked her in.

Fuck. It had been a good kiss.

He hoped like hell tomorrow-morning Iris wanted to try again too.

* * *

Sam juggled the coffees in his hands to unlock their hotel room door the next morning, and beams of bright sunlight filtered into the room. He'd purposefully left the curtains wide open so the sunlight would stream in.

"Is the princess awake?" he yelled as he closed the door.

"You are too loud," she hissed from the bed.

A knowing smile grew on his face. Yes, he wanted to kiss her again. A whole lot more than kiss. But teasing Iris was still his favorite hobby. "It's already ten a.m. Doesn't your fifteen-minute-chunk schedule have us going on a Benning Falls cidery tour?"

She sat up, rumpled, with her thick chestnut hair looking like cats had fought in it. Locks of it hung down on either side of her face. She'd woken up and changed into his oversized Bruins jersey at some point in the night.

"You have two coffees," she said slyly, her morning voice throaty.

It was lusty and would haunt his thoughts, he just knew it.

"You miss no tricks," he said, handing her the larger cup. "You said you love fall lattes, so I took a guess."

She took a sip and her face instantly lit up. "Oh my gosh, this is amazing!" she exclaimed as if he had delivered the most unbelievable thing to her.

"They make it there, I guess. The pumpkin spice syrup."

"Jesus." She took another long pull on the to-go cup. "This almost makes a hangover worth it if I get this."

He shrugged, feeling proud of himself as he grabbed a donut from the bag he'd bought and sat gingerly on the side of the bed.

That morning, he'd woken up again with her tangled around him, nearly on top of him. As he'd gently rolled her away, she'd grabbed for him, still asleep.

His chest tightened with nerves. Christ, they hadn't had a

serious discussion like this...maybe ever. "We should talk."

"Are you breaking up our fake relationship?" She snorted through her cup of coffee.

He willed her to meet his eyes. "If you want to chalk up everything to the spur of the moment and the alcohol yesterday, we will wipe the slate clean."

She bit her lip in response, looking unsure.

"But"—he inched closer to her—"you said you wanted to be brave last night. What did you mean?"

She pushed her hair out of her face with a hand entirely covered by the sleeve of his jersey. His cock jumped at that one motion, and he felt a new wave of possessiveness.

Maybe my shirt will smell like her perfume when I get it back. Her curves and that rumpled, sleepy look had him half-hard already.

She shook her head as if amazed at her own stupidity. "I didn't know it could feel like that. And it was only a kiss, and we're two adults who can do whatever we want, but..." She bit her lip. "Plus all of our history, and I know I'm not your type. I'm probably imagining things—"

"You're not imagining things," he interrupted her quickly, his heart beating outside his body. "And how do you even know my type?"

"I saw the girl you brought to Andrew's wedding. And the one who could be a swimsuit model at Alisha's."

Cozy Nights in Vermont

"Just because they were both blonde and athletic doesn't mean anything."

She rolled her eyes. "Please. They were gorgeous model girlfriends."

"You're drawing a definitive conclusion from two data points. So obviously, A, you need to go back to journalism stats class—"

She smiled and kicked him with her foot from under the covers. He grabbed her ankle, preventing her from pulling it back to her chest.

"And, B, you were right last night. That was a great fucking kiss. Maybe the best." His breath felt like it was trapped somewhere in his larynx. It would be so easy now to pull her the rest of the way closer to him.

Slide his hand into her hair and tug her mouth to his. Taste the sugar on her lips while he tried everything he could to make her moan.

She didn't yank her foot away, and he stroked her ankle with his thumb.

When you knew each other so well, every new stray touch felt intentional. Like it was a challenge to deflect back.

She hadn't moved.

"Even if I agree, I'm not... I'm not interested in anything that will tie me down ever again." She sipped her coffee, not looking him in the eye.

"Jesus, Bertone." He let out a sigh. "It was a kiss, not a marriage proposal."

She flung the pillow next to her and he dodged it with a smile as he squeezed her ankle.

She took a shaky breath. "This is my one chance, you know? The big leap into the big leagues. I don't want to fuck it up and get distracted, not right now. I can't let this chance pass me by again. I have to impress Ben."

Not everybody had a dad who made introductions for you when you got out of college. Who made sure you had the best internships, made sure that you didn't have to worry about paying your bills as you were starting out.

Iris was a great writer, and she deserved to not be distracted, even if they were potentially competing for the same role. His hand fell away from her ankle.

"Makes sense," he said quietly. "Just friends, then."

"After twenty years, we're finally friends?" she said with a sly smile.

"We'll consider it on a trial basis." He tossed the bag of donuts to her. "We'll need to skip the tour. See you at the car in an hour. Sumac Manor is next."

* * *

"How did this one get on the list?" Sam peered through the SUV's window at the ominous wrought iron gates in front of them.

"Probably the same way a cult got on it?" Iris said with a grimace. "Half-assed research skills from D&D's staff?"

Cozy Nights in Vermont

There were large wrought iron gates surrounding an old Victorian-style inn. Maybe it once was considered beautiful, but with the gray, chipped paint and the black trees surrounding it, a chill went down Sam's spine.

There was a post in the middle of the driveway that said "No cars allowed," interrupting their drive to the inn. No other cars were parked along the road.

Sam's stomach turned. "Why would somebody put this on the list?"

"They're a registered historical landmark? Remember, we're trying to find 'hidden gems.'" Iris shrugged, sipping on the remainder of her coffee. "Maybe it's charming."

"Maybe it's the scene of a gruesome murder," Sam offered.

"Welp." She slapped her legs. "Only way to find out is to investigate."

"There's the reporter I know and—" *Nope, not gonna say the L word.* "Uh, tolerate."

"Hey, we're friends now," she said before she slammed the SUV door. "Remember?"

She hefted her bag from where he'd popped the trunk of the SUV. Sam offered to grab it, but she waved him away.

"Go on, friend," she said over her shoulder. She looked cute today in her enormous scarf and cozy sweater. Her jeans hugged her round ass, and he let himself linger on it as she walked in front of him for a few seconds before getting his "friend" mode back on.

They'd driven farther north, and the day had an unexpected chill to it. Their shoes crunched on the long gravel driveway as ravens cawed around them. Inky purple-black leaves covered tall trees, blocking out the light.

"This is a working inn?" Sam asked. "Not, like, a haunted house?"

"They said they were going for..." She gulped, looking at what looked like a small family graveyard off to the backside of the house. "...romantic," she finished awkwardly.

The sun was beginning to set behind gray clouds.

He walked closer to Iris. "The associate editor that put together this list should have their head checked."

Iris pulled up her notes. "This is the 'Victorian experience,' giving romantic couples a taste of the past with all the amenities of the future."

"I hope amenities include cell service," Sam said, holding up his phone.

A small plaque on the right side of the large double doors read "The Sumac Manor Inn, Established 1860."

Iris pushed on the door handle, but it didn't budge. "Locked. Maybe they're closed?"

The door slowly swung open, and a tiny woman in a Victorian outfit appeared.

"Welcome," she said brightly, "to the Sumac Manor."

Cozy Nights in Vermont

She doesn't look so scary, Sam thought.

The woman looked like a grandmother playing Victorian dress-up, with pink cheeks and curly, gray hair. But Sam didn't trust her after the hijinks from the earlier stays.

"Why don't you come in? You're Iris, correct?" She spoke formally, enunciating each word carefully.

"Yes." Iris waved as she wrestled with her bag.

The woman turned to Sam. "And you're her husband?"

"Boyfriend." *Fake boyfriend,* he added in his head. *Emphasis on the friend.*

The tiny, older woman hesitated as she turned around, her Victorian skirts swishing behind her.

"Then we'll put you in two different rooms," she said, going to a large antique desk in the center of the foyer. No other people were around.

"No way am I sleeping alone in this place," Iris whispered to him as they followed her. "So, we just got married, 'kay?"

He didn't want to be separated from her either. He'd worry about her all night. "Sounds good to me, wife," he said loudly, lacing his fingers through hers.

The interior of the old house was grand, with tall ceilings and ornate woodwork. But every corner was filled with graying collectibles. And somehow, it still wasn't the worst place they'd been.

After convincing the tiny woman they were actually married and this was their honeymoon, she led them into their room. She floated as she walked, and Sam wasn't fully convinced she wasn't a ghost.

"I know you're going to love our honeymoon suite," she said in a reedy, happy voice as if this was the perfect place for their honeymoon night. She opened the door for them as they walked in behind her.

Hundreds of glass eyes stared at them. Dolls—big and small, fancy and damaged—all with their heads pointed at the door.

"Holy fuck!" Sam jumped and pulled Iris behind him. A pile of mismatched dolls sat on the chair, and another fifty lined the room. The four-poster bed had a floral canopy, and every flat surface in the room had multiple ceramic dolls on it. The entire room was shades of cream and faded burgundy with spindly old chairs and curtains with floral patterns.

"Now, Chessy and Elizabeth," she said, pointing to the two larger dolls on the bed. "They must stay in the bed with you. It's very important they stay right where they are."

"What happens if they don't?" Iris said with a quivering voice.

"Then you'll be fined. It's very important that the room stays exactly as is so no dolls get misplaced or damaged. This is a historic inn, after all."

"Great," Sam said slowly. Why was it always fucking dolls in these old places?

Cozy Nights in Vermont

"I'll let you get settled in. Breakfast is promptly at seven a.m. I will see you there."

"What time does breakfast end?" Sam asked.

"When all three of us are done eating." She giggled as if he'd lost his senses. "I will see you at seven."

As the host clicked the door shut, Sam listened for a lock to make sure they hadn't been locked in.

"The photos look so nice on their website," Iris said with a whine. "This might be a good time to share that I find old dolls creepy as fuck." She yanked her hand back from where it had brushed an especially old one with one missing eye.

"Same. But we can last one night, right?" He rubbed his chin, looking at the exits, thinking about how they could get out if any shit went down.

Iris shrugged. "Maybe the bed is comfortable?"

He sat down on it. It crinkled like it was made of corn husks, and he immediately sprang back up. "Nope. Nope, that's very terrible."

"Well, it's one night, and I guess it's part of the experience, right? I'm supposed to be adventurous. I'm a reporter," she said, psyching herself up to stay.

Goddamnit, she was cute.

"I'm going to wash the old doll dust off my hands," she said, shuddering as she walked to the ensuite bathroom.

The more time they spent together, the more he realized that what he'd initially thought of as annoyance was really irritation at the fact that she'd been off-limits.

A blood-curdling scream shot out of the bathroom. Sam's stomach hit the ground. He bolted in and flipped on the light, throwing his body between her and whatever had made her scream.

"Ah!" he yelled. He was greeted with a life-sized scarecrow doll propped up on the toilet. "I thought you were being murdered," he said, his hand hitting his chest, "but this is worse."

Iris had already started laughing. "I thought it was an old man—" she said, her gasps turning into hysterical laughs.

He leaned over, trying to catch his breath from the 180-degree shift from abject fear to the idiotic jump scare of a bathroom covered in *more* dolls. A smile crawled onto his face at her laughter and he chuckled. Her laugh was infectious.

"Thank you for rescuing me." She patted his back, as he still had her pinned behind him in the corner for safety.

"Oh, right." He moved to let her go. His heart hammered in his chest and he got lost in her navy eyes for a second. She stared up at him and suddenly shook her head to clear it, and walked to the sink.

He looked at his watch; it was close to eight o'clock. The check-in had taken forever after the not-a-Victorian-ghost had spent twenty minutes going over safety rules of the property.

Cozy Nights in Vermont

"Sleep in the car?" he said, looking at her in the mirror as she washed her hands.

"I would literally rather sleep in a sex dungeon. So yes, the car sounds great."

CHAPTER ELEVEN

IRIS

"Clovely is..." Iris faltered as they drove through the quiet town at 11:30 later that night. "Well, there's no other way to put it. It's cute as fuck. I can't believe it."

They'd run out the front door of Sumac Manor and to their car, speeding away. Iris had called all the inns, B&Bs, and hotels between Sumac Manor and Clovely, but no one had availability.

The town square was fully decorated for fall and lit with twinkle lights, despite the late hour. It felt safe and clean, like her soul probably wouldn't be trapped in a ceramic toothbrush holder doll.

She let out a full-body shudder as Sam put the car into park.

"Thinking about the dolls again?" he asked.

"It's their eyes, Sam. Their dead glass eyes."

"I know." He squeezed her arm before he hopped out of the car.

Sleeping next to him in the car was going to be less than ideal. Sam hadn't made it weird after their talk that morning, but she felt this crazy *pull* toward him.

How could she handle sleeping practically on top of him?

They parked outside of a quaint park with old-timey street lamps throughout it. It faced an empty baseball field, so they were completely alone.

"Is this illegal?" Iris asked as they lowered the backseats of the SUV in the dark.

"To sleep in your car in a public place? Shouldn't be, but..." Sam hefted their bags to the side so they could lie down. "You never know with these small towns. Hopefully no one will spot us."

She climbed through the open back door as Sam sighed behind her. He climbed in after her, shutting the door, and they rummaged through their bags for makeshift pillows and blankets.

"I have this scarf." Iris held up her coziest one.

"That cannot be a scarf." He laughed as he grabbed the huge tartan fabric.

Iris yanked it back with a smile. "They call it a blanket scarf for a reason."

"Alright, so we have a blanket." He pulled out his enormous flannel shirt. "I can add this."

"Nice," she said, taking off her chunky cable-knit sweater, planning to use it as a blanket. Luckily, she had on a long-sleeved shirt that would keep her warm-ish. She shoved her canvas bag into a makeshift pillow.

The SUV was mid-sized, so they only had a few inches between them. Sam shifted his bags until he got comfortable. They finally settled facing each other on their sides. The blanket scarf draped across their legs, and Sam's shirt lay mostly over her.

"Your arms aren't covered," she said.

"It's fine," he said with amusement, his eyes soft.

"Here." She turned over so she could be the little spoon. *What are you doing, Iris?*

Shh, other voice. I know what I'm doing: making a bad decision.

She tossed Sam's flannel over both of their shoulders as she nestled against him.

"Is this okay?" he said, putting his arm around her waist.

"Sure." Iris had a soft tummy that, as a teenager, she'd been self-conscious of. She'd decided as an adult, though, that it was cute, and she hoped Sam agreed. "Are you comfortable?"

"There's no corn husks, so it's already way ahead of Creepy Dollhouse Manor. Let's hope the windows on the SUV are dark enough to keep any perverts from peeking in," Sam muttered into her hair, squeezing his arm against her.

Cozy Nights in Vermont

Sam radiated body heat, and Iris snuggled in closer. It felt like the first moment of entering a hot tub, and her entire body shuddered from how good it felt.

"Are you warm enough?" he said, noticing her shudders.

"Yeah, you're really hot." *Ah, shit.*

He laughed.

"I mean, temperature-wise, you're literally very warm," she said as her cheeks turned red in the dark.

"Only warm?" he said, teasing.

"You could power a small Eastern European village with the thermal energy you put off." She turned to face him. "This side needs to be warmed now."

He wrapped his arm back around her and rubbed her back, trying to warm her up. "We could drive to a twenty-four-hour store and get a blanket or something."

Iris nuzzled into her bag/pillow. "The nearest one's like an hour and a half away. I already checked."

"Of course you did." His eyes connected with hers in the dark, and he winced as he moved. "My elbow is on one of the divots for the seat back."

She scooted over to the edge of the door. "Let's try the broken-mattress position."

He moved to his back and opened his arms, welcoming her into the position from the previous nights. She cuddled into his side and covered them back up with the shirt and her blanket scarf.

Her head lay on his chest, and she liked listening to the simple beat of his heart. "I'm going to put my arm around you because there's no other place to put it," she said defensively.

"Noted, friend."

"If you had bet me a million dollars a week ago that I'd be sleeping in an SUV with the guy who once called me 'Braceface Bertone,' I would have thought you were out of your goddamn mind," she murmured against his chest..

"Like that was any worse than your 'Last-Base Larsson' after word got out that I was a virgin my senior year of high school."

"If I remember right, Mandy Gilson helped you clear that up about a week later."

"Interesting," he said, squeezing her against him. "You were keeping tabs on me."

She smiled against his chest. "I was a reporter. Of course I was."

"What else did you notice?"

She shifted to finally meet his eyes. To finally address the fact that they were in each other's arms when they could be anywhere else in the entire world.

"I noticed when you went out of your way to treat the special needs kids like they were the coolest ones at school."

"Hey, they were." Sam shrugged.

Cozy Nights in Vermont

"But then everybody did." It was like a flip had been switched in the hallways when he'd started doing that.

He shrugged uncomfortably. "It's no big deal."

"And I noticed that when something really upset me, that was usually the one time you didn't dig in. And I noticed that you..."

She let out a little sigh. This was the hardest thing she'd ever admit.

"...you made me better."

"Yeah?" he said with a smile.

"It's like you run harder when there's someone to beat, you know?"

He nodded. "You made me better, too. Still pissed you got editor-in-chief senior year of college, though. I'll never let you live that down."

She shifted so her leg draped across his thigh, and he tugged her closer.

For warmth, she rationalized.

"What do you mean you're never going to let me live that down? I figured you'd be a cloud of dust after the end of this assignment."

"Nah." He tucked her head underneath his chin. "We're friends now, right?"

She felt the slow, mesmerizing movements of his hand idly caressing up and down her arm. His heart was close to hammering as she listened against his chest. Did he want her as much as she wanted him?

Her eyelids were heavy with desire. She wanted to rub her face on his muscle underneath her cheek. Mark him in some sort of instinctive, ancient way that said, "This is mine."

She swore she felt his lips brush her hair as he moved her head under his chin to get more comfortable. Her fingers stroked against the side of his layered shirts.

"Sam?" she asked.

"Mhmm?" was his sleepy response.

"My hands are cold. Would it be weird if I slipped them underneath your Henley?"

"Use my thermal powers as you wish," he murmured against her.

She slid her icy fingers underneath his shirt, but instead of only grabbing one layer, she accidentally grabbed two.

"Holy shit," he said, jumping at the contact with his bare skin.

"Sorry, sorry," she said, laughing.

"Your fingers are like icicles of death."

He pulled her hand up to his face and held it between his cheek and his hand. The stubble of his cheek grazed against her fingertips and she wanted to feel it with her cheek instead.

"Better?" He asked quietly.

Cozy Nights in Vermont

At least that was what she thought he'd said; all she could focus on were his lips as she leaned on one elbow over him.

"Sam," she said, her eyes roaming his face filtered with navy moonlight.

He stopped rubbing her fingers and licked his lips. The rise and fall of his chest quickened.

Need simmered all the way down into her core, and she squirmed for relief.

Fuck it.

"I don't want to be friends," she whispered, staring at his lips.

"Thank god."

Sam's hand threaded in her hair and crushed her to him, holding her head as he plundered her mouth.

She melted against him, licking into his mouth with a moan.

Yes, yes, yes.

His hands, his tongue, his arms were everywhere. He held her head and she felt precious, like he desperately wanted her *right there*.

He tasted salty and sweet, and she pressed her hips into his, shocked at the erotic feel of his open-mouthed kisses that were urgent, hungry.

Attraction and need consumed her. She wrapped her arms around him, needing to feel every muscle she'd stared at for so long. He rolled her over in his arms, and she broke away from the kiss, gasping.

"Fuck," she whispered.

His lips grazed her throat. "You okay?" he said, slowing down.

"Definitely, it's just… oh my god you're gonna get such a big head when I say this," she huffed.

"Try me," he murmured against her skin. He sucked on her earlobe, and she moaned shamelessly.

"Oh god…it's…it's never been this good," she sighed.

He pulled back with a raised eyebrow, victorious. "Yeah?" He looked wolfishly hungry for her.

She bit her lip and nodded.

"Good," he whispered as his mouth met hers again. He rolled on top of her, and she loved feeling all of his weight against her. She wanted him to pin her down and do unspeakable, amazing things to her.

His cock was hard against her hip, and she clenched her thighs on either side of his just thinking about it. She took deep, gasping breaths.

His hand started slowly, sneaking up the side of her hip to her waist line. Ever impatient, she grabbed it and moved it to her tits, wanting him right there.

He grasped her breast, pressing in and savoring the feeling. He dropped his head against her shoulder. "Fuck, you have no idea how long I've wanted to do that."

Cozy Nights in Vermont

A slow smile crawled on her lips. *He's thought about me.*

He swiped a thumb over her breast, finding her hard nipple poking through the soft fabric of her bra. She gasped at the tug of desire that shot straight to her clit.

"You have"—his thumb swiped and swiped, winding her up higher than she'd thought possible—"objectively the best tits I've ever seen," he huffed against her skin. He kissed her clavicle, then down to the top of her breasts. She'd worn a scoop neck shirt that evening and had never been more grateful for it.

The scratch of his stubble grazed her skin as he kissed and licked along the curved line. She raked her nails through his hair, and a new wave of his cologne scent sent her pussy into overdrive. She pressed his face into her as she writhed under him.

He slyly brushed the sides of her shirt onto her shoulders, exposing more and more of her tits. He pulled her bra cup down so she spilled out, and he stopped, laying his forehead on her breast.

"You okay?" she asked, raking her nails through his smooth hair again.

"Just..." He inhaled through his nose. "Trying to make this last as long as possible. You are perfect." He looked up at her with wonderstruck eyes. "I just, I need—" He cut himself off, kissing her breast as he pulled the other cup down, and he sucked her nipple into his mouth.

Her eyes rolled to the back of her head and her hips shot up with need, grinding against him.

"Do that until..." she gasped. "...until the end of time."

He pinched her other nipple, toying with her.

"Don't stop. Fuck," she moaned as he sucked on her, bringing her to a boiling point. He licked and licked until she was writhing under him.

She pushed him to his back, unable to take it any longer, and straddled him. Yes. Sweet relief, as her clit felt friction against the hard cock in his jeans.

Her shirt was half on, and her tits bounced as she ground herself against his cock. His left hand gripped her hip, rocking her harder against him, and his right caressed her breast. She closed her eyes, feeling worshiped. He moved up to her neck and pulled her down for a kiss, lips and tongues tangling.

This wasn't working out unspent lust. This was *more*. This was years of need and attraction and wanting. He stroked her cheek as he pulled away. "My Iris," he sighed, like a prayer.

He *never* said her name.

She bit her lip, and then his thumb ran over it, opening her mouth for him to kiss and take what he wanted. "You said my name." She kissed his neck, breathing in his scent by the lungful. "I thought you hated me for so long," she murmured against his skin, nibbling. Her hands threaded under his shirts so she could finally feel his chest.

He rolled her back over, pinning her with his thigh as he took his shirt off. "The opposite. I couldn't..." He kissed her breast, undoing her zipper. "It would have been too obvious. How bad I wanted you."

She raked fingers up and down his back, needing to feel him. She wanted him to blanket her forever with his Viking-descendant chest.

His eyes connected with hers as he slid his hand under the top of her panties. "Tell me you want it," he said with a low growl to his voice.

Fuck.

Me.

"So bad." She gasped as his fingers continued to slide. She stroked his cheek as her body hummed with desire.

He hissed out a breath as his finger, sliding against her clit, found her already so wet.

He lowered his forehead to hers, and his nose danced with hers. "Iris."

Her breath hitched at the sound of her name, and she marveled that Sam Larsson was doing exactly what she'd wanted him to do for so long. She kissed him, not knowing how else to say what she wanted—*let's live here forever, never stop, this is perfect.*

"Sam, I—" She moved her hand up to the bulge in his jeans.

"You don't have to," he said, kissing her as he circled her clit. She ground against his hand on instinct, arching her back to take in the overwhelming pleasure coursing through her body.

She sucked on his lip as she kissed him with everything she had and unbuttoned his jeans. His cock poked through the top of his boxers, and she salivated at feeling it against her palm.

She wrapped her hand around him, clenching her pussy.

"Fuck me," Sam cursed at the contact, catching his breath. "Sorry. *Shit*," he panted, watching as she brought her fingers to her mouth, licked her palm, and brought it back down to his cock to slowly pump him. "Christ, I thought you were a witch at one point. Now I *know* you are."

She moaned as he kept circling her clit. She pumped his cock, wondering what he'd taste like there. His eyes rolled back into his head.

"Stop," he panted, and she froze. "It's too much. I want...I want to focus on you. Waited too long for this."

This man. He's been waiting all this time?

She brought her hand back up to his bare chest, stroking the hair there. He circled her clit and—she gasped—found her secret spot that only she had ever found, teasing it.

"What was that?" he said with a sly smile. "Is that good?"

"Yes," she gasped again, back fully arched off of the seats. "Yes, more," she demanded.

He chuckled, moving his finger back and forth, back and forth, and she wanted to climb the walls of the car with need.

"Fuck, Sam," she screamed. "More. Moremoremore," she moaned. He drilled into her right in *that* spot and she thought she might explode. She crested up and up, expanding as he pressed himself against her.

He caught her mouth with his and she cried, moaning shamelessly against him as he drilled into her mercilessly. Until she crested with a scream, coming hard enough to whip her head back, shooting pleasure through her every nerve ending as she rode and ground against him.

Waves and splashes of pleasure lapped over her as the aftershocks of the best orgasm of her life faded.

He lay back on the seats and they looked at each other with miraculous wonder, unsure of what they'd just created. His hand wound into her hair as he kissed her gently. "I think you just broke the space-time continuum."

She rolled over onto his chest. "Or you did."

Long, slow, lazy kisses had her winding up. She hadn't forgotten about him, his cock nestling between her thighs as she straddled him. Slowly, she ground against him and he thrust against her. She sat up, scooting back and kneeling over him. His hands framed her wide hips, digging in. "Fuck, you look so good. Just like that. Just *my Iris*," he growled.

My Iris echoed deep into her, and she closed her eyes, savoring it.

Her top was still yanked down, and her hair was probably everywhere. But all she could think about was what his cock might taste like.

She grabbed for him, never breaking eye contact. She

rubbed up and down as he bit his lip, watching her, toying with her nipple. She needed to make this so good.

She scooted back and licked him from base to crown, making his fingers dig into her hair. Licking and sucking, she wet his cock until she could reseat herself over his thighs, straddling him as she stroked up and down, up and down with both hands.

A hungry look came over his face, like he'd eat every last bite of her, but he lasted a total of five seconds staring at her tits while she bit her lip with a building lust. "Iris," he panted. "Fuck...*fuck*." He came on his stomach, and she had a strange desire to lick up every drop against his abs.

He pulled her to him and held her there, kissing her forehead, her crown, his thumb stroking her cheek like she was the most precious thing in the world to him.

"We should have fooled around in an SUV fifteen years ago," she muttered.

She cuddled back against him and covered up, getting chilly. She leaned over her shoulder to look at him in the dark.

His brows furrowed again, he stared at her with an intensity she knew all too well. "What did I do this time? Are you mad?"

"I'm not mad." He shrugged.

"Yes, you are. Look at your face."

"I can't look at my face, it's *on* my face."

Cozy Nights in Vermont

"Okay, well what are you thinking?" Finally, she'd learn what irritated him so much that he had to scowl at her.

"That's the face I make when I think you're fucking adorable."

"It is not." She stared back at him in shock.

"It is too. That's what I was thinking. You're fucking adorable."

"...But, no."

"Yeah," he said, looking at her as if she had two heads.

"You know, if you had clarified that, about twelve and a half years ago..."

"Then what?" he said as she trailed off.

I'd have insisted you be mine. "Well, we wouldn't be sleeping in an SUV on the side of the park." She cuddled into his arms with a secret giddiness that bubbled inside of her, like popped champagne.

A montage of him scowling at her, after making a joke, or besting him in her speech for student council president, or when she'd stick her tongue out at him during the middle of a class argument, or during late nights in the bullpen in college.

This whole time, she thought, snuggling into the man behind her, who apparently had always been on her side.

CHAPTER TWELVE

IRIS

Cold sent shivers up and down her body, and Iris ducked her nose under the makeshift blanket in the gray morning light.

She lay against the heater formerly known as Sam. He was spooning her from behind, and although her back was toasty, her nose had frozen solid.

She sleepily remembered the absolute insanity that was five hours earlier.

This was going to make things very complicated when they got back to the real world—Discover & Dwell role, anyone?—but she wasn't gonna miss her chance. She turned around on the lumpy clothes they'd slept on and cuddled into his chest.

He groaned, tucking her head under his, then smoothed her hair down, kissing her on the forehead. She bit back a giddy laugh. *Sam Larsson kissed me on the forehead.*

Cozy Nights in Vermont

I should look for pigs flying in the sky.

A snort escaped her.

He looked at her with sleepy eyes. "Morning."

"Morning," she whispered back. There was a hazy glow of amazement around their words.

"Is my morning breath bad?" he whispered.

"No worse than usual," she said with a sly smile as she pressed up for a kiss. He chuckled as he rolled her over, pinning her down, sliding a thigh between her legs.

"Stay *right* there," she said between soft, slow kisses.

"Yeah?" he said, moving to her jaw, pressing up on his leg and putting more pressure between her thighs.

"I'm cold," she said, as she slid her fingers underneath his shirt.

"*Jesus Christ*, woman, I need to get you mittens." He jerked back from her hands but she pulled him back to her, those dark sandy eyes of his looking warm and friendly.

Breathtaking, she thought. *Didn't realize they could get better.*

A rap on the window startled them both.

"Wake up, perverts." A local beat cop peered into the driver's side window. They both ducked down and burst out laughing as he walked away.

Sam checked his watch. "I saw a diner when we drove in. Let's grab breakfast."

They shoved their clothes back into their bags.

"So how would you rate this inn?" He swirled a finger in the air to indicate the luxury that was the SUV backseat.

"Hmm." She smiled, thinking. "I would note the eco-friendly reuse of bedding, and the lack of dolls, or ferrets."

"And the front desk staff?" Sam stopped packing and pulled her close, eyes laser-focused on her lips. His thumb caught her bottom lip.

She leaned in for a slow, simmering kiss, and pulled back with a wink. "He's great with his hands."

* * *

Iris leaned back and stretched, full of pecan pancakes and scrambled eggs. They'd found the only place open—an enormous old log house converted into a restaurant—and had ordered a feast of a breakfast.

She cradled a cup of coffee near her face, happy to be warm again. "I think I'm sold on Clovely. A park you can fool around in *and* excellent pancakes."

"Come on," Sam said, throwing his napkin down. "Let's see if we can kill eight hours in a tiny town." He slung his camera bag around his shoulder.

"Oh?" she feigned confusion. "What's gonna happen in

eight hours?" A dull thump of need pulsed low at picturing what they might do together in a queen bed.

He wrapped his arm around her shoulders as they walked out into the crisp, fall air. "I'm going to request the fastest hotel check-in known to man."

They decided to walk through the town to explore every nook and cranny. They took the long way back into the town square, crunching through piles of newly fallen orange and russet leaves. The air had the beginning of a bite to it, and she reveled in that sharp scent of fall.

"This covered bridge has been here since 1847," she said helpfully as they stopped in front of a huge structure.

Sam nodded his head as he grabbed for his camera. "Do you know the historic dates of all the town landmarks?" he said as he snapped photos, changing his angle, crouching down below as they stood on the bridge.

"Only the ones that were built for presidential election campaigns," she said, scooting her boot in the gravel.

He stood, smirking, and pulled her in by the belt loop of her pants for a slow, long kiss that melted all the way down to her toes.

He held her chin up, his brows furrowed. "Turns out, I don't mind you being a know-it-all when I'm finally able to act on my impulses."

"Oh wait—I know this one," she said, pointing up at him. "You think I'm cute right now."

"Yeah, yeah, yeah," he said, spinning her toward the entrance to the covered bridge. He held up his camera. "Go be cute over there so I can finish up exterior shots."

After a twenty-minute impromptu photo shoot, she was fading fast. Two nights of crappy sleep meant she needed caffeine in her veins, so they stopped by a bookstore and coffee shop to get a pumpkin spiced latte, naturally.

They sat in big comfy chairs on the second floor of the used bookshop, overlooking the labyrinth of the store shelves as gentle rain hit the windows behind them. The bookshop smelled like aged paper and ground coffee beans, and a potbelly stove in the corner of the second floor popped and hissed with firewood. The store cat had found a warm spot in the window next to Iris and she decided that, yes, she would very much like to return to this exact moment in time as her own personal heaven if she ever died.

They'd played a game of picking out five books the other person should read as they'd waited for their lattes. Then, they'd do a debate-team-style pitch on why their book was better than the other person's and why they should read it.

"No, no, no," Iris said, waving her arms animatedly, as they were in hysterics over her selection for Sam. "You don't understand. The aliens look like people, but just a little different. No tiny gray men. So all their parts, you know, fit together. It's very sexy," she said, unconvincingly selling him on a sci-fi romance novel.

"And the humans want them to have two penises?" Sam said, cocking his head in disbelief.

"So, like I said, they have three, actually," Iris said as they both burst out in laughter, "and hello—of course they do. It's a fun, consensual time for everyone involved. Ten out of ten recommend."

"Fine, you've convinced me. I'll read alien smut," Sam said and held up his pick for her.

"You've got to be joking," she said with a straight face.

Sam shrugged. "Serious as a heart attack. This book changed my life"

She sneered at the title in her hands that he'd picked out for her. "*If You Want To Write*," she said the title out loud. "I do write. I know it's not as fancy as all the things you've done."

"I love your writing," he said earnestly. "But, it doesn't always sound like you. Maybe this book could give you the permission to be even more you. Because you are pretty great."

"Is that what it told you?" she said, holding it up and waggling it in his direction.

"You know I was always in my dad's shadow, and I thought I had to be like him." He shrugged. "That book gave me permission to be myself for the first time in my life."

Sam's dad had come in as a special advisor to the Dean of Journalism when she and Sam were both in college. And every time he spoke, Iris wanted to make the universal barf face. He was a smug asshole who treated Sam like a never-good-enough prop. And though Sam had irritated her for most of her life, no one deserved that, especially from their dad.

She'd realized her senior year of high school why her parents had always made a point to stop and congratulate Sam, even if he beat her at something. Because she'd never seen his dad show up for anything.

"Well damn," she said, leaning forward so he'd kiss her. His mouth met hers slowly, sweetly. "Looks like you convinced me too."

They sat reading their books for an hour, and damn him, Sam was right. The book was amazing. But a distracting thought kept rolling around in her head.

"So, what changed?" she said.

"Apparently my interest in alien romance. This is pretty good," he said, holding up the book she'd grabbed for him.

"No, I mean, you sat across from me for almost a decade. You saw me at weddings after that, a few industry events. And never once did you tuck a lock of hair behind my ear, or pull me in for a kiss."

"Just because I didn't do it, doesn't mean it didn't cross my mind," he said with a shy smile. "Sometimes when we'd argue ourselves blue in the face about what story to put on the front of the paper, or what to cut, or hell, what to order for dinner during the late nights. It usually crossed my mind that I might get my way, if I finally gave in to everything I wanted to do. But I would never. If somebody's in a relationship, they're off limits," he said, slicing a hand through the air. "The end, full stop."

Iris nodded with silent understanding as she grabbed his hand. *His dad.* It all made sense why Sam had never said anything, not wanting to be like his dad in any way. Bart had been there before they'd developed any attraction, and Sam had stayed away.

It finally stopped raining, and Sam looked outside over his shoulder.

"I'm gonna go outside and get some photos of the river."

"Enjoy yourself, I'm going to stay here and get started on learning how to write apparently."

"It's not a dig at your writing," he said, kissing her cheek before he left. She blinked several times to try to process the casualness of that. She turned to look over her shoulder to watch him walk away, and he winked at her as he walked out of the shop.

"Oh, he caught me looking," she said to herself, stamping her feet with giddiness.

> **Iris**
> I finally have sexy news.

> **Phia the Famous**
> NO WAY

Three dots appeared, disappeared, appeared, disappeared.

> **Iris**
> To answer your questions:

Elise Kennedy

> A. yes, it was him.
>
> B. yes, it was amazing.
>
> C. it's for fun, we don't know yet.

The bubbles stopped.

> **Phia the Famous**
> Well damn.
> But like, how wassss it? How are you feeling?

Iris tried to process what she was feeling. She was hungry, kind of cold, satisfied? And happy. *Weird.*

> Iris
>
> I think I feel good?

> **Phia the Famous**
> That's very odd.

It's nice to feel known.

> Iris
>
> Vermont is amazing. We've had a couple of weird close calls, but Clovely, the town we're in now, is blowing my mind with cuteness.
>
> We're actually staying here for the last inn as well. It's a farmhouse inn, a few miles outside of town.

> **Phia the Famous**
> The Texas heat is quite literally killing me

Cozy Nights in Vermont

How am I supposed to make soup when it's 112 degrees outside?

Publishing timelines are so stupid. Her sister was in the middle of prepping a rustic fall cookbook for next year, and her recipes were still in development.

Phia the Famous
I'm so behind *sob emoji*

Iris
I'd happily be a taste tester, if you wanted to fly your food out to Vermont.
Or you could "fall" in Vermont

Phia the Famous
???
Like fall down?

Iris
If people can summer in the Hamptons, why can't you "fall" in Vermont?

Phia the Famous
....
That's the dumbest thing I've ever heard.

Iris snapped a close-up of the calico cat next to her. Raindrops had pelted the window behind it, and a bright orange tree stood behind it in contrast. She sent Sophia the photo.

Elise Kennedy

> Iris
>
> You could be right here, making soup.

> **Phia the Famous**
>
> Oh my gggggggod.
>
> My ovaries just exploded with autumnal
> need.
>
> Okay fine. If you see a place that looks
> cute and isn't one bajillion dollars to rent,
> then perhaps I and my cookware will take
> a trip to the great Northeast.

With a smile, Iris grabbed the books she and Sam had been reading. Maybe she wouldn't be the only Bertone enamored with fall in Clovely.

* * *

"This is it. We found it." Iris's mouth hung open in disbelief.

"I don't even think we even have to go to the last one," Sam added with an amazed laugh.

She shook her head. "It's literally perfect."

The Clovely Inn had twinkling fairy lights draped around the banister of a wide, white wraparound porch. Decorative gourds sat on the edges of windowsills and at the front of the door. The porch railings were wrapped with handmade garlands that looked like real leaves. Hanging lanterns lit with flickering candles cast a warm glow in the gray early-evening light.

Cozy Nights in Vermont

The cobblestone pathway wound through a garden with rhododendrons and fall foliage in bright yellows, reds, and purples.

It looked like exactly what she pictured a perfect inn in Vermont would look like. Red shutters contrasted with the classic white of the wood siding. A pile of firewood sat beside the rocking chair, which had a blanket thrown over it for someone who might want to sit and stare out onto the town that extended from the inn. Inside, the warm glow of low lamps and firelight beckoned them out of the cold and damp air.

They walked through the garden and up the short steps to the front of the inn. A small filigreed sign welcomed them to The Clovely Inn.

"If it looks like a trash heap inside, or they want to recruit us, or harvest our organs, we're gonna say yes, right?" Sam said, turning to her.

"Obviously. Look at this place." She gestured to the hand-carved door covered in swirling maple leaves. "They know better than us what to do with them."

"Here goes everything," Sam said, opening the door.

The door opened to reveal a cobblestone entryway and an upscale wooden chandelier. The scent of cedar, clove, and cinnamon wrapped around them, like a friend they hadn't seen in years.

To the right, a huge open-style hearth crackled inside a dark, moody library that looked like it doubled as a lounge. Large velvet chairs surrounded the hearth, and shelves and shelves of books were displayed up the wall. Guests sat reading with a cocktail or chatting quietly together.

They turned to the left, and a wide, beautifully hand-carved reservation desk appeared. The live edge of the wood ran along the front, swirled designs etched artfully along it. The golden light of the lamps on the desk cast a cozy glow on the slate tiles on the ground. Two older men were laughing with a woman in a chef's coat as they approached the desk.

"Well, hi there!" one of the men said warmly, as if they were old friends who'd come to visit. He waved them in.

"Y'all come on in," the other, shorter one said slowly in a thick Georgia accent. The twinkle in his eyes made Iris think of an elf come to life. "You must be two of our guests today. We are so glad you're here. Let me check you in."

"My husband Alan will get you all squared away while I take your bags," the first man said with outstretched hands. Iris handed him her bag slowly in wonder. "Oh, and Chef Beverly made a fresh batch of cinnamon nutmeg cookies if you'd like some."

"I'm trying to perfect my recipe," Chef Beverly said as she extended a plate of thick, sugared cookies that looked like they could be shot for a magazine spread. "Would you mind helping me out and having one?"

Iris clutched Sam's arm. "If this is heaven, I'm glad I died."

"No," Beverly laughed. "This is Clovely."

Cozy Nights in Vermont

Iris and Sam each took a warm cookie with caution. She bit into it and actual tears sprang to her eyes as the cinnamon and nutmeg patched part of her soul she didn't know was bruised. The last forty-eight hours had been a roller coaster, and this was a hug in taste-bud form.

"Good?" Beverly asked, still holding the tray.

They just nodded, dumbstruck.

"Why don't I have a couple more sent up to your room? And maybe some decaf coffee, or a glass of wine?" Beverly said with a smile. "You look like you could use a pick-me-up."

"If you can make that wine into a scotch, I will do everything in my power to make the world a better place because you're in it," Iris said earnestly.

"I'll send up my personal favorite."

"Two glasses, please," Sam said with a smile.

"Now it looks like we have y'all with us for two nights," Alan said.

I wonder if they would notice if I permanently stayed here? Lived in the bushes and snuck in for Chef Beverly's castoffs?

Alan continued, "Our library and lounge is off to the side, and there's an unlimited stack of applewood firewood. We have a deck out back overlooking the river, with heaters and blankets. It's going to be cold tonight; if you need additional feather blankets, you call down and let us know. There is a hot tub on the premises; swimsuits are required." He winked.

"And for dinner, Bev here is making a mean pumpkin ravioli with squash blossoms and pureed cauliflower."

"It's better than it sounds," Beverly said with a wink, waving as she went back to the kitchen.

"Oh, there's Jerry now with your cart." His husband came around with a burnished, filigreed luggage cart, on which he'd set each of their bags.

"If you'll follow me, we'll take you up to your room." Still chewing on their cookies, they numbly grabbed the room keys from Alan as he waved them on and followed Jerry.

"I'm sure Alan gave you the rundown, but we're so happy to have you. We've only been doing this for about a year, so you let us know if there's anything we can do better. We'd love your feedback."

"Are you open to adopting a thirty-year-old woman with a lot of anxiety?"

Jerry laughed. A booming, warm sound. "I'll happily adopt you for the next two days. You let me know what you need, okay?" he said with a fatherly smile. "Alan and I never got to have kids of our own, so we try to take care of everybody else when they come through."

The elevator dinged to let them out on the second floor. They walked down the hallway, following Jerry.

"Well, here we are!" He popped their bags off the luggage cart. "Let us know how we can make your day better. It looks like one of the staff will be right up with your drinks."

"How do you know?" Iris said, cocking her head. Jerry had been talking to them this whole time.

Oh my god, I knew it; they're Fae. They're magic; this whole thing is magic. We're now trapped in some sort of fairy circle and will have to sacrifice our souls to get out.

Jerry wriggled his wrist, drawing attention to the smartwatch on it. "Staff intercom. The building may be over a hundred years old, but we like to live in the now," he said with a smile. "Enjoy your stay."

Bewildered, they walked into the room and stared at one another as the door clicked shut. "Did we have the most perfect check-in experience?" Sam asked.

"With the most perfect staff," Iris added. "They practically begged us to eat cookies."

A soft knock came at the door, and Iris opened it to reveal a young man with a silver tray carrying two glasses of scotch and a small dish of spherical ice.

Sam grabbed the tray as Iris tipped the server. He had an array of pins on his name tag, including a he/him pin, a 'pugs not drugs' pin, and a "Bly is Fly" pin with a caricature of Nellie Bly, one of the first female reporters in the late 1800s and Iris's personal hero.

She gasped as she clocked it. "Oh my gosh, I love your Nellie pin. Did you get that at the exhibit—"

"That toured last year?" His face lit up. "Yes." He held it out so she could get a closer look. "It was amazing, and was at the Burlington museum about fifteen minutes away."

"I'm so jealous," she said, stamping her foot. "Did they really have the outfit she wore to travel around the world in seventy-two days? And the original exposés she wrote? I heard her notes were included too."

He nodded, eyes bright. "It was so cool. I'm finishing a journalism degree, so it was life-changing."

"I've always wanted to see it. That's amazing," Iris gushed. "Good luck with your graduation," she said with a smile and a wave.

She let the door shut and turned to see Sam staring at her. He leaned against the closet door a few feet away looking hot and handsome with that furrowed brow and a sultry smile.

As he stalked toward her, she realized they were finally alone.

And maybe her wildest fantasies would finally come true.

CHAPTER THIRTEEN

SAM

A fire had stoked inside of Sam watching Iris nerd out on something she loved.

It was his singular aphrodisiac.

"Why are you smirking at me with those smirky, hot man lips?" Iris's eyebrow rose in challenge.

He chuckled as his hand found her cheek in the dim hallway light. "No reason."

"Oh, come on. What is it?" She stuck her chin out, daring him.

"You're pretty sexy when you can't help but nerd out." He crowded her in the doorway of the hotel room, staring at her lips.

Her jaw dropped in indignation as her eyes lit up with laughter. "I am not a nerd."

"Oh, yeah, you are, Bertone. A sexy, hot, know-it-all nerd." He leaned close, kissing her jawline, her neck. "You're passionate and smart. And your eyes turn this shade of navy, like an angry ocean storm when you want a fight." He pressed her back against the doorway of the room and her eyes crackled. "Like right now."

He pressed his lips to hers with a growing urgency. Tracing her lip with his tongue, he buried his hand in her hair. The silky feel of her waves felt best when he'd rake his fingers up through it and get that little moan of hers. "Your eyes light up and you come to life. You become... you."

She leaned her head away so he had better access to her neck. Her arms wrapped around him, pressing him closer, and he could feel her smile. "At least I'm not a sapiosexual."

He interlaced their hands and brought them above her head. She stared up at him with swollen lips, biting the bottom one through her smile.

"I bet you can't wait to tell me what that is," he said, capturing that mouth that tortured him. Her tongue met his, searching, seeking.

Christ, this woman was perfect. He needed to bite every last part of her, feel her under him. One hand held her wrists in place while the other moved to her breast, and she pressed into him, urging him on.

"Someone turned on by nerds," she said with a gasp as his mouth moved to her breasts, needing to kiss or lick or suck them. Anything. Iris's tits had haunted his thoughts for years, and he'd never get enough of doing exactly what he wanted. He ran a tongue between her cleavage. Her skin tasted salty and smelled sweet, like the vanilla lotion she wore.

He nipped her as he unbuttoned her jeans. "That's it, tease me more. It only makes me think of all the ways I want to fuck you." He slid her jeans down over her thick thighs, dropping to press a kiss to her panty line as he helped her step out of them.

He lingered there, wanting her scent everywhere as he pressed his face into her with a kiss. *Ten years* he'd been thinking about this. She wore dark purple lace panties, and his tongue itched to slide underneath her panty line where it met her skin. Take them off with his teeth.

Fuck. He was an animal. Just wanting to take and fuck and claim her. "I've dreamed of doing something for years," he muttered against her thigh, fucking gone for her.

"Yeah?" she said with a sly smile and an arched eyebrow as she caressed his face. "Is it finally winning an argument?"

His teeth playfully dug into her, delighted. "No," he warned. "It's this." He grabbed her upper thighs, lifting her up and tossing her onto the desk next to them.

"Holy fuck, Sam." She grabbed for him, and he yanked her ass to the edge of the desk so her panty-covered clit met the bulge of his cock in his jeans.

He ground her against him, their foreheads together. "Every time we'd argue in college, I'd have this flash in my head seeing all that passion. I'd imagine hauling you onto a desk." He pulled down her shirt and her bra, exposing her breasts. "And I'd taste it all for myself."

He kneeled and swept her panties out of the way. Her pussy was pink and soaked with desire. Spreading her legs wide with his shoulders, he held them apart and started teasing kisses along her inner thigh.

He teased hot breaths against her pussy, and her hips arched up to meet him, searching for him.

He held her more firmly in place.

"Larsson," she gasped. "I swear to god." She grabbed her nipple for relief.

"Bertone," he chastised. "I want my face soaked, but I didn't say I'd make it easy on you." He kissed above her panty line and nipped along the crease of her thigh, blowing on her clit as he passed from side to side.

She pulled his head down, but he resisted. He had to savor all that pink perfection glistening for him. He wanted her begging and wild for him. His hands dug into her ass. Iris had perfect, wide hips. He'd thought about bending her over and spanking her round, thick cheeks.

She moaned, sitting up and grabbing both nipples, her face pinched with need.

He nipped along her thigh, letting his stubble graze her skin. He swirled his tongue as he kissed her, moving closer and closer to her pussy. His hand moved to stroke closer and closer, just on the outside of her entrance. She clenched and sought his fingers, but he teased and teased.

He wanted to see *his* Iris. The passionate storm that was all-consuming.

His breath puffed against her pussy, hovering just above her clit and teasing her. It was wet and begging for his tongue as she ratcheted up.

With a whisper of a touch, his tongue barely made contact with her clit. Just enough to edge her into wanting more. To drive her out of her brain and into her body.

"Sam," she moaned, arching off of the desk with need. She threw her head back in agonizing pleasure at being made to wait. She lay on the desk, tits arched in the air as she grasped his hair. "Please, please, please," she begged him, losing control like he'd always wanted to see.

Moaning just for him.

Finally.

He let her push his head into the hot, wet heaven of her pussy. She gasped as he licked and sucked every inch, screaming in pleasure. His shoulders held her legs open, and she looked wanton and perfect as he ate and ate.

Her hips moved hard, up and down, up and down, riding his face.

A passionate storm just for him.

He licked up, finding her cheat-code spot from before. She cried higher, arching closer to him. He teased her with his tongue with tiny licks, slowly in and out of the corner of her clit. Edging her toward craving him.

"More," she begged, gasping as her hips bucked against him. He was stingy, though, wanting to prolong the agonizing pleasure.

Cock aching in his jeans, he was about to come from looking at the writhing, passionate mess in front of him. Her tits bounced as she bucked against him, searching for more and more.

He sucked punishingly hard on her clit, and she threw her head back, arching off of the desk like a live wire. *Christ, I can't take it anymore.* He gave in and lowered the zipper of his jeans, needing to tug on his cock while he watched the show in front of him. He'd always wanted her like this, wild for him.

He brought her closer and closer to the edge until she couldn't take it any longer, screaming and begging for him. Sweat slid down her breastbone as she grabbed his head, fucking his face. He licked it off her stomach, salty and so fucking hot. He slid a finger inside.

"That's my storm," he murmured against her thigh before he sucked her so hard she climaxed, screaming and clawing at him.

With more than a little pride, he reached in his pocket for the condom there. He tore it open and rolled it on, his mouth barely leaving her as aftershocks racked her body.

He stood and wrapped his hand around the back of her neck, bringing her face up to him. She met his mouth with a hungry kiss, and he teased his cock at her entrance. "You're my tempest, Iris. I want every scream and every claw mark. I want all of you."

Her stormy eyes connected with his as she held him closer, gasping. "Sam," she whispered, her eyes closed in pleasure. His forehead landed against hers as she grabbed his hand and put it on her heart. "You've always had me."

He slowly pushed into her—hot and tight perfection—and his eyes rolled back in his head from the pleasure.

Her legs wrapping around him, he slid in deeper, and they both gasped, marveling at each other. She was the wind and rain, whipping him bare year after year until they finally uncovered *this* between them.

Has it always been this simple?

He pulled her head back to meet his eyes. "I can take whatever you've got. It's me," he said with a slow kiss as she clenched *hard* around him. "*Fuuuuck*," he growled. "Yeah, like that. I want *you*, Iris. All of you."

He pulled back and slid in harder as her legs tightened. He pulsed hard, slamming his hips against hers.

"I know you're like me," he growled. He tightened the fist in her hair and she moaned, clenching around him. "All that passion inside needing to get out. You want to be fucked hard, don't you, darling? You need it."

Her mouth locked on his with a moan. "Yes, yes," she whispered.

He wanted to claim her, fuck her into being his. Fill her up and watch her drip with his cum.

Wrapping his hands around her thighs, he picked her up and fucked her against the wall, slamming and slamming into her as a lamp crashed off the desk. Her legs tightened around him, bringing him back harder and harder, with her scratching his neck, his back as she etched herself into him. Around him.

He needed more. Harder. "Need to feel you come around my cock," he panted.

He moved them to the bed. He sat down with her straddling him, and she sank down further with a moan. His hand wrapped around her chestnut hair, and he pulled back with a smirk. "Do your worst, darling."

She pressed him backward with a challenging eyebrow and moved over him with a slow, cat-like smile until her tits were over his face.

Ah fuck. He couldn't last long.

She was a goddamn dream straddling him, her hips round and thick over him so he could see his fingers dig in. Her breasts were full and ripe, needing his mouth on them. Begging to be sucked.

She ripped off her shirt and caged him with her hands on either side of his head, riding him hard, tits bouncing. He pushed her down onto his cock harder and harder while she ground her clit hard against him, and he wanted to feel her ripple around him.

Cozy Nights in Vermont

Sweat dripped off of her, and their bodies were slick with it. He sucked on her nipple as she slammed into him with abandon, grunting and moaning. *Fuck yes. Lose control with me.*

He pistoned inside her with an animalistic need, fucking her harder, faster, until she was moaning higher and higher. He slid a finger between them. He got one circle in on her clit as she broke and cried out, clenching his cock so hard that he saw stars.

"Iris," he groaned her name. A waterfall of pleasure shot down the base of his spine, and he arched off the bed with Iris on top of him, getting every last fuck in.

Collapsed on the bed in a sweaty, tangled heap, Sam wasn't sure if he'd maybe died. He held her head against his chest as she gasped for breath and leaned over for a long kiss on her temple.

Finally, my Iris.

***

It's her passion, Sam realized, *that has me by the balls.*

Iris was a curvy goddess with a face like a sultry angel, but he'd never get tired of her passion. Iris felt strongly about everything. She loved it or she hated it. She had no poker face, and she never lied as a rule.

That had to be it.

That was the reason he'd found himself planning out their future in his head.

That was the reason he'd thought about calling Ben and pulling himself out of the running for the D&D role.

She sat in front of him, gesticulating wildly as she listed the insights from her historical tour that afternoon.

"And then even though she'd been written in as a joke," she said, slamming her fist down on the table, getting excited, "she argued there was a loophole in the logic that women couldn't vote but could serve, and went on to be the first female mayor in the state. Annnnd I've completely lost you."

"No, no. I'm listening," he said, sitting back in his dining chair. "I feel like I can now finally tell you you're just adorable when you get excited, and I was distracted with some other thoughts."

"I knew as soon as we had sex, I'd lose all credibility," she said, smirking over her tea.

"Quite the opposite, in fact."

He broke off the end of what would be his third piece of pumpkin bread. They'd opted to attend the fall-inspired tea that afternoon. She'd been late to meet him, which had given him time to arrange a small surprise he hoped she'd enjoy.

"Your credibility is one of the sexiest things about you. Well, that"—he popped the pumpkin bread in his mouth—"and your bun-buns." He waggled his eyebrows at her.

She kicked him under the table as he laughed.

Cozy Nights in Vermont

He still couldn't wrap his mind around the night before and this morning, and *again* this morning. He smiled to himself. She'd pried herself away from him to attend the "can't miss" town tour as part of her reporterly duties.

"What did you do this morning?" She asked.

"Sorted through the photos to weed out the bad ones."

He'd also spent an embarrassing amount of time looking at the candids he'd snapped of Iris. Her laughing, talking with people who worked at the orchard or at the general store. He'd saved several, putting them off to the side. They could make good headshots for when she became a big-shot writer.

And, of course, he'd starred his favorite: one of the many in which she'd been staring directly into his camera while she flipped him off with what he now knew as eyes that didn't hate him. Eyes that were as hopeless about him as he was about her.

Iris pushed back from the table and stretched. "I should probably write this afternoon. Get some thoughts down from the past few days."

"But I was really hoping you could do something else with me this afternoon," he said with a wink.

Iris's cheeks tinged pink, and she leaned forward and whispered, "I'm a little sore from this morning. It's been a long time since I've..."

"Had your lede buried? Claimed your byline? Covered your local beat? Wrote a *nut graf*?"

"Oh my god, stop," she said, putting her hands on her face.

"I can go all day, got a million of them. But no, horndog, that's not what I had in mind. It's started to rain," he said, pointing to the window full of gray light in the dining room. "And I have it on good authority that the library lounge"—he stood and held out his hand for her—"has a tin roof."

"Ooh." She shimmied her shoulders as she stood.

He interlaced their fingers as they meandered out of the dining room. "And I asked Chef Beverly, who said they have fifteen Kentucky bourbons on hand."

"You somehow just got hotter," she said, curling against him.

He held up the bag he'd grabbed from behind his chair as they left. "I also went by the bookstore and got the new biography of Nellie Bly for you."

"Gimme gimme gimme." She made grabby hands at the biography.

Called it. Such a nerd.

"Finally, I took the liberty of pulling out your comfy pants and putting them on the bed upstairs. I will order us two bourbons on the rocks and be down here when you're ready to read by the fire, listening to the rain."

Yes, nailed it. I am the best fake-slowly-fading-into-not-fake boyfriend ever.

Cozy Nights in Vermont

She spun around to him with wide eyes and a smile, poking him in the stomach. "Oh...you *like me* like me, Larsson."

He swallowed a smile as he pulled her in by her belt loop on her corduroy pants. "What gave it away?" He leaned in, whispering in her ear. "Was it when I couldn't take my eyes off of you earlier, or when I wore your thighs like earmuffs last night?"

She melted against him. "Maybe I'm not that sore."

He kissed the top of her head, and she wrapped her arms around his waist, squeezing him hard. "Go," he said, swatting her ass. "There are comfy pants to be had."

She practically skipped to the elevator.

As Iris snuggled into his side ten minutes later, a blooming warmth settled somewhere in his chest. She was already knee-deep in the Nellie Bly biography.

They lounged on the velvet sofa as thick raindrops hit the metal roof of the library. The pitter-patter of rain intertwined with the crackle of the fireplace in front of them, warming their feet. Guests milled about, going to and from the reservation desk with soft, murmured voices—the perfect soundtrack to reading.

Chef Beverly had selected a smoky and sweet bourbon for them. As it hit his tongue, he felt the snort of Iris laughing beside him while reading.

He realized with a start that this was damn near perfect.

He'd backpacked Asia, shot assignments in the Middle East and Europe, and spent leisurely summers in the Adirondacks, but if he had to choose his favorite moment, he'd pick right now over all of them. He was sated, settled.

Happy.

He brushed his lips over Iris's hair and they lounged quietly. Nothing against the alien smut in his hands, but he reread the same two sentences over and over again as his mind whirled.

You're almost done with the trip.

It's never been better than this. You had the best sex of your life with the woman you've never been able to get out of your head.

He looked down at her as she was enthralled in the book, a finger caught in her mouth as she speed-read through it. *Such an adorable nerd.*

She was enthralling, all-consuming, sexy, funny, and talented, and he'd finally grown up enough to realize it. He'd read in his Psych 101 course that girls matured faster than boys through a combination of societal expectation and basic biology. He'd scoffed at the time, thinking that he was just as mature as any girl he'd known in college, but as a montage of their arguments flashed in his head, he realized that Iris behaved in much the same way that he remembered from seven years ago.

But he'd changed.

Cozy Nights in Vermont

Now he was smart enough to realize she wasn't someone to beat, and if he played his cards right, she might be the best partner he'd ever have.

The people he'd dated after college had largely been fine. But due to the instability of his job, he'd ended up having to leave them a month or two later. Now, however, he still had six months on his lease in Boston and currently had no plans of leaving. He wanted stability in his life, and if that meant turning down international assignments, then that was fine.

He hadn't breathed a whisper of what would happen after this was all over in a few days.

Just enjoy the ride, he told himself, but he didn't want to let her go.

He squeezed her closer to him.

She looked up over her shoulder with a smile. "This is the best night ever."

He rubbed a hand up and down her arm then tipped her chin up to kiss her. It was a slow, lingering, sweet thing. The spicy, sweet aftertaste of bourbon was on her lips, and he licked her bottom lip, wanting to savor it.

"Agreed," he said as he pulled away with a whisper.

His best date ever.

Sam realized with regret there would only be three more nights of this. Three more nights of a gorgeous woman who he loved to tease, running her ice-cold fingers under his shirt as they cuddled together.

Elise Kennedy

He sighed at the possibility that one of them would get the role at *Discover & Dwell*, which would make things awkward. He could see Ben favor a photographer/writer combo instead of just a writer.

Do I even want the job?

Maybe.

But one thing was certain.

After fifteen years of waiting for Iris, he wasn't letting her go without a fight.

CHAPTER FOURTEEN

IRIS

The nuzzle of a sheep's velvet nose was the most perfect thing Iris had ever felt.

"I wonder what the Boston municipal codes say about sheep as a city pet," she mused aloud.

The Chestnut Hollow Inn & Farm didn't quite live up to the Clovely Inn, but they were neck and neck in the cuteness category, thanks to Maaaaybel the sheep. The staff insisted everyone make the baaah sound to distinguish from Mabel the farmer (no sheep sound).

She and Sam had opted to take the barnyard tour before the hayride started. They walked through the rolling hills of the inn's farmland. It was a nearly self-sustaining farm-to-table inn, with vegetables, eggs, dairy, and meat coming from what they grew on the grounds.

It was the first day of their stay, and thus far, everything was a fall harvest dream.

Except that it would all be over soon.

She didn't want her time with Sam to end. They had one more night together, and then they'd go back to Boston. Her dream assignment would be over.

Only one day away from her carriage turning back into a pumpkin.

They hadn't talked about "what this was" between them, and she didn't want to reveal even a shred of clinginess to Sam.

They'd only slept together a few times (okay, seven, not that she was counting). For some people, that wouldn't mean much, just a casual fling. But whatever was between them felt like it was long overdue and serious, and not something she could just throw away as a vacation fling.

An old-timey awooga car horn interrupted her thoughts. *Head back in the game, Bertone. I can't stumble on the last inn just because I got dickmatized by my decades-long rival.*

She tugged on Sam's shirt. "Let's get a good seat for the hayride so you can take photos."

As Iris stepped up onto the tall milk crate to get onto the hayride trailer, she wobbled and nearly toppled over.

Two sturdy hands grabbed her hips—her ass, really. "Watch it," he said with that smirk she'd come to realize was not chastising but quite the opposite. Sultry, flirty.

She gained her balance as Sam gave her a little push on her ass, and she stepped into the trailer easily.

"Thanks for the lift," she said with a raise of her eyebrows.

He hopped up with a practiced, athletic ease. "Trust me." He smirked as he sat down, blatantly staring at her butt. "It was my pleasure."

It was a busy day, and the entire ride was full. Sam pulled Iris onto his lap to make more room for an extra couple.

"This okay?" he murmured.

"Best seat in the house," she said as she wrapped her arms around his shoulders. He kissed her cheek and situated his camera in her lap.

Has it been this simple all along?

Their friends and fellow newspaper staff had shouted "just kiss already" at them multiple times throughout high school and college as they'd railed against each other in constant disagreement. Sparks flew in passionate arguments as they insulted the other's logic, their hygiene, but never their character.

An older woman in her sixties in worn overalls hopped onto the footboard of the antique tractor hitched to the trailer. "Welcome, I'm Mabel. All right, first stop on our hayride is the pumpkin patch."

It was a crisp fall morning, and Iris cuddled against Sam's jacket. She put on every layer of flannel that she'd brought with her. Iris wiggled with excitement. "I don't think I've ever been to an honest-to-goodness pumpkin patch before."

They bumped and swayed as the tractor slowly rolled down a gentle hill toward a neighboring farm. Green vines crawled over the ground as they made their way to the center of the pumpkin patch where enormous gourds, yellow squash, and pumpkins stretched as far as she could see. Families milled about, picking what they could find.

The sun was shining on Iris's face, and she raised it up to catch more of it to warm her.

Sam squeezed her side. "Warm enough?"

"Never," she sighed. "But I'm glad I have my own personal space heater."

He squeezed her. "Your Christmas gift is going to be all compression socks."

Christmas? Well, that's a good sign.

Nope, nope. Don't read into this, Iris. Don't get your hopes up. He obviously will be doing things and going places in the world.

For all you know, you'll be begging the Scallywag to take you back.

"So, when we get back to Boston," Sam said, and her stomach dropped. "There's this museum exhibit I have tickets to. I think you'd like it."

A smile crept onto her face. Her mind whirled as he described a photography exhibit. She had absolutely no idea how to ask without sounding like a clingy maniac: *so we're dating now, right?*

Cozy Nights in Vermont

"You listening?" He jostled her. "Or are you rearranging our fifteen-minute-chunk schedule in your head?"

She stuck her tongue out. And then, because he was the only person that had seen all the worst sides of her and was still here, she just decided to go for it.

"So we're dating now, right?" she blurted out, suddenly holding her breath.

Fuuuuck fuckity fuck fuck.

The trailer stopped abruptly, as if appalled at how desperate she sounded.

He held onto her as they lurched, and he laughed, shaking his head in amazement. They'd stopped at the center of the pumpkin patch.

"I feel like I'm getting mixed signals here," she said with confusion. "You know what? Just pretend I had an out of body experience, and that scarecrow doll asked you that—"

"Iris." He kissed her cheek, slow and long. "I haven't felt myself with anybody like this in"—he paused—"ever. I've never had a partner in crime like you. And last night, and the night before." He cleared his throat.

There are kids around, after all, she thought.

"Well, it's never been that good."

"Really?" she said, shocked and surprised. Sam was a hot hot hottie, and she'd assumed he'd had orgy-level hot sex before her with how he'd fucked her their first time.

She clenched just thinking about it. *Goddamn.*

His mouth turned down in disbelief. "Has it been with you?"

"Oh, god, no." She laughed. "Bart was...well, a beige flag on all bases."

"So, yes, obviously we're dating."

A blinding smile appeared on her face. She could hardly contain it. "Really?"

"Unless you don't want to."

"No, no, no," she said quickly. "I just... you know. We're gonna be home soon, and I wasn't sure. I'd like to have a plan."

He laughed as he tapped her side to get up. They were the only two left on the hayride trailer. "Shocker."

They wandered through the pumpkin patch hand in hand. Young families walked through, picking out the pumpkins they'd use for decorations. The scene was gentle chaos, and Iris had never felt so enchanted looking at vines.

A gorgeous but older, in-need-of-repair farmhouse stood on the property with a small thatched cottage behind it.

"Look how cute that is," she said as they walked around the vine-wrapped patch. "It looks like a little witch cottage."

"That's mine." A tall man in flannel waved shyly as he stood by the pumpkin price sign. "I'm Blake. Jameson," he added at the end.

Cozy Nights in Vermont

Iris put on her reporter hat (mentally—she'd forgotten to pack literal hats for the trip). "This is the beginning of the season, right? You have a lot of pumpkins. Are you expecting a big crowd this year?"

Blake crossed his arms with a nervous smile. "I'm hoping so. The season was rough last year, and I'm trying to make up for it. We had some very persistent deer that ruined a bunch of the crop."

"Oh no," Iris said with genuine disappointment.

"Yeah, that and my renter officially moved out," he said, throwing a thumb over his shoulder. A small thatched cottage sat a few feet away from the farmhouse.

"Ooh." She thought back to her text exchange with Sophia.

The pumpkin patch was only ten minutes from Clovely, and Sophia would absolutely love the area.

"Are you still looking for a renter?" Iris asked with excitement.

"Uh, yeah. I keep meaning to advertise it, but there are so many other things to do here," he said, pointing at the acres of pumpkins.

"My sister will take it."

Blake's eyes bugged out. "Really? She hasn't even seen it."

"Then let's see it," Iris said with a friendly smile.

Elise Kennedy

Iris
I've solved all of your problems.

Phia the Famous
You found a butter that melts evenly?

Iris
I've solved *one* of your problems.

Iris sent photos of the worn but functional and warm kitchen, then a cute living room with old wood-trimmed windows that overlooked the pumpkin patch. The cottage was furnished with cozy hand-me-downs that looked like they'd been well-loved for a long time.

Phia the Famous
Are you moving?

Iris
No, you are

Sophia's face filled the screen.

Why doesn't she just text like a normal person? "Old millennials, I swear," Iris grumbled as she accepted the call.

"Did you just lease an apartment for me?" Sophia demanded.

"Not yet," Iris said with a smile at the two men standing in the kitchen with her. "Here, talk to the landlord who lives on a perfect, adorable pumpkin farm in the most amazing town I've ever been in."

Cozy Nights in Vermont

She gave the quiet farmer her phone. He stepped away and spoke in a soft, murmured voice, answering what she knew were Sophia's thousand questions about the kitchen.

"This took a turn," Sam said with a raised, surprised eyebrow.

"Sophia is miserable in Dallas and wants to escape to someplace that will get her in the mood for her latest cookbook."

"My mom still raves about her tortellini recipe."

"Aw, Donna loves her recipes?"

Sam rarely talked about his mom. Sam's parents had a very famous, very public fallout, and his mom had left their hometown.

Blake handed the phone back to her. "She wants to talk to you," he said with a grimace, massaging his ear.

Iris excused herself to the patio attached to the cottage.

"What are the chances that I'm going to be kidnapped and put in a basement somewhere if I live at this guy's cottage?" Sophia said, blunt as always.

"Pretty low." Iris peeked through the window. "Seems nice, and he's wearing a wedding ring. Plus, it's on an honest-to-God pumpkin patch. Come on, the kitchen has a gas stove," she sang the last part, tempting her sister. "And then you'd only be a couple hours from me. I could come over on the weekends."

Sophia hemmed and hawed.

"Phia, it is going to be 115 degrees this weekend in Dallas. You've worked your ass off for ten years. You can treat yourself to a fabulous work trip."

A long sigh sounded on the line.

"Think of the fall content you could make," Iris said, knowing the way to her sister's heart was through her work.

"Alright, fine," Sophia said with excitement.

Iris opened up the door before she could change her mind and called in, "She says she'll take it!" Addressing her sister again, she added, "I'll get his info for you."

"I can't believe I'm doing it," Sophia said, sounding even more enthusiastic now than she had a moment ago. "I gotta go pack, or maybe buy some sweaters. I'll talk to you later!" She ended the call in a rush.

Iris grinned at her sister's frenzied energy and shook her head.

Sam held out a hand to her. "We should go. I don't want to miss our ride."

As she and Sam rode back to the Chestnut Hollow Inn, she put her head on Sam's shoulder and tried to take a mental picture of a perfect fall day sitting on the lap of the most unexpected delight.

She could admit now that she'd nursed a crush on him ever since that first day in freshman lit. He'd always been cute, but now his features had matured and solidified into handsome. He'd seen her at her absolute worst—with no sleep, hungover at a 9:00 a.m. editorial meeting in college, or after a two-week long bout with the flu in high school—and he seemed to still want her anyway. She sighed as he held her closer.

"I think Jo and Oswald are going to get very good Christmas presents this year," she said with a smile.

He moved his head that was tucked over hers and kissed her on her temple. "From both of us."

* * *

As they walked back into the farmhouse, Iris tried to savor every part of the last day of her assignment. Sam had already captured photos of the rough-hewn exterior. The Chestnut Hollow Inn & Farm had been a working farm and inn for over one hundred and fifty years.

Iris loved the bucolic, real decorations they used. The bushel of apples in the corner was the one she'd seen a staff member use for an event the day before. Hand-tied rugs lay on clean, long, thick pine boards. When they'd walked in the day before, she and Sam had seen pies cooling on the windowsill and clutched each other's arms in shock. After assuring Iris and Sam multiple times that there were no ulterior motives and they were just a simple farmhouse inn, they'd finally relented, realizing they were free from the clutches of the ferret cult.

Afterward, they'd gone back to Clovely for dinner because Chef Beverly had made chicken pot pie for her signature Friday evening dish.

They were now cuddled up on the bed in their room, looking at Sam's photos. The room was bright, rustic, and had an airy quality with white linens and white shiplap walls.

Iris peered over Sam's shoulder as he shuffled through photo after photo on his laptop. He was still looking through the raw, unedited pictures, but she was amazed at his talent.

"You capture things the way my eye sees them," she said in amazement.

He shrugged. "I just try to find the best shot."

No sooner had he said that than her face came into view in a series of pictures of her laughing at him, staring into his camera lens.

"See?" He nudged her shoulder. "The best. How's the article coming?"

"I'm still drafting thoughts, but pretty good. Will you read it when I'm done? I want your opinion before I send it to Ben."

The editor at *Discover & Dwell* seemed nice, but she didn't know his taste yet.

Sam raised his eyebrows.

"You know, since you know him," she said defensively.

He leaned forward and kissed the side of her head.

She remembered she could be vulnerable with him now. "And...also because you're a really good writer. Oof, this is hard and new," she said with a smile, and he laughed, closing his laptop and wrapping his arm around her.

"What's hard about it?"

"Now I'm just going to say all the things that are always in my head all the time, and I forget that, you know, you're not going to use it against me."

"I never used anything against you," he said, pulling her to straddle him.

"Oh, falsehoods." She put her hands on either side of his head on the bed frame. "I could name five off the top of my head," she said as he pulled her down for a kiss.

His lips captured hers in that slow, simmering slide. His hands wrapped around hers as he held her there, her back arching into him as she straddled him, tasting him and inhaling that scent that was so happily familiar.

His head moved down to her neck, nibbling as he made his way to her breasts that were at eye level.

Iris felt a buzz between her thighs, and she pulled back. "You are three steps ahead of me."

He pulled out his phone with a raised eyebrow. "No, but... noted for later."

Ben, their editor, was calling. Iris sat back on her heels, still straddling Sam.

"Oh yeah, no, she's here with me," Sam said, answering the phone. "I'm putting Ben on speaker."

"Hey, I'm glad I got both of you at one time. Iris you can ignore the voicemail on your phone."

"Hi, Ben," she chimed in. "The assignment is going great," Iris said, wanting to sell herself well.

"Calm down," he mouthed, blowing out a breath to cool down.

"What's up?" she said, trying to play it cool.

"I don't know if you saw, but MacGlinnon, our parent company, just announced layoffs. I met with the team today and we've officially cut out any future roles for the staff. I wanted to let you know, Iris. I know we'd talked about the full-time role on my team, and I wanted to keep you updated."

"Oh, okay," Iris said. She met Sam's eyes. There was some relief in knowing they wouldn't be competing. But why had Ben only mentioned her name? Would Sam still go work at D&D somehow?

"How has it been working together?" Ben asked.

"Good," they both said, smiling at each other.

"Really good," Sam added.

"Oh, great," Ben responded. "I just had someone tap out, and I need a writer and photographer to cover a weekend in the Blue Ridge Mountains for the summer issue. It's urgent since we're behind. I'd like to see a draft of what you'll both turn in in a few days for this assignment, but let's consider you tentatively booked for the next one pending my review. You'll need to be there next weekend.

Cozy Nights in Vermont

Is that an issue?"

A sly smile grew on both of their faces as they connected with the possibility of another trip together—reporting, adventuring, and exploring this new thing between them.

"Sounds perfect," Sam said.

"Agreed. I'll have a draft to you by Tuesday morning," Iris said quickly.

They hung up with Ben, and Iris arched her left eyebrow, thinking.

What was going on with Sam? Had he somehow gotten a role at her dream company that wasn't downsized?

"Uh oh, I know that face," Sam said with a growing smile. "Out with it. What are you plotting?"

Iris narrowed her eyes. "Why did Ben only mention my name? Are you still going to have a role there? Or did you get hired into a different department already?"

Sam's cheeks tinged pink. "Uh, no. I told Ben I wasn't interested."

Iris sat back on her heels in frustration, hands on her hips. "But you said you wanted it. Is this because we slept together?" She pushed away from him.

"Iris, Iris," Sam said quickly, grabbing her hands to pull her back.

She got up so she could let the steam roll out of her ears in frustration. *Just like a man, doing something without even asking what I want.* "I don't want you to just let me have things, Sam. I don't want your castoffs. See, I knew it—"

"Iris, darling." He pulled her down back to the bed and put a gentle hand over her mouth. "I told Ben I wasn't interested because…I'm not. It has nothing to do with competing with you for it."

She took a deep breath, about to respond—

"I'd been searching for something," he said, cutting her off, probably sensing a monologue coming. "Searching for something that would make my life better. More…settled. I thought maybe a full-time role with a magazine would be it. But it turns out, I just needed you. Your tirades and your smiles and your teases."

She gulped, speechless for the first time in her life.

He needs me?

His thumb stroked her cheek. "I was searching for you all along, Iris. You are the only constant I need."

His eyes were full of something that looked a lot like love.

He needs me.

Like I need him.

She melted against him, and her lips found his. Strong, warm reassurance wrapped around her as he pressed her to him.

She hugged him fiercely, not wanting to let go. "I just want to live in this moment forever," she sighed, her face buried in his neck. She huffed his cologne like it was her personal air supply. "I never want to leave the most perfect two weeks."

"I mean, it wasn't *that* perfect. There was a cult, Iris," Sam said, and they both chuckled. "Plus, we still have one more fall activity to finish this afternoon before I have you again."

She cocked her head, ticking through her mental list. "There's nothing else to do." She grabbed her planner on the bedside table, flipping through pages. "Pumpkin patch, done. S'mores, done." *Done, done, done.*

He rolled off the bed and stood, holding out a hand. He was backlit by the setting sun, amber glints shining off his hair as he smiled down at her. How had her arch-nemesis turned into her dream come true?

She climbed off the bed, and he tugged her to the door. She stood, befuddled, as he wrapped a scarf around her. "I have it on good authority that you were looking forward to leaf angels, and you've been sorely lacking them."

She gasped. "Oh my gosh, I *was*." She hit his chest with astonishment. She'd completely forgotten about her personal fall bucket list in the chaos of the last two weeks.

"They're much—"

"Warmer than snow angels," they said together.

"I asked the groundskeeper if he'd leave out the big piles for us." He slid his shoes and coat on and held out her coat. "C'mon, time to fall in some leaves. But not until we finish thorough safety checks, of course."

Oh she was falling, alright. But into something much deeper, and far more permanent than a pile of orange and red leaves.

He held her chin as he pressed a lingering kiss to her lips and pulled back with a wink.

As they walked outside in the crisp air, they planned out their next adventure. It would be full of teasing, full of passion, and full of something that felt a lot like true love at last.

Finally.

THE END

FALLING IN VERMONT

For Star, my best friend's first best friend.

CHAPTER ONE

SOPHIA

Wind whipped around Sophia Bertone until her teeth chattered.

She fucking loved it.

Bobbing around curvy Vermont back roads in her rental SUV in the early autumn evening, the future finally seemed bright. Chilly air seeped into her bones, erasing all the sweaty, humid memories of Dallas earlier that morning.

Pools of boob sweat would be a forgotten, distant memory after her six-week fall stay in Vermont.

Maybe then, with the appropriate amount of festive weather, and if she got chilly enough, she'd be inspired to create the twenty-seven recipes needed to finish her cookbook manuscript. They'd been following her like possessed little ducklings for months, and every day her deadline grew closer.

Elise Kennedy

Sophia had met fame and fortune as an influencer on the internet ten years ago. She'd posted about cooking fabulous, cozy meals full of aesthetic vibes, feel-good ingredients, and cozy wisdom that she'd passed down from her Italian nonna. That success had led to a three-cookbook deal, the first of which was a mid-list success.

She'd scraped the bottom of the barrel with her second cookbook, and now she had barely anything left in the tank. This next one (probably her last, based on said bottom-scraping) was supposed to be a "rustic fall"-inspired set of recipes. She'd had little inspiration in Dallas, where autumn weather was more sweaty than sweater.

A six-week stay surrounded by every orange imaginable, preparing heaps of fresh squash, pumpkin, and apples is definitely the thing that's going to fix me.

On a whim, she'd decided to rent a small cottage on a pumpkin farm in Clovely, Vermont. Her sister had stumbled upon it a week ago on a reporting assignment and recommended it to cure Sophia's recipe-block.

I'll rent a snug little cottage with its snug little kitchen and snug myself into a pumpkin spice-infused coma until I beat twenty-seven recipes out of my brain.

Perfect plan, no notes.

The robotic voice of the GPS announced that she *Had Arrived*, but Sophia only saw large maple and pine trees surrounding a completely darkened, unmarked farm.

Cozy Nights in Vermont

"Wasn't this place a pumpkin patch?" she muttered, utterly confused.

A big white farmhouse stood behind the trees, but it was dark.

She'd quadruple-checked with Blake, the owner, about the kitchen essentials and her start date for her rental. This had been an under-the-table, not Airbnb situation because his renter in the furnished cottage had bailed. Her sister, Iris, had introduced them on the phone when she'd visited the pumpkin patch last week.

No signs of life were visible, aside from a lone flickering fluorescent light on the side of a barn.

Fabulous.

Sophia ordered her phone to call her sister as she slowly pulled the SUV onto the farm's crunchy gravel drive. The phone rang, and an out-of-breath Iris answered.

"Do you love it? Are you ready to fall in Vermont?" Iris asked, already knowing where Sophia was headed.

Sophia rolled her eyes at her dorky little sister. "I don't love that you're luring me to my death. The farm looks abandoned."

Iris giggled away from the phone. "Sam, stop."

"Oh, God," Sophia groaned. "You guys just had sex, didn't you? Ugh." Sophia shuddered.

"Don't be gross." Iris giggled into the phone.

Giggling. She'd never heard it from her uptight, Type A-est of the A sister. She was happy that her little sister fell for her photography partner, but a girl could still be jealous.

"Hey, I'm just glad you've graduated from your nunlike status to a normal lady with needs and wants." Sophia drove down the gravel drive around the side of the farmhouse, and a small building appeared with the lights on. "Oh, wait, we might have life."

A little cottage with an honest-to-god thatched roof was tucked behind the farmhouse. It was aglow with orange and yellow lights behind antique-looking lead-paned windows.

"Did you get lost?" Iris asked, still sounding distracted.

"No, I think I'm here. I just… stay on the line with me. I'm wary of rural men who don't leave their porch lights on."

Sophia parked and hopped out of the SUV, cradling the phone to her ear as she sneakily stepped up to the cottage in her sandals.

She'd worn a flirty summer jumpsuit with a cut-out crop on her soft tummy, flowing wide legs, and flutter sleeves that barely dusted the tops of her arms, all cinched down into a sweetheart neckline that tied in the bust. It highlighted every single one of her curves that she loved to show off and was a comfy dream to fly in.

It had been approximately Satan's Butthole degrees Fahrenheit that afternoon in Dallas when she'd left. The jumpsuit had a bra built in and her barely-there underwear didn't cover much, which meant the chilly breeze blowing through the thin material made her teeth chatter audibly into the phone.

"What's that sound?" Iris said.

"T-t-that's me," she whispered, creeping toward the cottage. "Isn't it amazing? I'm cold for the first time in a year. Now shh. I need to make sure he's not going to come up and murder me from behind." She looked around warily in the dark night.

She slowly walked up to the bottom of the kitchen window to peek into the cottage.

A large man filled the small space of the living room. Broad shoulders and a wide, broad chest were covered in dark, worn flannel. He had closely cropped hair in the back with a long swoop of wavy auburn hair on top, and he was built like a fucking tank.

Her pussy clenched involuntarily.

He moved a loud vacuum back and forth over the front of the hearth. A fire roared in the fireplace, and a black and white dog chased the cord of the vacuum as the man expertly whipped it around the living room.

The vacuum was loud, which would explain why the dog hadn't barked at her driving in. She crouched below the window, wanting to make a study of the hunky large man who vacuumed for strangers.

"Are you dead yet?" Iris asked.

"Shh, not so loud," she said, whispering, crouching so just her eyes would be visible. "I'm observing."

"And?"

"And...he bought me flowers?" Sophia said, seeing the beautiful, hand-cut wildflowers in an antique vase on a small butcher block kitchen island.

"Well, that was nice," Iris added.

The man, who Sophia assumed must be Blake, moved around the room fluffing couch pillows and winding the cord on the vacuum.

He had a kind face—open with round cheeks. His eyebrows knitted together as he moved through the space as if he was worried it wasn't good enough. His arms looked like they could throw her and two of her best friends on the bed, and Sophia was no featherweight.

His thighs looked like the thick rugby thighs she'd lusted over during the Olympics. They were nearly goddamn tree trunks. He had a broad chest with a belly that looked somehow soft *and* hard.

Fuck, he was hot.

She loved a fluffy man. Someone she could feed and then ride as hard as she wanted.

His thick arms gave way to muscular forearms full of freckles. His shirt had been rolled to the elbows.

"You still there?" Iris said loudly into her ear. Sophia lost her balance in surprise, trying to catch the phone after it slipped out of her hand.

She grumbled out a ladylike "fuck" as she dove for the phone, narrowly avoiding it splashing into an unknown puddle of dubious origin.

She careened toward the bushes, catching herself on the brick with her nails. *Damn, there goes seven-tenths of a manicure.*

"Yeah, yeah, yeah. I'm here," she said, out of breath as she grabbed the phone. "He's hot in that broken, fluffy man way."

"He *is* your type, but I think he had a wedding ring on," Iris said.

Damn. She hadn't been able to see that far away.

"Well, good for them," Sophia grumbled. A metal-hinged creak sounded above her head, and Sophia looked up with horror to see the kind face peeking out the window, staring down at her.

"It's easier to get in through the door," Blake said in a low rumble, smiling shyly. "I can open it if you'd like."

"Uh... I gotta go, Iris." Sophia dove for the end button.

God, she was so awkward. Why was she so awkward? Why was she crouching, watching a man like *she* was the serial killer in the situation?

"Sounds good. Sorry, I was just..." *Lusting after you?* "Thought I'd check out the foundation of the cottage to make sure that it's fine," she said finally. She stood up straight, shoving at her hair. "That's, uh, important to me."

He gave her a shy, confused smile as he slowly closed the window.

I wonder if my airline would take utter mortification as payment for an immediate flight back home?

She shame-walked the cobblestones up to the front cottage door. The door had long, thick planks banded together with metal and an arched top. Vines crawled up beside the doors and windows.

The entire front of the cottage was fucking enchanting.

Damn, I should have filmed this. She was always looking for more social content, and "Unbox My Cottage Rental" could have been an interesting angle.

As she walked up the steps, hot-probably-Blake-man opened the door and her jaw dropped. His shoulders fill the entire door frame.

"I'm Blake," he said in a low, warm voice and stuck out his hand. He had a full beard but she couldn't stop staring at his kind eyes that sparkled in the dim light.

"Sophia." She grabbed his paw of a hand, and a zing went up through her arm at the contact. His calloused hands were rough, but he shook her hand gently.

She loved the feeling of her hand being enveloped, and her body lit up like a Rockefeller Christmas tree in response. Her flimsy outfit was doing her no favors, though. She was keenly aware of her nipples poking against the fabric as she stared up into his sage-green eyes. He had auburn lashes, and she was momentarily distracted by the constellation of freckles across his nose.

"Come in, come in," he said suddenly, as if snapping himself out of a trance. "Let me show you around." He opened the door and gestured for her to follow him.

The cottage walls were rough-hewn logs, stacked together with some mud-like grout. The window panes were old and had bubbling, rough glass interspersed between lead detail. She felt like she'd been dropped into Snow White's cottage, sans seven tiny men.

Or maybe they were just all rolled into one hulking man.

"I thought you might like to have a fire, given this is the first chilly night," he said as they wandered into the living room. "Do you know how to operate the flue?"

"Sure," she said, shrugging.

No, I don't, but I'm an eldest daughter and we are experts at Googling things.

Blake walked into the small living room that flowed out from the kitchen. "I wrote down instructions just in case since you mentioned you'd never had a place with a fireplace before."

She wanted to shake her head like a dog with water in its ear. He remembered a small detail she'd said on the phone a week ago?

And *did* something about it??

"I also stocked some basics in the fridge—eggs and milk from the farm next door," he continued.

"Wow, that was so kind," she said, still surprised. Her last landlord had stared at her tits the whole time they'd talked, hocked a loogie, and then left her with the keys.

This is...

She clocked Blake's beefy arms as he wiped dust off a cabinet top.

...an upgrade.

He adjusted the logs in the fire with the sharp pokey thing that came with fireplaces. "I remember you mentioned that you're going to cook a lot here, and I thought you might want to get started. Plus, Mabel has the best eggs in the county." He shyly smiled over his shoulder.

"Is Mabel...your...chicken?"

His low rumbling laugh echoed into her rib cage and shuddered all the way down, far below her belly button. *Phew.* It had been a solid minute since she'd had a reaction like this.

I should've come to Vermont a lot sooner if they're all this hot.

"Mabel is the farmer next door," he said, clarifying.

We do not lust after a married man, Sophia. You're better than this.

She thought of how to silence her guilt: food. Food was how she soothed her soul and the souls of others. Her lasagna mended fences, her muffins healed bruised hearts. She was technically only half Italian, but her soul was all Italian grandma.

Cozy Nights in Vermont

She smiled as she leaned her hip against the kitchen island. "You have to let me make you something as a thank you. This is too much. Over and above, really, for a landlord. What dishes does your wife like?"

"Oh." He cleared his throat and scratched his head. "Um..."

Oh, shit. Did I say something wrong?

"It's just me," he said finally. "My wife passed a few years ago."

Her heart seized in panic. "Oh. Oh, no. I'm so sorry. Iris had said..." She looked down at his left hand as if by reflex and noticed there was no ring, but a tan line remained. As if he'd taken it off recently.

"It's okay." He shrugged with an embarrassed smile.

Oh no, she'd made this giant teddy bear of a man feel bad. *Shit, now I'm going to have to make him two things. Maybe a lasagna and a pie?*

"Let me help you with your bags," he said quickly, changing the subject. He tossed open the front latch of the door, and when it swung in two parts—a top and a bottom—she squealed with delight.

"I've always wanted one of these. It's like a fairytale cottage," she said, marveling that she could have the top of the door open while she baked, like a fucking Disney princess.

He chuckled at her dorky excitement.

The trunk of the SUV popped open, and she came back to earth from her fantasy.

"Wait, you don't have to get my bags," she said, momentarily discombobulated at her unknown fantasy come true. "They're heavy." She followed him out onto the gravel.

A cook was only as good as her tools, and she'd grown emotionally attached to her heavy orange enamel pot and perfect cookie sheets. They had scar marks from her many cooking and baking experiments.

He hefted one piece of luggage into his arm like it was a pillow, hoisted another over his shoulder, and grabbed her third small bag in his other arm. She imagined he might do something similar with a haystack.

Yum.

She did have a secret fantasy of men doing things she never asked them to do. She'd been a typical eldest daughter her entire life, being two steps ahead of everybody. Always being the organizer, always being the one in charge. If she didn't do it, who else would?

As it turned out? Blake the Teddy Bear Farmer.

She grabbed her purse from the car, walking behind him with a tilted head as he miraculously carried her three heavy bags in one go.

"I left some instructions for you on the table," he said as they walked into the kitchen. "Just little tips about the cottage. Some things can be finicky since the plumbing is old." He gently set the luggage down in the kitchen.

Cozy Nights in Vermont

She flipped through the neatly typed and stapled set of instructions. Her type-A sister would love this guy. "Thank you," she said, placing a hand on his arm, moved by his thoughtfulness.

She felt a gentle nudge against her leg and looked down to see the black and white dog looking up at her with loving, puppy-dog eyes and pinned-back ears.

"Oh my god, you are adorable." She bent over and the dog jumped up excitedly to lick her cheek.

"Whoa, down, Star. Sorry, she's not usually like this with strangers," he said with a smile and obvious affection.

"Star," Sophia echoed, seeing the star-shaped patch of fur on her chest. Star licked fervent kisses along Sophia's cheek, and her heart melted. She looked to be some sort of herding mutt with long, silky hair and intelligent eyes.

"She likes you," he said with raised eyebrows. "She's usually distrustful of strangers."

"Star seems like a smart girl who knows I might work on a dog-friendly biscuit recipe for her." She scruffled Star's ears and the dog's tongue lolled out of her mouth.

Now that was an idea she hadn't considered before.

I could probably get three or four recipes if I included dog treats. A glimmer of hope in the unending recipe marathon sparkled in front of her. *Maybe I'll meet my deadline. Maybe I'll actually finish this cookbook.*

She scratched up and down Star's body, swaying her hips from side to side, side to side, matching Star's helicopter-style tail wag. "You're just the best. *Est. Girl.* Is it okay if I make something dog-friendly for her?"

She looked over her shoulder at Blake. He'd taken off his flannel shirt and held it in front of him as he stood nervously behind the kitchen island.

His cheeks had turned pink, probably from the heat of the room. "Yeah, no, uh, I mean that's fine. No food allergies or anything. Just, uh, just the usual stuff."

"Luckily, I worked in a dog bakery in college, Star girl." Sophia scratched Star's head as the dog glued herself to Sophia's thigh.

"We should get going and let you settle in," he said, suddenly opening the door. "Come on, Star." He slapped his leg, and Star ran out the door.

Sophia stood up, surprised at his urgent tone. "Oh, sure."

He closed the lower door behind him. "Just call or text if you need anything," he said with a low rumbling in his voice. His eyes connected with hers briefly. "Any time." Then he spun around as if he'd seen seven ghosts and walked to his farmhouse.

His voice had been innocent, friendly even, but she let her imagination spiral out of control at the *any time* he'd added.

Sophia waved slowly, confused by his sudden departure. *Maybe I offended him?*

Her fingers traced the instructions printout as she leaned over to smell the flowers he set out for her. It was an odd feeling to have somebody two steps ahead of her, actually giving a shit about how she felt, and remembering what she'd said.

A hot man who took care of things before she even thought of asking? A dog she could pet anytime she wanted (probably)? And a fireplace all to herself?

No shared walls with any neighbors, crisp air filtering in, and the crackle of a fireplace. The worn butcher block counters and island had stains from pumpkins and berries past and small knife marks that made her unafraid to dive in and use the space for exactly what she wanted.

She burst into a running man dance move at how happy she felt.

She started brainstorming what she'd bake that night. A comforting treat for tomorrow morning sounded good, and maybe she'd make something for the beefy hunk who'd made everything so nice.

She peeked out the open half of the door, looking out at the pumpkin patch as Blake and Star walked to the darkened farmhouse.

She stared at Blake's bubble-like ass in his tight jeans and bit her lip.

All this, plus a view worth looking at for the next six weeks.

CHAPTER TWO

BLAKE

The slam of the screen door *probably* echoed in the quiet, dark farmhouse.

Star's nails on the old wooden floors *probably* click-clacked.

But all Blake Jameson could hear in the entryway of his kitchen was the blood rushing in his ears.

Holy fuck.

He panted, his head resting against the cool glass of his back door.

He barked out a laugh in surprise.

"Holy fuck," he repeated, eyes squeezing together. "Holy fuck, holy fuck, holy fuck."

His body had finally woken up after a three-year hiatus when he'd laid eyes on Sophia Bertone.

More than woken up.

Cozy Nights in Vermont

I got a surprise boner at a fully clothed woman, for chrissakes.

He wiped a hand over his face, trying to shake it off.

He'd seen plenty of gorgeous women in his life—met them daily at the pumpkin patch, saw them in town, even saw scantily-clad women on the internet without much interest.

And yet he'd stood there in a cottage kitchen with a raging fucking hard-on for the first time in years, all because, why? Because she had the most luscious, curvy body he'd ever seen? Because he could write a sonnet about her tits?

Because her smile reached into his heart and punched it back awake?

He turned around to see Star waiting for him in the kitchen. She sneezed to indicate her displeasure at not being tucked into her living-room bed yet.

"I'll be there in a minute. Go."

She huffed and tip-tapped her way back to her big fluffy bed in the living room.

He just needed a fucking minute. He'd met Sophia's sister last week. She was pretty, sure, but Jesus Christ, he hadn't expected her sister to bring him back from the emotional dead with the shock paddles of her smile and hips swaying side to side.

He squeezed the hard length in his jeans for relief.

Good to have you back, buddy.

After Angie died, all the joy in his life had gone out. With it, his ability to sleep easily through the night, to stomach romantic movies, and unfortunately, to enjoy any form of self-pleasure.

He'd only taken his ring off a week ago. He'd been using a saw and took it off for safety, but decided to try a few days without wearing it.

He was just happy he was attracted to anyone. Wanting to fuck a telephone pole would be preferable to the void of nothingness he'd felt for the past three years. He'd tried to date, but he hadn't been ready and hadn't felt anything for the poor women his family had harangued into blind dates with him.

Sophia was an explosion of color back into his world. She was serene and beautiful when she wasn't talking, but a bundle of life and light when she spoke. He still felt the glow of her touch on his arm, and he rubbed the spot, remembering how it had lit him up.

A flash of what she looked like bending over appeared in his brain. The curve and press of her tits against each other had made his mouth water, and he pumped his hand again over the outside of his jeans, his head on the back-door glass, his eyes closed.

"No, you're better than this. She's your renter," he murmured, standing and turning so his back was against the wall, out of sight of the doorway.

Why couldn't he catch his breath?

Cozy Nights in Vermont

Heaving, ragged breaths tore at him as he pictured her full lips, the riotous, curly chestnut hair falling out of her loose ponytail. It had looked silky and smooth. His hand flexed thinking of what it would feel like in his palm.

He thought about how soft her skin had felt against his as she'd grabbed his hand, and how he'd managed to be a gentleman for two fucking seconds and stared at her face rather than at her nipples poking through her top.

His cock jumped again as he savored that mental picture.

He'd rattled on like an idiot explaining the cottage so he didn't think about what her exposed soft stomach would taste like if he ran his tongue along it. How perfectly the jumpsuit would fall to the floor if he'd nudged the edges of it off of her shoulders. How her round curved ass would look in the thong she wore. It had jiggled as she walked, and he'd done everything he could think of not to stare at it as he showed her around the cottage.

He'd dug his fingernails into the palm of his hand to stay focused.

He'd never done anything like this—glance at a woman once for five minutes and have her imprint on every fantasy he'd ever had—but he couldn't waste the opportunity.

Fuck, maybe I'm not better than this, he thought, unbuttoning his jeans.

No, you're not going to objectify her.

Well, any further than you already have, he thought as he grasped his cock in his hand.

He huffed out a laugh in surprise. He thrust into his hand, amazed at how unfamiliar it felt.

Think of anybody else. Any other fantasy.

He stroked up and down as he arched his back off of the wall in pleasure. *Just concentrate on how good it finally feels.*

He reached into the small bathroom next to the back door for a pump of lotion. Warming it in his hands, he slid one hand down onto his cock and nearly doubled over at how good it felt.

Concentrate on the sensation. Smooth, slicking up and down, tighter and faster. Fuck, that feels so good.

Her hips swayed into his mind, but he pivoted to anonymous hips. The curve he wanted to bite. He loved women who had meaty, grabbable hips.

He pictured a woman bent over, her hips being grabbed from behind as she bounced back and forth. What it would feel like to squeeze her hips, then sink into her hot pussy. Moaning, taking his cock.

He stroked harder, pumping up into his fist. What if she was on her knees as he pumped into her mouth?

He pictured a generic gorgeous woman on her knees, but with each pump, she morphed into Sophia. Her red lips stretched around his cock, sucking hard. The curls of her hair falling along her face as she knelt below him, looking so fuckable.

Cozy Nights in Vermont

Fuck. He leaned against the doorway for support, lost in his fantasy.

He tried picturing another scene, but his mind drifted back to those red lips. Sophia's tits would bounce like they'd done briefly in the cottage.

And it felt too good.

Fuck, she was too hot.

He pumped hard, imagining the taste of her nipples in his mouth. How he'd want her riding him so he could stare at every bit of her. Hard, fast. *Throwing her down onto my cock.* Her tits would bounce and he'd catch one in his hand, squeezing it.

Flipping her over to bury his head between her thighs. Ripping panties off.

Fuck, she'd taste amazing. He knew it.

His balls ached and a curling in his spine ricocheted up at picturing her tits arching up as he ate her pussy, his face buried in her.

"Fuck me," he groaned as he came, thrusting into his hand until cum spilled onto his stomach and he pumped and pumped, savoring his wicked fantasy for one final second.

He caught his breath, not even mad about the mess he'd made. Forehead leaning on the wall, he huffed out a happy, surprised laugh.

That...

God.

That cannot become a habit.

* * *

"It's going to cost *how* much?" Blake scratched his head underneath his baseball cap as he stared at the tree specialist in front of him.

"About twenty-five hundred dollars. I gotta get a guy roped on a lift and chop off that yonder part of the tree."

Inappropriate thoughts long gone, Blake was in the midst of yet another unexpected cost on the farm.

A tree between the cottage and the farmhouse had gotten a case of oak wilt, and had started to die. Half the tree was looking creaky and unsteady. That meant spending money he didn't have on something he didn't want to deal with.

Money was tight right now, with his pumpkin sales down even more than last year. But, it had to be done. "I guess pencil me in for your next appointment." His sigh was bone-deep. The next available appointment was in two weeks, and Blake hoped he could make enough to pay for it by then. He saw the specialist off and then worked on raking the endless leaves under the maple trees.

He was still paying off Angie's medical bills, and though his parents had done gangbusters with the pumpkin farm for decades, the business wasn't what it used to be. There was more competition. Nobody just wanted a plain pumpkin patch anymore to pick up a few gourds or pie pumpkins.

Cozy Nights in Vermont

The last thing he had more of was time to figure out how to fix it.

The farm had been in his family for generations, and he couldn't let them down. He especially couldn't tell them he was barely making ends meet. Luckily though, he now had a renter again after Barb, his last renter, had left suddenly to care for her aging mom.

A nutmeg and cinnamon smell wafted out from the open, top half-door of the cottage, fifteen feet away from the injured tree.

As he saw the shadow of Sophia moving to and fro in the kitchen, happy as a clam, he was filled with shame thinking of how he'd fantasized about her last night.

Not cool.

Maybe his raw attraction was just a one-time thing. Just something to clear the pipes.

So to speak.

Caught up in the daydreaming about what Sophia might be cooking or wearing, what she might taste like, the crunch of gravel drew his attention away.

Thank god. He welcomed the relief.

A familiar antique, mint-green Chevy truck rumbled behind the farmhouse. His Aunt Beverly made weekly stops to the farm to gather produce for her kitchen at the Clovely Inn in town. He threw out a hand in greeting as he ambled over to the truck.

"Have trouble getting through the crowd out there?" he said with a sardonic smile, pointing to the empty pumpkin patch.

"Oh I'm sure I'm just beating the rush," she said kindly, hopping out of the truck and reaching into the back for her large basket. "You look like you have a spring in your step today."

She dusted her hand over his ball cap, knocking off hay from his work earlier that morning.

"Do I?" he said with a surprised look. Star ran up at full speed, barreling into Beverly's legs as she reached down to scratch Star's ears.

The bottom door of the cottage creaked open as Sophia walked through. She had on an oversized sweater that came down to the tops of her thighs, tight yoga pants, and boots. Her hair was in a high pony and had a scarf wrapped around it that made her look like Rosie the Riveter. She had a large basket full of muffins in her arms and waved to him as she walked up.

Her smile still hit him straight in the gut.

Fuck. Nope. Control yourself this time.

"Morning," he said, gruffly throwing a hand up in a hurried greeting.

"Just the man I wanted to see. Ooh, and my new bestie," she said as Star barreled toward her, running a circle around her and then giving her a quick lick in the face.

Cozy Nights in Vermont

She knelt down for a scruffle behind Star's ears. "I wanted to say thank you for the warm welcome." She handed him the basket of muffins covered with a tea towel. He smelled nutty notes of walnut mingled with sweet cinnamon and sugary, buttery scents.

His heart clenched. She'd made these just for him? He stared back at her, not sure what to say.

A soft cough to his right interrupted his thoughts.

Right, stop drooling over the goddess.

"Oh, uh, Aunt Beverly, meet my Soph—"

FUCK.

"My—my renter Sophia." He scratched his nose, hoping she didn't notice his slip.

"Hi," his aunt said, reaching out a hand and smiling warmly.

"Just got here last night." Sophia threw a thumb over her shoulder at the cottage. "Your nephew took very good care of me last night."

Blake choked on his own saliva, coughing out of thin air. "Sorry," he said, his cheeks growing pink with embarrassment.

Just kill me. Right. Fucking. Now.

"I'm not really used to all this country living. I needed to get out of the city and try to find some place where I could just think and stare up at the stars. I slept like an absolute pile of lead last night, so I haven't seen the stars yet. Then I woke up super early to bake something."

"Are you moving to Clovely?" Beverly asked. She had a twinkle in her eye when she caught his gaze.

"Just visiting until mid-November. Decided to 'fall' in Vermont, you know?"

"Ah, like summering. Clever," Beverly said with a chuckle.

"I had to get out of the heat and get inspiration for my cookbook; otherwise, it was going to be fifty recipes for standing in front of your freezer," Sophia said with a laugh.

Beverly lifted her eyebrows, impressed. "Wow, a chef. Whatever's in the basket smells absolutely amazing."

Blake lifted the tea towel, offering her one.

"It's one of my most popular recipes: Caramel Apple Streusel Muffins," Sophia said.

"You guessed right for a thank you. Streusel on anything is my favorite," Blake said, chancing a look directly at her bright, gorgeous face.

"Please, eat, eat." She clapped, eager to see what they thought.

They both grabbed an oversized muffin, the top of it spilling over the sides, still warm from the oven.

Gooey, buttery warmth landed on his tongue, and he'd never tasted something so delicious. The salty tang of the caramel against the powdery goodness of the streusel was perfect.

"Good?" Sophia said with wide eyes.

Blake could only nod. He was going to do it—he was going to eat seventeen of these today.

"Amazing," Beverly said, looking a little shocked.

"Oh, I'm so glad." She jangled her keys in her hand, now back to business, unaware that she'd just introduced him to the eighth wonder of the world in his mouth. "Can you tell me where good Wi-Fi might be in town? I need to upload some videos. The upside of being a content creator is I can jet off to Vermont whenever I want. The downside is I am handcuffed to good upload speeds."

"The inn in town has great Wi-Fi," Beverly offered. "The dining room is open to anyone. You're welcome to grab some lunch and do a little work on the side. People do it all the time."

"Oh my gosh, amazing. I can go visit all the produce stands that I've been researching on the way. All right. Enjoy your muffins." Sophia waved a hand, aiming a bright smile at both of them.

Blake waved back and stared as she practically skipped to her chic SUV. The curls in her ponytail bounced as she walked, and his eyes lingered on the curve of her ass and the tight leggings under her sweater.

His aunt cleared her throat. "So. When are you going to ask her out?" Beverly said, taking another bite, a knowing smile on her face.

"What are you talking about?" he said, scratching his ear. It was his tell, he'd been told.

"Come on, Blake," she said, sighing. She'd been one of the unfortunate people to try to set him up on a blind date. "You know Angie wanted you to be happy. Get yourself a haircut, clean up that beard, and ask her out. She's gorgeous."

"I can't do that," he said, walking toward the barn, wanting to be done with this conversation. "She's my renter. I don't want her to feel uncomfortable."

"You are clearly gobsmacked with that girl." She popped the last bite into her mouth and dusted off her hands as she walked into the pumpkin patch. "Gobsmacking doesn't come around every day, you know." She winked and started picking veggies without another word.

Unfortunately, he'd only ever felt gobsmacked one other time in his life.

And he'd married that woman a long time ago.

He stared after Sophia's SUV, torn. Angie had told him that she wanted him to date again when he was ready. She wanted him to be happy, and he knew that everybody deserved happiness again after grieving the loss of their loved ones.

But Sophia was only here for six weeks, and she'd leave to go back home soon. He didn't think he was strong enough to lose someone so special again.

CHAPTER THREE

BLAKE

Bzzt, bzzt.

Bzzt, bzzt.

…

Bzzt, bzzt.

A repeated buzzing pulled at Blake's mind as he rubbed his eyes. *That's a sound I should pay attention to,* he thought groggily.

Bzzt, bzzt. Bzzt, bzzt.

Oh fuck, my phone. No one ever texted him after 8 p.m. and it was… He glanced at the clock: 3:47 a.m.

He scrambled for his nightstand.

> **SOPHIA**
>
> help
>
> help
>
> help help help!!
>
> Wakeeee upppppp
>
> Oh it's Sophia.
>
> But WAKE UPPPPP

He shot up in the bed, rubbing his eyes to get a better look at the blurry screen. He scrolled to the beginning of the messages.

> **SOPHIA**
>
> Loud sound in kitchen.
>
> Think someone broke in.
>
> Can't get out. Don't want to call 911 because they'll hear me

Fuck.

He thundered down the stairs, jumping the last three and catching himself on the floor before falling. He dove for the slippers at the bottom of the kitchen door and threw them on, grabbing a baseball bat as he went.

He opened and closed his back door quietly, looking to see if anybody else was there. The cottage door was ajar, and his heart pummeled in his chest.

He ran to the back bedroom window. He'd call the police after he got her out safely.

Cozy Nights in Vermont

He tapped on her window at his eye level. She clutched her hand to her heart.

She unlatched the window quietly. "Jesus Christ, I didn't even recognize you," she whispered.

Oh, right. He'd trimmed his beard last night.

For no reason in particular.

Okay, maybe one reason in particular, who was staring at him in an oversized sleep shirt that looked four sizes too big for her with a loose, sleepy ponytail on top of her head.

"Come on," he whispered, wanting to get her to safety.

"What do you mean, 'come on'?" she said, panicked. "Call the police," she whispered through her teeth.

"I need to make sure you're safe first. It'll take them twenty minutes to get here. Sheriff Barnaby has three highballs before bed every night. It'll take him ten minutes just to see if he's sober enough to drive. Come on." He waved to her, holding his arms up. "I'll catch you."

She peeked out the window and stared at the five-foot drop. "Are you sure there's not a ladder somewhere?"

"Sophia," he said, urgency in his voice. "I've got you. Come on." He held out his arms to her, willing her to trust him.

* * *

SOPHIA

A crash sounded in the kitchen, and Sophia's heart leapt into her throat.

A gorgeous man—even if he dropped her—was preferable to whoever was invading the kitchen.

"Shit. Okay." She perched one ass cheek on the windowsill. It dug into her thighs as she slid her legs out the wide windowsill. "This always looks more romantic in movies."

The chilly wind wrapped around her, and she wished she'd thought to throw on a sweatshirt before climbing out the window.

It was just a few feet, but when you weren't used to jumping off anything, it might as well have been the Eiffel Tower.

"Here." His arms wrapped around her thighs. "Put your hands on my shoulders."

He grabbed her thighs and slowly, slowly slid her down his body, until her breasts were against his bare chest. He held her there, close against him.

They caught each other's eyes, breathing heavily from the panic.

His pecs were thick, beefy even, and gave way to a thick, muscular middle with padding around it. She wanted to bury her face into his chest. He held her firmly against him, snug and safe.

Her feet hadn't hit the ground yet, and she wasn't mad about it.

Cozy Nights in Vermont

"You okay?" he whispered softly.

She swooned at his low voice. *I think I left my stomach back in the room.*

Her eyes caught on his newly shaved face. Sexy, short stubble blanketed his skin. The moonlight reflected off of the curves of his wide, muscular shoulders, and he looked like a certified, corn-fed snack.

"I almost didn't recognize you," she said with a slow smile. "Yeah, I'm okay."

Maybe he'd stand here until morning so she wouldn't have to leave the pillowy muscles that held her so safely.

"Good," he said, clearing his throat and sliding her the rest of the way to the ground.

"Stay here," he said. "Or go inside my house. I'm going to investigate."

She balked. "Absolutely not." She wasn't standing in a dark, cold, foreign place.

"Yes, just stay here," he said, shaking his head as if she was crazy. "I don't want you getting hurt."

"I don't want *you* getting hurt," she said, raising her voice.

"Shh," he whispered, putting a finger to his mouth as he crept underneath the windows, walking around the cottage. She scurried after him.

"How do I know they don't have people in your farmhouse now?" she whisper-yelled.

"Star would have barked." He put a hand out to keep her behind him as he peeked around the corner. "Come to think of it, Star hasn't barked at all." He rubbed a hand down his face. "She always alerts me when someone comes into the patch. Maybe it's just an animal in the kitchen. Still though"—he double-checked the corner—"better careful than sorry."

They crept toward the front door, following the thuds and crashing.

They leaned in, listening hard. There was definitely rattling. "It doesn't sound like people," Blake said, lifting his bat. "And there aren't footsteps in the dirt. Stay back, okay?"

Sophia stood upright. "Like hell I will."

Blake sighed with resignation and slowly creaked the door open. She peeked in behind him.

He flipped on the light beside the door and yelled, raising the bat above his head.

All that greeted them was an empty kitchen.

"Wait." She pointed at the floor.

She'd left dough out overnight to rise, and there were suspicious tracks coming from the flour on the counter. They led to the pantry.

Rattling sounded inside of it.

She grabbed a large can of tomatoes on the counter.

Cozy Nights in Vermont

"What are you gonna do? Lycopene them to death?" Blake asked.

"Better than let you handle them by yourself."

He sighed but moved his arm so she stood behind him. It ignited something primal in her. Usually, she was the one charging ahead.

It was nice to be backup for once.

He yanked open the pantry door with a bat raised, and they both let out a primal scream.

Two raccoons with full bellies froze mid-chomp on her homemade granola bars.

Sophia let out a different scream, not expecting rodents in her pantry.

"Raccoons," she screamed, shoving at Blake.

"Get the door," he yelled as the raccoons scurried out.

"I don't want them in my kitchen. Oh my God, or my underwear drawer!" she screamed as she scrambled for the door.

"We got a runner," he yelled, darting through the living room after one.

She shooed one out, clapping at it, and it gave her a snide look, still clutching a granola bar.

Blake ran back, nearly knocking over a lamp. He and the raccoon took a hard turn out of the living room and through the kitchen.

The raccoon finally scampered out, and she slammed the door. Leaning against it with her full weight, she shoved at her hair.

Blake leaned over to catch his breath, the bat at his side. "How the hell"—he gasped—"did raccoons get into the pantry?"

She peeked into the walk-in pantry to examine the decimated shelves.

He poked his head in next to hers. "No holes," he said, crouching down, looking under the bottom shelf.

"How could two fat raccoons escape my notice after I was in the kitchen all day?" She shoved her fingers through her hair. She couldn't sleep tonight until she was sure they couldn't come back. "Yesterday, I was happily baking, enjoying the fall weather—"

Oh shit.

He raised an eyebrow at her.

She gasped. "Uh...I might have left the top half of the door open," she said sheepishly. "I wanted to be cold, and the oven was so hot and the fireplace was going, so I left the top half of the door open. Just a smidgen. Y'know, to feel more like a Disney princess or...uh, something."

A smile slowly curled onto his lips. "So you could feel like a Disney princess or something?"

"Or something," she said with a small smile, waiting for his anger. She'd endangered his property by letting vermin run all over it. "I'm *so* sorry."

"Maybe you could be like a Disney princess with the doors closed next time." He stood, bat over his shoulder, sporting a sexy smirk.

Gone was the bushy beard hiding his handsome face. His round cheeks complemented his strong jaw, and she was dazzled.

"I'm so sorry. I bugged you awake and then made you haul me out of a window. Then you chased wildlife around my kitchen-er, your kitchen," she corrected, "in the middle of the night."

Her apologetic smile threatened to burst into a bubble of laughter as she remembered the nonchalant surprise of the raccoons. As if she'd crashed their poker game.

Her fingers went to her lips, trying to keep a laugh in.

"What?" A smile now blazed bright on his face as he saw her biting back laughter.

Holy hell. If he was handsome before, he was devastatingly gorgeous when he smiled at her like that.

"It's just...the one on the left looked like Robert De Niro."

"Oh my God, he totally did," Blake said, realization dawning on him. Blake made a face with a downturned, disapproving frown, reminiscent of a certain famous actor.

She burst out laughing at the likeness, slapping his bare chest. "Exactly, but in raccoon form."

Their eyes connected as they laughed at the absolutely ridiculous situation.

"It was no problem," Blake said with a soft smile.

The sexiness of his dreamy eyes and beefy chest sizzled down to her toes, making a pit stop at her nipples.

Down, girls.

He shut the pantry. "I'm glad it wasn't anything worse. Chasing raccoons in the middle of the night was the highlight of my day."

"Really?" she said, fighting a yawn. "You're not mad?"

"No." He laughed and crossed his arms self-consciously. It only highlighted how sexy his arms were. He was muscular, probably from working on the farm, but there was a cushion of softness over the muscles that made her salivate. "It was probably the highlight of my whole fucking week, actually," he said with an exhausted, sleepy shake of his head.

"Why?"

"Because I got to hold—" He stopped himself and cleared his throat, glancing at her eyes with a flash. "Uh, hold the culprits accountable," he stuttered, squeezing his eyes together briefly. "I should go."

He wrenched her front door open.

"Hey," she called out.

He stopped on the doorstep.

A moment held between them, and she felt that flutter in her chest make its way up to her throat.

She wanted him.

Cozy Nights in Vermont

And she was pretty sure he wanted her too.

Normally she'd just be blunt. Ask for what she wanted. Shout, "Do you want to just bang it out already?"

She didn't do relationships, but she was excellent at just-banging-it-out.

Blake was far too sweet of a gentleman for her to say anything like that, though. She was blunt, but she wasn't going to scare him half to death with her Sophia-ness.

"Thank you," she said with a sleepy smile. His hazel eyes were full of warmth as he waved and shut the door.

Probably for the best.

If he knew what she really wanted, he'd never speak to her again.

CHAPTER FOUR

SOPHIA

A few days later, with the raccoon paw prints scrubbed from the countertop at least three times, Sophia angled her camera tripod at her latest recipe, a plate of buttery garlic rosemary focaccia.

She'd need to perfectly capture the light hitting the glaze of oil on the pillowy bread. Hearty slices sat on rustic stoneware pottery plates surrounded by a rosemary garnish. The effect against the butcher block counter looked effortless yet aspirational. In the background, a cozy candle burned to set the mood.

She'd already fallen into a quiet rhythm here. For all of her jet-setting appeal as an influencer, Sophia was a homebody. She was most comfortable in sweats, mixing something delicious together in the kitchen with a cocktail in hand and FaceTiming her little sister who absolutely hated talking on the phone.

Young millennials, she thought with an eye roll.

Cozy Nights in Vermont

She'd spent all morning going to farmers markets and produce stands to get the freshest ingredients. It was her small treat for making a dent in her recipes.

But everywhere she went, the remaining twenty-four recipes followed her.

They'd toddled behind her, reminding her she was behind as she walked through the farmers markets. They'd stayed with her, increasing her anxiety on a bike ride that morning exploring the countryside. The twenty-four recipes seemed to have strong feelings that she'd bought flowers instead of ingredients at the last farm stand, but she wasn't going to let them stop her joy of making time for herself.

"Forty days left, twenty-four recipes. I'll be fine, right? I can just make a recipe every other day," she mused as panic ran through her body.

She double-checked the camera angle before she hit record. Half her job as a content creator was just setting up B-roll cameras for her social media reels while hiding her baking chaos behind the camera. Her content had to look authentic, but polished. Fresh, but still hyper-relevant.

"I should be perfecting the soup section of my book. Instead, I'm making food look aesthetic," she grumbled.

She had no choice though. She had to keep her viewer numbers up, otherwise, her publishers could renegotiate her contract.

Scratching sounds at the window made her jump. Wind whipped through the farm and tree branches smacked against the windows.

A storm was brewing outside.

Even better for my rainy day aesthetic.

Her next shot would be a cute selfie as she took a bite of the bread. She checked her hair and makeup in the camera preview. She'd decided on a casual look, tossing her curls on top of her head, then artfully placing them in perfect spirals.

It had taken her forty-five fucking minutes to make it look so casual.

Her makeup was on point, as it always had to be for these. She was over-moisturized and over-contoured, but she looked barely normal compared to other content creators. She sighed, thinking of how much time and effort had gone into making herself look "barely normal."

It was honestly exhausting.

She'd even looked at local baking gigs in Dallas just to change up her routine. The thought of getting up at three or four in the morning to spend time with hunks of dough didn't seem so bad if she didn't have to wear perfect makeup, have perfect hair, and care about her posting strategy.

Back to business.

She'd record the voiceover later, so all she had to do was smile, wave, and take a bite. She hit start on her camera.

Cozy Nights in Vermont

A rattling sounded outside, and branches whipped against the windows again as the wind cranked up to a howl, making her jump. She pulled a face at the camera.

Maybe that's something I can use for later.

She turned back to the camera, checking her positioning, and grabbed a thick piece of focaccia bread, showing it to the camera. Obligatory nail tappies showed off the bumps and grooves of the bread, and she took a big bite.

The garlic and salt hit her tongue and settled into her soul. She savored the soft, pillowy goodness and was so proud she'd made something delicious.

She swiped the rosemary on her lip and winked at the camera as she licked it off her finger. She'd do some voiceover about how it was an extra treat to slow down and make something that made you happy.

Cshrrrrack!

The other-worldly sound interrupted her thoughts. A thousand cracks of a baseball bat were caught in the wind, and coming toward the cottage.

The living room ceiling—*holy fuck*—started to collapse.

Her heart seized as she registered that something was falling on the cottage.

She ducked beside the sturdy island, fearing for her life.

A booming crash sounded as debris and wind scattered into the living room. She tucked her arms over her head, hoping like hell that it wasn't going to come into the kitchen, whatever it was.

Bits and pieces fell around her, but then, beyond the howling of the wind, everything settled.

Gray sky poked through the cottage roof. Blake screamed her name and his footsteps crunched in the gravel running toward the cottage.

He threw open the door that had remained unscathed, and she waved an arm as she sat up on her haunches, brushing debris from her hair.

"I'm here. I'm fine," she added quickly. He looked around like a madman, eyes wild, and rushed to her, kneeling down.

He gathered her in his arms and crushed her against him, but then yanked her away. "Are you okay? Oh my god. I was in the barn when I saw the tree cave in the roof." He was out of breath, searching her body for injuries. "Are you hurt? Are you okay?"

"I'm fine," she said calmly, willing him to stop worrying.

Leave it to someone with chronic anxiety to be calm in a shitstorm.

He stood. "Come on. Let's get you out of here. It's not safe to be in here." He helped her up like she was injured and looked wearily up at the cottage roof that now sported a nature-made skylight.

The wind whipped around them as they walked out. "I ate a bite of focaccia, and then a tree crashed through the ceiling," she called over the wind, still trying to process the crazy last thirty seconds.

"Did you hit your head? Did anything fall on you?" he yelled, glancing over her as they walked against the wind.

"Blake," she said, putting her hands on his arms. "Breathe with me. I'm fine." She sucked in a breath and blew it out slowly to show him.

His eyebrows furrowed. The wind whipped around them like it was out for vengeance as leaves tumbled past. "I'll calm down when you're inside and safe." He laced his fingers through hers and pulled her toward his house. "It's entirely my fault. I should have had the tree removed months ago."

"Blake, it's not your fault."

He wrapped his other arm around her as they got closer to the farmhouse. "You could have been hurt or...or worse." He wrenched open the door, his voice catching above the howling wind.

He didn't let go of her hand once they were inside. She liked the feeling of his hand clutching hers as he led her through his entryway.

He pulled her into his darkened kitchen. "Are you sure you're okay? No cuts or scratches anywhere? Sometimes the adrenaline hides injuries." He looked her over, but she could only concentrate on his hand grasping hers. On the light freckles across his cheeks that seemed so at odds with his hulking stature.

"Oh shit," he said, looking at the side of her neck.

He turned her chin gently with his free hand and a shiver went down her spine at the contact.

"You're cut. Shit. I'm so sorry, Sophia." His voice was anguished.

"I'm fine," she laughed, feeling for the cut that must have been a mere scratch. Her finger had a small trickle of blood when she looked at it.

Oh. Maybe worse than it feels.

His hand broke away from hers, and she held it to her for some reason, wanting to keep the warmth he provided.

"Here, sit." Blake pulled out a wooden chair from the table and turned on the kitchen lights.

She hadn't been in his place yet, but now she gaped as she took in the kitchen.

"Whoa."

A long white wall of subway tile gave way to beautiful old cabinets that had been lovingly restored, a high-end designer fridge, and—

Holy Mother of the Food Channel Gods.

She gasped. "Is that a *Viking*?" she screamed the name in disbelief, walking to the oven and ignoring the chair.

"Uh, yeah. I think so," he said, seeming distracted. He walked to her with a first aid kit. "Here, do you mind if I...?" He gestured to her neck.

"Oh, sure," she said absentmindedly, running her hands over the sex god of ovens, the Viking Series 7. She'd stared at it on her computer multiple times over several glasses of wine, dreaming of what it would be like to use something other than the builder-grade oven in her apartment.

"This thing is gorgeous. I think this literal model is on my 'when I hit the lottery' vision board." She sighed with longing. "How did I not know you were a foodie?"

"I'm not," he laughed, clicking open the first aid kit. "My parents splurged on a redesign about ten years ago, but it's been lost on me since I took over the farm."

She popped open the smaller of the two oven doors. *I could make lasagna and roast vegetables at the same damn time.* "This was your parents' place?"

"They took it over from my grandparents. When they decided it was time to retire, I took over."

"Wow." She mentally cataloged what she could make that used all eight burners on the stove. "Do you know that this thing heats nearly instantly?"

She resisted the urge to moan as she saw one had the wok attachment. *The wok attachment, for chrissakes.* Jesus, it looked practically brand new. "This oven is ten thousand dollars' worth of homey goodness."

"My mom has expensive tastes, unfortunately. Hasn't always been a great fit for a husband who is a farmer, but my dad tried to spoil her. All I know is that it heats up frozen pizzas pretty well."

She gasped. "Blasphemy. Frozen pizzas in this thing? Not even fresh homemade ones?"

"'Fraid not. Ready?" A gentle hand lifted her chin. "This may hurt a little."

"Can't sting as badly as how you've misused the Jaguar of ovens."

The corner of his mouth curled up at her teasing.

She liked the feeling of his fingers brushing her throat as he took care of her. Her eyes fluttered closed at that little bit of contact, but she flinched as the warm gauze hit her cut as he cleaned it.

"So what kinds of things should I be making in this oven?" he said, probably to distract her.

It worked.

"Ooh," she thought with excitement, wiggling around. "Maybe some homemade bread. You could use a big Dutch oven to do a peasant-style loaf. Very Jean Valjean. I'd insist you flavor it with the rosemary that I got from Mabel."

"Mabel the sheep?" he said in a soft voice, smiling. She could almost feel the puff of his breath against her cheek as he put antibiotic ointment on her cut.

Delicious.

"If I got it from Mabel the sheep, I would have said 'Maaaaaaybel,'" she said, making the obligatory baaaa sheep sound. Maaaybel was the local superstar animal at the Chestnut Hollow Inn and Farm next door. Sophia had met both farmer and sheep Mabels when she'd stopped to check out their farm stand.

"Okay," he said, stepping back. "All done."

"Thank you." A small shiver traveled through her body and her teeth chattered. Weird. She pulled her sleeves over her hands and wrapped her arms around her middle. "Why do I feel cold?"

"I think you're in shock." He reached into a hall closet.

"Psssh." She waved him away. "I'm not in shock." That was what other people experienced. She could handle practically anything.

Though she hadn't realized she'd had a wide cut on her neck...

"A roof almost fuckin' *fell* on you, Sophia. You're allowed to be in shock. Here, this should be clean." He held a thick flannel shirt open for her, and her insides flip-flopped.

If my system is already in shock, I don't think I can handle an honest-to-goodness gentleman on top of it.

She slid it on and he tugged it up onto her shoulders. The warmth of it felt like heaven. It smelled like him—that cologne and ivory soap scent of manliness, maybe with a hint of wood smoke. "Thank you," she said quietly, wrapping the shirt around her.

"I'll call Mabel and see if she has an open room at her inn. Or my uncles at the Clovely Inn." He looked out at the cottage where half a tree stuck out of the roof. His brow scrunched with worry as he turned around, looking pained. "I'm not sure when I'll be able to get the roof fixed. It'll definitely take more than a couple of days."

He wiped a hand over his face, letting out a loud sigh. "But I'm not sure if either of them will have availability for a whole month. They're usually booked solid this time of year." He looked down, chewing on his cheek. "I can give you your money back so you can go home early."

He looked pained as he spoke to her, like a thousand different worries were sitting on his shoulders.

But I don't wanna go home.

She'd sublet her apartment in Dallas, and she desperately didn't want to go back yet. The air here was too crisp, the veggies too local, the man in front of her too handsome.

She'd planned to spend Thanksgiving with Iris and her new boyfriend Sam in Boston a couple hours away. It seemed silly to fly all the way back with her stuff early, only to have to crash with a friend for four or five weeks and come back.

She looked around the gorgeous kitchen—the designer fridge, the oven porn behind her.

Ample granite counters would be perfect surfaces for rolling out heaps of dough and chopping endless vegetables.

She peered over the countertop into the open-concept living room. A large cobblestone fireplace wound its way up the wall. Comfy sofas sat facing it. The old farmhouse kitchen table had decades of character built into it.

And she'd have a kind, sexy roommate to talk to.

One that worried about her, even when he didn't need to.

Cozy Nights in Vermont

"What if...I stayed here?"

"Here?" he echoed, his eyes going wide. He gulped. "In this house? Where I am?"

It looked like his brains had been dumped into a deep fryer.

She shrugged as she looked around the kitchen. It was spotless. He'd probably be a better roommate than most women she'd roomed with. "It's a big farmhouse. Is there a guest bedroom?"

He huffed out a surprised laugh. "Uh, yep. Across the hall from my room. We'd have to share a bathroom, though."

She thought back to the conversation she'd overheard between him and his aunt.

Okay, the one she'd *eavesdropped* on.

He was already worried about money on the farm, and she hadn't seen many people stop by for pumpkins, despite other farm stands being overrun with tourists.

"You could even keep the rent money." She bit her lip, starting to get her hopes up. She'd get to see him every day, get to spread her wings in this gorgeous farmhouse kitchen on a dreamy pumpkin farm.

"I can't let you do that. I mean, you're welcome to stay here." He scratched his ear in what looked like panicked thought. "But you can't pay me to stay in my place. I'd love for you to..." He shook his head, blushing. "I mean, you'd be welcome to stay here."

Elise Kennedy

"Your kitchen is amazing." She placed a lingering touch on the stovetop. "A lot more space than my kitchen at home, and better tools."

She opened the fridge door to take a look, and her face fell as she saw rows and rows of nothing but packaged protein shakes. She ripped open the freezer and saw stacks of microwave TV dinners and frozen pizzas.

"Where is your food?" she said, turning around with concern.

"Right there." He shrugged, crossing his arms.

"These are nutrients. Where's your *food*?" She peeked behind the rows of bottles filled with perfectly balanced macros, but likely zero happiness.

He closed the fridge door. "I just don't really know how to cook."

"Do you *like* drinking only protein shakes?" She scratched her head, dumbfounded.

He huffed out a laugh. "No, but they're fast. I usually don't have free time. I just chug one and keep going to do whatever needs to be done."

She grabbed his arms, shaking him for emphasis. "But you deserve to feel good when you feed your body, Blake. Food is life. Food is *love* in your mouth."

His cheeks went red at that.

Oh god, she loved doing that to him. She realized how close she was to him—nearly toe to toe—and took a step back.

Cozy Nights in Vermont

She could be a little *intense*; she knew this.

"Well, that settles it. I have to move in. I have to feed you. Otherwise, my 4'11" Italian nonna will rise from her grave, crawl here from Sarasota, and haunt me until I do."

He smiled at her, looking a little embarrassed. "I'd love anything you'd care to make, but you don't need to worry about me." He grabbed the jacket he'd tossed off when they'd come in. "I'm going to go look at the damage in the cottage. Is there anything else you need tonight?"

You, holding my chin again while you take care of me.

"My computer's on the kitchen table," she said. She was tempted to add "a red thong" to see him blush again, but she didn't dare. He'd take her too seriously and risk injuring himself. "Oh, and Kim Carbdashian."

He halted in confusion. "Kim what?"

"She's my sourdough starter in the fridge."

"And you're getting your money back," he shouted as he walked out.

"Not unless I can take this oven with me back to Dallas," she shouted back.

The back door clicking shut was his response.

Star trotted up to her and leaned her full body weight against Sophia's legs.

"Hey, Star girl." She got in close for a cuddle. An overwhelming wave of exhaustion came over her, and she yawned into the dog's fur. A small tongue lick grazed her cheek, and she smiled into the cloud of black.

"You gonna give me a tour?" she asked, as Star's mouth opened with a smile, panting her puppy breath onto Sophia's face. "How about I get a tour of the couch first?" she said tiredly.

Maybe this whole ordeal had tired her out more than she realized. She'd been hustling nonstop since she'd arrived five days ago.

As she curled up on the comfy overstuffed couch, it seemed to fold her in, and she settled under the heavy, soft blanket that Blake kept on the edge of the couch. She was thankful for being safe and warm in a cozy old farmhouse as Star settled onto her legs.

The image of Blake ripping open the cottage door and running toward her flashed in her mind as she processed the last twenty minutes.

She sighed, thinking about how he'd crushed her to his chest and the overwhelming wave of safety she'd felt when he'd gotten there.

Maybe, if I'm lucky, he'll hug me one more time.

CHAPTER FIVE

BLAKE

UNCLE ALAN
Blakey, tell us about the cutie patootie that Bev saw you with. 👀

UNCLE JERRY
Oh my God. Alan, stop torturing my nephew. —JERRY

UNCLE ALAN
He's my nephew, too, according to the state of Vermont and our marriage license, sourpuss.

AUNT BEV
Sorry 😬
I'm just so excited that maybe you're ready for dating!!!

UNCLE ALAN

And stop signing your texts Jerry!!!!!!! It makes you sound old as Moses.

UNCLE JERRY

No. —JERRY

Blake rubbed his temples.

His uncles and aunt took their family duty very seriously. Aunt Bev was constantly shoving food in his fridge he never asked for, and Uncle Alan, Uncle Jerry's husband, was always prompting him to get out there and try again. He loved them for their warmth and how much they cared for not only him, but for other people.

He just wished they cared a little less about his dating life.

                                              BLAKE

                              She's just my renter.

Uncle Alan started to type back.

                                              BLAKE

                     And this isn't the go ahead for any more blind dates!

UNCLE ALAN

Bein' a sourpuss must run in the Jameson family... :|

His Uncle Jerry had bought the old Clovely Inn, and he and Alan had painstakingly restored it. Once it got going, Beverly had joined as the head chef, and after only being open for a year, they were putting Clovely on the map.

Blake crossed his arms with an uncomfortable half-smile as a family walked up to the pumpkin patch. He gave them a small wave. His prices were posted, and he didn't like to crowd people as they shopped.

Honestly, he just wanted to be out in the fields, not watching over his pumpkin patch like an awkward hawk.

"Do you have a place where we could take pictures?" the mom asked. A little girl in pigtails in a plaid fall outfit clutched a pink teddy bear held the mom's hand as she stared at Blake.

"Uh... sure. Wherever's fine," Blake said without really knowing what he was supposed to say.

What was it with families wanting to take pictures with his vegetables?

"Oh, okay," the mom faltered. The family wandered over to where some pumpkins were piled up and knelt down doing a selfie-style picture.

As long as they don't take a picture of the tarp on the cottage roof. He was embarrassed by the cheap, bright blue plastic covering the hole.

He'd been on the roof early that morning nailing down a temporary tarp to keep the weather and birds out.

"Actually, would you mind?" the dad called to him.

Blake sighed. He was a farmer, not a photographer, damn it.

"Uh, sure, though I'm not great with these kinds of things." He never wanted to screw up somebody's holiday picture.

He took the photo, grimacing the entire time, and another car rolled to a stop in his small gravel parking lot beside the pumpkin patch.

He checked his watch. It was about time for Mabel to bring her load of tourists from the inn next door.

He'd been distracted all morning thinking of the terror he'd felt yesterday at seeing the tree limbs falling on the cottage. He'd run faster than he thought possible trying to get to Sophia in time.

She'd been nonchalant and cool under pressure, despite having a house fall down around her.

Seeing her wrapped up in his blanket on his couch guarded by his dog—safe and sound—had been the best kind of gut punch. He'd felt a quiet, thrilling satisfaction at pulling the blanket over her and tucking her in last night after he'd brought in her things.

She'd slept hard through the night and was still on the couch the next morning. But shock did that to you.

Anytime Angie had had an emergency, he'd felt the same overwhelming sense of drowsy exhaustion when they got back home, having dealt with whatever brought them into the hospital.

I can't lose another person, he thought, the image of Sophia on the ground flashing in his head.

Cozy Nights in Vermont

He had to stay far away from her, the only woman who had ripped back the curtains of his monk-like existence with her bright energy.

It would hurt too badly when she left.

He needed to stay as far away as possible while also sleeping across the hall from her.

Fuck.

The screen door slammed, and Star trotted over to the woman in question.

She looked fresh and sexy with a slouchy sweater on, torn jeans, and Converse sneakers. Her hair was thrown into a messy bun, and she had streaks of flour across her apron.

He wished she had just a dash of it against her cheek so he'd have a reason to touch her there. Wipe it away with his thumb.

He had the sense that no one had ever truly taken care of Sophia. That she took care of herself—but he couldn't help himself. He *wanted* to take care of her. That was just who he was. It was what made him happy.

Stupid, stupid. That's the opposite of what I should be doing.

But still, he wanted her to feel welcome and safe despite the adventure-filled last few days at his farm.

"I wanted to say thank you," she said, gesturing with a decorative plate that his mother had left. On it was a heaping pile of golden, sugar-covered donuts.

He smiled. He wasn't used to having somebody make a fuss over him.

"You didn't need to do this." It didn't keep his fingers from plucking a donut off the top though.

"It's my new take on an apple cider donut," she said, looking eager for him to take a bite.

As the spicy cinnamon sugar hit his tongue, he knew that even before he bit into it, this donut was going to change his life.

He savored the dense, sweet, vanilla burst with apple notes that washed pleasure over him. He shuddered at the contact.

"Wow," he said, opening his eyes wide with amazement. "That's...that's the best donut I've ever had. Don't tell Aunt Bev." He took another small bite, wanting to savor it.

"Shut the front door," she said with a bright smile, smacking his arm.

The simple touch left a glow on his bicep, radiating warmth into his bone marrow. He loved that she casually touched him.

Craved it.

She jumped up and down. "Really? I've had too many samples, so I can't actually tell anymore."

"Donuts!" one of the kids from the families wandering through the pumpkin patch screamed.

Cozy Nights in Vermont

A second kid from the other family started running toward them. "Can I have one? Are these for us?"

Kids these days. But looking at their hopeful faces, he couldn't hog them all to himself. "Are they allowed to try some free samples?" he called over to the parents.

"Oh, of course." One of the moms smiled. "That's so nice that you give out free samples here."

"This is my apple cider donut. It's a new recipe that I'm trying out," Sophia said, breaking a donut into small bites with a plastic knife she'd brought out.

After the kids each slurped up their samples, the grownups gathered around them picked out ones too.

Well, damn.

"Oh my gosh, it just melts in your mouth," one of the men said, holding a big pie pumpkin that the family had picked out.

"I'd love to buy some for our oldest. Our teenager decided to sleep in today," one of the women said with a roll of her eyes.

"Oh, I'm just testing out recipes. I don't have anything for sale. Yet," Sophia added with a nervous smile at Blake. "But you're welcome to take another one for the road. And don't worry," she said, leaning over to Blake with a wink, "I have more in the kitchen for you."

He liked that she worried about him, and loved it even more when she acted as if they were partners sharing a secret.

He rubbed a hand on his chest where it ached to hold her. In the middle of a workday, no less.

This was a goddamned nightmare.

"Dad, are we gonna get the big pumpkin?" one of the little boys asked a man whose mouth was full of donut.

Blake stared expectantly at the man eating the donut Sophia had made for *him*.

"Uh, sure," the dad said, swallowing a bite. "Could you help me load it into the car?" he asked Blake.

Hot damn, that was his two-hundred-dollar showpiece he didn't think he'd sell this year. Blake smiled, amazed at what a few donuts could do. "I'll even help you buckle it in."

The two families settled up, and he was surprised to see they bought more than average. Sophia chatted with the families as he loaded the enormous pumpkin into one of the SUVs, and she sparkled as she entertained them.

It didn't seem like an accident that his customers left much happier than normal.

As both families drove off, they stood side by side and waved.

Sophia bumped her hip against his playfully. "I hope that was okay. I panicked a little. I wanted them to tell their friends to come and spend all the money."

Blake rubbed a hand on his chin, still getting used to the shorter stubble. "It's a smart idea. It's what other pumpkin patches do, but it's never been my forte, putting all of this fall stuff together. I just like farming."

She sighed wistfully. "I love cute fall shit," she said with a wry smile. "It's part of the territory of making lifestyle content. Maybe I could spruce up an area over there for photos. I saw them taking pictures." She pointed to the old trailer he'd left out with pumpkins on it. She hit his arm with a happy realization. "Oh, and maybe have rotating samples as a special treat." She looked absolutely gorgeous when she lit up with her ideas.

Hair blew across her face, and he reached up to push it away.

No, don't be a weirdo. You're just roommates.

He awkwardly changed course and scratched his chin instead.

"That's awful nice of you to offer," he said, hoping she didn't notice his awkwardness, "but you're busy with all of your recipe stuff, and the social whatchamacallit."

"That *is* the technical term. C'mon, it'll be fun," she said, tugging on his arm. "This will give me motivation to get through all the recipes I need to create. It's so nice to see people actually eat my food for once and not just look at the like count on my posts." Her smile was tinged with sadness as she clutched the plate to her chest.

He'd do anything, anything in the whole fucking world—turn cartwheels if he had to—to see happiness replace that sad smile.

"I mean, if it would make you happy," he said, more truth slipping out than he wanted.

"Really?" she said, clapping her hands. Her cheeks had gone ruddy in the cold, looking like they'd been pinched. Her ruby-red lips were picture-perfect in her face-cracking smile.

His eyes were probably goddamn cartoon hearts at this point. "I mean, we'll have to get some permits or something. I don't know. I'll call around."

He shoved his hands in his pockets so they didn't do something stupid.

Like pull her in for a hug.

Or more.

"Thank you!" Unexpectedly, she wrapped her arms around him and squeezed for a nanosecond, then jogged back to the farmhouse.

My plan for staying as far away as possible?

He sighed wistfully as she played with Star while she jogged.

I think it just went to shit.

***

SOPHIA

Artfully placed pumpkins sat on hay bales at different heights in front of an arch of orange maple trees, creating a perfect frame for family photos. Sophia could practically smell the pumpkin spice coming off her camera screen.

Since the farm was quiet that afternoon, she used the space she'd styled for the pumpkin patch photographs as her backdrop.

And she wanted to scream every curse word she knew when she messed up another. *Goddamn. Fucking. Take.*

I hate this fucking dance.

Any happy fuzzy feelings left from the day before vanished as Sophia stomped over to hit stop on her camera.

Why did dance moves have to make videos go viral? Why couldn't she just monologue about how delicious brie cheese was?

"But no, I have to make stupid dance videos so I get stupid fan engagement so I can pay my stupid fucking bills," she muttered as she hit restart.

She sighed, a bone-deep tiredness seeping out of her pores. "You picked this. You could have been an accountant. Coulda had your own condo in the arts district, but no. You had to go live that hustle life being your own boss."

No 401k for me, just 401 fucking tasks I have to do.

"I just want to make butternut squash soup," she whined, putting her phone back on her tripod. It turned out that getting a food truck permit was shockingly easy (maybe unsettlingly easy), and Sophia's samples would be up and running within a day or so.

She went back to her marker, checked her reflection in the camera preview, and hit start using her remote thingy. A beat in her ear synced with the track, and she started the dance over.

Again.

As her arms moved up-down-side-side, like an air traffic controller making love to a windmill, a mean comment she'd read that morning flashed in her head.

You'd think she'd spend less time cooking and more time exercising, ThatBiiiiitch6969 had commented under a recent video.

She tried to focus on the song.

I tried her gazpacho recipe and it was absolute shit. My dog didn't even wanna eat it lololol, 12turtleluver had said a week ago.

Her lip quivered.

She shoved her arms down into a T-like position and then shook her hips with a saucy little smile, but the tears started forming and her lip wobbled.

"Fuck," she screamed, kneeling and curling into a ball in frustration.

A scroll of all the mean things she'd ever read about herself ran through her brain. God, she was so *tired* of it all.

Cozy Nights in Vermont

A sob escaped. She just wanted a life where she could focus on things that meant something.

"Ugh, so annoying," she said, getting mad at herself. "Get your shit together, Sophia. This is what you worked for."

She wiped her eyes and stood up. *Maybe the cold air will hide my puffy eyes.*

"Are you okay?" Blake walked toward her with a bulky table in his arms.

She wiped her eyes again and put on a bright smile to feel like she was in charge.

Strong.

"Is that for our food stand?" she said brightly. "Sorry, your food stand."

"It's ours," he said with a smile, his eyes lingering on her lips for a second before he took a big breath. "Uh, yeah, I made a table that has a holder for your soup since that's first up on your recipe list. So the crockpot wouldn't slide off and burn anyone. You know how the kids run around. The little one is for your coffee."

He set it down, but his eyes caught on her face. "You sure you're okay?"

"Oh, it's fine," she said, waving him away as her voice wavered. "Just one of those days."

She started to lose control of her grip on the tears and he looked pained.

"I hate to see you cry. Do, uh..." He shifted nervously as if debating with himself. "Do you want to talk about it?"

"Oh." She shook her head as if she was being silly. Usually guys just let her wave her hands at feelings and didn't comment on it. "Yeah, I'm just, um..."

He looked so earnest and sexy in his flannel shirt layered over a light gray Henley. The green in the flannel brought out the olive green of his eyes.

She looked down at the perfectly placed little square holder he'd nailed to the table for her coffee cup. He'd even cut out a little hole for the handle. No one had ever made her anything like that. He'd worked all morning just because she'd said it might be nice to try getting people's thoughts on her soup in a few days.

She let out a big sigh. "It's just...I have to do this stupid dance."

"A dance?" he said, looking at the camera.

She nodded. "I don't want to because...I don't think it's who I want to be anymore." Her lip wobbled.

Keep it together, Sophia. Shove it deep down inside.

"That sounds really hard," he said softly. He stepped closer, staring down at her with concern.

She nodded, trying to keep it together. "I've just really enjoyed my time with your customers, and I have nineteen recipes left that I should be working on and um..." She gulped. "...I'm losing followers and everyone hates me, and..."

Cozy Nights in Vermont

Her eyes kept being drawn to the little coffee holder.

How had she gone her whole life with no one ever having done something that nice for her? Made her something she didn't even know she could ask for?

"I just want a life where I can focus on cooking for people, and not what Ilovehorses5000 in Arizona will think about my dance moves." She buried her face in her hands. "I don't know why I'm telling you all this, but it's just been inside, you know?"

"You don't have to have it together all the time. It's okay to cry." He rubbed a hand on her shoulder. "Is there anything I can do? I'm a pretty bad dancer, but I can try if it'll make you happy."

She heard the smile in his voice but knew he wasn't joking.

Not even a little.

A laugh burst out from her. *It's okay to cry* and *'Is there anything I can do?* Those weren't words that she'd heard in that order in a long time, maybe ever.

I just feel so lonely. She squinted up at him as she realized what he could do. *I'm gonna kick myself for this.*

"Can I..." She gulped. *Oh God, I hate this. I hate this.*

But I need this.

"What?" he said with concern.

"...Can I have a hug?" she said, squinting with embarrassment as she looked up at him.

"I happened to be an excellent hugger, so. Sure." He shrugged with a slow smile.

She looked at his shoulders that were the size of a Mack truck, his beefy but soft arms, and the chest she wanted to sink into.

She bet he was a good fucking hugger.

She wiped her eyes self-consciously, not wanting any mascara runoff on his shirt. "All right, but I need a hug that means business. None of this gentle patting crap, okay?"

He smiled and drew her in against his chest. She wrapped her arms around the thick of his middle. He had a soft belly that met hers, and she squeezed hard around him. He squeezed her hard back, enveloping her into his chest.

He was tall, and his head cleared hers as she settled in.

She'd once read that characters at theme parks were told to return a hug until a child was ready to let go. That was what she wanted right now—somebody to hug her and never let go until that deep aching loneliness finally went away.

His hand smoothed in small circles up and down her back, and she cuddled in, feeling at home.

He was warm and solid, and didn't think it at all weird that the woman sleeping in the bedroom across from his was such a fucking weirdo that she needed a hug from a practical stranger.

Cozy Nights in Vermont

And just when she thought, *I shouldn't bother him anymore,* his hand smoothed down her hair and rested on her head, cradling it against his chest.

Dopamine flooded over her, cascading down her shoulders in glittery waves of happiness.

Oh God, was this as good as her life was going to get? A paw of a hand resting against her head, smushing it against a beefy chest?

Because this... She sighed. *This is really fucking good.*

A deep knot somewhere in her stomach relaxed. She inhaled his spicy, clean scent, and the feel of the flannel against her cheek felt like heaven.

This man was a walking weighted blanket intent on destroying her nerves and anxiety.

What are you doing? She was probably embarrassing him with how she was clinging on, though he just kept patiently stroking her hair.

After she memorized the feel of the fabric against her cheek and what his arms felt like around her, she finally dropped her arms. She stepped away, embarrassed but not sorry.

"Thanks," she said with a small laugh. "What do you think of the styling of the photo spot?" she added, quickly changing the subject. Needing to distance herself from how needy she'd felt. "Unfortunately, the nearest craft store is like an hour away, so I had to improvise."

He looked past her at the display. "It looks perfect."

"I thought we'd move the free sample stand over here," she said, gesturing to a spot across the courtyard area where people tended to wander and pick their pumpkin, "so that it would be closer to the kitchen where I can run and get refills."

"Yeah, that'll make it easier for the generator as well."

"Generator? What, for the crockpot?"

"No, so you can have heat when you stand here."

She pshawed. "I don't need that."

He crossed his arms as his brows knit together. "It's getting colder. I need you to be warm."

"You don't have to worry about me," she said, waving away his concerns as though she regularly stood in fifty-degree weather for hours at a time. She didn't like the idea of somebody going out of their way for her.

"Sophia," he said, arching an eyebrow at her. "You don't have to use it, but it's going to be there." He walked back to the barn.

"All right, sass pants," she called back.

"Just selfishly want to keep you alive for more apple cider donuts," was his response.

She ran her hand along the table. *He made something just for me,* she thought as butterflies flew around her heart.

Maybe I should care just as much about my happiness as he does.

Cozy Nights in Vermont

Now there was a novel thought. Making sure *she* was happy, rather than caring about what everyone else thought. Not what her publisher thought, or her agent. Not her followers, or other content creators.

Maybe she should do more of what made her happy. *Like working on the fall decorations, and less of what I'm supposed to do.*

Wasn't this what it was all about anyway? Making food that made people happy? Social media was just a delivery mechanism, but she'd let it run her whole life.

She decided to split the difference. A lot less time worrying about her social posts, more time making good food.

Grabbing her tripod and camera, she walked to the farmhouse to experiment with delicious ingredients. Maybe make her favorite creamy chicken dumpling soup.

What else would be fun while I'm here? She thought about the hunky man who'd disappeared into the barn.

A wicked idea sparked in her head. She pressed her lips together to stifle a burst of laughter at how happy it made her.

Seducing my roommate would make me very, very happy.

CHAPTER SIX

SOPHIA

A few days later, the fall morning was brisk and fog loomed on the edges of the fields. Sophia cozied into her scarf, nuzzling it over her nose and delighting in being cold as people milled around the pumpkin patch.

Attendance had doubled overnight as word got out that the Jameson Family Farm was now a proper pumpkin patch experience with free donut bites, hot drinks, and a photo area. The coffee had been Blake's idea to make sure she wouldn't freeze to death. Though her toes stayed toasty thanks to the heater he'd rigged up.

She'd been inspired to make something sweet that morning, so she put out three versions of a molasses cookie recipe she'd been struggling with onto the tables. She couldn't decide what it needed. More molasses? More cloves? Neither and just make it chock-full of walnuts? Hopefully Blake's customers would help her decide which of her recipe risks was the best bet.

Cozy Nights in Vermont

Blake had been actively avoiding her the last two days; she could feel it. She'd walk into the living room, and there'd practically be a dust cloud from him running away. He'd even taken his protein shakes and whatever food she could convince him to grab to the barn.

But there had been a *moment* between them, she was sure of it.

Maybe even several moments.

When he'd burst into the cottage, he'd been so protective he'd looked feral.

Which was silly. I'm an eldest daughter extraordinaire. No one protects me. I protect myself, thank you very much. I have for thirty-two years, and I will for thirty-two more.

Young women walked into the pumpkin patch, taking silly videos as they laughed together. A persistent irritation tap-tap-tapped on her shoulder, reminding her that she should be monetizing her content right now. Recording the vibes, making cute faces, buying the trendiest thing so she could put it in a video.

But she needed five more minutes of the chill wind against her skin and the smell of woodsmoke in the air.

Five more minutes of families wandering through the vines, picking the pumpkin or squash they'd take home and make their own. Maybe they'd bond over pumpkin guts spilled on the kitchen table. She bet the boy holding the small pumpkin over his head would ask his dad to carve a scary face.

What Blake grew and sold here was *real*. It made its way into people's family memories.

She wanted that sense of purpose for herself, desperately.

But how?

A group of older ladies browsed through the pumpkin patch, all done up in their cute fall sweaters. Their bobs of white and gray hair in chic styles stood out against the oranges and reds of the maple trees. Two wandered over with small pumpkins in their arms.

"Ooh, are these the free treats made by a famous chef?" one of the ladies said with a twinkle in her eye. "The owners at the inn told us to make a pit stop here."

"I don't know about famous, but I'd love your opinion of which cookies you like better," she said, pointing to the three trays. "I'm testing out which recipe I should put in my new cookbook."

The woman tried a bite and waved her friend over. "Mary, you'll love these. Come try."

A woman with iron-gray hair and a sour face walked up. "I wish it wasn't so cold today. And that the car was closer to the pumpkins," she said to Sophia with a resigned sigh.

Looks like Mary's having a rough day. What a treat for me.

The older woman looked irritated, as if Sophia had done something wrong to her. "Are these full of sugar? You young people make things too sweet."

Cozy Nights in Vermont

Swallowing a growl and an eye roll, Sophia pointed to her recipe number three with the biggest smile she could muster. "This batch has less sugar than the others, but more molasses and cloves. I'd love to know what you think."

Mary huffed, taking a small cookie and biting into it.

Sophia steeled herself for the reaction.

The older woman went still. Her brow furrowed in surprise.

Sophia waited, holding her breath. Then Mary blinked eyes that had turned...teary?

Is...is she crying? Oh shit. "Is everything okay?" Sophia asked, her chest tightening with nerves.

Mary took another quick bite and chewed thoughtfully, then closed her eyes. A wide, happy smile replaced her frown. She clapped her hands together with excitement, and a tear ran down her cheek.

She wiped it away. "Blanche," Mary called to one of the ladies. "C'mere. Hurry."

The first woman looked as confused as Sophia felt. "Mary, are you okay?"

Mary ignored her and grabbed the plate, holding it out for a woman with long gray hair who walked up in more hippie-like attire.

Blanche bit into the cookie and gasped, bending over with animated surprise.

"Doesn't it taste just like Mom's?" Mary said through a wavering voice.

Blanche clutched the cookie to her chest. "Oh my god. Ohmygod it *does*," she said in a wobbly voice, a tear coming to her eye.

This was not what I expected when I accidentally over-poured the molasses this morning, Sophia thought with surprise, trying to get a handle on the situation.

Blanche turned to explain. "We've tried and tried to find our mom's gingersnap recipe. Tried a thousand different versions but we could never get it right." She shook her head in amazement as she took another bite.

Mary stood nibbling on the cookie, lost in her own thoughts. Sophia could see the ghost of the girlhood still inside of her, even decades later.

Maybe that never went away.

"She'd make these every day after school." Mary huffed out a laugh, shaking her head and closing her eyes, savoring it. "It's like she's right here."

Oh, my heart. These women were easily in their seventies, but all it took was a single bite to bring them back to their mom's kitchen.

Sophia found her own eyes tearing up. Food was life, indeed. How many times had she thought of her nonna when eating *tortellini in brodo*?

This. *This* was real.

What she'd made finally meant something to someone.

"It's a molasses cookie, actually," Sophia said with kindness. "Plus, I used extra strong cloves and about half the sugar as normal."

Blanche slapped her forehead. "That's why our attempts never tasted right."

"Can I buy the rest?" Mary asked suddenly, looking nervous—as if Sophia would dare take away the memory of her mother.

"Please, take them," Sophia said, offering an empty Tupperware container. "I'm happy to share the recipe, if you'd like."

Blanche clapped her hands and Mary nodded emphatically with wide, teary eyes.

Sophia grabbed their email addresses and copied the recipe from her notes app, noting the modified ratio she'd used, the specific cookie sheet, and even the brand of ingredients so they could replicate it at home.

She double-checked that they received the email. "Let me know if you have any questions, okay?" A thought occurred to her. "Would you..." Sophia's voice faltered.

She stared at the women who had no idea what impact they'd just had on her. "Would you be okay if I named the recipe in my cookbook after your mom?"

Blanche sniffed as she grabbed Mary's hand. Mary nodded with a watery smile. "Minnette was her name."

"Thank you," Sophia said. "Minnette's Molasses Cookies it is."

Elise Kennedy

They exchanged thank-yous and hugs. Mary walked away holding the cookies as though they were precious cargo, smiling and bubbly.

A memory crashed through Sophia's brain watching the women walk away. Back in her childhood suburb, she walked with her nonna to deliver a lasagna to a family down the street who'd had a baby. Or bringing a pot of pastina with its tiny, cheesy noodles and fragrant broth to their neighbor who'd been so sick he could barely stand. Or wrapping delicate, wafer-thin pizzelle cookies for the tattooed mailman who'd always made sure her nonna's steps were cleared when it snowed.

Or, or, or, she thought as the slideshow of memories shuttled past faster and faster. Seeing their faces light up was always Sophia's favorite part.

She sighed wistfully. She'd found what she'd been looking for.

Maybe someday she'd get to feel this bubbling happiness in her heart every single day.

* * *

Wet orange leaves slapped under Sophia's bourbon-colored boots as she walked along a Clovely side street. She'd woken up early and decided to treat herself to breakfast.

She'd slept pretty well, but had a lucid, hot—*hot*—hot sex dream about Blake.

Again.

Cozy Nights in Vermont

In the dream, he'd taken her from behind in front of the fireplace, and it had felt real enough that she'd been confused when she woke up.

And so horny that it hurt.

She had to get out of the house and away from his pheromones to clear her head.

What would be more wholesome and distraction-free than a New England inn on a rainy autumn morning?

The Clovely Inn was wrapped in charm, with twinkling fairy lights draped along the banister of its wide wraparound porch. Decorative gourds and pumpkins were bunched in groups along the outside of the porch for festive fall decoration. The morning was gray and misty, and the lanterns leading up the cobblestone walkway glowed with warmth.

A path meandered through a small garden bursting with vibrant fall colors: bright yellows, reds, and purples. The path led to a beautiful hand-hewn door. The red shutters stood out against the classic white wood siding. It was exactly how she imagined a perfect Vermont inn.

As she was about to step onto the cobblestones, Blake walked around the curved porch of the inn with armfuls of hay bales.

Jesus, he was handsome. A beanie was pulled down over his wavy hair, which somehow emphasized his handsome face more.

She wanted to kiss the freckles on his cheeks. See him blush. Back him into the barn he was always in and kiss his pumpkin-covered brains out. Maybe beg him to reenact her dream.

She still hadn't figured out how to seduce him since he would barely stay in the same room as her.

A warm smile grew on his face as he saw her, and he nodded in greeting. "You're up early," he called as he lifted three hay bales from his truck.

He had on a long-sleeve Henley shirt with the sleeves pushed up, and his forearm rippled as he held the heavy bales, walking them to the side porch.

Hot.

She wandered to the back entrance of the inn where his truck was, now wishing she'd done more than pop her hair into a messy bun and slide gloss on her lips. "Thought I'd work on my content this morning and grab breakfast in the dining room."

The back door of the inn opened. A small man with a dapper haircut in a half-zip sweater came out.

"Ooh Blakey, these will be perfect," he said in a slow, thick Georgia accent, clapping at the hay bales and pumpkins stacked on the large wraparound porch.

"Sophia, this is my Uncle Alan. Uncle Alan and my uncle Jerry own the inn."

Alan had a warm smile with a twinkle in his eye that gave him an elven look. He clasped her hand in both of his. "Well, aren't you just pretty as a peach?"

She liked him instantly.

Cozy Nights in Vermont

"Sophia is here working on her cookbook," Blake said with a proud smile, leaning on the side of his truck as he took off his work gloves. "When she's not dazzling the pumpkin patch customers."

"Blakey has told us all about what y'all are doin' at the farm. I sent a van load of tourists your way yesterday who wanted a Vermont pumpkin patch experience," Alan said with delight. "So what brings you here on this fine drizzly morning?"

She hefted her tote bag higher on her shoulder. "Thought I'd get a little work done, and grab some breakfast if the restaurant's open."

"It sure is. You just come on in with me, darlin'." He took her arm as they walked around the porch to the front entrance.

Blake turned back toward his truck, but Alan was faster and grabbed his arm. "You are not gonna let this gorgeous young lady have breakfast alone, are you?" He arched an eyebrow at Blake.

Blake sighed. "She's busy—"

"Nonsense. Everyone needs to eat breakfast." Alan shooed Blake up the inn's porch stairs. They followed behind him.

"So you're Blake's uncle?" She looked from the short, petite man to the tall, could-lift-a-tree-if-necessary man in front of her. She didn't see the family resemblance.

"By marriage. But Jerry and I have been together for decades so I feel like Blake's my very own." He patted

Blake's arm as he held the door for them, and Blake beamed down at his uncle.

Adorable.

"Breakfast this morning is heaven. Bev made a quiche and these pumpkin spice latte muffins I just can't keep my hands off of," he said with a sparkling laugh.

He ushered them inside, and Sophia was dumbstruck as she crossed the threshold.

The scent of expensive cedar and white tea wrapped around her. To the left of the entry, a huge open-style hearth crackled inside a masculine library that looked like it doubled as a lounge. Large velvet chairs surrounded the hearth, and rows of books ran up to the fifteen-foot ceiling.

As she crossed to the dining room, following Alan, they passed a beautiful live-edge reception desk. Her boots echoed on the slate tiles, and she was discombobulated at the comfortable yet opulent feel of a small, historic inn in Vermont.

"Now, have you been here before?" Alan asked.

"Uh, no," Sophia said, stuttering as she took it in. "This is gorgeous."

"Jerry and I just had a ball redoing it, and then we finally convinced Bev to move back to do the kitchen, and voila! Oh, there's my better half," he said, waving to a tall man.

Sophia could see the family resemblance as the broad-shouldered man with graying auburn hair walked through the lobby. His face was warm and fatherly as he smiled at Blake.

He held out a hand to Blake to shake and clapped him on the shoulder. "Thanks so much for bringing all the pumpkins and hay bales over. They look just perfect."

Alan leaned over to her and whispered conspiratorially. "I'll be damned if we lose another Fall Festival contest to Sally's Salads. Now," he clapped his hands. "Why don't we all pop into the kitchen to see Bev? I think you met her, right Sophia?"

Alan looped his arm through hers and took her through the dining room. "She said she'd met a gal that had caught Blakey's attention."

Her eyes went wide and she pressed her lips together, trying not to freak out.

Blake sighed. "Uncle Alan—"

"We just love Blake," Alan interrupted, as he pushed through the double-swing doors. "We like to check up on him to make sure he's eating an actual meal. Ah, shoot." He looked at his smartwatch as a beep went off. "I gotta see to the checkout desk. Show her a good time, Blake."

Blake looked like he wanted the earth to swallow him up, thoroughly embarrassed by his family. "Sorry," he mouthed, but his eyes danced. She could tell he secretly loved his family's teasing.

Beverly set an overflowing basket with bright green carrot tops on a food prep station. "Did he show you his protein drink collection?"

Blake wiped a hand down his face, rolling his eyes. "Come deliver hay bales, they said. It'll take five minutes, they said…"

"Yes," Sophia said to Bev, hand slapping down on the metal prep table. "Horrified."

"Horrified," Beverly echoed back as she squeezed Blake's side in a warm half-hug. "You wouldn't believe the amount of times I've tried to teach him how to cook."

"And I appreciate it, but I'm fine. You don't need to worry about me." He shook his head, crossing his arms with a resigned nod. "Alan promised Sophia a tour of the kitchen."

"I'm sorry to interrupt. I'm sure you're busy," Sophia said, knowing any distraction in a kitchen could cause chaos.

"Oh, it's fine," Beverly said with a smile, leaning her hip against the prep counter. "I'm waiting on the last quiche to bake before I start on lunch. Actually, while you're here"—Beverly turned to the stove where a pot simmered—"I could use another set of trained taste buds."

"Oh, I'm not formally trained or anything," Sophia said, embarrassed.

Bev ladled a chicken and herb broth into a bowl and gave Sophia and Blake each a tasting spoon. "Based on what I ate at the farm, I think you qualify. Plus, I'm recovering from a cold so my taste buds are a little off. Something is missing in the soup I threw together."

Sophia was excited to actually collaborate with somebody. "My nonna and her friends would make sauce and then quiz me on what ingredients were missing, so I feel right at home."

"Sounds like you *were* formally trained."

"Yeah, just by the little Italian grandma mafia."

She and Blake dipped the spoons into the bowl. Blake shrugged. "Tastes good to me?"

Sophia took a taste, thinking through the seasonings, how the flavor profile was balanced. Too salty? Too overpowering?

"It's good. It's a little...thin," Sophia said finally, searching for the right word. "It needs more umami flavor. So... mushrooms?"

Beverly took a new tasting spoon and dipped it into the bowl. "It *is* mushrooms," she said, snapping. "Thank you. It was driving me nuts."

A server pushed in the swinging double doors. "Table sixteen has offered to name their firstborn child after you if they can have the recipe for the muffins."

Beverly threw her head back and laughed in surprise. She walked to an old wooden writing desk and pulled out a pre-printed card.

"I get this more than you'd think," she said over her shoulder. "Here you go, but tell them to use my middle name, Ann," she called after the waiter as he sped away. "Beverly is a terrible name for a baby."

"That must feel so amazing," Sophia said in awe.

"There's something really satisfying"—Beverly had a dreamy smile as she pulled out mushrooms from the fridge—"something primal about feeding people. It can turn a bad day around, fuel people, inspire them."

"Could I get a special-order plain omelet?" the waiter said, popping in from the swinging double doors.

Blake started toward the door. "Sorry, we'll get out of your hair."

"Stop by any time," Beverly said with a wink as she turned around to collect the eggs from the gorgeous see-through chef's fridge.

"You are so lucky to have them," Sophia said as they walked into the dining room. "And they obviously love you so much."

Blake stuffed his hands in his pockets. "I love 'em back, even when they tease me. Sorry about all of that. They just want me to find any red-blooded woman and produce lots of great-nieces or nephews for them to dote on."

A shiver went down her spine at picturing Blake being a dad. Giving piggyback rides, teaching them how to plant vegetables, fiercely protecting them. "They'd be lucky kids."

He looked up in surprise and then shook his head. "I'm just trying to stay on top of what's already at the farm. The—the work, I mean." His eyes darted briefly to her lips, and he took a step back as he bit his lip.

And there went that blush again.

Cozy Nights in Vermont

God, what she wouldn't *give* for him to be on top of her.

Maybe her whole down payment of the house she was saving for. A kidney. Her cast-iron skillet.

Anything.

"Maybe we should check out the competition. See how your pumpkin patch is doing compared to other ones in the area," she offered.

He smiled at that. "Yeah? You'd do that?"

"Sure," she said with excitement as she pulled out a chair. "Let's go tomorrow. We can see how to up your pumpkin patch game."

He stood, hands in his pockets at the table.

"Aren't you having breakfast?"

He looked over his shoulder. "I'd love to, but I gotta run three more errands after I finish unloading here. And hey," he said before he walked away. "It's *our* pumpkin patch game now, okay?"

She smiled, liking being included. "Okay. I'll see you at home."

He swallowed. "See you at home," he said with a bewildered smile and walked out.

Home echoed in her chest.

Blake felt a lot like home already. That was a dangerous thing for someone who was leaving in four weeks to feel.

She pulled out her social media planner with resignation.

Elise Kennedy

The existential pit of dread in her stomach loomed large. She stared at the blank page, utterly at a loss. No energy left to think about what could be funny or cute or could gain her more followers.

I could do a countdown, she thought feebly as she sipped the Clovely Inn's version of a hazelnut latte.

The blank page screamed judgment at her as she looked down. She'd be here all day trying to think of the forty new videos she'd need to make for the upcoming month.

The eighteen recipes tapped on her shoulder, insisting they were more important.

And more fun.

What if...what if I just allowed myself to focus on the recipes?

The thought of deleting her account, the one where all her followers were her bread and butter, was so enticing.

No, I just need a little time.

Instead, she edited together clips in a random assortment that she'd taken over the last few days with some moody music.

Over it, she put the text, *BRB—Gone Falling in Vermont for 2 weeks.*

Before she could change her mind, she punched the post button, her heart thundering in her ears. When she saw the confirmation of the post appearing on her feed and a few likes start to trickle in, she gulped.

Cozy Nights in Vermont

I've really done it. I've really given myself two weeks of no content creation time. I can just focus on what I need to do, and maybe—she looked around at the dream come true she was sitting in—*maybe enjoy myself.*

She deleted the app from her phone and immediately felt like thirty pounds of pressure had been lifted from her chest.

She needed to go—do—make.

She grabbed a muffin as she dashed out of the dining room after leaving cash with the waiter.

She had things to make.

As she got close to the pumpkin farm, cars unexpectedly lined the road.

What the heck?

Getting closer to the pumpkin farm entrance, she realized people were waiting to get in.

Technically, the pumpkin patch opened in two minutes, but Thursday mornings were usually slow. *Blake must still be in town running errands.*

She slowed her car to a stop, flabbergasted, and rolled down her window as a dad with two kids in touristy-looking sweatshirts peered in. "You might need to park back on the road."

"I, uh...live here. Work here." *Really, really want to bang the farmer here.* "I can let you in."

Elise Kennedy

The dad stood back. "That would be great. Oh, are you the lady with the amazing cookies? My mom told us about you."

A smile blazed onto her face. "Uh, no cookies today, but happy for you to try other things I'm making." She'd been planning to make pumpkin croissants to sample that afternoon but she'd have to do with the leftover baking experiments from her apple crumble tart misadventure last night.

The crowd parted, and the dad swung open the small gate so she could drive through. The crowd—crowd!—flowed in behind her.

She wiggled with happiness as she drove in, too excited to talk to all their future customers.

CHAPTER SEVEN

BLAKE

Blake tossed and turned in bed.

Sophia's smile as she chatted with his family would appear every time he closed his eyes.

And he hated it.

And he *loved* it.

He threw off the covers, put an arm over his face, and tried to fall back asleep.

Think of all the chores you need to do tomorrow. What you need to grab for Star at the fancy pet-food store.

He'd never been a great sleeper, but it was unsettling to sleep by yourself after so many years next to somebody else. Star was no help either. After her nightly ten-minute cuddle, she'd hop off and settle in her oversized, furry princess bed.

As soon as he'd start to fall asleep, he'd picture Sophia joking with his customers when he had come back to the farm. He'd been blown away by the business her smart ideas had generated.

Or how sexy she'd looked in her clingy sweater with a flushed face last night as she cooked.

His stupid body and his stupid heart picked the worst time to come back to life for a woman who was too good for him.

She was carrying so much on her shoulders. He'd noodled and found her social account. She was funny and bright and made people happy. For every unkind comment, he wanted to hunt them down, throw them against a wall, and make them eat their words.

Maybe literally.

He wanted to help her, make all her worries go away. He wished he didn't feel so protective of her. She was a grown woman for chrissakes, probably with a Roth IRA thing and dental insurance. She always had her shit together. She was strong, not even fazed when a house fucking fell on her.

But who took care of the strong ones?

He flopped onto his stomach, burying his face in a pillow as he pictured what Sophia had looked like that morning. The curve of her thighs and ass in tight yoga pants peeking out from her oversized sweatshirt that said *Kale*. He'd wondered what she'd had on underneath it.

Cozy Nights in Vermont

No, you've already had your fun tonight. He allowed himself one lurid fantasy of her per day. That was it—no more. He wasn't going to become obsessed.

Become more obsessed?

His clock now clicked to 3:10 a.m. *Might as well get the day started.* There was always something to do on the farm.

At least he wouldn't have to see her in the morning over breakfast. He'd already be out of the house.

The less time he spent with her, the less he was tempted to daydream about her later. How she bit her lip when smiling mischievously, that pillowy bottom lip he wanted to bite. How her eyes sparkled when she teased him.

"Nope, shit. Doing it again," he muttered. He threw on sweatpants to go downstairs and start the coffee pot.

Star was snoring in her bed and didn't even budge when he walked past. *Some guard dog you are.*

As he slowly walked downstairs, he realized the dim light wasn't from the night-light, but from the kitchen.

Dim lights glowed under the cabinets. Every single baking ingredient he'd ever seen in his life was spread out over the granite countertops. Piles of sugar and flour sat beside bowls, cups, measuring spoons, and ladles. A pot was on the stove, and a mapley, caramelly sweetness perfumed the air.

In the middle of it all was Sophia, headphones on, dancing like a maniac with her eyes closed. She wore a loose burgundy T-shirt that hung past her elbows and down her thighs. Her back was to the stairs and she was bent over, shaking her ass to a beat he could barely hear, throwing her hips back from side to side and knees bent.

Oh my god.

She started twerking, leaning over the countertop and making her ass cheeks jiggle as she pushed against the kitchen island, her back still to him.

Fuuuuck.

She dropped down to the ground, sliding up sensually until she was thrusting against the kitchen island with a smooth, practiced ease that belonged in a nightclub.

Or his bed.

His cock instantly stood to attention, with him wanting to grab, caress, take her, but he stood transfixed—stock-still in the kitchen at the foot of the stairs, unable to move.

Her purple underwear peeked out as she bent over again to do that ass-jiggling thing that would haunt his memories for the rest of his fucking days.

Je...sus. He had to stop staring. "Sophia," he called.

Her breasts swayed side to side as she closed her eyes, dancing, lost in the music.

She turned to face him with her eyes still closed. She bit her lip and shimmied her shoulders, making every part of her sway under the loose T-shirt that was now the sexiest piece of lingerie he'd ever seen. Her breasts bounced and she moved her hands up her hips, stomach, and then grabbed them.

"Sophia," he yelled louder as he finally tapped her shoulder.

She opened her eyes and screamed.

She flailed backwards, and he grabbed her arm before she toppled ass over teakettle.

Throwing a hand against her heart, she righted herself.

"Sorry," he said suddenly. "I just, um..."

She ripped her headphones off. "Oh my God, you gave me a heart attack," she said, laughing and bending over. The billowing T-shirt around her puffed forward as she caught her breath.

Her hair looked like caramel chocolate in the dim light and was captured in a low, messy bun. He wanted to pull it free and run his hands through it.

Bubblegum pop blared in her headphones, and she tapped her phone to turn it off. "Now I'm really not going to sleep tonight." She laughed, rubbing her hand on her chest.

You and me both, he thought as he padded to the fridge, trying to hide his hard cock. "What are you doing up?"

Think about anything other than her tits bouncing underneath her soft T-shirt.

He concentrated every brain cell on filling his water glass at the fridge.

Breathe in, breathe out.

"I tried baking the anxiety away for a few hours. Made a great bourbon maple frosting recipe, but that wasn't working. So, I tried dancing the anxiety away. Sorry if you saw more than you bargained for."

He took a gulp of water and thought about throwing the rest on his face just so he'd calm the fuck down. His cock was hard as a wrench in his pants.

He gasped as he chugged water, setting the glass down too hard. "Did it work?"

"A little," she sighed, looking sad as she leaned next to him, licking a spatula with frosting on it.

He cock throbbed as her tongue swiped along the spatula.

"Plus, I have just a tiny bit of the kitchen to clean up. I was a *little* messier than usual," she said with a sardonic smile, licking the spatula clean.

"Nah," he teased, tracing the movement of her mouth with his eyes. He wanted to see her eyes sparkle again. "This looks about normal for Sophia, goddess of kitchen chaos."

Her jaw fell in mock outrage as her eyes lit up. "I am not chaos. This is a well-honed"—she grabbed a big pinch of flour from a pile on the countertop and tossed it at him—"system."

He shielded himself with a laugh but flour poofed over his skin. "A system implies less"—he threw a larger poof of flour back at her—"collateral damage. Lest we forget the raccoons you let in." Flour streaked across her face and shirt.

Her eyes ignited with playful fire. "How dare you toss Raccoonbert De Niro in my face. That's it." She dove for the cocoa powder but he caught her wrists in time and yanked them down on either side of her body, pinning her back to the kitchen island.

"You're not playing fair," she huffed with a smile and licked her lips.

"All's fair in love..." His voice died as her eyes caught on his at that word.

His thumbs stroked the pulse points of her wrists as they stood toe to toe.

Her breasts rose and fell, matching his own ragged breaths.

A streak of flour had landed on her cheek. He wanted to kiss it off. Wanted to run his hands up under her shirt and finally know what her belly, her hips, her breasts felt like.

She was heartbreakingly beautiful and he needed her like his next breath.

Her eyes held his with intensity.

"Did you call me a goddess?" she whispered, staring up at him.

"Mmhmm." His thumb came to her cheek, stroking the flour away. Her skin felt like velvet, and he stroked and stroked.

She closed her eyes and leaned into his hand. Thick hazelnut eyelashes fluttered closed against her pale skin. He wanted to memorize each one.

His thumb traced her soft, round cheek. "You're gorgeous, strong."

Her dusky bottom lip pouted out and he couldn't help it—his thumb wandered to it. Her eyes fluttered open, the heat of her breath against his skin making him burn hotter.

He stroked her bottom lip, pulling it down, the need inside of him clawing at his control. "A body begging to be worshiped."

He stepped between her legs, needing to feel the brush of her hard nipples against his chest.

He didn't give a shit if she saw how hard his cock was for her.

He cupped her cheeks with both hands.

She leaned into him, arching up against him.

"Please," she breathed, barely a whisper. He was an inch from her face, and he just wanted a little more.

"Please what," he said, his nose stroking the end of hers.

She grabbed his hand from her cheek and brought it to her breast, squeezing her hand over his in a slow, deliberate grasp. "Worship me."

His knees almost buckled, feeling the heavy weight of her tits that he'd dreamed of.

Cozy Nights in Vermont

Fuck it.

His hand dove into the messy bun of her hair. His mouth took hers, hunger and need taking over.

She tasted unreal, like she was already his.

He sucked her lip, raking his teeth across it. Wanting to claim her.

He licked into her mouth, needing to taste all of her. Her tongue met his, ravenous, feral.

Her nails raked down his scalp and—*fuuuck*. He moaned, trying not to come as waves of pleasure lapped over him.

His hands moved to her hips, grabbing—claiming.

"Yes," she sighed against his mouth.

The sweetest sound he'd ever heard.

He thrust his hips against hers. She moaned, and he palmed her breast again, desperate for her. Her arms snaked around his neck as he kissed her, and kissed her, and *kissed* her.

Hair cascaded around her shoulders as it fell out of her bun. A cloud of vanilla perfumed around him. He'd always think of her now when he smelled it.

Shudders wracked her body as he sucked along the curve of her neck. He made a map of all the places on her body where she seemed to crave his touch.

He moved her to straddle his leg, and he grabbed her hips, pulling them toward him. A carnal part of him wanted to know what she tasted like, what her scent was.

Wanted it on him.

He grabbed her hips, thrusting her against his leg.

"Yes," she sighed. "More. Please." His arm snaked around her waist so she could ride him.

His other hand moved back to her breast, needing to memorize the feel of heaven. He teased her nipple, and it was a hard gemstone under his fingers. "You were so gorgeous that first night it almost killed me. With your perfect ass jiggling in my face." He growled against her mouth. "Couldn't think of anything else." He rubbed her nipple back and forth, slower, harder. "For three"—flick—"fucking"—flick—"days."

She cried out his name, and goddamn, if that didn't make his cock weep.

He raked his teeth down her throat. Nipping, biting, worshiping.

Her low moan would be his nightly meditation.

"I came that night," he said, "thinking about you. Fuck, you're so hot."

He kissed her, needing to make sure this was real. She kissed him back, her tongue licking against his.

The heat of her pussy against his thigh was too good.

He needed more.

Just a little more and then he could stop.

He needed her on him.

Cozy Nights in Vermont

His hands traveled down to her ass cheeks. "I stared at this for weeks, wondering what it would feel like." He squeezed as he thrust her against his leg. She moaned out a sob.

Fuck, it felt even better than he could have ever imagined taking her in his hands.

He lifted her onto the island as bowls and ingredients clattered to the ground. Her legs wrapped around him as she ground herself against his cock in his sweatpants, the tip of it now peeking out from under his boxers.

Her hands raked up and down his arms as he grabbed her hips.

He rocked her against his cock, grinding through the layers of her panties and his sweatpants. "Holy fuck," she whispered. "You're huge. I *need* it," she mewled.

He could feel the heat of her and it was too good.

"Not done worshiping your collarbone yet," he muttered as he licked into the hollow there. He rocked her hips into his and she gasped, clawing closer around him.

"Have an IUD," she panted, "and I was tested before I left Dallas."

His mind screeched to a halt.

They were careening toward sex.

Because that's what adults do, have sex whenever they want, he realized.

He was essentially fucking her with clothes on *right now*.

Fuck, fuck, fuck. He'd lost control.

His heart pounded outside of his chest for an entirely different reason than Sophia's perfect tits.

This was panic.

Panic at losing control and almost giving in. Getting in too deep.

He ripped himself away, coming up for air as ragged breaths clawed through him.

"I'm sorry," he said. He took a step back. "I don't know what I was—"

"Sorry?" she said. She tightened her legs, bringing him back toward her until he could feel the heat of her against his cock through his sweatpants. "Just be sorry you stopped."

She pulled him back down for a slow, melting kiss that built and built.

This woman tasted like vanilla, and cinnamon.

She tasted like *home*.

He growled, wanting to take all of her, wanting to squeeze every bit.

Fuck. Stop.

He pulled away, anguished. "I'm sorry. I can't," he said, knowing he sounded insane. "I'm not sorry for kissing you. I'd do it all day if I could. But I can't. This is... I mean, we can't."

Cozy Nights in Vermont

She dropped the tension in her legs so that they hung on either side of his hips.

"I knew it. You're making out with one of your other roommates, aren't you?" she said with a wry smile, tracing her finger along his stomach, playing with the hair on his chest as she chewed her cheek.

He grabbed her hand, cradling it to him.

"Sophia, you are..."

Perfect.

"...leaving in a month, and I can't risk getting attached. *More* attached. I already feel..." He sighed. "I care about you. Sex is a big deal to me. And I shouldn't have lost control. I haven't really dated...well, since I moved here." He didn't want to get into the past. "I had a couple dates that went nowhere because I didn't feel like this," he said, his eyes connecting with hers, hoping the weight of his words was clear. "And *this* was entirely unexpected."

Her eyes grew wide, understanding this was bigger than casual sex for him.

He wanted to spill out his heart. But she'd run for the border if she knew how deep in it he already was.

I'm afraid I might already be falling for you and already can't stomach you leaving.

I can't imagine anyone more perfect than you, and I don't want to know how good life could be with you.

"This is all just new for me," he said finally.

"You wouldn't be interested in a roommates with benefits situation? I could be your practice run," she said with a teasing smile.

"Soph." He cradled her chin, and she leaned into it. Her wide, dark toffee eyes broke his heart. "You're no one's practice run. You're the whole fuckin' championship."

He'd love every minute of "benefits" until the part where he watched her drive away.

"I'm sorry," he said with a shake of his head, seeing the instant disappointment on her face that was about as subtle as the lights on the Vegas Strip. It broke his heart. "I want to. I'm just not ready to lose anyone."

He stepped back but held her hand in his, slowly kissing her palm. He savored the scent of the butter and cinnamon on her skin and the soft feel of it against his lips.

That would have to last him for a long while.

Before he changed his mind, he turned around and ran up the stairs, two at a time, with a hard cock and a breaking heart.

CHAPTER EIGHT

SOPHIA

"He ran away, Iris."

"He didn't run away," said her sister's tinny voice. "It's so loud. Where are you?"

It was dusk and the crowd at the Finch Family Orchard was hopping. "A fall orchard thingy. If he could have done back handsprings to get away faster, he would have. Blake kissed me like a caveman claiming his mate and then ran away. That's how bad of a kisser I am, apparently."

"I've always told you that you have terrible breath," Iris said, a smile in her voice.

"You're a butthead." Sisters were the worst.

"An apple orchard sounds romantic. Are you two on a date?"

Sophia looked for Blake and saw him still in line for their hot spiked ciders. He looked so handsome tonight. He'd blushed when asking what time she wanted to leave to scope out the competition.

For research purposes, he'd made sure to add.

"This is business research," Sophia responded.

"At night?"

"Yes."

"Are you wearing makeup and a bra? If so, then it's a date."

Sophia huffed. "It is not a date. Especially after said running-away. Now, what does it mean?" She chewed her fingernail, hoping for her sister's insight into the enigma that was human behavior.

"I'm sure he's just nervous. You said he hasn't dated anybody?"

"He went on like two dates, but it seems they ended in hearty high fives."

She stared at Blake as he chatted happily with a guy next to him. His smile was wide and it took her breath away. His eyes found hers through the crowd. *Shit, caught me staring.* She waved and his smile went even wider.

"He said he couldn't lose another person. He talked about me leaving, and...I just thought we'd have fun, you know?"

"Hmm," Iris said with a knowing voice.

Sophia's eyes narrowed so she could listen harder to her genius sister. "What do you mean '*hmm*'?"

Cozy Nights in Vermont

"You know, you're...casual. You don't like commitment," Iris said, a blinker sounding in the speakerphone.

"Yeah, because—"

"Soulmates are a myth, and"—Iris finished for her—"all the good ones are taken. Yeah, I know. I've met you. But he's not some douchey, weird bro you picked up at a bar. He seemed like a really nice guy when I met him a few weeks ago."

"Wait a minute. This is all *your* fault," Sophia said, realizing she could blame her little sister for her not-heartbreak heartbreak.

Pussybreak? Is that a thing?

"Sorry, I'm k*hrrrt*"—Iris said, mimicking static with her voice—"going through a tunnel. I'm k*hrrt* losing you."

"Iris, do not hang up. Do *not* hang up on me."

"Oops, oh no. I'm losing signal. Love you, bye!" Iris said, and the line went dead.

Sophia had to laugh at her sister. Iris was her best friend, and sometimes she wanted to wring her neck.

This *was* all her fault.

Sophia's pride had stung when Blake had bounded up the stairs. She respected his choices though. It must be an odd experience starting over after so long, and not everyone could hit-it-and-quit-it like she could.

She'd have to be content simply being roommates.

Didn't mean she couldn't have one-handed fantasies as she went to sleep like she did last night.

After finally falling asleep on the couch at the lovely hour of 5:00 a.m., her body had woken up after four whole hours of sleep, tucked under a pile of blankets, with a note beside the coffee table that said he'd restocked her favorite local creamer. The coffee pot was on, and there was a mug beside it waiting for her.

Mixed signals much, man?

Blake appeared through the crowd looking like the sexy Brawny towel guy coming toward her with two steaming cups.

"This is quite a crowd," she yelled over the noise as he handed her the cider. "I'm glad we came here to scope out the competition. They definitely know what they're doing."

The Finch Family Orchard had a large hay bale maze, face painters, a band, two food trucks, string lights strung throughout the entire seating area, and a pumpkin patch and apple orchard to pick from for families.

They strolled through the edge of the apple trees as the sky turned into a deep violet. He smiled down at her with that dreamy look. "Yeah," he said, shaking his head suddenly. "I don't know why I didn't think of it sooner. I guess I was just too embarrassed or something."

Oh no. She didn't want him to feel bad. "There's no need to be embarrassed. You'd need an army of people to do something like this."

Cozy Nights in Vermont

"Jeff and his family have been doing this for decades. It's an institution."

She wanted to put her arm through his as they walked, but she refrained. *Not a date.*

"One summer I worked on the round hay baler for Jeff's dad. He hired the whole football team. It was backbreaking work on old equipment."

She allowed herself a lingering glance at his chest and arms. He was easily 6'2", and she could imagine him destroying on a defensive line.

Maybe that was where he got his protective streak.

"It feels almost impossible to try to catch up to something like this." He sighed, looking around him as he sipped his hot cider.

"Let's think about how to do it your way." She needed to keep him hopeful.

They meandered past the hay bale maze entrance. "Definitely not the hay bale maze. You have no idea how long it takes to set that up." He shook his head as if reliving a memory.

"Part of the football team duties?" she said as she sipped her spicy, rum-laced cider.

"The first time we helped, we accidentally trapped ourselves in it."

She snorted apple cider through her nose. The rum warmed her chest in the chilly night air. "Well, next year we'll do something that has no hay involved."

He went quiet.

She turned around and bumped his hip. "What? Did I drip cider somewhere?" She looked down at her sweater.

"No, it's not that. It's just, um..." He shook his head.

"What?" Oh fuck. "Right. I mean, you will do whatever you want next year." She winced in embarrassment. "I didn't mean to insinuate you'd want me to come back, and—"

"You can stay as long as you want," he said quickly.

Whoa. Her eyes went wide.

His eyes went wider as he realized what he'd said. "I mean, you can always come back and visit. The cottage roof will be fixed, and..." He scrubbed a hand down his face and sighed. "You know what I mean."

Fuck. She guessed they couldn't ignore the elephant in the apple orchard forever. "You'll probably be dating up a storm by next year," she said, trying to add a little levity and elbowing him. "You'll be the Clovely Casanova. Ooh, should that be your new dating app bio?"

"I've never been on a dating app. It seems overwhelming."

Her jaw dropped open. "That is desperately unfair. You haven't lived until you've been ghosted by a creepy guy you weren't even really interested in. Ooh, ooh"—she hit his arm for emphasis—"or the guy who was great to chat with, but when I didn't want to pay for his four cocktails and two burritos because I'd only had water, he said *I* was, quote, 'what's wrong with feminism.'"

Cozy Nights in Vermont

"You?" he said with arched eyebrows. He guided her through the foot traffic with a gentle hand on the small of her back.

"Yes, me. I am the Achilles heel in the third-wave feminist movement because I wouldn't buy Chad extra large margaritas after *he* asked *me* out."

Blake shook his head in disbelief as they wandered to a quieter area of the Finch Family Orchard. She was sad when his hand dropped from her back.

"The bar is in hell, that's all I'm saying. Any single woman would sell her skincare routine for a chance with a nice guy who's tall, good looking, hot, kind, with a gigantic"—she faltered, *Not gonna finish that thought*—"uh, soft spot for his dog."

His eyes connected with hers, and though they sparkled back at her in shared humor, there was a veil of sadness she could see.

"What if I only want one woman in particular?" he said in a low voice as they stopped in the shadow of an apple tree. His hand rested on a tall branch as he hung onto it and stared down at her. "Who is gorgeous, and funny, and smart?"

She swallowed. She wasn't used to a man who told her how amazing she was. She bit her lip. "She'd be a really lucky woman."

A slow smile grew on his face, and her breath caught as his eyes trained on her lips. He started to lean down—

"Coach Jameson!" shot through the air.

Blake paused in surprise, turning his head toward the shout. A group of gangly teen boys waved their whole arms at him. "Ah, fuck."

Sophia pulled back with a bark of laughter. "Coach?"

He put his hand on her back, clearing a path through the throng toward the group of high school boys at a picnic table.

They looked like actual babies. *How do high schoolers get younger every year?*

"Coach, I didn't know you had a girlfriend," a boy with a wobbly, cracking voice called.

Blake squeezed her side before he dropped his hand from her back. "This is my friend, Sophia. Sophia," he said, over the chorus of *oohs* as they catcalled him, "this is the JV football team."

"Coach! Coach! Did you see me tackle the running back at the game last week?" a kid with glasses and a mop of curly hair said with big eyes.

These boys clearly worshiped the ground he walked on.

"I'm sorry, things have gotten crazy at the pumpkin patch."

"Hey, is that your girlfriend?" another kid from the end of the table yelled at him with attitude.

"Braden, is it respectful to talk about somebody as if they aren't there?" Blake said authoritatively.

Cozy Nights in Vermont

"Nooo," he said with an eye roll. "Sophia, you his girlfriend?"

"Why? You single?" she said with a sarcastic eyebrow waggle back to him, and all the boys went oooooh, shoving the kid at the end.

"We like you," the first boy said, pointing at Sophia. "You should come to the next game."

"Hey, you boys behave, okay? Who's driving?" Blake asked. The rest of the boys started to walk away, but a lanky kid jangled keys with an adorably dopey grin.

"What's the rule to stay on the team," Blake said with a warm, firm tone.

"Seat belts on, eyes on the road," the boy answered confidently.

"And?" Blake said with an arched eyebrow.

"And call a coach before you do something stupid," he said, rolling his eyes in embarrassment. "Oh my God, we're fine, Coach J."

Blake gave the kid a fist bump before he started jogging after his friends. "Be safe!" Blake called.

"They *like* like you," Sophia said with shock and awe. "How has this never come up?"

Blake bit back a smile, clearly proud of himself. "I mostly do summer training camps with them. Fall gets too busy to deal with the team travel. I played with Marcus, their coach, in high school. Mostly, I'm there to reinforce responsibility. If they manage to learn something about football in the meantime, even better."

"How do you manage it all? Isn't summer busy with farming?"

"Yeah," he said. "But when I moved back, Marcus knew I needed to be around people. Herding thirty lovable dummies with raging hormones who want to beat the shit out of something took my mind off of things for a bit."

They meandered through darkened apple trees toward the farm exit. "You don't talk about her a lot."

"It's still hard," he said, looking down. "But I promised her when she was sick that I would try my best to be happy. It was important to her that I keep going, you know? She and I were together for twelve years. We met in college and then got married. That's why dating has seemed so daunting. It's just not a skill I've ever had as an adult."

Her heart broke at how lost he sounded. "You are the kindest man I've ever met. You have absolutely nothing to worry about, whenever you're ready. I'm sorry if..." Her cheeks reddened with embarrassment. "...if I pushed you. I didn't realize."

He gave her a sad half-smile that lingered. "Let me go get the truck. You stay here."

"Oh, it's okay. I can walk," she said, shrugging it off.

"I don't want your shoes to get muddy. It's not safe to be on the road with all the cars crowding in like this. Please," he said, turning back with a plea in his voice. "Just let me take care of you, okay? Roomie," he added as an afterthought with a sad smile and jogged back to the old teal truck parked a quarter of a mile down the road.

When was the last time a man wanted to actually take care of her? Or spend time with her? Not try to see her bank account statement or get in her pants and be ashamed to take her out? Some guys in Dallas loved a full-bodied woman, but only in secret.

Blake drove back and slowed the truck down in front of the entrance.

She cocked her head in confusion as he hopped out and jogged around to the passenger side door. "What in the Leave It to Beaver are you doing?"

He opened her door with a mischievous smile.

"Just being a gentleman," he said as he grabbed her hand, helping her into the cab. "Never know when one of the football players is watching."

She felt her insides flutter. He slid into the driver's seat.

The last time a man had opened the door for her was her prom date approximately 110 years ago. "This wasn't a date...was it?"

Subtlety had never been her strong suit.

"Who said it was a date? I just opened the door for you."

That's what people do on dates. He'd also paid for her. "I'll send you money for the drinks and snacks." She held up her phone, but there was barely any signal.

"But you don't have to," he said with an arched eyebrow.

He turned onto the sloping roads back to the farm. "Why don't you like people taking care of you?"

She shifted in her seat. Guess he wasn't that subtle either. "I just don't want anybody to feel burdened."

"Is that because you feel burdened taking care of others?"

Ouch. Direct hit.

"You know, if this pumpkin farming thing doesn't work out, might I suggest being a therapist?"

"I like taking care of other people because I like how it makes *me* feel," he said with a low rumble as he drove with one hand at the top of the steering wheel.

Ugh, he even drove sexily.

He did seem to love taking care of people, thinking back to how he'd talked to his football players, all the things he'd done for her.

It was an experience entirely new to her.

As an eldest daughter, she was used to planning and making and doing for other people rather than for herself. She could name on one hand, maybe even one finger, the number of times a man had been on top of it enough to not only take care of himself, but her as well.

He slid a sidelong glance at her. "Does it make you feel good to take care of other people?"

She shrugged. She was her parents' unofficial therapist. She was the one who organized all of the family events, and her constant nagging was probably the reason Iris had finally fallen for a guy. "They need me."

"What if they just want to love you instead of needing you?" he said with a shrug.

Fucking shrugged.

As if he hadn't just dropped an atomic bomb into her brain.

She looked out the window as the odd words clunked around in her head.

Just love me...not...need me.

But what would there be to love if I didn't help them?

She decided to ignore it for now. No time for her world to turn topsy-turvy with a brand-new concept like that.

"Feeding people makes me feel good," she said, answering his first question instead. "It's easier to make something special you know someone will love than to say all the words."

He agreed, nodding sagely. "Sometimes actions are better than words."

She bit her lip as she smiled, looking out the window.

Like opening a car door.

CHAPTER NINE

BLAKE

"Thanks for letting me borrow these." Blake hefted a long table and bench into a trailer attached to his truck.

They needed more seating for the crowds they were starting to attract. Sophia had had the bright idea of renting picnic blankets to folks wanting to bring their own food and drinks to spend time under the maple trees in the pumpkin patch, but he'd felt bad after seeing a couple of older folks struggle to get up and down.

Mabel, his next-door neighbor and owner of the Chestnut Hollow Inn and Farm, hefted a small bench onto the trailer for him. Mabel shrugged. "Yeah, no events until Thanksgiving, so return 'em whenever."

"Hey, be careful of your shoulder," Blake said. "Let me do this."

Mabel was in her sixties and strong as a horse but was recovering from rotator cuff surgery. "Eh, the doc says I gotta exercise so it doesn't get frozen," she said, rolling her stiff shoulder.

Mabel was a farmer at heart and lived in overalls. She had long, flowing hair that crimped in natural waves, and she wore it loose with big men's work shirts over it. She was no-nonsense, like most Vermonters, and showed her love in actions rather than words.

He'd known Mabel ever since he could walk. He was a lonely kid on a farm, bored out of his mind, and regularly came over to Chestnut Hollow to escape farm duties. She'd tuck him into a corner with a piece of apple pie and whatever farm dog they had around at the moment, listening to his troubles even then.

"Heard you got somebody special over there," she said with a knowing smile.

Blake blushed thinking about the morning a few days ago. "I mean, I don't have her," he said, hefting up another table and some chairs.

"I don't know, you've got a spring in your step." She smirked as she tossed up another bench onto the trailer.

A question nagged at him. "Hey, uh," he said stupidly, scratching his head.

He and Mabel didn't do feelings. She was part colleague, part adopted family, part mom, part hardened farmer with that thick candy shell exterior that hid a gooey middle.

Feelings weren't really part of their repertoire.

She leaned on the trailer and chewed a piece of gum, looking at him nonplussed. "Come on, out with it," she said, slapping her legs. "I gotta go feed Maaaybel here in a minute," she said with an eye roll, making the sheep sound. Her staff had demanded that their latest baby sheep be named in her honor. "The damned thing only answers when you say her name that way."

He chuckled at how much it irritated her, but he knew she loved it, deep down.

He kicked a leaf on the ground. "After Gus passed..."

She threw her head back with a knowing look, closing her eyes. "I wondered when we'd get to this." She sat on the bottom of the trailer and patted the edge for him to sit.

Her husband Gus had passed away when Blake was in high school. He'd been a sweet and kind man.

It had been a devastating blow.

"You've never dated," Blake said.

"You don't know what I get up to in the evenings," she said with an eyebrow raised.

"Alright, fine, maybe you're hittin' the strip clubs, who knows," he said.

She bumped his shoulder with hers. "Nah, they couldn't handle me," she said, crossing her arms. He barked out a laugh in surprise.

"I threw myself into work," she said, gesturing around her. Her inn had tripled in size and popularity since he'd been in high school. She had more rooms, more activities, more streams of revenue in the farm. "It never made me stop missing him though. I met lots of nice people. Some of whom have been interested in me for some reason"—she shook her head—"but I never felt that spark, you know? I just had the one, and that was enough for me. Do you feel a spark?" she said with that authoritative tone that made him feel like he was twelve again.

He rubbed at his chest where it ached.

"Ah." She nodded sagely.

He didn't even have to say anything, it was so obvious on his face.

She nodded her head. "It can be a bitch, not being prepared for it. That's how it was my first time." She slapped her legs and stood up.

"Return these whenever," she said, gesturing to the benches and tables all loaded up onto the trailer.

"Mabel!" one of her farmhands called. "Maaaybel is loose again."

She sighed with tired resignation. "Would you believe that they wanted to name one of the baby horses Neighble?" she said with a disbelieving shake of her head. He chuckled with her.

She slapped him on the shoulder as she walked past. "And Blake, just know, it's been eighteen years," she said with a sad smile, "and if I found a spark today, I wouldn't ever let it go. Might have been nice to have somebody help chase the sheep."

She sauntered over to the sheep stables, calling out, "Maaaybel! Maaaybel!" as she wandered over the meadow and down through the red and orange trees.

A baby lamb burst out of the bushes and came running up to her with a happy cry. She grabbed it and lifted it, and Blake shook his head in disbelief.

She seemed happy enough, but maybe her life could have been even better had she taken the risk.

She threw a hand up as she walked away back toward the sheep stables, and Blake considered how special the spark was that was waiting for him back at his farm.

The spark that felt a whole lot like his future.

"I can't believe the turnout we've started having," Sophia said, thwacking garlic with the blunt edge of the knife. Her cheeks were rosy, and hair had escaped from her ponytail as she'd buzzed around the kitchen.

He tried so hard not to stare.

They'd been working for an hour, prepping vegetables for what he expected to be an even bigger turnout tomorrow. He was dazzled by how smart her ideas were. The little changes she'd suggested with practically no additional cost to him had resulted in people spending a lot longer at the patch and picking up extra veggies. That, combined with the free snacks and coffee they offered, meant his sales had hit an all-time high.

Cozy Nights in Vermont

It was really the least he could do to help her with her vegetable prep. The fact that she swayed as she cooked, her hips bouncing to and fro as she worked, was just an added benefit.

"It's all because of you," he said, concentrating on the butternut squash in front of him.

"Psh." She rolled her eyes at him over her shoulder. "I don't think I planted gorgeous maple trees people want to walk through, or built a beautiful farm. Didn't grow acres of pumpkins."

"Those have always been here," he said with effort on the last word as he made another big chop on the butternut squash. Jesus Christ, no wonder his didn't sell that well. *What a pain in the ass to prepare.* "Your maple butter scones? Those are what people want."

Your smile? That's what makes them stay.

Her attention moved between the food bubbling on the stove, stirring each one. She had six simmering pots of various versions for her ginger carrot soup and cranberry sauce for tomorrow. "Oh, I had an amazing idea in the shower." She turned around with a big smile.

"Does your brain ever turn off?" He marveled at her, able to keep track of every dish and also have a separate conversation.

"No. So—" She paused as he laughed. "What if you have a pumpkin carving party?" She whipped her wrist like a champion jump roper as she started to magically spin egg whites into a meringue in front of his face.

"A...party?" He could barely keep up with her.

"Well, for your customers. You know how much of a pain it is to carve a pumpkin. What if they can do it here? Then they'll want to hang out, grab snacks. We can rent blankets or sell drinks. Maybe sell stencils."

He chopped the butternut squash into the cubes she'd requested. He was trying to keep his eyes focused on the squash in front of him and not on every single one of her curves bouncing in her slouchy sweater.

She had on a clingy, black-and-white-striped shirt that left little to the imagination as it spilled over her shoulders. Her apron was tied high on her waist, emphasizing the curves of her hips and her tits.

How did this woman make everyday items the subject of his new obsessions?

He caught himself staring at her bare skin when she was engrossed in conversation as they prepped vegetables. He licked his lips, wishing he could still taste her from a few days ago. Ever since his dick had woken up, it hadn't turned off when she was around. He actually would have described himself as a gentleman before this. Kind, considerate, not a creep, but no. Now he was here, fantasizing about fucking shoulders.

Well, not fucking shoulders. Oh God, was that even possible? Ugh, he needed to get a handle on this.

Somehow, in the time it took him to cut a half of a squash, she'd already made three dishes. A beep sounded from the giant, fancy oven.

"Ah, the cheesy bread. Could you get that? I have one more minute of cardio left over here," she said as she puffed, whipping the egg whites and sugar into submission.

He grabbed rows of long, cheese-covered bread out of the oven. The bubbling gooey heaven smelled like if garlic bread and cheese pizza had had a baby. His stomach growled. "What do you want me to do with it?"

"Cut it into small, bite-sized pieces please." She tossed ingredients into her bowl and whipped the meringue further.

He ate a bite of the cheese bread after he cut it, and it melted in his mouth. It was part herby goat cheese, part garlic and sea salt.

She slid a cookie sheet with small meringue dollops on it into the small second oven in the enormous double oven. She wiped her forehead, glowing with happiness as she looked at him eating. "Good?"

"This should be studied for the perfect flavor combination," he said, pointing to the bread. "Is this a new recipe for tomorrow?"

She popped a small bite into her mouth, licking her finger as cheese spilled over. His eyes tracked the movement.

"Oh, it's just for a snack. You said you didn't have much lunch and I thought you'd be hungry. Here, try it with this." She slid a tomato soup-like dish at him from the pile of ingredients on the island. "So no? Yes?"

"Very much yes," he said, dipping a second bite of the cheese bread into the tomato soup. He sighed in pleasure. How had he lived on protein smoothies for so long when warm, delicious food was just waiting for him?

He opened his eyes, and her glossy lips were curved into a smile, looking like she'd been studying him. "I like seeing you happy. And eating satisfying food. I meant, do you want to do the pumpkin carving thing? I can figure out logistics." She popped another cheese bite in her mouth.

This woman. She'd already done so much for him. How could he ever repay her? "Don't you need to focus on your cookbook? I don't want you getting behind because of me."

"I'm making a good dent in the recipes," she said, washing her hands. She then scooped up a handful of minced garlic and popped it into a simmering pot. "Just about ten more and then I'll be set."

And then she'd be gone. How would he survive it if she left? He needed to start planning on what he'd do in November. Maybe he and Star would take a road trip. Get away from the kitchen he'd forever associate with her. Her smile, her kindness, her curves.

He crossed his arms as he leaned back against the counter. "An event could be fun. I don't want you to risk your deadline for me."

"Cooking is all about taking chances. Sometimes they really pay off—Minnette's Molasses Cookies, as an example."

Cozy Nights in Vermont

She'd told him about it, and he'd seen her try to hide her tears of happiness. He'd fallen just a little more for her that day.

"You're good at taking chances," he said, realizing that was a theme with her. "You started your own content creation business. Made a cookbook."

He never took chances.

And where had it landed him? Alone, despite knowing the most beautiful woman in the world wanted to sleep with him.

She shrugged. "Yeah, I guess I have the 'why the hell not?' gene. It usually works pretty well, until I say it too many times in a row." She drizzled cranberry sauce onto a dish. "Then I stand in a pumpkin patch crying to a hot farmer because I'm overwhelmed."

She winked at the shared memory as she moved back to the oven to check on her soup.

The need to hold her was a physical ache inside of him.

Why don't I ever take risks? What could my life look like if I did?

"Oh, can you grab the meringue bites? They bake so fast," she said as she salted the soup after tasting it.

He leaned over her shoulder after closing the oven to smell what she stirred. "Smells good."

"This is just a base. You want a taste? It's chicken stock and some herbs from your garden." She scooped up a taste with a spoon and held her hand underneath.

He thought about telling her he could feed himself, but then he wouldn't have a reason to be so close to her. It tasted buttery and savory, like tonic for his soul.

"Wow," he said with an awed breath.

"It's a twist on one of my grandmother's recipes," she said. "This is what she would make for us when we got sick. I thought we'd try this with the base, and then maybe add pureed butternut squash in to give it a creamy spin."

He stood close. Probably too close for a roommate. "You're really good at this," he said softly.

"Tell that to Ashleybabezzzz who thought one of my recipes tasted like, quote, 'trash,'" she said with a sarcastic smile as she turned off the burners on the stove.

He could see the hurt in her eyes, and anger thundered through him. "They said that about you?" He had half a mind to make an account, find Ashley's comment, and then tear her a digital new one.

"Oh, it's okay. Don't look so mad," she said, rubbing his arm. "It's part of the deal."

Light spiraled out from her touch across his body.

Her hand lingered on his arm until she turned away and dropped it.

But he leaned forward and caught her wrist.

She stopped in her tracks.

Cozy Nights in Vermont

Their breaths stilled as he stared at his hand, sliding it down to hers.

His chest rose and fell as he weighed the need clawing through him against everything he knew he shouldn't do.

The risk.

She was leaving soon.

Three weeks.

He'd never had a casual relationship, and she'd somehow crawled under his skin in less than a month.

He drew his gaze to her face, and those big almond-shaped eyes stared back—they were his favorite shade of bourbon brown in the low kitchen light.

Her cheeks were flushed from the heat of the stove, and the color rose high on them. He wanted to lick the rosiest patch to see what she tasted like. Nip at earlobes that held dangly metal earrings that swished as she swung her head. He wanted to pull her hair out of the messy bun on top of her head and bite her plush lip. Sink his hands into her wide hips again.

"Maybe roommates with benefits..." He stepped toward her, his chest aching to hold her. "Maybe...maybe it could be a good first step into casual dating for me."

She nodded, transfixed, staring at his chest, eyes barely open with lust. His hand had moved to her waist, and he dug his fingers in. "I need you," he said, catching a growl in his voice. "I haven't thought straight since I tasted you.

Barely slept. Dreamed about feeling every part of you again."

"Maybe if we just clear the air," she whispered as his hand slowly slid down to her ass, and she leaned into him. "Just bang it out. No pressure."

He squeezed her ass cheek hard—fuck, she felt so good.

She sighed, running her hands up his chest, clawing at him, grabbing at the fabric there. "Just keep it casual."

Sure, a casual, earth-shattering night as he fucked her again, and again, and again.

"Oh fuck." His heart dropped. "No condoms." *Goddamnit.*

"It's fine." She shook her head. "Birth control. Got tested before I left Dallas," she said, panting.

He allowed himself a soft kiss on her temple, his nose tracing her cheekbone slowly. Her grip on his shirt tightened, pulling him down closer to her. "Got tested before my first blind date. Are you sure? I'd happily spend all night with my head between your thighs."

She sucked in a breath and bit her lip, nodding. "Can I make one request?"

"Literally anything," he puffed against her skin, trying to stop himself from coming right here, right now.

"If you come," she whispered into his ear, "leave it in."

He sucked in a breath.

"I like the feeling of it dripping down my legs."

Cozy Nights in Vermont

Fuuuuck.

"*Goddamn, you're my dream girl,*" he muttered as his hand wrapped around her neck, crashing his mouth down on hers.

CHAPTER TEN

SOPHIA

Sophia tore at the buttons on Blake's shirt, needing him now.

His hand clutched her head as his mouth plundered hers, and she kissed him back. She licked and sucked his lip into her mouth, tasting the butter and herbs from her soup.

She unbuttoned his shirt, wanting to rake her hands against his chest. Oh *fuck*, his chest. She could spend the next three weeks sinking her teeth into his sexy, plush muscles.

Her pussy clenched. *No, we have more important work.*

She tore off his belt, wanting to see if the cock she'd felt against her a few days ago was as big as she remembered. She'd come that night thinking about him coming all over her, stroking an enormous cock at her.

His mouth never left hers as his hands grabbed at her greedily, squeezing, pressing. She fumbled with his jeans, pushing them down onto his hips. Finally, she felt the outline of it, and holy fuck, it was huge. She dove under his boxer briefs, wanting to feel it in her hands, taste it.

"Soph"—he pulled away—"this will all be over if you do that." He turned her around by her shoulders and untied her apron, which was knotted in the back. The apron fell to the floor, and he leaned her back against him, his ragged breathing in her ear. His arms wrapped around her. Her hands twisted up into his hair.

"Fuck. Your tits," he growled. "Did you wear this sweater to torture me?"

Her sweater gaped open, and he would be able to see straight down her shirt.

And her strategic lack of bra.

His hand grabbed her breast in a hungry, claiming grasp, pulling her back against him.

"Yes," she panted. She'd wanted him to fuck her. So badly.

She shoved her flowing sweatpants off, and they fell to the floor as he buried his face in her neck, sucking and biting on the curve of it.

He locked an arm around her waist and, with the other, slid into her panties.

"Fuck, Soph. You're soaked." He slicked two fingers around her clit, and her knees buckled. She grabbed his neck, arching against him. He moved his fingers, making her leg twitch as he expertly fingered her clit. Her jaw dropped at how good it felt as she sobbed.

He growled. "So wet it feels like I already came all over your pussy." He dove his fingers in deeper and cupped her as she moaned.

She couldn't catch her breath, *holy hell*. She needed more.

Turning around in his arms, she pushed his shirt off. He raked his hands up and down her back as he captured her mouth, until his hands wrapped around her thighs and lifted her up.

"Jesus." She wrapped her arms around his neck and her legs around his waist. His mouth never left hers as his hands dug into her ass. He walked them slowly to the couch in the living room as his cock pressed against the soaked lining of her panties.

He sat on the large leather couch, and she straddled him. She grabbed the edges of her sweater to take it off, but his hand stilled her.

"Let me," he said, his eyes transfixed on her body.

He slowly lifted the slouchy, soft, nearly see-through sweater until her lower stomach pooch was exposed.

His thumbs stroked along the edge of her stomach curve. "This okay?" he asked, his eyes never leaving it.

She held her breath. "Y-yeah," she said, not sure what to make of it. Most men ignored anything that wasn't her tits.

"Jesus," he murmured. His large hands framed her hips, and his thumbs stroked harder, more boldly, into the soft squish of her. "You are so sexy. This," he said, tracing the bottom curve of her stomach where it met her thighs, "is so sexy."

"Really?" she panted with surprise.

"When I said your body was worth worshiping, I meant all of it, Soph. This," he bit his lip with an *ungh*, as if keeping himself at bay. His hands explored, caressed every dip and groove of her stomach. "Have you seen a classic painting of a gorgeous woman, or a sculpture without one?" He pulled her up so she knelt on her knees, bringing her belly up to his mouth.

He nipped and licked at the soft curves that met her hips, and her world tilted at the feeling of being treasured. "Makes me want to drag you back to a cave and feed you berries."

She smiled and looked down at him, caressing his face. His eyes were bright and happy. *Free.*

He pushed her sweater up to her rib cage, trailing long, slow kisses as his hands squeezed her ass. He nipped along the sides of her curves there, moaning as he traced her stomach, the indents of her abs, nipped where her skin curved more. She was clenching around nothing, needing him but moaning at the feeling of being lost in pleasure.

Blake pushed the sweater up higher until it sat just on her breasts.

"Fuck. Me." His eyes were trained at her tits, and the under curve of them peeked out from her sweater. "You are a goddess. I just need…" He licked under a breast, running a tongue under one, then the other, finally burying his face against her sweater-covered tits. "Just need one to two weeks here."

His cock was at full attention, weeping through his boxers. She licked her lips, wanting to taste him too. "Only if I get to return the favor."

He pressed her shirt up over her breasts, and her nipples were hard points, begging to be licked and squeezed.

Blake sucked in a large breath. He shut his eyes, throwing a hand over his face. "I…need a minute."

She smiled, raking her hand through his hair. "Everything okay?"

"It's…it's too much. I'll come right now if I don't." He let out a slow breath, his eyes still covered.

Warmth and confidence glowed inside of her. She'd never felt more powerful or hot.

I almost made him come with my tits. She bit her lip, wanting to edge him on. She leaned down to whisper, "Have you ever come thinking about me?" She tossed off her sweater and took out her scrunchie.

"Obviously," he growled. "Every fucking day."

She mussed up her hair, bit her lip as she sat back on her knees, and pulled her panties to the side so he could see her pussy and clit. She let her finger rest there, teasing it.

"Did I look like this when you came?"

He opened his eyes, and hunger lit them aflame. "Goddamn." He moved and gently tossed her onto the leather couch. "Are you trying to kill me?" He spread her legs wide to get a good look at her pussy, with her panties still pulled to the side. His gaze never wavered.

She could feel her wet arousal slide down as he tore her panties off. His wide shoulders spread her legs further as he kissed his way up her thighs until she was fully spread in front of his face.

"Soph, look at how wet you are. Goddamn. You've already made my couch a mess." He pulled her legs apart wide, and she could feel it seeping onto the couch, pooling at her ass. He peered up at her with a feral need. "That's my girl. Drench it."

Jesus.

It's always the quiet ones.

She arched her back, wanting to press more slickness out for him. It trickled down and he cursed, never taking his eyes off of her pussy as he bit her thigh, hard enough that she arched her tits higher and higher. She grabbed her nipples, needing relief. He held her legs wide, taking his sweet fucking time getting to her pussy.

"Blake," she whined. She felt so empty. Had dreamed of his cock ever since she'd felt it against her.

"One taste," he murmured. "One taste of how soaked you are."

Finally, he spread her pussy wide as his tongue dove into her entrance.

She arched off of the couch as she clenched around his tongue hard, the warmth and wetness of him nearly making her come. He slowly—so slowly—licked in one slow lap up her pussy.

His tongue lay flat against her clit as he shoved his face against her, gripping her hips for leverage. The end of his tongue twirled around her clit, and her back arched in pleasure. Her nails sank into his thick hair. He lapped and lapped, his wide tongue destroying her clit. She clenched hard around nothing and pulled at him.

"I want your cock," she sighed.

He kneeled on the couch over her, tugging down his boxer briefs. The sides of his abs clenched as he tossed off his t-shirt. The gentle curve of his belly met the tip of his cock, and a bead of precum sat on the end of it, having rolled down.

Holy. Hell.

His cock was long and thick with pronounced veins. Her mouth salivated as she sat up, wanting a closer look.

"What?" he asked, tugging on it with a sly smile.

"Oh, you *know* what. You're...huge." She licked her lips. "I want to taste."

"Will it make you wetter?"

Cozy Nights in Vermont

She nodded, wide eyes looking up at him.

"Then spread your legs as you do it."

"Fuck," she whispered, so turned on by him. She knelt, spreading her legs as far as she could, feeling the wetness soaking onto his couch.

"That's my girl," he said. He grabbed her head and pressed her to his cock.

Fuck yes. She took the tip, the salty drip hitting her tongue. Even with her mouth wide, she could only fit a few inches in. She closed her eyes, savoring it as she sucked.

"Christ," Blake said, pulling out of her mouth slowly. "No more." He wiped the side of her mouth with his thumb, tracing her bottom lip. "Otherwise I'll come down that pretty throat."

"Don't threaten me with a good time."

"On your back. Now."

Jesus. Her pussy clenched. "I like bossy Blake."

He kneeled between her legs and slowly notched in. He was *thick*, and the fullness tugged at her. She sucked in a breath, getting used to him.

"Can't last," he breathed. "Will make you come after," he said as though holding back a freight train of need.

She wanted to see him come so badly. Needed it. Wanted it all over her. She loved that he loved her cum kink.

He slowly slid in, but she wrapped her legs around him, digging her heels in. With each inch, they breathed together. "You're doing so good," he murmured against her breast, nipping it.

He was finally fully seated and she squeezed, wanting to feel all of him.

"Fuck, Soph." His head dropped against hers. "Feels...feels like I was made for you."

Her arms had wrapped around him and his mouth found hers. She loved that he tasted like her, and their tongues danced as she squeezed around him. He moaned, pulling back.

"You don't play fair," he said with a smile.

"Just want to feel you come," she said as her hand went to her breast. "Being pumped full of it—"

He groaned as he pulled back, sucking a nipple into his mouth as he thrust into her. She arched from the dual sources of pleasure. Her hand found her clit, but he pulled it back.

He hooked her leg around his arm and leaned up so he could stare at her pussy. "Let me," he said, biting his lip. His thumb stroked her clit as he thrust inside of her. He flicked it mercilessly. She cried out as her orgasm built, throbs of need pulsing, pulsing, pulsing through her.

"I can't wait to fill your tight, needy"—thrust—"hot pussy with cum."

"Yes," she sobbed. "Fill me. Please."

On a shuddered curse, Blake thrust hard into her, bracing

himself on the couch arm. She could feel the heat of his cum inside of her as he stilled.

His head rested on her breast as he kissed his way across. "I am brain-dead, but I know one thing," he murmured. "You are the dead sexiest woman I have ever seen," he whispered. He kissed her, sucking her lip into his mouth, tracing it with his tongue.

Drawing her desire up, and up.

He slowly pulled out of her, angling her hips up, and she felt cum start to trickle out of her.

He kneeled on the carpet beside the couch, placing kisses down her belly.

"Now..." He spread her, knelt between her thighs, and raised an eyebrow.

Bossy Blake was back.

He pushed the cum trickling out back into her. "Don't spill a drop."

Fuck. Me.

He buried his head between her thighs, and instead of one long lick, he worshiped each dip and valley of her pussy, thrusting his fingers into her. "Jesus, Soph, my cum looks so good on you."

Sophia arched with a moan, biting her lip. She squeezed her nipple.

His fingers worked their way inside of her as his tongue circled and circled her clit. She screamed in pleasure, grabbing the couch arm behind her. "Fuck, yes," she panted. "More. I need more."

"My girl needs more," he murmured and moved his fingers covered in dripping cum to her mouth. "Open."

She whimpered as she opened her mouth and sucked his fingers, salty wetness on her tongue. She squeezed her pussy, shoving his head down. She needed to be eaten. Needed every bit of him.

His fingers went back, pushing in the cum dripping out of her as he sucked on her clit, harder—

"Yes," she panted.

And harder—

"Yes, yes, yes—" Her muscles contracted harder and harder, pulling her higher, needing more.

Until she crested as Blake sucked hard, squeezing her nipple, and she screamed through her whole body, throwing her back against the couch as she rode his face until her body froze, throbs of pleasure radiating out of her.

She collapsed and coiled into herself as aftershocks wracked her body.

Blankness, happiness, warmth. The only thoughts in her brain were the lack of them.

Blake gathered her up, and she crawled toward him instinctively. He threw a heavy blanket over them.

"My...I can't..." She couldn't form thoughts.

Cozy Nights in Vermont

A beep sounded in the kitchen. "Daaaamn," she moaned against his chest. She didn't have time to think about food. She just got fucked three ways till Sunday.

He shifted her onto the couch. "I'll get it."

"Mmmm," was all she could muster.

She dozed until the couch sank and warmth surrounded her as Blake cuddled her into him. She leaned her head back, her hair probably a rat's nest of sex hair. "You are... wow. I think you could do that professionally."

He burst out laughing, gathering her tighter. "A high compliment."

She was dazed, looking at the fire he must have started while she dozed. "Truly. But, bad news." She cuddled into his chest.

He stroked her hair as he looked down at her with concern. "Not interested in any more?"

She pushed up and straddled him, kissing him just to show him how much she cared. "The opposite. I don't think it's outta my system yet."

He pressed her into his chest so she cuddled against him. She could feel herself dripping onto him, and she loved it. And if he kept stroking her hair like that, she'd fall asleep in a second. "Hard to believe we've only known each other for three weeks."

"Twenty-two days," he murmured against her hair. "But, you know. Sure, three weeks."

She smiled up at him. His olive green eyes were warm and happy, his hair a mess from where she'd tugged on it, standing up in unruly tufts.

Oh no, this is dangerous. She could very, very easily fall into something other than friendship with this man.

Or had she already started slipping?

The man that was kind, and sexy, and looked at her like she'd hung the moon. "I can't believe I've been here for twenty-two days. I've barely seen the sights of Vermont since being here," she said as she played with his hair.

"I can take you to my favorite spot in a couple of days when the weather clears," he offered. "It's not far."

She twiddled a wave in his hair that threatened to curl. "Like a date?" she asked innocently, not sure whether she hoped he'd say yes or no.

He squeezed her against him, placing a kiss on her forehead.

"Consider it a benefit."

CHAPTER ELEVEN

BLAKE

Blake's feet hit the bottom of the staircase right before Star's did.

He was dead on his feet after yet another terrible night of sleep, but he had to get an early start. He'd promised to install the large painted sign Sophia had worked so hard on, and today was his least favorite day of the month: bookkeeping.

She insisted his business would increase if tourists drove by the farm and actually knew they could stop. He'd hit his forehead with how obvious an improvement it was. They'd worked all night painting the sign she'd designed. They'd then taken a very long, very sexy shower together.

Like he did every night since they'd first had sex, he'd kissed her goodnight and dropped her off at her bedroom door. He didn't want to subject her to his tossing and turning. At least one of them could get a good night's sleep.

As he rounded the corner, in the early, dim light he saw Sophia looking like his every fantasy. She was in a long rumpled sleep shirt, half sloped over her shoulders, with her messy bun still looking like cats had fought in it. She stirred a giant bowl that smelled like home. Clove, pumpkin, and vanilla perfumed the air. Every kitchen surface had some ingredient on it.

If she was here permanently, I could wake up to this every morning.

Her cheeks were rosy from the heat of the oven, and she had a sleepy smile on her face. "Morning, roomie," she said in a low, throaty voice.

His heart clenched, and he wrapped his arms around her from behind as she stirred the contents of her bowl. He buried his head in the curve of her neck, inhaling her vanilla scent, kissing her there. Couldn't get enough of it.

Only three more weeks of her here.

She leaned into him, and he squeezed her, trying to savor this memory.

She set her bowl down and turned around to wrap her arms around him. "Did I wake you up? I was trying to be so quiet."

They hadn't officially outlined the rules of their "with benefits" arrangement, but he was glad she hadn't seemed bothered that benefits included kisses, hugs, and as much sex as their tired bodies could handle.

Cozy Nights in Vermont

He bundled her against him. "I woke me up. Just like always."

Star huffed and stamped her paws, eager for breakfast. She stood by her food dispenser, demanding her kibble with specials on top, which were stupidly expensive meatballs that he splurged on because she was the best dog.

"I'm comin', I'm comin'," he grumbled in the direction of her food station.

Sophia looked like she'd fall asleep standing up as she stirred her batter.

"Hey, you don't have to make anything today. We can cut back if you need to rest." He didn't like seeing her so tired.

"No, no, I couldn't sleep either," she said, cracking one eye open as she stirred.

Her cheeks and lips were a dark rosy color, and he fought every nerve in his body that urged him to walk over, toss her over his shoulder, and go back to bed together.

"I'm exhausted, but I'm nervous about whether I can get everything done. What if I can't find enough recipes that are really mine, you know? Really me on the page. It's the best part of my day to talk to everybody and ask their opinions."

"What are you making today?" he said. Star inhaled her kibble, and he sipped his coffee waiting for her to finish so they could go to the barn.

"Everything pumpkin. Pumpkin muffins, pumpkin donuts, pumpkin bread. Tonight I'll try my hand at pumpkin ravioli."

"Mmm," he said noncommittally, thinking pumpkin ravioli sounded like a punishment. But if anyone could make it good, it was probably Sophia.

"I can't help it, you have amazing pumpkins," she said with a shrug, "so we're trying everything. Where are you off to at the crack of dawn?"

"I'm gonna put up your sign—looks good, by the way."

"Yeah? We have so many good things coming up." She started bouncing on her toes, waking herself up. "I wanted everybody to be able to find us, and I thought you deserved a face lift." She stumbled over her words. "I mean, not you, you're very handsome. I meant the farm."

Very handsome.

The most gorgeous woman in the world thought he was very handsome.

He let that bombshell roll around in his head, gripping the counter so that it wasn't obvious his world was tilting.

Yeah, they'd had sex. Yeah, he still dreamed about her every waking moment, but a sneaky voice in the back of his head thought, *I'm just convenient. Just a distracting toy for her to play with while she's away from home.*

She poured batter into a greased muffin tin. "Also, don't forget we're going to pick up the pumpkin carving kits later today."

He craved one kiss before he left to go to the cold, empty barn. "I won't forget," he said, staring down at her lips, which she bit.

She beamed back. "I already got ten insta-vite responses for the event."

He shook his head, amazed at her. Tilting her chin up, he kissed her with a slow, lingering nip. She tasted like coffee, and he inhaled her scent he'd never get tired of.

He wanted more, desperately. No time to get distracted this morning. "I don't know what I'm gonna do when..." *When you're gone.* "Uh...when all this is over and we have free time," he said, changing his mind. *Don't sound desperate.*

She kissed him quickly and went back to her recipe. "You know what I thought we should do before Halloween? A pet costume contest. Maybe at the same time as the pumpkin carving day. Make a whole thing of it."

His eyes went wide. *A pet costume contest?* His brain spiraled trying to understand the logistics of how he could do something like that.

"Oh, don't make that face. It'll be so cute, and I just did a one-off little post with Star the other day because I was so excited for the Pumpkin Treat-o's I made for her, and people asked about bringing their dogs to the farm."

Upon hearing Treat-o's, Star's tail slapped on the floor. "Now look what you did," he said with a shake of his head.

She grabbed one of the orange bone-shaped biscuits she'd made and broke it in half for Star. "You can't help that everyone loves you, can you?" Sophia asked as Star politely gobbled up the treat from her hand. "It'll help celebrate the end of the season, you'll get rid of the rest of your stock, and I'll get to see several dogs in costumes. It'll be a great time."

"If it makes you happy," he said with a smile full of wonder, "we should do it."

She fist pumped and shook her ass. "Yuuus. I was hoping you'd say that. I'll handle everything." She pecked his cheek as she went back to her recipe.

It was like living with a sexy, industrious energizer bunny.

He tapped his leg for Star to follow him out to the barn before he lost his control and really did haul Sophia back to bed.

As he stepped outside, the crisp air that slapped him in the face was far more effective at waking him up than the coffee in his cup. His boots crunched on leaves that were starting to turn brittle in the near frosty morning. Fog settled over the hills and fields, looking magical meandering through the pines.

The old barn had been standing on the Jameson Family Farm for well over a century, but about thirty years ago, his father had put in a small office leading out of the back of the barn. He'd installed a huge bolted safe to the concrete where Blake fed in the cash every evening after they closed. The safe was waist-high, and he absolutely hated unlocking it every month only to see a few measly bills at the bottom.

As Blake sat down in the small office, he tried to figure out what felt so different than the last month. Normally he dreaded this part of the job, tallying up just how much he owed everyone and seeing if he needed to dip into his savings yet again.

An unexpected feeling registered as he sat down. *I'm... happy?*

It almost didn't matter how much money they did or didn't have in the safe.

Business had been so good in the last few weeks due entirely to Sophia. He hadn't tried to get his hopes up because honestly he rarely kept track of what they earned day-to-day. It all netted out at the end of the month anyway.

He dialed in the code for the safe—his parents' first-date anniversary—expecting to see a few more bills than normal.

A flood of money spilled out of the safe as he opened the door, and Star barked in surprise.

How...what...

What the actual fuck. He'd been so distracted by the joy that Sophia had brought that he hadn't thought much of what he'd put in the safe every night.

After counting them all up and double-checking his math,

he realized they were ahead of schedule for the entire season.

So ahead that he might be able to repair the cottage and still actually make a profit.

He laughed, scratching his head in wonder.

He'd have to show Sophia how grateful he was to have her in his life.

* * *

That night, Blake turned onto a small country road as his old Chevy bumped through the dips in the road. His hand was on Sophia's thigh, and he couldn't remember a time he'd been happier in the last few years than he was then.

He'd driven them further and further into the backroads, far away from any other houses. The night was pitch black, and only the Chevy headlights illuminated the bumpy country road in front of them.

It was one of his favorite places on a clear night like this.

Sophia was texting on her phone like a madwoman.

He squeezed her thick thigh and sighed in pleasure at the feeling of it. "Everything okay? You might lose signal soon. Gets a little spotty out here."

"Just...thought of how...to fix...the ravioli," she murmured as she typed. "There. Phew." She sighed and put her hand over his. "I will not be deterred. I'm gonna crack it tomorrow."

Cozy Nights in Vermont

"It was good," he lied. They'd dined on leftovers before leaving. His fridge was at max capacity with delicious food.

He'd volunteered to eat everything...other than that.

"It was not," she said, squeezing his hand. "But thank you for trying to make me feel better. Tomorrow is another day. Where are we?" She peered out the window.

"This is an extra plot of farmland the family has. I haven't needed to plant it, but it's here if we ever were able to expand operations."

She leaned her head on his shoulder. "Did you always want to be a farmer? You said you moved here after Angie died."

"Sort of." He pulled off onto the patch of dirt in the middle of the field. "As a kid, I wanted to get as far away as possible. See some of the world. But I realized, the world isn't that great. Coming back is something I always dreamed about as an escape when I worked in an office."

"You? In an office? I can't believe it."

He shoved the gear stick into park. "Took after my mom. Was a CPA for about eight years."

She tossed her head back in surprise. "What the what?" she shrieked. "And that doesn't stand for Certified Pumpkin Analyst?"

He laughed, kissing her cheek. "Don't think I can handle numbers?"

"No, I'm just trying to picture a tie around your flannel shirts. You're so at home on the farm, I can't picture you anywhere else. I was an accounting major too. And I hated it way more than you did, because I only lasted for one year. Luckily a couple of my videos went viral with my first big recipe, and I've been hustling on my own ever since."

"I hated being trapped in an office," he said, his hand scratching his chin. "It felt like I was suffocating. I wanted to be outside, move my body. Not sit behind a desk and stare at a screen all day. I missed this."

"A pitch-black field?" She looked quizzically at him.

He smiled. "Not quite." He hopped out of the truck. "Just stay put. I need to get some things ready in the bed of the truck."

Her eyebrows rose. "If you're going to murder me, I'm going to be so mad at you."

He unfurled the air mattress he'd tossed in his truck bed and hit the button on his portable pump to start inflating it.

While the pump worked, he tossed two blankets over the air mattress and tucked two more off to the side.

He'd grabbed a few of the battery-operated flickering candles Sophia used for decor on the snack and drink tables. He turned them on and scattered them around the air mattress.

Candles don't make something a date. It's for...safety.

Cozy Nights in Vermont

Yep. Safety.

The thermos of hot toddies he made? Well, maybe that's edging toward a date.

He walked to her side and opened the door. "Time for you to experience some of the Vermont sights."

"Is this one of those things where you teach me to hunt for a pretend animal?" She narrowed her eyes.

"No, I'm not hazing you like some fifth grade Boy Scout. Come on." He held his hand out for her as she stepped out of the truck.

He squeezed her hand. "Now, look up."

Her jaw dropped.

"Holy...stars," she whispered.

His field was next to a registered dark sky state park. Bright stars blanketed the sky in an unimaginable density.

"It looks like when I spilled powdered sugar over the pumpkin loaf today."

He loved how her brain worked. "There's hardly any light pollution out here, and new construction is prohibited near the state park so that people can come from all over to see the stars like this."

"Blake, this is...I can't even process what this is."

It's a date, he thought with a tinge of shame at going back on their agreement. "C'mon, there's more."

He pulled her by the hand to the truck bed. "Let me help you up. I thought we could stay awhile."

"...Blake." She turned to him with wide eyes.

Oh fuck. Had he done something wrong?

"You did this for me? You even grabbed the little candles."

He scratched his ear, nervous he'd fucked up whatever good thing they'd just started. "Uh...yeah? We can go home if—"

"No." She swirled on him, her voice full of awe. Her hands came to her face as if she was processing it. "This is so thoughtful. I love it."

I love you.

Fuck.

It had been on the tip of his tongue.

Jesus.

Apparently, his soul, his cock, and his brain had all gotten together without his permission to create a laser beam of attraction and had aimed it at a total of two other people in his lifetime.

And number three was staring at his old beat-up truck as if an air mattress and some lights meant he was special enough to be with her.

So much for casual dating.

"Let me help you up." His hands came to her hips, and he lifted as she jumped, causing her to fly up and backwards.

Cozy Nights in Vermont

She burst out laughing as she landed.

"Did I say jump, woman?"

She cackled. "I was helping. I'm not used to being with a guy who can toss me around." She crawled onto the air mattress, and he enjoyed the sway of her hips in her jeans as she crawled.

He hoisted himself up and reached for the thermos.

She settled under a quilt and looked up, her eyes big—full of awe. For the first time since he'd met her, she was quiet.

"You said you'd always wanted to stare up at the stars and just think for a little bit, so I thought this was the best place I could find to make that happen," he said, pointing up.

"You remembered that from when I first got here?" she whispered under her breath.

He handed her a mug with the steaming drink he'd brought.

"Look at you," she said, impressed. "Thought of everything. Is this a hot toddy? Mmm." She cradled the mug. "I love the touch of cinnamon in it."

He lay down on the mattress next to her and poured a small one for himself since he'd drive in a bit.

"This is...unreal. I'd look up at the stars sometimes at home—at your house," she corrected. "But it's not like this."

He fucking *loved* that she thought of his house as home.

"Sometimes when I was a teenager, or after I moved back, I'd come out here and think. Easy to remember you're just a speck of dust in it all here."

"What made you want to move back to your homet-t-t-town?" Her teeth chattered.

He lifted his arm and tucked her into his side as he pulled his blanket onto her. "I had good memories growing up on the farm as a kid, and it seemed like good timing with my parents wanting to sell. It's been in our family for a hundred and fifty years, and I couldn't bear the thought of it going to some New York tech bro who wanted to escape the city. It felt good to get some space from my life before that too, start over somewhere familiar. But I always feel like I'm two steps away from failing my family," he said quietly.

"What? How? You're doing great. Need I remind you that a small child literally fell over from trying to carry too many pumpkins today."

He snorted. "And the fact that his face was painted a pumpkin, just...cherry on top." Sophia had convinced him to hire the local art teacher to come and do face painting for an hour in the afternoons, and the kids had been delighted by it.

"There's just always something that I feel like I should have done better. Like I should have had the tree taken care of when I first noticed something wrong with it." He shook his head. "I wouldn't have forgiven myself if something had happened to you."

Cozy Nights in Vermont

Her head rested on his chest, and she grabbed his hand. "You take your responsibility in the world very seriously. It's a refreshing change from the 'I'm forty-five and maybe I'll start settling down sometime soon' guys I've been knee-deep in for the last few years."

"Even though I'm stressed and think I'm usually failing, the worst day on the farm is still better than my best day behind a desk. Especially lately," he said, squeezing her to him.

She sipped the rest of her drink and set her mug to the side. Staring at him with an intensity that echoed inside of him, she reached her hand up and scratched her nails gently along his short beard.

"Why did you shave? When I first moved here."

Ah shit. His beard had been to his shoulder when she'd moved into the cottage. He'd taken the not at all subtle advice of his aunt and gotten his shit together, pronto.

"That's enough questions for today," he said, squeezing her closer so that her leg fell over his. "How about we just stare up at the stars?" he said with an embarrassed smile.

She pushed up to straddle his lap, the blanket falling off of her. "I'm more interested in my question."

Her chestnut curls were thick and tumbling over her shoulders as she impishly smiled at him.

"I should have known you'd be trouble," he muttered as his hands came up to grasp her ass, pulling her toward him. He hoped her small moan meant she wanted more of that.

Her hands were warm as they framed his face. "I mean, you can't seduce a woman," she said, leaning down, her breath over his lips, "and then get mad when she's been thoroughly seduced."

Her lips were plump and full like perfect berries, and his hand came up to her chin to hold her in place while he took her mouth. His cock was already rock hard at the mere taste of her.

His tongue traced her lip. A *cupid's bow*. He had to remember that for when she was gone. Had to remember how perfect his life was right now. And maybe that was all that mattered.

Her tongue met his as he grabbed her ass. Fuck, he wanted her. Constantly.

He kissed down her jaw, needing to hear her. She sighed out a small moan as he sucked on her earlobe, rocking against him.

"Blake," she panted, pulling back. "Why did you shave your beard when I first moved here?"

Her eyes searched his. Their hot breaths were clouds of desire around them in the air.

"Isn't it obvious, Soph?" he said, his thumb caressing her cheek. "I wanted to do whatever I could to have a chance with the most gorgeous woman in Vermont."

Cozy Nights in Vermont

Her eyes scanned his face as she pushed a hand up into his hair. He closed his eyes, savoring the cascade of pleasure down his spine.

"I..." She paused, looking like she'd changed her mind. "Kiss me."

He pulled her down to him, his arms wrapping around her. She raked her hands up and down his scalp as their tongues fought, ratcheting up their need and desire.

Needing to feel the world's most perfect pair of tits, his hand moved to her waist and pressed up, grabbing a handful of her breast like she'd done with him that first night they'd kissed. She spilled out between his fingers, and fuck, he'd never get tired of this.

"You are"—he kissed down her neck—"gorgeous."

She moaned as he rocked her harder and harder against him. "Fuck, I might come from this," she sobbed.

And a *pop* sounded in the quiet night, followed by an aggressive *hsssss*.

They stilled in surprise and burst out laughing. "What I'm hearing is a timed challenge," he said against her mouth.

"Yeah?" she said, unsure and panting.

He rocked her harder against him as air hissed out of a hole somewhere.

She moaned.

He rocked her harder, and harder.

"Fuck," she cried. "Yes."

He yanked her sweater down and found her nipple, sucking hard as he rocked her harder. "Louder," he ordered, shoving the other side of her sweater down and exposing both of her nipples. He was about to come just from this sight.

"Yes," she screamed as she rode him. Her hands were on either side of his head against the cab of the truck as her tits bounced in his face.

Need curled in his spine, and cum erupted out of his cock as he lost control.

She moaned, but she still moved against him. He kept rocking her, wanting her to come so badly.

"That's my girl. Tell me what you want." He squeezed her hard buds, pinching and twisting them as she humped his cock.

"Did you come?" she panted, rocking against him.

His cock twitched as it calmed down, thinking of her kink. "Yeah. Does my girl need it?"

She threw her head back and sobbed, "Yes."

He unzipped his jeans, reaching in to find the slick of cum against his skin. Gathering it onto his fingers, he grabbed her breast and slicked his finger around and around her hard nipple with it. She moaned at the contact.

"You feel so good covered in my cum," he growled into her ear.

She moaned. He sucked her other nipple into his mouth

and gripped her hips with all his might, throwing her back and forward against him.

"Fuck," she shrieked in a long cry, coming against him. She rocked and rocked until she slowed.

She stilled right as her knees and his ass and thighs hit the bottom of the truck bed, the air mattress having officially died. They burst out laughing again.

"We made it," she panted, pumping a fist in the air.

God, he really, really did love her.

He pulled her sweater back up so she didn't get cold and pulled her down for a long, slow kiss as they smiled.

Whatever happened between them, for the rest of his life, he'd remember a perfect night full of stars in his favorite place, with the woman who'd made him believe in love again.

CHAPTER TWELVE

SOPHIA

Lo-fi beats pumped through Sophia's headphones as she stared at a blank piece of paper in the dining room of the Clovely Inn.

Who knew that writing the introduction to a cookbook would be the hardest part she'd faced thus far in her scramble to get it finished?

The first two introductions she'd written had been easy. They'd been about her initial fan base, then about the launch of the first cookbook. This was maybe the last cookbook she'd ever do, and she felt the weight of responsibility in each of the empty lines on her notebook page.

Should she talk about her parents? Her grandmother? Her sister?

Her trusty enamel pot?

Cozy Nights in Vermont

Maybe she could convince the publisher to skip it, because who even read cookbook introductions anyway?

She nibbled on her salad as she made a word cloud, starting with her loved ones. Her pencil decided to write the words Star and Blake, which then turned into writing "I heart Blake."

Nope. Nope, nope, nope. It's just a casual dating thing.

She had to rip the whole page out and start all over again.

Get your head in the game. The first two cookbooks had been labors of love, and for some reason, this one had felt like pulling teeth.

Maybe because it didn't feel true.

She wasn't normally surrounded by end-of-season fresh vegetables in a farmhouse or a gorgeous restored inn. She never surrounded herself with flannel and pumpkins and chilly morning walks. She usually sat in her condo, staring at a screen in five-second increments as she swiped, trying to get content ideas.

She felt like she actually had *lived* for the first time in years, being away from the grind of strategic content creation.

A few days ago, she'd broken her rule and posted a silly video with Star enjoying her pumpkin treats. She'd decided to use it as engagement bait for pre-ordering her third cookbook that would include the recipe next fall.

Elise Kennedy

She logged in once she got on the inn's Wi-Fi to check the comments as a guilty pleasure, and of course, they were all abuzz after her first post in weeks (aka a lifetime online).

Soooo cute.

Was that your dog?

They couldn't wait to try the recipe.

Was she alive?

They missed her.

And then there was always the flip side:

Why does she think she's so special?

That dog looks purebred. You should adopt, not shop.

That could kill the dog, you have to list all the ingredients.

Never feed your dogs pumpkin.

No, pumpkins are good for dogs.

This one time, my dog ate pumpkin...

"Neeeevermind." She'd forgotten how much brain space all those opinions took up. She promptly closed the web page and opened up her notebook instead.

Maybe I'll work on photos.

Her recipes would be photographed in a professional studio, but the editors liked mixing in her personal photos too. It added a layer of authenticity that her audience appreciated. As she waited for her phone and computer to sync with the Wi-Fi, she finished the fresh autumn salad she'd ordered.

Roasted sweet potatoes had a touch of heat and cinnamon, and they contrasted with the fresh greens, pecans, and savory gorgonzola cheese.

Cheese, she sighed, savoring the creamy, sharp bite of it. She could probably do an entire cookbook dedication just to the dairy available in the state of Vermont. *I'm pretty sure they've outlawed processed American cheese slices at the border.*

She closed her eyes, savoring the interesting contrast with a bit of apple and pecan.

"It looks like you're having a moment," Beverly said, appearing in front of her as she wiped her hands on her apron.

"This tastes unreal," Sophia said, pointing to the salad. "Bits of fennel layered in? I would have never thought to do that."

"It's nothing compared to what I've been hearing about what you've been serving. You've made quite an impression on Clovely," Bev said, sitting down beside her at the four-top.

"My kitchen staff raved about your cheddar and sage biscuits. The new server said I should 'try to copy your recipe' before I explained to him that's not how this works," she said with a laugh.

Sophia grabbed her phone. "Here, let me write it down for you."

"Oh you don't have to."

"No, it's my pleasure. Honestly," Sophia said, jotting out the recipe from memory. "And interestingly, the one with the half cheddar, half pepper jack cheese was the winner. It's been so fun to actually see people eat what I'm making. Get their feedback, see what they like, see the stories behind it. Food has so much emotion."

And then it struck her. That was what she had to write about—all of the emotions and memories she associated with each of the recipes. She'd need several pages to talk about how much she'd treasured her time here.

"I've loved being here. There's nothing like a pumpkin farm in the fall." Or a very hot, very sexily capable farmer. "I'm supposed to leave in a few weeks, which feels too soon." She sighed and fiddled with her salad.

Beverly nodded. "Where are you off to next?"

"Uh," Sophia faltered, not mentally ready to move on from her life as it was right now. "My sister's apartment for the holidays. Then eventually, back to Dallas."

God. It filled her entire body with dread just thinking about it.

Beverly patted her hand. "We'll miss you here, and I hope you'll come back anytime. We've never seen Blake happier," Beverly said with a sad smile.

Cozy Nights in Vermont

Sophia's heart dropped at the thought of leaving. She bit her lip, unable to speak. Too many thoughts crashed in her head at once.

Do I really have to leave? Why go back to a city that doesn't fit anymore? What if when I move here, everything goes sour with Blake?

Wait. When she moved here? When had her brain jumped the tracks to moving here?

"Oh, speak of the devil," Beverly said, looking over Sophia's shoulder at the handsome man filling the dining room doorway.

Blake wore a dress shirt that hugged his muscles and jeans that hung perfectly on him.

His face lit up when he clocked them just staring back at him, and it gave her goosebumps. *Goosebumps.* Who even was she anymore?

"Thought I'd find you here," he said.

Beverly slapped the table and moved to stand. "I'll leave you to it." She patted Blake on the shoulder as she walked back to the kitchen.

"Are you coming to have a very late lunch with me?" Sophia gestured to an empty seat.

"Nope, you're coming with me."

"Ooh, surprises," she said, wiggling her shoulders in excitement. She shoved her things in her canvas tote bag, happy to have a distraction from her work. "Is it a sexy surprise?" she whispered, getting up, and his eyes simmered with unspoken heat as he looked down at her.

"No," he murmured, his eyes on her lips. "It's a long overdue token of my appreciation. Here, let me take that." He grabbed her heavy tote bag and offered her his hand as they walked through the lobby.

"Damn," she said, turning to the door. "I was really hoping it would be a sexy surprise."

They walked slowly down Clovely's Main Street. As they crossed each street, he'd quietly step in between her and the road.

She shook her head as she bit back giddiness. It was an old, silly, leftover custom of gentlemanly manners, but damn if it didn't make her insides flutter.

They passed the general store where she'd found the best maple syrup she'd ever had in her entire life, as well as an odd assortment of home goods. It was rare to find beeswax candles, apples, and bear spray all in one convenient location, but Roy's Hardware Store seemed to have its finger on the pulse on the heartbeat of the town.

Leaves blew in the chilly wind, and purple and yellow mums lined the streets. Each of the businesses had gone all out for the local Main Street decorating competition. A few Halloween decorations were spotted here and there, but this town seemed to linger in the dreaminess of autumn.

Cozy Nights in Vermont

"Have you been to Bookslingers?" He hefted her tote bag onto his shoulder, completely unfazed by holding the neon pink bag covered in flowers.

She bit her lip, finding that oddly sexy. "Not yet. I've just been running between every business that sells groceries and the farm."

"Come on, I wanted to show you something."

There was a puddle at the crossing point, and he held her hand out so she could jump over it. She was getting too used to having somebody there with her, one step ahead of her.

She felt a dangerous tug on her heart, huddling against him as the wind blew.

The clang of the antique bell on the door sounded, and that magical musty smell of a used bookstore mingled with the scent of freshly brewed coffee and a fireplace somewhere in the back.

Thick, deep chairs were scootched this way and that into corners, and small children played at a toy area in the corner while some townies wandered through.

A young woman with teal highlights turned from the register with a smile.

"Hey, Abby," Blake said with a wave. "This is Sophia."

"I am such a fan." Abby fanned her hands in excitement. "I've watched all of your videos. I'm obsessed, truly. You are entirely the reason I purchased brand-new spices after mine had been lingering for a decade in my cabinet."

Sophia lit up as she pulled Abby in for a quick hug. "Oh, wow, it's nice to meet you. I don't get to talk to many people that follow my content in real life."

"I haven't had a chance to get out to the patch yet, but I've been hearing amazing things about all of your recipes that are going into your new cookbook. In fact..." Abby waggled her eyebrows at Blake. "Come with me."

They followed her through the store up to the front where special books were on display. Sophia gasped as she spotted a large stack of her first book, *New Italian Comfort*. Her cookbook was rarely sold in small bookstores, since she wasn't famous or anything.

"What is this?" She glanced at Blake, who was beaming.

"I asked Abby if she would do me a favor and order lots of copies so I could try to pay back all of the kindness that you've done for us since you've been here."

Several dozen copies sat underneath and on top of a large oak table with a small, handwritten sign that said "Local(ish) Author."

She'd never found her book in a bookstore outside of the one signing her publisher had set up. For the first six months after her first cookbook had come out, Sophia had always looked anytime she'd been in a bookstore. But shelf space was limited in most stores, and her cookbook was one of thousands. She was just an influencer, and a small one at that.

She'd never stumbled upon it like this.

She was gobsmacked and had to take a quick photo—not for posting, but just for herself. Just to savor the moment of being appreciated and seen.

"They just came in yesterday, and I sold three this morning," Abby said with a smile.

"I'm taking five," Blake said, piling them into his hands.

"Do you want to sign some?" Abby's hopeful smile was contagious. "Let me get a Sharpie."

Sophia turned to Blake, who had his arms full of the heavy cookbooks. "You don't even cook. There's no recipe for a protein powder shake in there."

He shrugged. "Maybe there should be. Do you think there's a rustic fall protein shake recipe you should add into your next one?"

She bumped his hip with hers. "You'll know I have been lobotomized if you ever see that in my cookbook. Blake..." She laid a hand on his arm. "This was very nice."

"You wouldn't take my check, and I know that your social media thing is paused. I just wanted to show you how much, um—" He cleared his throat. "How much we all care about you. How much I..." he faltered.

"Here you go," Abby interrupted brightly, coming back with two Sharpies. "Let me grab a pile and you can sit down in that comfy chair and sign your little heart away."

As Abby gathered up books and walked them to the chair, Blake's unspoken words lingered in the air as he stared at her with furrowed brows.

It would be so, so easy to get lost in his eyes.

"I'll meet you at the front, Abby." Blake grabbed one more book and walked to the register.

Sophia settled into the overstuffed armchair with fifteen heavy books and closed her eyes, savoring this moment. She was signing her books in a cozy little bookstore on a perfect autumn day, just the way she'd always dreamed about.

She soaked in the moment as she lovingly signed her name with an XOXO in big swoops on the page.

She and Blake carried the signed copies back to the display table, and Abby put up a "Signed by the Author" placard in front of her books.

Abby fussed over the display, trying to make it perfect. "Blake said your second cookbook is coming out in a few months. Do you want to schedule a signing? We'd love to do something here for you."

"I've been waiting for almost a year for it to come out. Sure," Sophia said without thinking.

Wait. Sophia looked up at Blake, and her mind froze. *I won't be here anymore.*

"Uhh, well, maybe. Let's just see how things go," Sophia said noncommittally. "Though I guess I can always come back and visit," she said quickly to Blake. "I mean, they have trains and cars and planes to Vermont, right?"

"Okay, let me know and we can set something up. I'll ring

you up when you're ready," Abby said, gesturing at Blake to come with her to the checkout counter.

"Sorry," he said quietly to Sophia as they were walking out, "I hope that didn't make you uncomfortable. I'd mentioned the idea to Abby and I just...didn't think."

"It's fine," Sophia said, squeezing his arm and trying to wave away the awkwardness. "It's easy to forget that I'll be gone in a couple weeks."

He was quiet for a few moments before he finally cleared his throat. "Not for some of us."

Her stomach dropped, and she hated seeing that sadness in his eyes. She slyly smiled at him, trying to lighten the mood. "Is Star taking the news poorly?"

"She was inconsolable," Blake said with a dry smile. "She specifically requested at least one container full of Pumpkin Treat-o's before you leave."

"As if I would leave her anything less," she said with a smile, feeling like she was on even ground with him again.

They stopped at the end of the street and the last of the setting sun glinted against his auburn waves. His hair caught in the breeze, and she wanted to kiss him so badly. Wrap her arms around him and live in the scent of ivory soap and woodsmoke and crisp air forever.

"I was wondering if an early dinner might be included in roommates with benefits?" she asked. An old log cabin that looked like it'd been turned into a restaurant was across the street.

Elise Kennedy

With only two weeks left, she needed to maximize every minute with him.

That wasn't any more of a date than anything else they'd done, right?

"Only if my roommate likes to split dessert," he said, wrapping an arm around her as they walked toward the restaurant.

CHAPTER THIRTEEN

SOPHIA

They'd had a quiet dinner at the log cabin restaurant, where they'd talked about their days, Star, Sophia's love-hate relationship with social media, and everything in between.

Everything other than if she'd come back for a bookstore signing in a few months.

They'd gotten home, and Sophia realized she felt more like part of a couple with him, wandering through the house, turning off the lights, and tucking Star in, than she had in any other relationship she'd had in years.

They shared a bathroom as they both got ready for bed, brushing their teeth at the two sinks. This was only a semi-regular occurrence, given that she was a night owl and he was an early bird.

He brushed past her with a hand on her waist to go to his bedroom across the hall, shirtless and in his pajama pants. She licked her lips. She wanted all of that so near her, feeling an urgency she hadn't felt after being here for a month.

Only two weeks left.

"I was wondering," she said suddenly, twisting her large nightshirt in her hands and biting her lip out of nerves. "I was wondering if the roommate benefits might extend to sleeping next to each other."

He looked nervous. "I don't wanna bother you. I toss and turn all night long."

"No, I know. You've told me, but..." Her eyes darted around the room, not wanting to admit that she desperately missed cuddling. "I don't get to just be with people very often, you know?"

He stepped closer to her, in that way he had when he wanted her—when he was about to take her.

Ah, fuck it. "It's hard to trust new guys, and it's been a long time since I've just gotten to cuddle."

Her pulse quickened, and he slowly pressed a kiss to her temple, threaded his hand through hers, and tugged her to his bedroom.

Star settled down onto a giant fluffy white bed in the alcove near the door.

"Star's bed looks more comfortable than mine does across the hallway," she said with shock.

"She's very particular," Blake said through a yawn as he tossed off his slippers and his watch, pulling back the covers. She was far too tired to do anything sexy tonight, and he looked like he was about to fall asleep sitting on the bed.

"Any requests for your wake-up benefit?" he asked, looking at her with tired, happy eyes.

"What benefits are included with wake-up service?" she said with an eyebrow waggle and a yawn.

"Hmm, dealer's choice." He crawled under the covers.

She leaned over him, giving him a flirtatious look. "Let's just say I give you permission to wake me up any way you choose," she said, biting the inside of her cheek. She hoped he'd actually do it. She loved the idea of being fucked awake.

He looked skeptical but devilish. "Any way?"

"Any way." She bit her lip, clenching her thighs together at the possibilities.

"Even if it's with my head between your thighs?" he asked with a smile as his hands rubbed up and down her leg.

"I'll be disappointed if it's not." She stared at his lips long enough to make him lean in for a quick kiss, and she wiggled with excitement.

She ran a hand along the king-size bed as she went to the other side. "I hadn't planned on there being an acre of bed here."

"I'm a tall guy," he said, leaning on his elbow. She wanted to sink her teeth into every inch she could see on him. His eyes were closed though, and he looked completely dead on his feet.

She threw back the covers, took off her sleep shorts, and slid in bed, settling onto a pillow.

His eyes were closed as he spoke. "You're very far away."

"I think there's a toll pass in between you and me."

He snorted as she settled down, fluffing her pillow.

The sheets smelled like him, and she enjoyed the cocoon of feeling completely wrapped up in the safety of his scent. He turned the light off beside his bedside table.

He was more than an arm's length away in the king-size bed. Not what she had hoped for for her first cuddle in ages. But *he's a terrible sleeper, and you can't bother him and make it worse.*

Just as she considered moving back to her own bed, she felt Blake's hand move under the covers, hook around her thigh, and pull her to him.

He sighed, letting out a happy hum, as if tucking her in safely was all that he wanted before he fell asleep.

"Are you sure I won't bother you?" she whispered.

He just sighed, tucking her head under his chin. "I just needed you."

A smile bloomed on her face, and she curled into him.

His arm wrapped around her, tucking her closer against him so that her thigh slid over his. He let out a long, heavy sigh of contentment.

And no sooner had she gotten comfortable, hearing the

soft thud of his heartbeat underneath her cheek, than she heard him snore beside her.

* * *

Longing, craving clawed at her. Sophia registered that something was happening.

A hot, wet thickness moved on her pussy, and she needed it. Yearned for it. "More," she whispered through parched lips.

A cloud of desire blanketed her, and she needed to be filled.

Heavy weights bracketed her thighs, holding her open so anyone could lick her hot pussy. "Yes," she called out. She needed it. She wanted them all.

Her legs twitched, and she came back into her body, feeling soft sheets against her skin.

Someone was sucking, licking her pussy.

Fuuuuck.

Blake had been eating her while she was asleep. Yes. Just like she'd wanted.

So fucking hot to wake up to his head spreading her.

Just like she'd asked for without shame.

Because she knew he loved making her happy.

His shoulders pinned her thighs down, and she tested his

hold on her. Loud, obscene slurps and licks carried from under the covers.

His arms were an iron grip, and she couldn't wiggle out easily. Hot, horny need surged at that. That he was pinning her down to eat her until he was good and ready to be done.

She squirmed, arching up into his face, and she dove her hands under the covers. She wanted to feel him.

"Hands on the headboard," he murmured. "You're supposed to be asleep."

She panted at feeling exposed, at being told what to do. "You're too good. You woke me up."

His fingers slid inside of her, and she gasped at the feeling.

"Gotta get you ready to be pumped full," he said through licks and sucks, teasing her clit.

Fuck.

"I had to say thank you," he said, blowing on her clit—actually driving her mad—as she wanted to fuck his face so badly. "I slept for seven hours straight for the first time in years."

He sucked hard on her clit, and she arched off of the bed, crying out with a shriek. "More," she pleaded.

But Star ran to the window that overlooked the pumpkin patch in the bedroom and barked with alarm.

Cozy Nights in Vermont

"Star!" Blake yelled back, ripping the covers off. "Down." She continued to bark, turning into yips of excitement, recognizing somebody.

Blake cursed, looking up at Sophia. "Sorry, she never does this." He walked over to the window on the side of the bedroom and peeked out.

"Is everything okay?" Sophia asked, coming back to earth as her pussy throbbed.

She gathered up a comforter around her so she was covered and walked over to the window. She peeked out from behind Blake's back.

They looked out the small gable window of the house. Jerry and Alan stood by the farm gate and waved up at them.

"Morning!" Jerry yelled up.

Blake opened the window. "What are you doing?" Blake called down.

"Bev said you both looked exhausted yesterday, and you needed a break. So, take your time and sleep in this morning," Jerry called back.

"You don't have to. You don't know where I keep anything," Blake yelled.

"Young man, I was working on this pumpkin farm decades before you even existed." A few cars had already parked along the road, deciding to stop in early.

Jerry waved at them to go back to bed. "Just take your

time; I don't want to see either of you down here for another two hours. And send my best girl Star down."

Sophia shrank back to the bed. She yawned and laughed behind her hand as Star thundered down the stairs and out her doggy door hatch.

Blake waved and shut the window. "Family," he said with a surprised shake of his head.

"It must be nice to have people here who care for you so much." She threw back the covers so he could crawl in.

He settled onto his back and pulled her against him. "It's been nice, even if they are a little nosy."

She chuckled as she burrowed her way into his chest, placing kisses along his pecs, the curve of his stomach, wanting to taste every part of him.

She looked up at him with wicked eyes.

"Soph," he said, holding her face. "My family is down there. They might think we're having sex if we don't go down."

She huffed out a laugh. "Of course they think that. So let's have sex since they're already thinking it." She made a *duh* face at him.

He raised his eyebrows. "Pretty solid logic, actually." He grabbed for her, pulling her up to his chest.

"One of these days I'll actually convince you to let me prioritize just your pleasure," she murmured into his chest as she straddled him.

Cozy Nights in Vermont

He peeled off her t-shirt and sighed, shaking his head. "I don't know what I did to deserve you, but I'm not gonna ask any questions." His hands sank into her thighs, grabbing handfuls of her. She loved that he loved her body just as it was.

His cock was already hard against her heat, and she pushed up, then slowly, slowly sank down on it.

"Mmmm," she sighed with her eyes closed. "I've dreamed about doing this since the moment I saw you."

He let out a huff of surprise as he rocked her against his cock. "No way." He pressed up, taking her breast into his mouth.

She clutched his head against her. "Yes. Thought about riding you that night when I came. Thought about you fucking me and taking me however you wanted."

He paused. "However I want?" His eyes darted to the tall mirror on the wall by the bed.

She smiled and pushed off of him, already feeling empty and needy. She walked over to it, leaning against the wall seductively. "What did you have in mind?"

His wet, dripping cock twitched. He pressed off of the bed and turned her to face the mirror. They were naked and safely out of view of the window. They looked soft and really fucking sexy together in the mirror. He stroked his long cock where she could see it.

He reached a hand around her and stared at her in the mirror as he grabbed the edge of her lower belly pooch hard, then fucked up into his hand. "Goddess. That's what you are. Look at you. Look at how hard I am for your perfect body."

Her mouth salivated, wanting him so bad.

His eyes turned dark as he leaned into her ear and his hand slid between her legs. "Now, bend over and spread your legs."

Oh.

God.

How had she thought this man was a gentle giant? He was a demon sex god about to destroy her pussy with the feral look in his eyes.

She bent over and spread her legs wide, placing her hands on the wall beside the mirror. Her tits and belly hung down, and he stared at their reflection.

"I dreamed about fucking you just like this," he said, sliding into her. She clenched around him as he slid down, further in. "Where you'd take it so well, beg for more."

He thrust against her; her tits and tummy swung from the force, and it reverberated against his middle and chest. "Yes," she moaned.

"Just like that."

He grabbed her hips as he thrust harder and harder, his eyes laser-focused on her in the mirror, his bottom lip caught between his teeth.

"This was my first sex dream of you. Fucking me from behind," she moaned.

Cozy Nights in Vermont

His jaw tensed, and his hand moved to her shoulder for more leverage. "Does my girl like being taken from behind? Fucked hard?"

A guttural moan was all she could manage as he pumped hard.

He pulled her back so her arms dropped, and he gathered one arm behind her back. He hooked his arm through hers to hold her upright, and his other hand grabbed her shoulder.

He started fucking her hard and fast, thrusting against her as they both watched her tits bounce harder and harder in the mirror.

Her hand found her clit, and she rubbed hard, drilling herself where he could see.

"Jesus," he ground out and thrust faster. He leaned over to whisper in her ear. "You want me to make you a cream pie, don't you?"

She moaned in response, unable to form words.

"Beg for it," he growled as he fucked her hard. "Show me how much you want it."

"Please, fill me," she cried out, clenching around him as she shook from his hard fucking. "Please, please. Come all over me," she shrieked the last word as she came, feeling his hot load shooting up inside of her.

They stilled, his lips on her temple, and panted in the mirror, staring at each other with small, shocked smiles, looking like sweaty, happy messes. She could feel it drip down her legs as he pulled out.

He gathered her up in his arms, still facing the mirror, burying his face in her neck. "That feel good?" he murmured.

She knew he was referring to the hot, wet reminder dripping between her legs.

"Yes," she sighed. "I like feeling...like yours."

His eyes met hers in the mirror, and he tilted her chin to look straight at him. "You are mine," he said, panting, "for however long you want to be." He kissed her, his tongue tracing her bottom lip, his hand supporting her head.

For however long I want to be.

CHAPTER FOURTEEN

BLAKE

People swarmed the farm, and Blake had to take a minute as he registered what a difference a month made.

Families walked through the last of his pumpkins. They picked up butternut and acorn squash and pie pumpkins with the baskets that Sophia had found around the farm. She said the baskets added to the "aesthetic," whatever that meant. Soft indie folk music played from a large speaker he'd borrowed from Abby at the bookstore. It set the mood on the busy, gray fall afternoon.

Sophia had found a second face painter, and half the kids running around looked like pumpkins and zombies come to life. And though he liked the sound of kids laughing and dogs barking—the pet contest was today—he decided his favorite sound was the soft hammering of the cottage roof being fixed.

A burst of laughter sounded out near the snack table. Sophia laughed loudly, throwing her head back, as she talked with Mabel, who had already been wrapped around Sophia's finger. In a true Italian fashion, she shoved food and samples of soup at people, begging them to tell her what they thought.

She only had three recipes left to finish, and he was so proud of her.

Small and large dogs on leashes and even a few cats wandered through the grounds, with some dressed as hamburgers and another one dressed as the perennial favorite, a ghost. His personal favorite was the dog dressed as a pumpkin.

Sophia had wrangled local judges, including Mabel, Abby, and Uncle Jerry.

She practically glowed as she corralled everyone. It was completely beyond his comprehension, he thought, hauling more hay bales over to the seating area, how she'd managed to pull all of this together.

Members of the JV football team ran back and forth from his house to the snack tables, and she directed it all with the air of a congenial four-star general. Sophia had been exhausted running back and forth, and he'd decided that the boys on the team could use a little extra cash now that the JV season had ended.

He dodged Braden who ran past him.

"Gotta get more soup, Coach!" he said, running in with an empty tray.

Sophia walked over with a basket of small tools and newspapers. After the pet costume contest, they were going to do pumpkin carving where they'd set out stations so that guests didn't have to clean up their own pumpkin guts mess. And he could admit his pumpkin-carving abilities were on the higher end of amateur. You didn't grow up on a pumpkin farm without *some* set of skills.

"Hey, thanks. It looks like you're having fun," he said, taking the basket from her. He pulled her in for a quick hug and forehead kiss.

Her cheeks went pink, and he noticed folks staring at them, whispering. As far as the town of Clovely was concerned, Sophia was a short-term renter.

Little did they know how permanent his feelings were.

"Oh, sorry." They hadn't done any sort of public affection.

"No, I liked it," she said, looking a little embarrassed. "Roommates can do forehead kisses, right?"

He nodded. "For sure, that's what my college roommate and I used to do all the time. Forehead kisses before we went to class."

She threw her head back and laughed at his dry delivery. He loved making her smile, making her glow. Her arms were still wrapped around him, and he wanted to live in this moment forever. All of his worries had disappeared, and his life in Clovely had never been brighter.

"Do you want another one?" he said with a slow smile.

"You know, when the mood strikes." She shrugged with an impish grin.

But the mood always struck around her. He placed a lingering kiss on her hair again, squeezing her against him. He rubbed up and down her arms. It was chilly today. "Are you staying warm enough?"

"No, and you know what? Even after four weeks, it still hasn't gotten old. I literally can't remember the last time I was a sweaty mess. Well"—she stared up at him with a sultry smile—"outside, at least."

The picture of her working up a sweat last night would be with him until his deathbed. "Hey, you look happy," he said suddenly.

"Hey, I am happy," she said, as if just realizing it herself. "This is so fun. Did you see all of the dogs?" She jumped up and down in excitement.

"My personal favorite is the pumpkin dog."

"Oh my gosh, I know, though I am a little partial to the wiener dog," she said as a tiny, rat-like dog toddled beside them, wearing a giant hot dog bun, looking a lot like a literal hot dog. "I can't wait for you to see Star's David Bowie costume I got her."

"Hey, Coach Sophia!" Elijah, one of his defensive linemen, called over.

"Coach?" Blake said with a laugh, squeezing her.

"I couldn't convince them to just call me Sophia. They insisted."

He nodded with approval. "Good men."

Cozy Nights in Vermont

Elijah jogged over, and Blake finally dropped his arms from around Sophia, already missing the feel of her.

"We're out of that rosemary stuff for the soup samples?" Elijah said.

"Shoot, I forgot to get more. Would you be able to supervise?" she asked Blake, gesturing to the tables. "I can run to the general store."

He looked over now at the two tables filled with grab-and-go items and samples. "Why don't I go for you?"

"No, no, I want to pick out the herbs myself. Oh shoot," she said, realizing as she grabbed for her keys in her pocket, "I have to go get gas, too. Shit. It might be a little while." The only gas station was half a mile outside of town, in the other direction.

"I filled up your tank for you," he said offhandedly.

She stopped in her tracks. "You what?"

"I had some extra gas in the barn, and I saw your tank was empty. Is that okay?"

She blinked back tears unexpectedly. "That's really nice. Sorry, I think I'm just overwhelmed." She wiped the corner of her eye. "I'm just not used to being taken care of."

"Well, I like taking care of you." He pulled her in for a quick hug and another forehead kiss. She said it was alright, right? "The guys and I got it covered. Go," he said with a squeeze.

He watched the woman he loved walk to her car, blissfully unaware of his feelings.

The fear of losing her became palpable in his chest.

He had to tell her how he felt. Even if she left on the spot and he never saw her again, she needed to know how deeply she was loved just for being herself.

* * *

The next day, Blake was working in the barn, finishing his trays for seed propagation before he went back out to see how the cleanup was going.

He decided to try growing carrots for next year. Maybe he could finally give Aunt Bev her farm-to-table vegetable dream if he figured out how to grow enough different crops.

The pumpkin patch was closed today. They'd needed all the time they could get, given the massive cleanup of the pumpkin carving stations. He heard the barn door roll open and the familiar clomp of boots walking toward him.

Sophia looked like a cozy angel today with her big flannel scarf wrapped around her neck and her cheeks pink from the cold.

"Did the guys get everything cleaned up?" he asked, not able to take his eyes off her curves as she walked toward his work area.

"There was a threat of a pumpkin guts food fight," she said with a smile and an eye roll. "But yes, they were very good helpers while I worked in the kitchen. They're all on their way home."

Cozy Nights in Vermont

He'd thought the farm had seemed quieter.

Yesterday had been amazing. They'd barely had time to catch up before they'd both fallen into his bed, cuddling in the chilly night. He'd been up early and wanted her to sleep in after all her hard work.

The less time he spent with her, the more likely he'd keep his mouth shut about how much he loved her. But there she was, standing in his barn, fiddling with a piece of hay between her fingers.

"You know, I think the pumpkin sage gnocchi was the favorite because I doubled the sage. I wonder if I could do a twist on it next time. I mean, the next time that we have another big weekend."

The season was coming to a close, and he only had maybe two dozen pumpkins left. Halloween was in a few days. "I figured next weekend would be the last time we'd be open," he said with a pained smile.

"Oh, right," she laughed. "People don't really need pumpkins after Halloween, huh?"

"Maybe for the odd pumpkin pie for Thanksgiving, but no. Things will slow down here."

"Right," she said. "Silly. I just didn't think about it ending. Guess it'll give me time to finish up the last few recipes, though I'll miss seeing everyone." Her eyes looked sad even as she smiled at him.

He pulled her in for a hug, wanting to make that sadness go away.

"Hey, I saw the cottage roof. It's looking good," she said with a squeeze around his middle.

Please don't ask to move back. "It has to cure for a couple of days, but it should be good as new by next Thursday."

"I hope you don't mind me still staying in your house. I've gotten far too used to the very sexy Viking to go back. Both the oven kind and the one right here," she said with a squeeze and a smile, burying her face in his chest.

He was happy she wanted to stay. But *will she stay after I tell her how I feel?*

He remembered the piece of paper for her burning a hole in his pocket. He took off his gloves, covered in dirt. "Speaking of the cottage, I have something for you." He pulled out the small piece of paper from his pocket.

She opened the paper.

"We've made more money than ever in the last month. You've helped my farm get back in the black. I had enough to repair the cottage roof, and I even paid off the last of Angie's medical debts. I can't tell you—" His voice caught, but he cleared it. "—what a weight off my shoulders this has been. It's all because of your hard work, and amazing ideas. And even better food. Please, I need you to take this."

She stared at the piece of paper with his scrawled handwriting on it—a check made back to her for the rent she'd paid and groceries she'd bought.

Cozy Nights in Vermont

She looked up at him with an earnest face that broke his heart.

That face he wouldn't get to see in less than two weeks.

"I just wanted to see you happy," she whispered.

"You make me happy," he said, his hand coming to her cheek. She leaned into it.

"Blake, I don't want this." She slapped the piece of paper on his chest.

And I don't want to be in love with you, he thought. *But here we are, and I can't stop it.*

"We don't always get what we want," he said. picking the piece of paper from between her hand and his chest and shoving it into her pants pocket. She smiled against his chest.

"It's good you don't know how paper works." She reached into her pocket and looked up, kissing his cheek on her tiptoes. And as she smiled against his cheek, he heard the sound of the check being ripped in half.

"Soph, come on," he said with a huff.

Her mouth twitched. "So that's when my nickname comes out? When you're frustrated with me?"

"No," he said quietly, pushing locks of hair that had fallen beside her face and stroking a thumb along on her cheek.

Quite the opposite.

Oh god, it was getting hard to hold it back.

"Then what?" she said with a warm smile, her hands wrapped around his middle, looking utterly gorgeous—happy, perfect.

Her round cheeks were perfection, and he pressed a slow kiss to each side.

Mabel didn't have a chance like this in nearly twenty years.

And in the end, didn't everyone deserve to know when they were loved so deeply?

"I'm so sorry for what I'm about to tell you," he said, his brows knitting together as his insides danced. "I know it's not what we agreed on."

This was not what he'd set out to do this morning.

"Is it that you'll write me another check?" she said with a worried smile. "'Cause I'll just rip that up, too."

He laughed. "Sophia," he said in a low, needy breath, taking her face in his hands. "I am so in love with you, and I'm so sorry. I told you we'd be casual, when I'd already started falling for you when you were crouched under the cottage window. I fell in love again when you spoiled Star." His eyes scrunched together, and he knew he was acting like a giant coward. "I think I fell more in love with you when you swung your hands at the fat raccoons and screamed bloody murder. Definitely fell in love with you when you were so kind to my family."

He opened his eyes, his chest heaving. "I think I've been falling in love with you every day, every moment, since I met you, over and over again. I can't stop it any more than I can stop breathing. It's just how I'm built."

Her mouth had fallen open.

He was like a fire hose—he couldn't stop it. "I love every bit of you. The messy, the chaotic, the lovely, the curvy, the anxious." He caressed her cheek because, miraculously, she was still there and not a giant cloud of dust from running away. "I love your fears and your hopes. I've tried to fight it, tried to push it away, but your puzzle pieces fit so perfectly to mine. You have a big life with big opportunities, and I'm never going to stand in the way of that."

He took in a ragged breath. "But you should know how deeply you are loved. You brought me back to life because of how much I love you."

His chest heaved from spilling out the most words he'd ever strung together. "I'm so sorry to…to spring this on you," he said, shaking his head. "I just needed you to know how much you mean to me."

Uncharacteristically quiet, she stared up with big caramel eyes with a mixture of wonder and…was that horror? Panic?

Oh God, I'm never going to see her again after this.

She's going to shove her pans and her pots into her car and then take off for the border of New Hampshire.

CHAPTER FIFTEEN

SOPHIA

Static filled her ears.

Or was that the sound of an out-of-body experience?

How had she missed all the signs?

A montage flashed through her head: him running after her when he'd thought she wasn't safe, in the bookstore, whenever he'd pulled the covers over her and tucked her in, too many times to count over the last month.

"I, um." She needed to say the right thing.

This was a precious, crystalline gem of a man. She'd never want to hurt him, and she'd fight anybody who wanted to.

But how did she even respond to this?

How did she even *feel* about this?

"I need to go for a drive," she heard herself say.

He nodded, as if processing much faster than her.

Cozy Nights in Vermont

"Yes, a drive, I think. Um, you know, to get some produce," she said, backing away, a response of *"I love you too"* on the tip of her tongue. But no, she had to be sure. She didn't want to just say something to make him happy.

He was too important.

"I'll be back, okay?"

"Do you want me to warm up your car? It's cold."

"Yes," she said. "No, wait, I have to do this on my own. I have to think about this. Thank you though. Can I get you anything? Toothpaste? Baking soda?"

A cohesive response to the most romantic declaration of love I've ever heard?

"No," he said with a slow smile.

She bit her lip. "Aren't you worried I'm gonna walk out and never come back?"

"No." He walked to open the big barn door for her. "You love your cast iron enamel pots too much," he said, a knowing look on his face.

He looked down at her with what was now such obvious love in his eyes. She mentally facepalmed herself at not seeing it before, or maybe not wanting to believe that it could happen to her.

She pushed up on her toes and pressed a long, lingering kiss on his cheek, then ran like a giant coward to her car.

Elise Kennedy

As she turned on the SUV, the gas gauge that had been hanging out at nearly zero for over a week jumped all the way up to almost full like it had yesterday.

There it was. She barked out a laugh—or was that a sob?—as she shook her head.

She turned onto the road, trying to process everything, and yet, there he was in the gas gauge of her car. Her roommate who apparently loved her, having taken care of her one more time before she'd even thought to ask.

For some reason, tears pulled and clawed their way up her chest and into her throat, threatening to spill out onto her cheeks.

Why couldn't she ever make sense of her emotions? Who cries after a perfect man declares his overwhelming love for you? Me, an idiot, that's who.

She drove the only route she knew back to Clovely, wanting to see the comforting, familiar sites she'd visited every few days. Driving by the farmer's stand with the great cucumbers. The You-Pick apple farm that had an adorable honor system money box drilled into one of the trees.

Her brain was on autopilot as she wound her car through the streets filled with historic homes. She drove until she found herself outside of a small park.

It had old-style lights on it, and in the gray, low light of the afternoon, they had flickered on, illuminating paths through the trees.

Cozy Nights in Vermont

She called Iris, who picked up after one ring. "Hey, how's—"

"I ran away," Sophia said.

"*Now* you ran away?" Iris responded in confusion.

"Yes." Sophia's voice caught. Finally the tears caught up to her eyes and started to spill over. God, she hated this.

Hated not knowing what she was feeling.

"Are you crying? Where are you?"

"I'm at a park," Sophia said in a wobbly voice.

"Where? Are you okay?"

"In Clovely."

"That's a good park," Iris said, laughing for some reason.

"Everything is ruined," Sophia responded.

"Why, what happened?" Iris said with concern and surprise.

"He—" Sophia heaved a sob.

"Loves—" Another sob.

"Meeeeee," Sophia said, unable to form a more coherent sentence.

"I think...I think I love him back—"

"Then why are you crying?" Iris said, exasperated.

"I don't know..." Sophia hiccuped. "...because I think he really, really loves me, and it's overwhelming. And then I think maybe I've never actually been loved. Just for me. I hoped I could take all these butterfly feelings he gave me and not think about them. That somehow time wouldn't pass and I wouldn't have to leave him and I wouldn't have to admit that...maybe I do believe in soulmates."

She shook her fingers out to try to regulate herself.

"And?" Iris asked.

"But what if I'm wrong? What if I throw away what I worked so hard for?" Sophia wiped her face with her sleeve.

"What, being single and alone?"

"Okay...ow," Sophia said in response.

"What would you throw away? Your life in Dallas?"

"It all seems tied up together. My life, my influencer persona, and the cookbooks. I don't know...I'm just not sure if..." She trailed off, unsure of what she was unsure of.

"Sophia, it doesn't have to be all or nothing. Just stay a little bit longer; just try it out. I'm only a few hours away. In fact, I thought maybe I'd come and visit you next weekend. We finally got back from our assignment in Iceland yesterday," she said through a yawn. "Need I remind you I threw away ten years of my life on my idiot ex-boyfriend?"

"Because you didn't listen to your big sister."

"And then what happened after two weeks? I knew I was in love with Sam."

Cozy Nights in Vermont

"Two weeks, really?" Sophia said with awe.

"Sometimes I think that's how long it's supposed to take. Maybe less. If you know, you know."

"He said he knew"—Sophia felt embarrassed admitting this—"when he first saw me."

"Ohh," Iris swooned on the phone. "No waaaay. That's so fucking adorable. He was such a quiet guy when I met him, almost embarrassed to be around us."

"He is quiet," Sophia said with a smile. "And also funny, and so sweet, and so thoughtful. And *hot*."

"It's never too late to start over and try out a new life somewhere else. I should know." Iris had spent many years with her ex-boyfriend in Buffalo and, after getting dumped, had started over her new life in Boston a year ago.

"I wouldn't be starting over, really," Sophia said, fiddling with her steering wheel. "I'd just be continuing."

"See, that's not so scary."

"Maybe I started over without even realizing it, because I loved it so much."

Loved *him* so much.

"Will you still make your cookbook deadline?" Iris asked.

"I dunno. It seems sort of small in comparison to figuring out you're in love and maybe upending your life."

"See?" Iris said with a laugh. "Now you have new anxieties to replace those old anxieties."

"I just never—" Sophia laughed as she rolled her head back and forth in the car. "It never felt like this, you know? Like I might die and also burst into tears and barf and dance if I said I loved him back."

"What do you really want?"

"A martini." Sophia rubbed a hand on the bridge of her nose.

"And then tomorrow, what do you wanna wake up and do?" Iris asked. "Tell me your best day ever."

Sophia sighed. "I wanna wake up, do a bunch of things I cannot talk to my sister about with a hot farmer."

Iris laughed.

"And then bake a bunch of pies or muffins, or braise a lamb shank, make some roasted broccolini. Feed it to people that I get to talk to, see that they love it, encourage them to eat more. Go to a bookstore, play with Star, have an amazing dinner overlooking orange and red trees, and do it all over again."

She laughed, realizing that was all possible. She could do that tomorrow, and the next day, and the next day, if she was just willing to start over.

All the pieces clicked into place and she saw the edge of the inn across the park.

She knew exactly what she needed to do first.

"I gotta go, Iris. Love you." She started the car and drove to the Clovely Inn, where she spotted Beverly just opening the back door, heading inside before the dinner rush.

"Beverly!" she said, calling as she parked her car and jogged over.

"Walk with me." Beverly hung up her bag and coat on the old wooden hooks at the door.

"Hey, Chef," an older man called from the line prep counter, "Marco called out sick today, again."

"Oof, that flu. The price you pay for having little ones in daycare." She chuckled. "We'll just have to work extra fast and hard. What did you wanna talk about?" she asked Sophia as she washed her hands at the sink, having donned her chef's coat and tied her apron around her waist.

"Um." Sophia had never pitched herself into a job. In fact, she'd had exactly one job interview ten years ago for an accounting job that she'd fucking hated.

"I'm hardworking," Sophia said, diving in, "and, um, I've built my own business, doing influencer campaigns, marketing."

Beverly nodded with a smile as she grabbed vegetables from the gorgeous glass fridge and a wooden cutting board. She set them out with a sharp chef's knife on the prep table and then grabbed a second apron.

Sophia kept rambling. "Everyone loves the recipes that I've tried out at the pumpkin patch. My standout was the butternut squash and bacon soup, paired with a hearty, rustic bread. And then of course, the pumpkin pie bites.

You can't beat a pumpkin pie bite when the pumpkins are fresh from the farm," she rattled on as Beverly picked up a paring knife and set it beside the four carrots, two stalks of celery, and broccoli heads on the counter.

Sophia prattled on, not sure how to actually say the "Can I work here?" part.

"You know, I'm not afraid of hard work," Sophia said, wringing her hands.

"Mhmm." Beverly nodded, searching through the fridge-scaped fridge, then pulling out two bunches of herbs.

"Oh, that sage is going to go soon; you might want to include that," Sophia said, peeking over her shoulder.

"Good idea," Beverly said as she grabbed the herbs. "You're a hard worker, yes, continue." Beverly rummaged through drawers until she came to what looked like a bin full of potatoes.

"And I've always wanted to work in a kitchen, or a bakery, anywhere with other people, because I think I like people. I realized that maybe I created a life where I don't really see anybody or talk to anybody or get to feed anybody in Dallas."

"Hold these," Beverly said, putting the potatoes into her arms, piling more and more on as Sophia talked. Beverly grabbed two onions. "Yes, you're a hard worker. You want to work in a kitchen?"

"I can do anything. Start as a dishwasher, or a server, an, um, unpaid intern." Jesus Christ, she was normally more eloquent than this. Sophia smiled through her grimace, so completely embarrassed. "Whatever I can do to get my foot in the door."

"So you can do...what?" Beverly asked, setting onions down on the large prep table and gesturing for Sophia to set down her potatoes.

"So I can become a baker, I think, and enjoy feeding people, and I don't know, just being a part of the whole process."

"Excellent, that's a great idea," Beverly said as she tied an apron around Sophia's waist.

"It is? So, can I work here?" Hope teetered on the edge of Sophia's soul.

"Your paid trial started ten minutes ago. Wash your hands and chop these vegetables for soup." She winked and walked past Sophia, already on to the next seventeen tasks.

"Really?" Sophia said, spinning around.

"Before I change my mind," Beverly called in a singsong voice over her shoulder, walking into the walk-in freezer.

Sophia dove for the hand soap. A scent had never smelled sweeter than the cheap Dial soap as she washed her hands for her first ever cooking job.

As she thoughtfully peeled the carrots and potatoes, diced just the way her grandmother had taught her, she thought of what she'd say to Blake when she got home.

To their home, as she thought of it now.

How she could explain that she ran away to understand just how much she loved him back. That the kind of love he was offering was too overwhelming for her to think about, outside of building a life with him.

She paused, chopping as she actually imagined leaving him. Never seeing him again.

It was a physical impossibility. She would have turned back at the county line.

How could she explain that she had to put all the puzzle pieces together at once—her career, her goals, her life, how much she loved him, what their future would look like together?

She knew in her bones that she needed to be here with him and their Star girl forever.

Carrots sliced, she moved on to the broccoli.

But Blake isn't a talker, he's a doer.

He'd been showing her he loved her since the moment they met, and now she had some catching up to do. She happily dreamed, as she chopped vegetables, of how to surprise him that night to convince him she loved him back.

CHAPTER SIXTEEN

BLAKE

Blake and Star walked down his sloping field in the navy cover of night.

He'd taken some tools over that Mabel needed to borrow. He'd chatted long enough to where Mabel insisted he stay for dinner. After a single beer, he'd poured his heart out, telling Mabel what had happened. She'd said she was proud of him but then had firmly kicked him out after dinner to go deal with his choices.

Blake chuckled as he shook his head, avoiding the gopher holes that were always on this side of the field between the two properties. He walked back through a thicket of pine trees on the well-worn path between Mabel's farm and his, thankful for neighbors who would be here even after Sophia left.

"I always got my best friend, right, Star?" Blake said as Star glanced up happily, tongue lolling out.

And in the end, it's fine, he thought. *What's important is that I know I can fall in love again.*

I know I can recognize a good, kind person and feel something for them and picture moving on with my life.

Really, that was the biggest victory of all, he realized with a pop of laughter. He'd been working himself to the bone for the last three years to avoid the loneliness.

But what else was he supposed to have done? Soulmates didn't appear out of thin air.

Until they did.

He'd write her a note if she wasn't back yet. Uncle Alan had texted the group chat with a quippy little joke that Blake's lady friend was working hard on the Clovely staff with Beverly, so he knew she was safe at least.

He'd tell her she could just forget about him ever saying anything. Just take it as an honest compliment and nothing more, and they could go back to being just roommates.

Less than two weeks would pass in a flash, and then he'd have a bittersweet memory to treasure after she left.

It wasn't what he wanted, but it was what he'd take if that was all she wanted to give him back.

As he walked out through the thicket of pine trees and his farmhouse came into view, he was surprised to see her car in the driveway and the cozy lights of the kitchen glowing.

He'd lived alone for so long, it was odd to see somebody in his house when he wasn't there. He had to face her sooner rather than later, but he gulped, feeling butterflies in his stomach.

He couldn't be rejected if they never talked about it.

I should double-check the seedlings' heat lamps are working. I'll just do that until she's asleep.

Star huffed by his side as if to say, "Coward," but she had loped up to Sophia's car and sniffed around with a tail that grew happier and happier.

Star ran to the back door, prancing, excited to go in. How was he going to explain to Star that Sophia had to leave in two weeks? Her new favorite person, making her favorite treats, would be gone.

Star whined, wanting to be let in.

"Fuck," he muttered.

"I guess I can't escape." He turned on his heel, willing himself to face his fate.

His heart felt like it had dislodged, and he was now carrying the shattered, jagged pieces in his hands. They clinked with each step to the back door.

This is the last time I listen to Mabel.

Feeling like he was walking up to certain doom, he slowly opened the back door of the kitchen. Star bounded up the short stairs.

"There's my Star girl!" Whines accompanying heavy foot tappies meant Star had found her second favorite person ever.

Elise Kennedy

Shit, she's here. Maybe I'll just go back out to the barn.

"Are you coming in?" she called out to him.

With a resigned sigh, he walked up the stairs.

This is my house. I can go through the kitchen and up to my bedroom if I want. And go straight to bed and never talk to anybody ever again, especially not make eye contact with Sophia.

Blake walked through the kitchen and who was he kidding? He couldn't just glance—he needed to stop, take his fill of her.

He cocked his head in confusion as he tried to understand what he was looking at.

"Why is there a pumpkin pie with a bunch of candles on it?"

"Well, this is as many candles as you had," she said, wringing her hands, "and it's not a pumpkin pie. It's a new recipe. Oh shoot!" she said and clapped her hands. "Hold on." She grabbed a bowl as she crumbled streusel-like bits around the top of the pie, and sprayed dots of whipped cream around the edge.

"I made a new recipe," she said, crumbling it around, careful not to hit any of the candles in the center. "It's a pumpkin caramel streusel pie. I, um, I call it, the boyfriend pie?" she said it as a question, staring at him nervously.

His heart leapt, but he wouldn't get ahead of himself.

The boyfriend pie.

Cozy Nights in Vermont

Blood thundered in his ears at what it might mean.

She walked toward him, looking nervous. "Um, it's a new recipe. Exclusive to this house. I am not putting it in a cookbook, or a post, or sharing it with anybody." Her lip quivered as her eyes filled. "It's just for you," she whispered.

And just like that, all the jagged pieces of his heart melted into a puddle.

"Just for me?" he repeated, trying to understand what she was saying. He reached for her hand, pulling her toward him. He needed to hold her. Needed to wipe that tear off her cheek.

She nodded, sniffling. "It has pumpkins from your pumpkin patch, and the clove for, you know, Clovely. And you have this spicy scent to your aftershave and it makes me so happy," she said, closing her eyes, looking nervous for some reason. "So I added nutmeg. And I know you said that the streusel topping was your favorite, and so I worked that in, and"—she swiped part of the whipped cream from the pie on her finger—"and whipped cream for..." She bit her lip and gave him a flirty look. "...well, reasons."

A laugh rumbled out of him; he was completely overwhelmed.

"And, it's just for you."

Food was how she showed love; he knew this. But what did it all mean?

"The boyfriend pie is just for me?" he asked, trying to clarify.

"Yes," she said with a bright smile. "I'm so glad you understand. I'll grab some plates." As she turned around, he grabbed her belt loop and hooked her back to him.

"For all the talking you do," he said, pulling her toward him, "you don't say very much."

He crowded her against the kitchen island, and he took it as a good sign that she wasn't bailing.

"Are you, Sophia Bertone, asking me to be your boyfriend?" He hoped it came off cool and flirtatious, not like she held every bit of his heart in her hands.

"I mean, obviously. Didn't you hear me list—"

He couldn't wait any longer. He swooped down to catch her mouth. He savored his first taste of his girlfriend's kiss. It was sweet and laced with spices, and her lips trembled as his thumb stroked her soft cheek. He pulled back, not fully accepting that this was real.

"I love you so much," she whispered, her lip quivering.

An entire jolt shot through his system. "Soph, you don't have to say that just because I did. I just wanted you to know."

"I had to think about it, because I've been just doing one thing after another. Just focusing on getting things done. Getting my recipes done, figuring out my influencer work, and it was easy to push my feelings away. But I've been

Cozy Nights in Vermont

falling for you ever since you got me the good eggs for my cooking that first night."

"Yeah?" He leaned down, needing to feel her skin against his lips. He kissed down her neck.

"You listened, and cared about what I thought. And you were vacuuming; that was a big plus."

He rumbled out a laugh, squeezing her tight against him.

She held his face. "You've never once judged me. You accept me, and you're so, so kind. You're sexy, and smart, and I've felt more cared for in the last four weeks than I have in my entire life. You know how when a place is so big, you can't see the edges of it? It just extends as far as the eye can see? That's how...that's how this feels. Overwhelming. I can't conceive of a time and space where I don't love you like this." She put her hand over his heart. "I didn't know I was in it until I was in the middle of it, and I never want to leave."

He kissed her, wrapping his arms around her and lifting her up so she wrapped her legs around his waist. He loved the feeling of her surrounding him, of her safe in his arms.

"So, you'll stay?" His eyes searched hers, and she squeezed her arms around him.

"For as long as you'll have me," she said with wide eyes and a nervous voice.

"What if I sold the Viking?" he said with a smile, sitting her on the counter beside the boyfriend pie.

Elise Kennedy

She narrowed her eyes. "I would throw it a funeral, but I'm still staying. It does not build me tables nor look good in flannel." She picked up the pie and offered it to him to blow out.

He blew out the candles. "What if Star decided she'd had enough farm life and went to live a spoiled city life with Bev?"

"Then I'd insist on visiting Bev every day. But I'd still live here."

He dipped a finger in the pie, sucking it off his finger. The creamy spice of the pumpkin was perfectly complemented by the sweetness of the caramel. "Jesus, this is so good. Are you sure you don't want to share the recipe?" It was sinful heaven.

"Trust me, I don't want anyone else knowing exactly how to eat the boyfriend pie. That's half the food experience, serving something properly." She pulled off her top, revealing a lace bra.

Whoa, this was unexpected.

"Step one, after letting the boyfriend pie cool to room temperature, offer him a sample."

She swiped a finger into the creamy pie, holding out a perfect taste to his mouth.

He licked it off of her finger, savoring the taste of her skin and the creamy spicy sweetness of the pumpkin pie.

Her curly hair was frazzled in his favorite kind of messy

Cozy Nights in Vermont

bun, and her eyes were scorchingly mischievous as she smiled at him with an eyebrow raised.

He definitely liked where this was heading.

A smile curved on her lips as she reached around, unhooking her bra as she stared at him.

His cock stood to attention and he held back a low growl of need.

"Step two"—she scooped up a small handful of it and smeared the creamy pie onto her nipples—"Make sure to serve it on a dish he'll lick clean."

His mouth salivated at her heavy teardrop tits that were ready to be licked. He dove down to suck and lick her nipple as the spice and flavor mixed with the taste of her skin. He greedily licked every drop off, feeling like an animal whose primal urge to consume and fuck had been ignited. He sucked her second nipple, holding her breast up to his mouth and sucking hard to get every drop off.

She pulled his head up to her lips as she grabbed for his belt, ripped it open, and reached for his cock. He fumbled with her jeans doing the same.

"More," he groaned.

"Step three of serving boyfriend pie," she said, biting her lip. "Ask if he wants whipped cream." She ran whipped cream along his favorite curve between her belly and hip. He licked it off as his cock weeped, pushing down her panties to lick every part of her curves.

"Fuck, Soph." He pushed down her jeans until they were on the floor. He needed to taste her, have her like he'd wanted to that first night. He licked down onto her clit as he pressed her thighs against his head.

He pushed down his boxers as he pumped his clean hand on his cock. He stood and notched himself at her entrance, and as he slid in, he lifted her, her legs wrapping around him. He walked them slowly as she clenched around his cock, dripping onto it, until they were in front of the fire.

Slowly, lowering her down, he thrust into her as she arched off of the rug. "I love you, Soph," he murmured into her throat as he licked there. "I love every"—he thrust into her as she arched higher—"single"—thrust—"part of you." He worshiped her shoulders, showering them with kisses. Kissing down to her elbows, licking there. She clenched around him.

"Now I want you on top of me," he said with a wicked grin.

He rolled them over so she straddled him, his favorite sight. "I love you, my bossy Blake," she whispered, smiling, her hand coming to caress his face as she kissed him. "Especially when you boss your way into taking care of me." She nipped at his throat, kissing down to his chest. "I'll never stop trying to protect this heart."

She rode him with open, vulnerable love in her eyes.

He caressed her cheek as she leaned into it. "My dream girl," he whispered as she rode him harder and harder.

She leaned down as he bundled her against him, needing to press every part of his love into her. She kissed him,

Cozy Nights in Vermont

her lips never leaving his as they crested together, showing the other just how much they were loved.

CHAPTER SEVENTEEN

THANKSGIVING

SOPHIA

"And then, they brought ferrets out," Iris said, slapping the farmhouse kitchen table, making the Thanksgiving centerpieces wobble as she talked about her reporting travels. "Ferrets."

"They get it, honey. Ferrets," Iris's boyfriend Sam said, rubbing her shoulders.

Sophia beamed at her sister from across the table. She loved having them stay for the last week in the newly reopened cottage.

The kitchen that she now thought of as hers as much as Blake's was bursting with love. She and Blake hosted an informal Thanksgiving get-together at their house. Her parents had already planned a trip to Italy for the holiday, so Iris and Sam had decided to come to Vermont to visit their favorite small town during their travels.

Cozy Nights in Vermont

It had only been a mere eight weeks since Sophia had entered the state of Vermont, but she felt like she'd been here a lifetime.

Felt like these were *her* people. Like she'd found a place where she belonged.

"Tell us more about the dolls," Alan said. Sam and Iris both gave a full body shiver.

"That's why your inn was so magical," Iris said, patting Alan's hand. "When we found Clovely, we knew we'd found something special."

Sophia squeezed Blake's hand on her thigh as he kissed her head.

"I'm really, really, really grateful that you found Clovely," Blake said to Iris, even as he looked directly at Sophia.

Oh, her heart.

It had never recovered from the shock of having a perfect man love her so completely.

And she hoped it never would.

A knock on the door interrupted things, and Star let out a howl. She'd been having a ball running back and forth between all of her favorite people.

Blake grabbed the door, and Mabel popped in holding a pecan pie.

"Happy Thanksgiving!" she said, and a chorus of voices greeted her back. "They're finally settled down enough at the inn. I thought I'd come over for whatever meat you've left on the bones."

Beverly and Sophia both got up instinctively to fix Mabel something.

It had only been three extra weeks of considering Clovely home, but Sophia knew in her heart of hearts that she was here to stay. She'd put in a month at the Clovely Inn so far and loved it. Beverly was an amazing head chef, and Sophia had learned so much already.

Blake came up behind her and rubbed her shoulders as she fixed Mabel a plate. She'd been up early preparing things yesterday and then had done a rotation at the inn, subbing in for the normal baker who was on vacation. Add in all of the manual labor of massaging the dough, and her shoulders ached from being in overdrive.

She fucking loved it.

"Can I get you anything?" Blake said, digging into her shoulders with his thumbs.

"Oof, that," she said, leaning into it.

The last few weeks with Blake had been magical. The pumpkin farm season had settled down, so they finally had time to do this novel thing called relaxing. They shared each other's hobbies. He'd tried his first face mask; she'd cheered on the Clovely High School varsity football team to their county-wide victory, shouting along with Blake.

Her cookbook was finished. The final manuscript of all

fifty recipes and her introduction had been sent in only one day late.

Aside from committed partnerships that she'd already agreed to before she'd upended her life, she now only posted on social media for fun. She'd told her followers about the change in her life, and most were exceedingly happy for her. Star made regular appearances on her posts now, much to the joy of everyone, Blake especially.

Her account lost a few thousand followers, but you know what?

Those people could fuck right off.

She was happy now.

"Is Star's plate ready?" Blake asked.

Tippy tappies sounded on the tile beside Sophia's feet as she gathered bits and pieces that she'd saved off to the side before they'd been seasoned. She made Star her own Thanksgiving plate without any of the bad stuff, wanting to make sure she spoiled her as much as Blake did.

The beeper went off.

"Oh, my apple fritter tarts are ready." She passed them out with dollops of whipped cream on top. Blake had sent her a wicked wink as he'd licked his off.

God, she loved him.

Getting seven hours of sleep each night cuddled up together had been a game changer for him. He now had energy to spare and big plans for his crops (that she didn't fully understand but enthusiastically supported) for that spring. Even now, Beverly was quizzing him over a glass of wine on how to get more of her supplies from the farm for the summer menu.

Sophia had already started secretly planning how to make the next fall the best one yet. She wanted to put the Jameson Family Farm on the map so Blake would never have to worry again.

She hadn't seen a protein shake in the house in weeks. He'd slow down to eat lunch and dinner as she enjoyed feeding him delicious food, showing him just how much she loved him every day.

Star ran through the room, darting between many of her favorite people as they chatted in the kitchen.

And as Sophia registered that the kitchen was filled with people she could feed and the man she loved and who loved her back to her very marrow of her bones, she felt so terribly grateful for the gift that was fall in Vermont.

THE END

Acknowledgments

Thank you so much for staying with this project even as it was delayed. I haven't experienced kindness and grace like I have with the readers + reviewers in bookstagram.

Special thanks to Mr. Kennedy who talked me off a (metaphorical) ledge when I thought about quitting altogether. It turned out that much like a four year old at 3PM at Disneyland, I had had too much of a good thing and was just overwhelmed with it all. I regret that exercise, time with friends and family, and taking care of yourself really do work. I'll be slowing down my publishing schedule so I don't reach that point again (hopefully).

Thank you to my amazing ARC team for their kindness and warmth as I navigated some tough themes and burnout in August. I appreciate you more than you can ever know: Kristina Holmes, Reed Towne, Sara Rawson, Persephone Hawker, Meagan Vogus, Amanda Brown, Kaylee Holland, Jennifer Gibson, Alexus Smith, Kailey Huber, Rachel Kent, Kelsie Wheeler, Terryn Winfield, Stephanie Toot, Katie Anne Ranney, Jenna Rhiannon, Melanie Granata Egan, Nicole Scarborough, Tiffany Amber Schwartz, Laura Jones, Kelly King, Bianca Sevidal, Rania Laham, Alizae Cratch, Grace Casteel, Laura Lee, Amanda-Jane Savage, Kaylene Ledger, Božena Stojanovič, Nicola

Butler, Allison Thommen, Sarah Gwerder, Janina Majeran, Mary McCabe, Melinda Mauro, Thuy Cu, Chloe Simpson, Lisa Christensen, Oasis Donnelly, Jenny Ellis, Jen Williams, Jenna Baker, Shaafia Kasmani, Kailyn Glassmacher, Eva Bower, Caitlin Timm, Trish Meade, Cristie Lynn, Lottie Sheppard, Caitie Parker, Marianne Kay, Ashley Babineaux Medina, Susan Dara, Heather Kelley, Rachelle Leblanc, Cynthia Cabrera, Lyna Nguyen Stanley, Riley Collins, Jennifer Castillo, Celeste Velocci, Chelsea Higley, Sam Nelson, Melissa Letts, Kimber Kennedy Alexander, Sasha M Fountain, Ashley Marie Vaccaro, Karli Jordan, Jane Litherland, Amanda Preece, Sarah Elyse, Julie, Jenna Coulson, Christine Fass, Lauren Giacalone, and many others! (Interested in being an ARC reader? Fill out my general interest form!)

About the Author

Elise Kennedy is an author of cozy, spicy, heartfelt small-town romances. She lives in the midwest with her (very) patient husband and two perfect pups.

* * *

Visit **elisekbooks.com** to sign up for Elise's newsletter for new book announcements, freebies, and more!